GYHARD HEARD A FOOTSTEP BEHIND HIM. . . .

He forced himself to turn. Three soldiers of the Sixth Army blocked his retreat. All three carried crossbows that tracked him unerringly despite the black leather bands that covered their eyes and prevented him from jumping to another body. His heart began to pound. As he couldn't go back, he went on.

The remainder of the army, similarly shielded, waited in the area around the tower wall. He couldn't count the number of crossbows aimed at his heart. He tried, then decided it didn't matter when one would be enough. A slight figure dressed in black beckoned to him from the top of the wall.

Suddenly he stared down at where he'd been and, from that exact place, Vree stared up at him.

"Time to die," announced a familiar voice.

No. Before he finished turning, a noose settled around his neck.

Vree smiled and pulled it tighter. "Long past time to die. . . ."

NO QUARTER

TANYA HUFF

DAW BOOKS, INC.
DONALD A. WOLLHEIM, FOUNDER
375 Hudson Street, New York, NY 10014

ELIZABETH R. WOLLHEIM
SHEILA E. GILBERT
PUBLISHERS

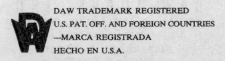

For Cap'n Dave Nelson, who taught me the most important lesson I learned in seventeen years of formal schooling by giving me my first C in English. When I protested, saying another student had written a much worse paper and gotten an A, he replied: "If that student had written your paper, they'd have gotten an A. But from *you*, it's worth a C."

Chapter One

Motes of dust spun in the sunlight slanting into the upper hold through an open hatch. At the edge of the shadows, a slight, dark figure held a round shield, turning it this way and that so its polished surface caught the light.

"And I thought Bannon was vain," Vree muttered.

It's not vanity, Gyhard protested.

As the quiet voice in her head spoke with unusual seriousness, the ex-assassin, late of His Imperial Majesty's Sixth Army, snorted but continued tilting the shield.

There. Hold it there.

Vree stared into the makeshift mirror, feeling as though she were seeing her features for the first time. Her dark brown eyes looked too big for her face. Her chin was ridiculously pointed. Six days at sea under an unrelenting late summer sun had darkened the deep olive of her skin. She looked thin and much younger than her almost twenty-two years.

*You *are* young.*

Her lips pressed into a thin line. *You told me you couldn't hear my thoughts.* When Bannon had shared her body and it had been her brother's voice she heard, their thoughts had merged and, with their thoughts, their identities. It had very nearly destroyed them both. With Gyhard, however, it had been easy to draw the line between them. Until now.

I can feel strong emotions, Vree. Gyhard's reassurance was almost gentle. *So can you. There's no need to panic.*

You don't know ...

I have a good idea. He'd been there from the beginning. As Governor Aralt, the leader of a rebellion whom Vree and Bannon had been sent to assassinate, he'd stolen Bannon's body. When Vree had appeared, carrying her brother's life, her brother's kigh, tucked in with her own, he'd blackmailed her into helping him get close enough to a young Imperial prince for him to make yet another trade. But a broken piece of his past had taken the prince and they'd ending up chasing him across half the Empire. Together. He'd seen how close she'd come to losing herself in sharing herself with her brother. *I'm not Bannon, Vree. His weaknesses aren't mine.*

Neither are his strengths. Until Gyhard had driven them apart, Bannon had been the center of her life. No. Her teeth ground together. Gyhard had not driven them apart. For reasons she could not yet admit, she'd chosen to save his life by making it a part of her own and now had to face the consequences of that decision. Forcing the tension out of her shoulders, she stared down at her reflection. *Are you done?*

In a minute.

What do you think you're going to see?

Who I am.

*Who *I* am. ... Did you hear that?* Brows drawn in, she set the shield aside and started for the ladder leading up to the deck.

Hear what?

Lookout's spotted a sail. Callused fingers and toes barely touched the polished wooden rungs and a heartbeat later, Vree crossed the deck to a knot of sailors gathered at the rail. "What is it?" It was the one sentence she could say in Shkoden and be certain she'd got it right.

"Pirates."

The word was close enough to Imperial that she understood the meaning before Gyhard finished his translation. Shading her eyes with her hands, she peered back along the side of the ship. Just moving into the current behind them was a sleek, two-masted, narrow-hulled vessel.

"The *Raven*." It sounded like a curse. Two sailors spat over the side, giving water to the sea for luck, and a third traced the sign of the Circle on her breast, muttering, "Probably bin followin' us since the outer islands." When the lookout confirmed the identification a moment later, the crew of the *Gilded Fancy* raced to defensive positions.

Vree put herself in the path of a running sailor and he skidded to a stop. The third night out, she'd barely managed to keep from killing their best knife fighter when he'd challenged her right to the long dagger she wore. After her easy victory, the crew treated her with the same wary respect she'd received from those around her most of her life. While they might not know what she was—had been—they'd been made very aware of what she could do. "Can we ..." She hated having to search for words but her Shkoden was up to little more than the most basic of conversations. *Gyhard, how do you say, outrun her?*

When he told her and she repeated it, the sailor

shook his head, scalp locks whipping his ears. "No stinking way. They're in the same stinking current, ahead of the same stinking wind, and they're built for speed which we sure as fish shit aren't."

"What will . . ."

He didn't wait for her to finish. "Happen? They'll board us. Anyone who survives the fight'll go over the side. Less, of course, they've got some stinking skill Edite i'Oceania . . ."

i'Oceania?

She's claiming the sea as her mother, Gyhard explained. *It's probably not true.*

Probably?

". . . thinks she needs—healers, or sail makers, or stinking carpenters. You, don't know what she'll do about you, but the hucksters, his stinking Lordship, and his stinking Lordship's servant, she'll hold for ransom."

The hucksters were a pair of Imperial merchants and His Lordship was a Shkoden noble, who was involved in some way with the ambassador at the Imperial court. Vree knew nothing more about any of them, nor did she really care. As the sailor ran off to join others performing complicated and inexplicable maneuvers with a rope—the decks looked like an anthill stirred with a stick—she took another look at the *Raven*.

Even in that short time, it had pulled closer—close enough to see that all exposed timber had been painted a deep matte black.

That's conceit, Gyhard growled. *All that black paint must've cost her a fortune. No wonder she turned pirate.*

Conceit. Vree frowned.

She felt Gyhard stir uneasily within the boundaries of her mind. *What are you thinking?* he demanded. *Vree . . .*

I'm thinking that there may be an alternative to going over the side with a pirate's ax splitting my skull.

What alternative?

She turned from the rail. *The usual one.* Ignoring the chaos growing around her, she made her way past frantic men and women fighting to get the last bit of speed out of the *Fancy* to the arms locker where the armsmaster was methodically setting out bundles of barbed arrows. As he'd spent some years in the Empire and spoke fluent Imperial, they'd not have to waste any of their rapidly decreasing time on translations. "Tell me," she demanded without preamble, "about Edite i'Oceania."

"Good at what she does," he grunted, not bothering to look up. "Almost as good as she thinks she is. Shkoden navy controls most of the sea-lanes through the Broken Islands, but they can't catch her. And the Circle knows they've tried. From what I've heard, her crew adores her. They should. She's made them rich. They'd die for her." He pulled oilskin-wrapped packets of bowstrings out of the locker. "And some of them are going to."

"What about her? Would she die for them?"

The armsmaster laughed, but the sound held little humor. "Her type thinks they're immortal."

"How would she respond to a knife at her throat?" The tone of Vree's voice lifted the armsmaster out of his crouch and turned him toward her. "Would this pirate call off an attack in exchange for her life? Would her crew listen if she did?"

"Aye, the crew would likely listen," he said slowly, studying her face, a slow realization dawning. "But i'Oceania wouldn't give that order. If she's taken alive, she'll die ashore and she knows it. You kill her, though, and her crew becomes the stinking rabble it was before she forced order on it. Captain Edite's the only thing holding that murdering bunch of cutthroats together. If she dies, they'd fall apart. If they fall apart . . ." His eyes still on her face, he closed his fist around the hilt of his short sword. "I can beat them."

Vree nodded and spun about on one bare heel.

"Assassin."

She paused.

"Do it quickly or there'll be no point in doing it at all."

Down in the forecastle, ignoring the fire crew readying its station, Vree unrolled her pack and began buckling on the wrist sheaths that held her throwing daggers. Up above, she could hear the armsmaster shouting orders. As she understood it, the captain—a thin and hairy man she'd barely seen—commanded all nautical situations and the armsmaster commanded defense. It would never have worked in the Imperial Army, but it seemed to work at sea.

If the armsmaster commanded, then the *Raven* was close.

You're very quiet, she said a moment later as she regained the main deck.

I thought we'd agreed that it would be best if you told no one what you were.

*I didn't *tell* him.*

*You gave him enough for him to figure it out. He

must've been suspicious ever since you won that knife fight . . .*

Teeth clenched, Vree cut him off. *Look, you can jump into the nearest slaughtering pirate if this body dies. I can't. So shut up and stay out of my way.*

I can't talk you out of this?

No.

She had a mental image of Gyhard spreading his hands—Bannon's hands because those were the only ones she'd ever seen him wear. *Then I guess I'm along for the ride. Wait a minute! Where are you going?*

Surefooted despite the constant movement of the ship, Vree started up the rigging by the stern mast. *You know that long thing sticking out from the front of the *Raven*?*

The bowsprit.

Whatever. Swinging up onto the bottom spar, she moved out to the end. The armsmaster had obviously said something to his bowmen, for the three she passed stared at her wide-eyed and twisted out of her way as much as their position some fifteen feet above the deck allowed. *I'm going to jump from the end of this crosspiece thing down onto it.*

You're going to what? Each word was carefully and separately enunciated. He sounded impossibly calm.

There's enough rope coming off it that it shouldn't matter if I miss a little.

Are you out of your mind! The calm had disappeared so completely it might never have existed. *That is *not* possible!*

Rolling her shoulders, Vree squinted back at the *Raven*, now close enough to make out the individual pirates crowding the rail. She could almost see the single line that held them together. The line she was about to cut. *It's not impossible, just very difficult. In fact, I'll aim for that rope between the whatever-you-called-it and the front mast and not worry about my footing. I can swing straight from there to the deck.*

*No you can't. *No one* could do that.*

Vree merely shrugged and watched with interest as a flaming ball of pitch landed with an angry hiss and a gout of steam just short of the *Raven*. Familiar with the huge siege engines the Imperial Army used, she'd been fascinated to discover, upon exploring the ship, a much smaller catapult on the carved stern of the *Gilded Fancy*.

The *Raven*'s answer was a canister of metal fragments. The *Raven*'s armsmaster was a better shot. Vree heard the impact; heard wood splinter; heard someone scream; could smell smoke.

What happened on the *Fancy* was no longer her concern.

All her attention shifted to the enemy.

*Vree! Listen to me! You *can't* do this! I don't care how much training Imperial assassins go through; you can't jump from a moving ship to a moving ship!*

Concentration broken, she snapped, *How do the pirates intend to board us?*

That's different!

Only in degree.

They'll wait until they've dropped sail and grappled!

I haven't time to wait, and I know what I'm capable of. You don't. So shut up. And if you try to take over even an eyebrow, I'll push you right out of my head! Do you understand me, Gyhard?

I don't want to die, he said softly, ignoring the threat neither of them wanted to explore.

Good. That makes two of us. But as his concern was in her head, she had to feel it. And the feeling was a distraction. Because assassins couldn't feel. Not while they were working. *Gyhard . . .*

At least they won't be expecting it, he sighed, surrendered, and drew back until he was barely a whisper in the depths of her mind. Vree suspected the whisper would remain even if Gyhard's kigh should find another body.

She forced her attention back to the *Raven*. Looked through the arrow fire. Ignored the howls of both pain and fury. Found a wild-haired woman in a scarlet shirt and boiled leather armor conducting the attack, a sword in one hand, and a basket-hilted dagger in the other. She marked the defenses and defenders she'd have to pass and found two of the pirate ship's other officers.

Compressing her focus, she shifted her gaze to the bowsprit.

The world became a rope, two sets of movement, and the distance between them.

The distance narrowed.

A grappling iron clanged against the side of the *Fancy,* only a hand's span short.

Vree jumped.

She was holding the rope but still falling when the *Raven*'s reinforced bow rammed into the *Fancy*'s side. The rope took up most of the shock, her arms the rest. Her right hand lost its grip, gained it again as the rough hemp burned a line across her palm, but the dagger in her wrist sheath twisted out and into the sea.

Shit!

She let her weight on the rope swing her in over the deck. As the ship rose, cresting a wave, she dropped, rolled, and sprinted for the stern.

Survive to reach the target. She'd been seven when she'd started training. Bannon had been six. They'd survived the training—two out of three didn't. She couldn't remember how many targets they'd survived to reach.

The world became a scarlet shirt and the pale column of throat above it.

In the confusion of boarding, few of the pirates noticed her. Those that did, she avoided although one took a wild swing and slashed a shallow cut diagonally across her back.

When Vree reached the sterncastle, a narrow three steps above the main deck, she leaped, without pausing, up and over the railing, landing directly in front of her target.

The captain broke off bellowing orders and began to laugh. A large woman, carrying very little of her weight as fat, she towered over the short, slender Southerner. "Have you come to challenge me, little sprat?" her voice cut through the bedlam and heads began to turn on both ships. "I think not."

Her heavy sword slammed down into the deck, splintering the wood, but Vree had begun to move before she'd finished speaking. Virtually too fast to follow, the point of her long dagger slipped in under Edite's left ear, drew a graceful line across the captain's throat, and slid out from under the right ear. She finished the motion by flicking her remaining wrist dagger down into her hand and sending it hilt deep into one of the brilliant blue eyes of the sailor on the tiller.

Edite scowled and began to choke, covering the immediate area with a crimson spray. Sword and dagger fell from fingers that curved to clutch futilely at life. With her windpipe and all major blood vessels severed, she didn't live long. As she slammed into the deck, still twitching, a roar went up from her crew. As one, their prize forgotten, they turned on Vree and, screaming with rage, they rushed for the stern. A few, already on board the *Fancy*, returned to join the enraged mass. A high-pitched voice, shouting for them to continue the attack, was ignored.

An ax splintered the deck at Vree's feet and a javelin cut through the place she'd been an instant before. Fortunately, most of the howling pack forgot the missile weapons they held in the desire to personally rip their captain's killer limb from limb. Backing rapidly into a corner of the stern, Vree's hips hit the rail. The first half-dozen crew members charged toward her past their captain's body, faces twisted in identical masks of hate.

Vree!

She hit the water in a clean dive some distance from the *Raven*'s ebony hull and stayed deep as long as she could.

I didn't know you could swim.

The relief in Gyhard's mental voice was so great that Vree very nearly laughed aloud. *The Sixth Army's garrison was at Harack, on the coast. When I was eleven, we had to swim about five miles back to shore in the middle of the night.*

*When you were *eleven*?*

Bannon was ten. The swim wasn't so bad, but the sharks were annoying.

Sharks!

This time she did laugh as her head broke the surface, the water pulling her dripping hair back off her face. *I'm kidding about the sharks.* Bobbing up and down the swells, salt burning in the cut across her back, she turned until she could see the battle raging on the two ships. Although she thought she could hear the *Fancy*'s armsmaster yelling orders, she had no way of knowing who was winning.

If the garrison was by the ocean, why didn't you know what a bowsprit was called?

Because it wasn't important; we had too many other things to learn, and a ship has no throat to slit. I guess we should go back and ...

Large hands closed around Vree's waist and dragged her under. Released her, grabbed her shoulders, and pushed her deeper. As the water closed over her head, she fought a heartbeat's panic, then pointed her toes and pushed up against the water, trying to go deeper still. It almost worked. Her attacker lost his grip on her shoulders but caught a painful handful of her hair.

Taken by surprise, her lungs were nearly empty. She needed to breathe.

Most assassins died after taking out their targets, success having made them careless.

Her chest burned. A primal panic clawed at the inside of her mouth and throat.

The sea closed around her ribs and squeezed, trying to force her to inhale.

Through slitted eyes, she could see a huge, dark shape in the water above her.

Facing her.

Throwing the strength of arms and shoulders into a backstroke, she drew her legs up and, knees touching her own forehead, drove both feet past his arm and slammed them up under his jaw. Pulling herself over and around, she sucked in great lungfuls of air as her face broke the surface and finished the circle, coughing, gasping, with an unnecessary dagger in her hand.

I think you crushed his throat.

Forcing her breathing to slow, Vree sheathed the dagger and started swimming for the ships, ignoring the choking, thrashing pirate just over an arm's length away.

Aren't you going to finish him?

He's finished. And I'd rather not put more blood into the water. Arms and legs growing heavier with every heartbeat, all she wanted to do was get back on board the *Fancy* before the last of her energy gave out.

I don't understand why they're carrying on like this.

Through Vree's eyes, Gyhard watched as the crew of the *Gilded Fancy* celebrated by lantern light. The captain'd had two casks of sweet Imperial wine brought up on deck and most of the toasts drunk had been to Vireyda Magaly, the savior of the ship. Gyhard could feel her confusion and recognized its source. While any of the Seven Armies might rejoice at the removal of an enemy commander—for the lack of a battle no lives were lost—they'd been trained to make no fuss over the assassin who, after all, had only been doing her job. But Vree was no longer in the

Imperial Army and she'd just done the impossible.
You've never worked with an audience before. Usually, the people who see you don't survive the experience.

She shifted uneasily. *So?*

So, you do impressive work. He remembered the first time he'd seen her kill; by the time he'd thought she should start moving, it was all over. Her concentration, he'd just discovered, was as complete as it appeared—nothing got in her way. Fueled by that concentration, her speed was terrifying. If he ever took control of her body, the difference would be night and day, her deadly grace lost. *If he ever took control of her body* . . . He buried the thought as deeply as possible, lest she feel it.

He'd wanted to remind her back when she'd been worrying over how assassins couldn't feel, that she wasn't an assassin any more. Except that only an Imperial assassin with years of brutal training both mental and physical behind her could hope to make that jump, and as she obviously intended to make it and he had no choice but to go along . . .

In the corner of her vision, he caught sight of the two Imperial merchants and felt the memory of hair rising off the back of his neck. Although both merchants held heavy metal goblets, their expressions were anything but celebratory and when one of them, believing herself unobserved, glanced at Vree, she was scowling.

In the Havakeen Empire, assassins were named the blades of Jiir, the goddess of battles, and their terrifying, deadly skills were controlled by the army. The citizens of the Empire were constantly assured that assassins were not only rare but safely sheathed, killing only on order of their commanders. Trained from early childhood that the army was their only family, assassins never left ... home.

As an added reassurance to a nervous population, it was well known that if, in spite of incredible odds, they should desert, they would be targeted and quickly killed.

But Vree had been trained with her brother and that attachment had been strong enough to break all the rest. She'd killed the man sent to kill her and had bought her freedom from His Imperial Majesty with the life of his youngest son.

Gyhard, though born in Shkoder, had lived most of his hundred and thirty-six years—most of his lives— in the Empire and could understand the fear on the merchant's face. *This* assassin was not sheathed by the army and she'd just made her own decision to kill— without orders. If that were possible, how could anyone be safe?

How indeed, Gyhard wondered. When the celebration was over, it would only take a couple of voices to turn the admiration to fear. *"Listen to me, I come from the Empire, I know ..."* She was too fast. Too deadly. Too impossible to stop. And they had all seen what she was capable of. Assassinating both merchants before the warnings could start seemed a bit extreme even if he could convince Vree to do it. Besides, after the afternoon's exhibition of her abilities, the authorities wouldn't need a bard to discover who'd wielded the knife—Vree was deadly but hardly subtle.

As Vree turned slightly to watch a sailor juggling three torches, an ax, and a dead chicken, Gyhard took a better look at the merchants. There was nothing obviously wrong with the male of the pair; young enough, reasonably good-looking. Suppose he could convince Vree to push him into the male merchant? Once there he could easily silence the rumors by arranging an accident ... except that even should Vree prove willing—which she wouldn't—Gabris and Karlene had made it clear what the bards would do if he acquired a body by taking a life.

"As we can neither remove you nor bring you to justice for the lives you've so callously ended as long as you remain in Vree's body, you have, for the moment, found sanctuary. You'd best not forget what you owe her for that." Karlene's voice had made it a warning, not a reminder. *"But this is where we draw the line. If anyone else dies because of you, anyone, the bards will see to it that your kigh goes back into the Circle so fast you won't know what hit you."*

That Karlene and Gabris were a very long distance away in the Empire meant little when they both Sang air and distance meant nothing at all to the kigh.

He felt Vree's foot tapping in time to the music as a battered squeeze-box, a fiddle, and a pair of pipes began to play. The army had gone to a great deal of trouble to present the assassins as weapons; perhaps it would help if Vree were seen as flesh and blood. *Why don't you dance?*

To his surprise she shifted uncomfortably. *Don't you start.*

Start what?

The whole time Bannon shared my body, he kept trying to push me into having sex with someone, anyone. You. Karlene. He didn't care just as long as he got to experience it from the other side.

It's just a dance, Vree.

He could feel her tension as she chopped a hand at

the leaping, stomping, sweating bodies that filled the deck. *If you think this won't end in a sacrifice to the horizontal gods, you never spent much time expecting to die.* She snorted. *How stupid of me; of course you didn't. If you expected to die, you just . . . jumped ship.* Wiping damp palms on her cotton trousers, she added, her voice flat, all sarcasm gone, *Not for Bannon. Not for you.*

It didn't take much to recognize where the tension originated. First Bannon. Then him. *It's been a while, hasn't it?*

Shut the slaughter up!

Vree, I'm not your brother. I don't want to be with you—in you—while you're with someone else. The thought of her wrapped in the arms of a man or woman, taking what he couldn't give her, drove daggers into his heart and twisted. She might not know how she felt about him, but he knew exactly how he felt about her.

Don't say it.

They could feel each other's strong emotions.

Vree . . .

No.

When the *Gilded Fancy* made her way into Pitesti Harbor—the only harbor in the Broken Islands deep enough for a merchant ship of her draw—followed closely by the *Raven*, the hysterical reaction on shore could be both seen and heard from the foredeck. Bells rang out, fishing boats ran themselves aground, and the broad pebble beach curving between the town and the sea began to empty.

"Fools think they're being invaded," the armsmaster snorted, jerking his head at the masts where the flags of Shkoder hung limp and unreadable. "Think i'Oceania's crew has both ships."

Vree glanced toward the *Raven* where the late captain's body had been lashed to the bowsprit. The surviving pirates were secured belowdecks and the sailors now guiding her in past the breakwater were a skeleton crew off the *Fancy*.

On shore, the beach began to fill again as archers took up their positions behind the curved shields of overturned dories and siege engines were uncovered at both ends of the crescent.

"Pitesti was the last place to fall when Shkoder took the Broken Islands," the armsmaster told her, leaning unconcernedly on the rail. "They're proud of that. Obviously, they don't intend to fall again."

Vree squinted at the town silhouetted against the setting sun. "I'd feint at the harbor, land troops on the other side of the island and take the place from behind."

The armsmaster nodded. "You and King Mikus."

Should we be worried? As far as Gyhard could tell, the catapults were being loaded with what looked to be bales of hemp soaked in pitch.

Under the circumstances, it seemed a reasonable question, so Vree repeated it.

"No, we're just at the edge of their range." As the armsmaster spoke, the anchors were dropped. "Captain'll send a boat in. With any luck they won't sink it."

From the expressions on the faces of the boat crew, they were aware of their danger; postures visibly relaxed when the keel scraped gravel and the mate stepped safely ashore. Her hands out from her sides, she moved a body length from the boat, and stopped.

There seemed to be a lot of shouting going on although no one on either ship could make out the words. After a moment, she half-turned and waved an angry hand toward the harbor.

As though the mate had commanded it, a sudden evening breeze unfurled the crowned ship of Shkoder flying from both the *Fancy* and the *Raven* and a last, long ray from the setting sun bathed both ships in a golden light.

The cheering carried clearly over the water and the bells of Pitesti began to ring again.

"Always said Kirston had a touch of bard. Couldn't have done that with more style if she'd Sung the kigh." The armsmaster pushed off the rail. "You'd best get ready. They'll likely want you ashore."

"Why?"

He chuckled, the sound almost fatherly. "You killed Edite i'Oceania. That makes you a hero in these parts, Assassin."

I wish he'd stop calling you that.

Vree nodded slowly. She didn't know why but the armsmaster's reinforcement of her past made her uneasy as well.

Bonfires were lit on the beach that night, but most of the sailors, exhausted by the effort of bringing two ships safely to harbor with what remained of a single ship's crew, crawled into their hammocks and stayed there.

The next morning, the town council and the captain of the *Gilded Fancy* hung Edite i'Oceania's body in an iron cage on the harbor headland.

"And she'll soon have company enough," growled an old woman. Dry fingers wrapped around Vree's forearm and drew her away from the crowd clustered under the dead woman's dangling feet. "I'm Ilka i'Gitka, the eldest on the council. You're the Southern girl who cut that second smile 'neath her chin, aren't you?" Before Gyhard could finish translating or Vree could answer, she went on, "Slip of a girl like you doing what the entire Shkoden Navy couldn't; that's going to make them feel like a bunch of unenclosed fools, isn't it? Looks good on them. We'll have the trial this afternoon, you'll tell your story—that's you, the *Fancy*'s armsmaster and anyone else who feels like they've got an anchor to drop—the pirate scum'll tell their story, then we'll likely hang the lot of them. Until then, you let folk make a fuss of you, you hear? Few enough heroes in the world as it is."

A muffled exclamation drew them both around. The man who'd made the noise was staring wide-eyed at Vree.

"Looks like you've made an impression on young Tomas," Ilka cackled.

Did she say *young* Tomas? Vree frowned. The man was at least forty; possibly older, the broad faces of the Northerners made judging age confusing.

Look at the robe, Vree.

Tomas' robe hung off his narrow shoulders in full folds of green and blue. Other than a white splash of seagull shit, Vree couldn't see anything special about it.

He's a bard!

Oh. Bards knew. In ways she couldn't understand, they could sense both of the lives she carried. Even injured and in the dark, Karlene had known.

Make friends with him, Vree. He keeps these people connected with the world and his opinion carries a lot of weight.

She set her jaw. *Why should I care what he thinks?*

Gyhard watched through her eyes as the pair of Imperial merchants came ashore and, keeping as far from the assassin as possible, joined the crowd. He hadn't wanted to tell Vree his suspicions, but now he had no choice. Quickly, he outlined the damage he thought the merchants could do.

Vree's hands curled into fists. *The next time you see danger at my back,* she said, her mental voice an edged weapon, *tell me or this slaughtering ... thing we have won't last very long.*

I just thought ...

No. You didn't think. I can't protect myself against enemies I don't slaughtering well know I have. She turned to the councillor, who'd been talking about bards and heroes and how the former could create the latter while she and Gyhard had been holding their silent conversation. A quick bow cut off the flow of meaningless words. "If I may be ..."

Excused, Gyhard broke in. *Not dismissed. Let's not remind people of the army right now.*

"... excused, the bard and I have ... something to talk on."

Discuss.

That's what I said. Her tone made it clear he was far from forgiven.

As Vree approached, Tomas stopped nervously cracking his knuckles and tried, not very successfully, to smile.

The Bardic Hall in Pitesti occupied the seaward corner of the top floor of the four-story Healers' Hall. It was the tallest building in the town and Tomas' balcony—a ten by twenty cedar-covered section of the third floor roof—had an unobstructed view out over the harbor. As he Sang, Vree watched the leaves of potted herbs flutter against the wind and wondered what Karlene would tell him.

His voice quavering just a little, the bard Sang a gratitude and sent the air kigh on its way. Although the salt breeze was cool, he wiped a dribble of sweat from his brow before he turned to face his guest. Guests. "We won't get an answer for a while," he explained. "Would you like some, well, lunch?"

Well, would I?

She could feel Gyhard's approval. *Lunch is good.*

Lunch is all. I don't care how friendly we need him.

*Having touched Bannon's mind, I can see how you might have gotten this impression, but not *all* men think about sex *all* the time.*

"And if it's all right, I'd like my partner to look at you," Tomas continued, taking her silence for assent. "He hasn't a full healer's talent, but he's a good diagnostic and I'd like to show him proof that the fifth kigh exists. That is, if you and, uh . . ."

"Gyhard," Vree prompted.

He has the worst memory of any bard I've ever met.

I don't think he wants to remember.

"Yes. Gyhard. If the two of you don't, well, mind?"

"No." When his face fell, Vree frowned. "Yes?" When he only looked confused, she sighed. "The words in your language get . . . mixed." Hands spread, she said very slowly, "You may bring your healer."

"Good." The bard finally managed a smile. "I hope you like fish."

What do you man, he doesn't want to remember?

Isn't it obvious? This whole slaughtering fifth kigh thing, you being here in my body, has screwed up everything he thought he could be sure about in his entire life. Vree perched on the edge of a huge fan-backed wicker chair and, out of habit, adjusted her daggers. *You're good at that.*

Vree, are you about to begin your flows? You seem unreasonably angry.

Jiir forbid I should be angry at you for destroying my life? For nearly killing my brother? For deciding what I do and do not need to know about potential danger?

For loving you?

Yes. No. She sagged into the chair. *I wish you'd quit bringing that up. It doesn't have anything to do with . . .*

You?

Oh, shut up.

Gyhard tried to remember how close they were to the next dark of the moon. There were aspects of occupying a woman's body that had never occurred to him during the previous six lives he'd lived. He thanked all the gods the Circle contained that he wasn't facing those complications alone. If Vree had made it to his/Aralt's chamber before her brother and he'd taken over her body . . . He shuddered.

Brow furrowed, Tomas listened to the message the kigh brought out of the Empire and tried to keep from glancing over his shoulder to where Vree—*"No, Vree and Gyhard,"* he corrected himself silently—sat talking quietly with Adamec. His partner had been first skeptical and then, after laying on his hands, ecstatic. He'd had a thousand questions. Tomas only had one.

"You can trust Vree completely," Karlene told him through the kigh. *"She'll kill to survive, but I believe that's it. Ignoring for the moment the implication I would've even considered sending a maniacal murderer to Shkoder—Imperial assassins don't work that way. If anything, they're too controlled. All she wants is to talk to our healers and see if there's anything they can do to find Gyhard a separate life."* The kigh paused and their ethereal noncolor seemed to darken. *"Gyhard, on the other hand, you can't trust. He's spent over a hundred years jumping from body to body—I don't know how he does it; I wish I did—and this is the first time he's been in a willing host. It's also only the second time he hasn't killed the host and the first time with Vree's brother Bannon was, as I understand it, a fluke. He says he loves her, but I personally am not sure I believe him."*

Tomas grinned a little at that as the emotional nuance the kigh gave to the words indicated that Karlene herself had an intimate interest in the tiny, Southern woman.

"Even if he does love her, I doubt it would be enough to change his basically amoral nature. This is, after all, a man who has removed himself from the Circle. We can't do anything about justice as long as he's sharing Vree's body but he seemed to believe Gabris and me when we explained that if yet another host died because of him, that would be it. I explained the whole thing to Captain Liene, and if I'd known Vree'd be stopping at Pitesti, I'd have let you know as well. Final chorus—as long as it's Vree in control of her body, I wouldn't worry about it."

"*You* wouldn't worry about it," Tomas muttered after Singing a gratitude and dismissing the kigh. How was he supposed to tell who was in control of the assassin's body? With two kigh in a place where there should be only one, all nets came up empty. Why did he have to be the first bard to deal with this situation? *"All right, third bard,"* he amended, granting first and second place to Gabris and Karlene. Not for the first time, he felt completely inadequate. Although most bards who anchored the country at a Bardic Hall Sang all four quarters, he'd been given Pitesti because he Sang the two most common, air and water, very strongly and because King Theron and the Bardic Captain had agreed that a returning native might be more acceptable to the Broken Islanders than a perceived foreigner.

As he turned, he heard Adamec say, "I wish you could stay! There's so much we could learn from you! So much we could learn to do deliberately instead of instinctively."

"Trained instincts," the young woman replied, "can be a powerful ... tool."

Crossing toward them, Tomas wondered what she'd intended to say. What had been discarded in that pause? Weapon, perhaps? *She doesn't look dangerous,* he mused. *With that pointy little face she looks almost fragile.* Then she stood and the way she moved suddenly made him think of several deadly predators. It took him a moment to find his voice. "If we're going to be on time for the trial," he managed at last. "We'll have to leave now."

Vree nodded but remained where she was. "What did the air spirits, the kigh, tell you?"

"Well ..." He weighed the information and separated what he thought he should pass on. "Karlene says I should trust you."

"Are you going to?"

Meeting her steady gaze, Tomas saw strength and vulnerability about equally mixed and found himself in sudden sympathy with this strange young foreigner. "Yes," he said, a little surprised by his reaction. "I am."

I wonder what Karlene told him about me, Gyhard muttered.

Vree snorted. *I think you already know.*

"Bertic a'Karlis step forward."

Vree watched in horror as the armsmaster obeyed the bard's command.

"Bertic a'Karlis, you will speak only the truth."

Are they going to do that to me? She remembered the terrifying feeling of being held by an invisible fist the night they'd broken into Karlene's chamber at the Healers' Hall in the Capital. She'd broken the spell by having Bannon take over her body, but she didn't have Bannon with her now.

Calm down, Vree. They just want to make sure they're getting at the whole truth. People's lives are at stake here. Don't worry, it doesn't hurt.

I wasn't worried about it hurting, she snapped. *I don't want anyone controlling my body ever again.*

He won't be controlling your body. In a minor way he'll be controlling your mind.

That makes me feel so much better.

They don't need your testimony as such, but if you refuse, you'll be playing right into whatever rumors those merchants started.

They'd definitely started something. Vree could feel

the hostility rising from whispering clusters scattered through the crowd and wrapping around her like a dark fog. She'd seen mobs work before and couldn't ignore the danger.

"Vireyda Magaly, step forward."

It wasn't as bad as she'd thought it would be, but without Gyhard's constant murmur of comfort, she doubted she'd have been able to stand it. When it finally ended, she was covered in a clammy film of cold sweat.

As Gyhard predicted, her cooperation, combined with the apparent approval of Tomas and his partner, returned the hero status the Imperial merchants had nearly managed to destroy.

The *Raven*'s carpenter and sail maker, impressed from captured ships and tortured to maintain their compliance, were set free. Unfortunately, the sail maker was no longer exactly sane. Three women in the early stages of pregnancy were taken aside—their sentences commuted until their babies were born. The rest, condemned out of their own mouths, stood bound on the beach before the council. Most of them looked numb, a few cursed softly, a couple wept. They all wore the marks of rotten eggs and fruit. The crowd had stopped throwing things only after the council had threatened to move to the privacy of the council chamber.

From her central seat in the semicircle of driftwood chairs, it was clear that Ilka's position as eldest not only allowed her to run the council but also everyone on it. "You're lucky we're not on the mainland," she declared, looking as though she considered them lucky indeed. "On the mainland you'd have to go through all this again before the king at a Death Judgment. Fortunately for us, our distance from His Majesty ensures a certain autonomy in dealing with the sort of people who have, over a period of some years, slaughtered, individually and collectively, upward of two hundred men, women, and children. In short, in dealing with scum like you." She stood, accepted a staff carved with an entwined pattern of kelp and crowned with a leaping dolphin, and slammed its metal-bound butt three times into the smooth stones of the beach, "By the power invested in this council by Theron, King of Shkoder, High Captain of the Broken Islands, lord of a whole bunch of places that don't mean fish shit out here, I pronounce sentence—hang them."

The crowd released a collective, satisfied sigh and Vree thought she saw Tomas wince as he said, "Witnessed."

"Of course she's dangerous. She just put an end to the most vicious crew of mass murderers we've had in these waters since my grandfather's time." Ilka nodded in satisfaction as the seventh pirate was hoisted kicking and writhing into the air at the other end of the beach, then turned her attention again to the pair of Imperial merchants. "Tell me something I *don't* know."

"Honored Councillor, you don't understand." Although he spoke Shkoden fluently, the merchant's accent put strange inflections on the words. "Assassins are trained only to kill or be killed, for them there is no middle ground and they are never away from the army. For this one to be as she is, deciding to kill as she has, is wrong."

"Very wrong," affirmed his companion. "It is as though a sword moved through the world, striking and killing with no hand wielding it."

The elderly councillor studied them, weighing their fear. "How do you know there's no hand wielding her?" she asked at last. "Perhaps she's been sent to kill someone in Shkoder, no one saw fit to tell the two of you, and you've just blown her cover to the other side. That's treason, isn't it?"

The young man paled. Frowning, the woman shook her head. "Assassins travel only as part of an army. They are targeted and released by the army. The Empire is not at war with Shkoder, nor do we wish them to be. War is very bad for trade."

"It is that." Hand disappearing into her robe, Ilka scratched at the white line of an old scar, received the day Pitesti fell. "So what do you want me to do about this wild sword of yours? If she's too dangerous for Shkoder, she's an unenclosed sight too dangerous to hold here. Even if we had a reason to hold her. Which we don't. And besides, she spent the morning with the bard and if she was any kind of a threat, he'd have told me."

"We know nothing of bards, Honored Councillor, we merely thought that someone should be told what we know of assassins."

"Well, someone's been told. In fact . . ." The sudden shrieking of a pirate brought face-to-face with his own imminent death cut her off. She waited until the noise stopped before continuing. "In fact, from the whispering I've been hearing, hasn't just about everyone been told? Didn't it occur to you that she could get *annoyed* about that and, if she's as dangerous as you say, maybe you'd be better off not attracting her attention?

You think on that, and I'll think on what you've told me. Ass-kissing bottom feeders," she added after the two recognized a dismissal, bowed, and scurried away.

"Still," she sighed, a pair of pirates later, "personal admiration probably shouldn't stand in the way of national security. Kaspar!"

A balding fisherman hurried over to her chair. "Yes, Grandmother?"

"Wasn't there a Shkoden diplomat of some kind on the *Fancy*?"

"I think so, Grandmother."

"Go find him, and tell him I want to talk to him."

Imrich i'Iduska a'Krisus, diplomatic courier between the Shkoden ambassador to the Empire and King Theron, stroked the point of his beard and frowned. "We've been on the same ship for nine days; I wonder why they didn't bring this information directly to me."

"Because you're an officer of the Shkoden court, and I'm a sweet, approachable old lady." She threw up her hands. "How in the Circle should I know? The point is, you have the information now. Forget it or pass it on, it's all the same to me."

Vree stood out on the bard's deck and watched the dark silhouettes of the hanged pirate crew swinging in the night. Although the air was warm, she shuddered.

Tomas, who'd been about to ask if she wanted something to eat before Adamec started in on her again, saw the movement and asked instead, "It bothers you?"

She shrugged without turning. "It is a slow, painful, messy way to kill."

"You're saying you could've done it better?" He

couldn't stop the incredulous question, recognized how insulting it sounded, and hoped Karlene's assessment of the assassin's temperament was correct.

"I am not ... an executioner. I say, it is a slow, painful, messy way to die. And, yes, it bothers me."

The bard swallowed and risked touching her gently on one shoulder. "It bothers me, too."

When Vree turned to face him, her face was carefully expressionless and her tone matter-of-fact. "But they expect it to bother you. Please tell Adamec I will be in ... soon."

He could possibly have Sung his way past the barriers, but he suspected he wouldn't have known what to do with what he found, so he merely nodded and went back inside.

Vree? What's wrong?

I'm in a strange country, speaking a language I barely understand, and I want to go home.

We can.

No. She stared at the harbor without really seeing it. *I miss the army.* Her fingers dug into the soft wood of the railing. *I miss Bannon. I have no one around me I can trust.*

He didn't so much understand her pain, as share in it. *You can trust me.*

The sound of the rope rubbing against wooden cross beams drifted up clearly from the beach.

Vree?

Chapter Two

"Vireyda Magaly."

Vree turned and, even in the midst of the chaos on the docks, easily identified the woman who'd spoken her name. It almost seemed as though she could see a line drawn in the air between them.

Bard, Gyhard murmured.

That would explain the robe. But his single word had sounded nervous and Vree regretted the sarcasm. All at once, she found herself wondering how Gyhard felt about returning to Shkoder. He hadn't asked for her interference back when he'd left Bannon's body. She'd just grabbed him out of nothingness and since then she hadn't once considered that he might have feelings that didn't involve her—for all that she refused to acknowledge his feelings that did. The sudden realization froze her in place.

Go on. She's waiting.

Gyhard, I ...

Not now. Something in his tone suggested he could read the direction of her thoughts and found himself mildly amused by them.

If he didn't want to come here, he should've said something before *we left the Empire.* Less easily defined emotions lost in irritation, Vree gritted her teeth and made her way toward the bard. The quartered robe covered a stocky body, condensed by age but far from frail. Above the robe, deep lines bracketed eyes and mouth in a well weathered face and her hair hugged the angles of her head like a steel cap. She leaned on a heavy, no-nonsense cane that to Vree's practiced eye had enough heft to make an effective club. Amidst the seemingly formless pandemonium that surged back and forth against the harborfront of Elbasan, the elderly bard stood surrounded by a nearly visible circle of competence and calm.

This is someone, Vree thought with relief as she ducked under a swinging net of cargo being unloaded from the *Fancy's* hold, *who can tell me what to do.*

Weight on her cane, fingers drumming against the quartered pattern carved into the handle, the Bardic Captain dragged her attention from the pair of kigh the young woman carried—despite the urge to begin investigating them immediately—to the young woman herself. She was younger than Liene had expected. *But then again, these days,* the captain grunted silently, *everyone is.* She was also smaller than expected and her lack of height, combined with her youth and the pointed features, resulted in an almost fragile appearance.

But there was nothing fragile in how she moved through the confusion on the docks. She used exactly the space available, sliding from opening to opening, never in anyone's way, never allowing anyone to be in hers.

Assassin. Liene turned the word over in her mind. She'd never met a person who'd taken a life who hadn't been, at least for that instant, insane. Karlene had insisted that the Empire had turned this young woman into a weapon without destroying her. Perhaps. Karlene had also insisted that her personal feelings had nothing to do with that analysis. Not likely.

Now this assassin was in Shkoder, asking for help; offering in return a chance for bards and healers to study the suddenly impossible to ignore fifth kigh. And it had to be done in Shkoder not the Empire where an assassin would be no more than a part of the military infrastructure for, in spite of the evidence, the citizens of the Empire barely believed in the original four kigh.

Original four kigh. Liene shook her head. That seemed to imply a possibility of further discoveries. A sixth and a seventh kigh perhaps? Perhaps. All things were enclosed in the Circle. *But for now,* she told herself emphatically, *we have enough to concentrate on without adding further complications.*

Upon dismissing the kigh who'd brought Karlene's message, Liene had gone over every recall in the Bardic Library that mentioned Imperial assassins. It hadn't taken long. Although bards had gained access to the Havakeen Empire twenty-two years before when Princess Irenka had joined with the Empire's crown prince—now Emperor—not one of them had met an assassin until they'd encountered Vree and her brother. Apparently, as few people had the necessary combination of skills it took to kill on command as had the perfect pitch and desire to Sing the kigh. Uncomfortable with the analogy, Liene hastily put it aside.

A small amount of the available information had been gleaned from the military. The rest, unfortunately, was nothing more than rumor and hearsay. When she'd had the kigh contact Aurel, the bard Karlene had replaced at the Imperial court, he'd expressed doubts that assassins actually existed.

No doubt of that now. The young woman who turned to acknowledge a shouted farewell from the *Fancy*'s stern with a truncated wave, had danger wrapped around her like a crimson cloak. Danger to what, though; that was the question.

Was Vireyda Magaly a danger to crown or country? Karlene believed not and, more importantly, Gabris had agreed with her. But they had both warned her to watch Gyhard i'Stevana.

"According to Gyhard, unless Vree pushes him, he can't jump to another body without killing the body he's in. He says he has no wish to do that, but then he's not likely to tell Vree otherwise, is he? Vree has agreed not to help him if it means the taking of a life, but we have little doubt that while he is in her head, he'll attempt to convince her otherwise. He has been outside the Circle for so long, we cannot trust him." The kigh had grown very agitated at that point, making the rest of the message difficult to understand.

"We suggest, Captain, that the bards and healers both watch him closely."

Liene snorted, remembering. Neither bard had been able to suggest how they were supposed to watch a man reduced to kigh and sharing a body with another.

As the young woman drew nearer, it became more and more difficult to be aware of anything but the two kigh she carried.

A good thing I came myself, the captain mused. *A younger bard might lose the larger picture in the smaller. Might find a pair of kigh completely overwhelming.* Bardic Captain for twenty-nine of her sixty-eight years, Liene considered herself long past the possibility of being overwhelmed by anything. She held out her fist as the ex-assassin stopped an arm's length away. "Liene. Bardic Captain."

Touch the bottom of your fist to the top of hers and tell her your name.

She knows my name, Vree protested, shifting her weight forward onto the balls of her feet.

It's the way they introduce themselves in Shkoder. Just do it.

He was definitely nervous. Under the circumstances, Vree decided to do as he suggested and ignore the tone he suggested it in. "Vireyda Magaly. But I am always Vree."

"Vree." Liene nodded. She'd noted the signs of a silent conversation and, abruptly, decided to acknowledge the situation. Ignoring it wouldn't make it go away. *More's the pity.* "And your companion?"

Vree started and glanced around. No one in the surrounding crowd of buyers, sellers, sailors, and city folk seemed to paying them any attention. "Uh, Gyhard i'Stevana."

Maybe I didn't want them to know.

You think Karlene or Gabris hasn't already told her? She's their captain.

It isn't a military organization, Vree.

Then why are they using military rank?

She's like the captain of a ship.

Then she's still the person in charge and they'd still have told her.

"Is Gyhard not able to speak for himself?"

"No." When Liene's eyebrows rose, Vree found herself elaborating. "Not without I give him control of my body."

The captain half smiled. "Unless. Not *unless* you

give him control of your body. Which, as I understand it, is probably not a good idea."

As she didn't seem to expect a response, Vree waited.

"Is that all you brought with you?" Liene used her cane to point at Vree's pack.

"Yes."

"Good." She half-turned and, still using the cane, pointed to a cluster of stone buildings just visible above the slate roofs of the city. "That's the Citadel, there on the top of that hill. That's where we'll be walking to." The last phrase emerged like a challenge and when the expected protest wasn't voiced, the Bardic Captain shook her head in disgust at her own defensiveness. "Most of the bards and some of the healers seem to think I can't walk across a room anymore, let alone halfway across the city," she snorted as Vree fell into step beside her. "My joints stiffen up in the damp, especially my hips and knees, but I've walked across this whole country in my time and I *won't* be coddled."

Am I supposed to say something? Vree asked, a little confused.

I don't think so.

"Kovar thought he should be the one to come to the harbor to meet you." Her cane hit the damp cobblestones of Upper Dock Street with unnecessary force and a young man pulling a wheeled dolly loaded with bales of raw cotton moved hastily out of her way. "I had to remind him that I remain Bardic Captain until Third Quarter Festival and he can just live with it."

What is it about you and old ladies? Gyhard wondered as they followed the captain around the edge of the Dock Market, the roar of buying and selling making audible conversation impossible. *All of a sudden, you seem to be attracting them. First in Pitesti and now here.*

Maybe it's something Bannon left behind. He was always the one getting pinched and patted.

Probably enjoyed it, too. He watched through Vree's eyes as Liene exchanged noisy greetings with half a dozen people, questioned the price of a pound of jasmine tea, and arranged for it to be delivered to the Bardic Hall at the lower price all without breaking stride. *I'm curious about why the Bardic Captain herself came down to meet us.*

Vree glanced up at the stone towers of the Citadel rising from the center of Elbasan like a crown. Although the steepness of the hill made an estimate difficult, it looked like they had some distance to cover and, with the captain's age slowing them down, they were going to take a while to cover it. *Seems like we'll have plenty of time to find out.*

Remember you've got to . . .

. . . make a good impression with the bards. She sighed. *I know. But I can't be something I'm not.*

Be yourself.

Yeah. Right.

The bitterness took him by surprise.

The noise of the market became a background growl as the two women turned onto a narrow avenue and started the long climb up the hill.

"Cotton Street," Liene explained, following Vree's gaze to where thick skeins of thread dyed all the colors of the rainbow hung twisting in the breeze between the open shutters of a shopfront. "Use to be West Wharf Street, but about fifteen years ago everyone started calling it Cotton Street and about five years ago the city council finally changed it. They buy bales of the stuff raw off the ships from the South, spin it, dye it, weave it, and sell it all around here. Don't sell a lot of it, mind, as the price is one unenclosed amount higher than the linen coming locally out of Vidor. The cloth doesn't last as long either." Then her voice changed, and it suddenly became impossible not to pay attention to what she had to say. "Lower Dock Street, then Hill Street to the Citadel would've been more direct, but at this time of day there'd be people all around and we need to talk without being interrupted. What do you want from us, Vree?"

"Karlene ..." Vree began defensively.

The Bardic Captain shook her head. "No. I've heard her version, now I want yours."

"Gyhard ..."

"Forget Gyhard," the older woman commanded. "Or if you can't forget him, disregard him for the moment. What do *you* want from us?"

I want everything to be like it was before. Except she didn't. Not really. Or she'd have let Gyhard disappear into oblivion.

"I want Gyhard to have a body for his own." Ignoring Gyhard's soft, *Of his own,* Vree clutched the hilt of her dagger with her left hand, fingers opening and closing convulsively, and added, "But no one can die for it."

"Why not?"

She saw the face of Edite i'Oceania, a crimson line of death across her throat; Commander Neegan's face, her father's face, finding his only possible peace as her blade found his heart; Avor's face, a friend's face, as

he realized he was going to die; too many faces to
remember the names or the reasons. Her own face,
reflected in a polished shield.

What do you think you're going to see?

Who I am.

Who I am . . .

"Vree?"

She blinked and realized that she'd stopped walking.
The captain had moved a few paces ahead, had
turned, and was watching her. She couldn't read the
expression on the older woman's face and had no better idea of the expression on her own. Her arms were
folded tightly over her stomach, as though she'd been
slashed in the belly and had to hold in her guts.
Slowly, she released the white-knuckled embrace she
had on each elbow and held out her hands. "There
has been enough death. I don't want to see death
when I look at him."

To her surprise, the Bardic Captain took a step forward and enclosed her fingers in a gentle grip. Vree
found herself looking into a dark gaze that reached
past all the years of blood and all the training that
had come before to find a seven-year-old who was
suddenly no longer a child. It hurt more than any
wound she'd ever taken. Somehow, she found the
strength to drag her eyes away.

Liene released the girl's icy fingers and began walking toward the Citadel once again, her only outward
reaction to the pain she'd seen a spasming of the hand
that held her cane. Never good with emotions uncon-
fined by chord and chorus, this was far more than she
was capable of dealing with. More, she suspected, than
the Healers' Hall could deal with. *Karlene has a*

greater perception than I gave her credit for. This child is so tied in knots she's no danger to anyone but herself.

She'd intended to ask a lot of other whys, but they were no longer necessary.

"I don't want to see death when I look at him."

It was a love song with enough tragic potential to rip out hearts and tear them into tiny, bleeding pieces. Teeth clenched, Liene wished she'd sent Kovar to the docks so that she could've received these first impressions filtered through his recall.

Gyhard felt Vree tremble and silently cursed his inability to hold her, to comfort her. He hated the Bardic Captain for what she'd done and his anger sizzled around the parameters of his existence. If only he had hands. . . .

Don't.

He forced himself to withdraw although he knew at that moment she couldn't have stopped him from taking control.

The moment passed.

Are you all right? he demanded, fighting to suppress the anger for both their sakes.

Don't leave me.

If he'd still had a body, that quiet plea would've left him struggling to breathe. This was the first time, since the initial impulse that had gathered up his kigh, that Vree had shown him her heart. If confronted, she probably wouldn't admit to the thought but he'd heard it—felt it—and nothing, not hatred, not anger, was worth hanging onto in the face of it. *Don't leave me.* Catching hold of them before they could fade, Gyhard gathered the words up and locked them away in his memory. Then he waited.

He felt her chin rise. *I'm fine,* she told him,

lengthening her stride to draw even with the Bardic Captain again. Her tone implied she didn't care if he believed her or not.

"I half expected that you'd be carried off the *Fancy* on the shoulders of her crew," Liene observed, stepping aside to allow a tailor's apprentice, arms loaded with a bolt of sea-green fabric, to pass. It suddenly seemed important she find a subject with a little distance.

Vree shrugged. "They were happy to come home. They made me a hero in the Broken Islands. That was enough."

"From what Tomas told me, I imagine it must've been." The image of a row of hastily-constructed gallows, filled as quickly as they were built, rose in Liene's mind. The crowd of dead behind the young assassin grew. "You speak Shkoden very well," she said, searching for yet a safer topic.

"Gyhard taught me."

The older woman stifled a sigh. It appeared there were no safer topics. "Well, he did a good job. I assume he translates for you, too?"

"Less now."

Liene grinned at Vree's tone. "Don't like depending on other people, do you? I can appreciate that." Then she frowned. "Gyhard hears through your ears? Sees through your eyes?"

"Yes."

"Then we shouldn't talk about him as though he isn't here." She turned that over, examined it from all sides. When she spoke again, they'd moved some distance up the hill. "From what Karlene has told me, I think you and he and your brother have proved that the body is merely meat worn by the kigh and that

what we all consider the person, *is* the kigh. So." She
took a tighter grip on her cane, forcing herself to give
credit where credit was due. "Gyhard, thank you. Although a number of the bards speak Imperial, none
of the healers do. You've made all our lives less complicated." Sweeping a piece of trash into the gutter,
she snorted. "Well, less complicated as regards language, at least."

*I'm not sure that granting me any kind of individu-
ality is such a good idea.* Gyhard lightly touched the
place where he ended and Vree began, felt her recoil,
and drew back. *If I'm given a little, I may be tempted
to take the rest.*

You can try.

Vree, I'm serious.

*Then we'll deal with it ourselves because I'm not
going to tell her. It's obvious she thinks I'm, we're,
unstable. We don't need to prove her right.* Conscious of Liene's gaze, Vree added aloud, "He says,
you're welcome."

The Bardic Captain shook her head. "No, he
doesn't. Didn't Karlene tell you that you can't lie to
a bard?" With everything filtered through Vree, they'd
have no way of telling if Gyhard was lying—a realization that left the captain feeling distinctly less than
happy—but they could certainly tell when she was.
"Now then, what did he actually say?"

Okay. That's it. Ever since Ghoti, Vree'd had to
continually draw lines between herself and the world.
Time to draw another one. *How do I tell her that's
none of her slaughtering business?*

Vree!

Never mind. This woman was the head of all the
bards; Vree'd dice with the gods on the odds the

Bardic Captain understood Imperial. "That's none of your slaughtering business," she repeated aloud, glad to be speaking her own language again and discovering an unexpectedly pleasant freedom in no longer being bound by the rules of rank. A similar response to an Imperial Army Captain would've resulted in six lashes and time in the box.

The Bardic Captain understood Imperial. She stopped in the middle of the street. Her cheeks flushed an alarming purple as she spun around and glared into Vree's face. "If you want our help—" she began.

Vree cut her off. "If you want to study the fifth kigh, we're going to have to trust you enough to let you poke around in our lives. If you want that kind of trust, you're going to have to give it in return."

"Gyhard i'Stevana has removed himself from the Circle!" Liene snapped.

"And we're asking you to put him back in. Doesn't that count for anything? All we want is a chance to start over, and if you're not willing to give us that chance, then we're on the first boat out of here and you can whistle up information on the fifth kigh without us."

It wasn't a bluff. Liene suspected assassins were unable to bluff. And, it was the truth. All they wanted was a chance to start over. At least, it was all Vree wanted and if it wasn't what Gyhard wanted, she believed he did. Still standing in the middle of the street, disregarding the audience they'd attracted, the Bardic captain drew in a deep breath and released it slowly, releasing her anger and her suspicion and her fear at the same time.

Then she held out her fist. "Liene. Bardic captain."

Vree stared at it for a long moment. "Vireyda Magaly. Vree," she said at last, touching it lightly with her own. "Gyhard i'Stevana."

"Welcome to Shkoder."

"Thank you."

"That Southerner giving you trouble, Bard?" a heavyset woman called from a second-floor window. "You want I should come down there?"

"No need," Liene replied, her tone suggesting the curious return to what they'd been doing before the shouting started. "But thank you for the offer." She waited until her champion waved cheerily and withdrew, before turning her attention back to Vree. "Are we all right, you and I and Gyhard?"

"I think so."

"And what does Gyhard think?"

Muscles still tensed, Vree's gesture took in the end of the argument. "That starting over's a good idea."

We'll have to play a careful melody here, Liene thought as they continued up the hill, squinting in the late afternoon sun. *This child has been tuned so tightly she's going to start breaking strings. I guess it's a good thing I* didn't *let Kovar meet her at the dock,* she decided silently to herself. *If I don't stay on top of this, it's never going to work. Someone's going to have to remember there's more involved here than the fifth kigh.*

"She threatened you?"

Liene drummed her fingers on the edge of her desk. "She threatened to leave. Which is her right, she's not a prisoner."

The waxed ends of his mustache twitching, Kovar slapped his palms down on the polished wood. "But she lied to you!"

"If someone called me an unmitigated horse's ass—which, upon reflection, is how I was acting—would you tell me?"

"Of course not."

"You'd lie to me."

He didn't pretend to misunderstand. "It's not the same thing."

"Ah." Liene nodded. "One rule for you. A different rule for her."

Kovar sputtered for a moment and finally grabbed onto the one affront he was certain of. "She is voluntarily carrying the kigh of a man who removed himself from the Circle!"

"True. Which means there's a great deal we can learn from them concerning the fifth kigh." She leaned back in her chair, considered putting her feet up on the desk, and reluctantly decided her hips weren't up to it. "They help us, we help them—which, if you'll recall, was the whole point of them coming here—and we all act like civilized people while we do it."

"How civilized is assassination?" the younger bard demanded.

"How civilized is prejudice!" Liene snapped. Painfully conscious of how her own preconceptions had caused her to react, she was determined Kovar would be less inflexible. The bards had not come across in the best of lights this afternoon.

"Are you trying to tell me that you met this woman completely unconcerned about her past?"

"I'm trying to tell you that after I met this woman, her past became unimportant. She followed orders, exactly as she was trained to. Frankly, I'm a lot more concerned about the people who trained her."

"You have a point," Kovar murmured after a moment's reflection. Liene was pleased to note that he'd stopped reacting and started thinking. "But what about the past of the kigh she's carrying?"

"That," Liene admitted, "I am concerned about. But if Vree can't control Gyhard, we can. If only for her sake, he deserves a chance."

"For her sake?" Kovar shook his head and dropped into the wood and leather chair facing the desk. He directed a searching gaze at his captain's face. "You sound like Karlene."

Liene spread her hands, the gesture clearly allowing the comparison. "The girl's beautiful, intense, and tragic. I can understand what Karlene saw in her."

"Beautiful, intense, and tragic," Kovar repeated, rubbing the creases out of his forehead, unable to maintain suspicion in the face of his captain's certainty. He sighed deeply. "Then she's just what we need around the Bardic Hall."

"Afraid you'll have the youngsters falling in love?"

He looked up from under his hand and his mustache lifted as his mouth curled into a weary smile. "No. I'm afraid I'll have to spend the next dozen years listening to overheated, overwritten ballads. If there's one thing a bard can't resist, it's a tragedy. You'll be well out of it."

"I'll be retired, not dead," Liene pointed out curtly.

The ends of the mustache lifted higher as the smile grew. "I beg your pardon." Then he sobered and stood. "I suppose I'd better meet her—meet them—before they're surrounded by healers."

"Kovar."

He paused by the door, turned, and lifted an inquiring brow.

"Remember what Vree said about trust. They *have*

to trust us in order for us to learn anything, so we're going to have to offer trust in return. Keep in mind who they were but deal gently with who they are."

Shadow screening her from the courtyard, Vree studied the wall below her second-floor window. *I could get down that,* she said with satisfaction as she straightened.

Why do you want to?

I don't. But I might need to. Bannon wouldn't have had to ask. Bannon would've understood. *Let it go, Vree,* she told herself sternly. *Even if you'd let Gyhard die, you and Bannon couldn't have gone back to what you had. You'd come to know each other too well.*

You know, talking to yourself seems a bit redundant under the circumstances, Gyhard told her dryly, wishing he'd been able to pick the content out of the buzz of thought. *Are you expecting trouble?*

Expecting trouble keeps you alive. A squint into the small fireplace showed the chimney too narrow to climb although it appeared to open up into the larger stack just past her fingertips.

Vree, what are you doing?

Checking.

For what?

Escape routes.

But we aren't in any danger.

Now.

Unable to get past the surface agitation to the cause, Gyhard muttered, *You weren't this paranoid on board ship.*

*I understood the rules on board ship. I stay out of the way, I let them do their jobs, they take me where

I've paid to go.* The heavy plank door opened in and would be easy to secure from the room. Not so easy from the corridor. *And they don't want us here. Their captain made that plain.*

They want us, but they're afraid of us. Of you, because you're an assassin. Of me, because I'm outside the Circle.

Outside the Circle? What the slaughter does that mean?

It's a religious thing. I'm sure they'll explain it, he added caustically.

I want you ... She froze, head cocked to one side. *Someone's coming.*

I hear them, but, Vree, you aren't the only person in the Bardic Hall. Other people will be using the ...

A brisk rapping cut him off.

Vree checked that her knives were accessible, swore softly when she remembered that one of her wrist daggers lay on the seabed in the Broken Islands, and positioned herself where she'd have the greatest freedom of movement should there be a fight.

Are you going to tell them to come in? Gyhard asked when the rapping grew louder. *Or wait for them to break the door down?*

Wait.

Vree!

I'm kidding. A quick glance over her shoulder defined the distance to the window, just in case. "Come in."

By all the gods in the Circle, it's true! The girl is carrying two kigh! Kovar stood in the doorway, fingers clutching the latch, trying to sort out what his eyes told him and what he knew. One slender young woman stood facing him in the center of the small sitting room, but two separate people occupied that space. Until this meeting, he'd dealt with Karlene's incredible tale purely intellectually. Having taken over most of the day-to-day administration of the Bardic Hall, he'd made arrangements for the girl's stay, he'd set up schedules with the healers, he'd worried about bringing both an assassin and a man who'd dared to remove himself from the Circle into Shkoder. Upon coming face-to-face with the unarguable evidence, however, he found himself far more overwhelmed than he'd believed possible. *Two separate and distinct kigh! What we could learn from this!*

Would it be rude to tell him to close his mouth? Vree asked, not sure whether she should be amused or annoyed.

Almost as though he'd heard her, Kovar's mouth snapped shut and he released his white-knuckled grip on the latch, jerking his fist forward. "Kovar."

"Vree." She moved toward him just enough to touch her fist to his, carefully avoiding his gaze. "And Gyhard."

And Gyhard. Two kigh. "Did Liene mention me?"

"Yes."

He couldn't remember her stepping back, but she stood, once again, in the center of the room. "Were you told about the necessities?" How would a male kigh react to a female body? Or was gender a result of physical form?

Privies, Gyhard explained.

"Yes."

"And the dining hall?" Would she have to eat enough to sustain two lives?

"Yes." Vree's pulse began to slow as the inane dialogue convinced her this tall, balding man with the impressive mustache was not a threat.

"The bards who have rooms in this part of the hall are all out Walking, so you should have plenty of privacy. If you need anything, just ask." He paused, then added. "Either of you."

"Thank you."

"I have a thousand questions to. ask."

Vree waited, the bard's last statement so obvious she didn't think it needed a reply.

About to begin on the first of the thousand, Kovar stopped himself. Something about the young woman's stance, so clearly defensive, reminded him of his daughter the day she'd arrived at the Hall to begin her training, her talent an inheritance from a father she barely knew. Superficial differences between the two disappeared beneath a shared, desperate bravado. It would be distressingly easy, he realized, to lose sight of the needs of one kigh in the wonder over two. "You've nothing to be afraid of, Vree," he said gently.

Startled, Vree looked him full in the face, her need to keep a distance between herself and these strange new people lost in her need to find out just what he meant. He didn't seem to be mocking her. "I'm *not* afraid."

"I beg your pardon." Four years learning to be a father to Olexa as much as many more years of bardic training made the apology believable. If the captain, by her own admittance, had not been welcoming, it was time to remedy that. "The bards and the healers are both very glad that you're here, Vree. You and Gyhard. By allowing us to study your unique kigh, you're doing us a tremendous favor and we'll do everything we can to take care of your problem in return."

"Uh . . ." To her horror, she started to shake and could feel tears burning behind her lids. *Gyhard, why is he being so nice to me? I haven't done anything for him.*

You're doing him a favor—he said so himself—besides, he's a bard. They're supposed to be nice. Gyhard struggled to keep his own emotions under control lest his anger push Vree over the edge. The mere fact that she couldn't deal with someone being unexpectedly nice to her told him more than he wanted to know about her life before he became a part of it. He wanted to grab Kovar by the shirt and shake him until he was sure the bard understood. *Do you see what they've done to her?*

Behind his gentle smile, Kovar gritted his teeth, certain he saw another intelligence flash for a heartbeat in Vree's eyes; pure animal rage one moment, gone the next. Gyhard. All at once, he thought he understood what Vree was afraid of. *She's carrying a kigh that's been over a hundred years outside the Circle.* Before he could say anything—before he had any idea of what to say that wouldn't make her situation even worse—the sound of a gong struck twice filled the building.

"Dinner gong," he explained, amazed at how still Vree had gone. "I'd be pleased to have your company this evening."

Heart pounding, Vree struggled through her confusion and finally nodded. Anything would be better than facing a roomful of strangers alone.

Not quite alone.

No, she allowed. *Not quite.*

"So what will it be? Do we arrive late to get the reactions over all at once, or do we arrive early so that you only have to go through it one bard at a time?"

"Reactions?"

"To the pair of kigh." Kovar spread his hands and smiled encouragingly. "I'm afraid there's no way around it, you're going to be the center of attention for a while. Unless you'd rather I had something sent up? You could eat in your room."

"No." Her chin rose. "I don't hide from confrontation."

"Well, with any luck, it won't go any further than acknowledgment."

Considering that Vree's reaction to confrontation usually involved knives, Gyhard sincerely hoped the bard was right.

Three or four heads turned when Vree and Kovar entered the dining hall, reactions turned three or four more and, in a moment, every one of the dozen bards in the room stared openmouthed in their direction.

During the heartbeat of absolute silence, before the babble could begin, Kovar took a step forward. Using enough Voice to hold their attention, he said, "This is Vree, a citizen of the Havakeen Empire who has graciously consented to assist us in our studies of the fifth kigh. Yes, she *is* carrying two kigh and if you must know the whole story, Karlene has sent us a copy of her recall which will be in the library by tomorrow morning. If you have any questions, bring them to either the captain or myself. **Do not pester Vree with them. Is that clear?**"

Heads nodded.

"That said, I expect you to make her feel welcome. She speaks Shkoden fluently . . ."

He has a loose definition of fluently, Gyhard observed.

". . . but it wouldn't hurt for some of you to use this opportunity to practice Imperial." His voice lost its overtone of command and picked up a distinct note of amusement as he added, "That's all; enjoy your meal."

Her expression carefully neutral, Vree followed Kovar across the dining hall, skin crawling under the heated focus of a dozen intensely curious pairs of eyes. Assassins worked unseen and not even the greenest of recruits was fool enough to satisfy curiosity by staring at the blades of Jiir. Vree could hear Kovar's footsteps against the plank floor and her own blood roaring in her ears; nothing else.

The silence stretched and grew brittle.

Then a very, very old woman in a wheeled chair leaned toward her neighbor and said, in what she imagined was a whisper, "She's a pretty little thing, isn't she?"

The silence disappeared in the mutual embarrassment that followed. By the time Vree set her plate of cold beef and vegetables on the table across from Kovar, she was the topic of every conversation but no longer the center of attention.

That's your third old lady.

So? Vree watched Kovar carry a piece of meat to his mouth on the tines of an implement she'd never seen before and carefully imitated his action. *What is this thing?*

How would I know?

You're from Shkoder.

A hundred years ago. And I was never in Elbasan and I never actually met a bard before Kars.

That's why you're so, she settled on, *tense. You keep being reminded of Kars.*

*I'm so *tense* because everyone around us would as soon Sing me back into the Circle as look at me.*

I think you're overreacting.

I'm not the one planning to climb up the chimney, he snapped. He didn't want to be reminded of Kars—not by Vree, not by the bards. Unfortunately, what he wanted didn't seem to matter because every bard he saw reminded him not only of Kars but of how he'd failed him twice; the first time by pushing him into insanity, the second by leaving him there. Gyhard didn't know whether Vree had felt his reaction through their close contact or had come to it on her own; either way he didn't like it much.

But it's okay if you know what I'm feeling?

Stay out of my thoughts, Vree.

Strong emotions, remember?

You going to answer Kovar's question or sit there like an idiot?

Vree jerked and found Kovar staring at her from across the table. "I'm sorry. Could you repeat, please?"

He waved a hand at her plate. "I just wondered how you liked the food."

"The food?" She looked down and realized she'd eaten most of it. "It's, uh, fine. Better than army cooking." She couldn't actually remember how anything tasted, but it seemed a safe comparison.

"And Gyhard?"

"He tastes what I taste."

Kovar leaned forward, trying not to appear too anxious. "And do you like the same things?"

Conversations died as every bard still in the dining hall waited for her answer.

Vree's ears grew hot. She had no idea what Gyhard liked.

You never asked.

You could've told me!

She felt the memory of a shrug. *It wasn't important. Besides, I was busy learning about you.*

What? And I'm not supposed to learn about you?

Kovar sat back. "I'm sorry; have I started something?"

Before Vree could find the words, the double doors to the dinning hall slammed open and a short, dark-haired figure charged in.

"Is she here? I heard she was here!" Without waiting for a reply, the young woman—girl—swept her gaze across the remaining occupants of the room. Quarry spotted, she flung herself forward, racing to Vree's side, her eyes gleaming. "You *are* here! And you *do* have two kigh! This is so amazingly amazing. When they told me you were coming, I just couldn't believe it. I'd have been here sooner, but I had garden duty this afternoon."

"This is Magda i'Annice a'Pjerin," Kovar interrupted. If he had anything more to say, not even bardic training gave him the chance to say it.

"Maggi. Almost everyone calls me Maggi. You're Vree, right? And Gyhard? Captain Liene told me all about you." She grinned as she took in Vree's expression. "You have no idea who I am, do you? I'm the healer, well, all right, apprentice healer who Heals the fifth kigh—it has something to do with my mother

saving my brother's life before I was born, but they're
still trying to figure out the particulars. Karlene *must*
have told you about me. I'm the one who's going to
find Gyhard a body." She shoved a thick fall of curls
back from her face with weed stained fingers. "I think
that what you did was the most romantic thing I've
ever heard of."

Vree blinked, as stunned by the delivery as by the
actual flow of information. *I feel old.*

She felt Gyhard twitch. *You feel old?*

Chapter Three

Vree's eyes snapped open and she stared at a crack in the rough plaster ceiling over her head, momentarily uncertain of where she was. Then she remembered. Senses extended, she swept the tiny bedroom. There was no danger. She was alone.

Not quite alone.

Vree–ee . . .

Wha–aht? she mocked, throwing back the thin blanket and sliding out of bed. The braided straw mat gave way to painted boards underfoot as she made her way silently into the sitting room. In the liquid light of early morning, she could see that none of the carefully arranged furniture had been moved during the night.

Gyhard gathered his scattered thoughts, flung out of sleep by Vree's sudden, complete, and irritating return to consciousness. *Do you have to wake up so unenclosed quickly?*

Yes. The single hair she'd laid across the latch remained in place. *Wake slow. Die fast.*

So you've said, he muttered, wishing he had teeth to grind. *But you might take under consideration, nothing's trying to kill you.*

You don't know that until you're awake.

You do this wakey-wakey thing to me on purpose, don't you?

No, she replied as she pulled a long-sleeved shirt over her head. Without the weight of wrist sheaths and throwing daggers, her arms felt unnaturally light. *It's training.*

Yeah. Right. Training. Why can't you train yourself to wake up a little slower?

Vree grinned and headed for the privy at the end of the hall. *Because I don't want to.*

Similar conversations had become part of their morning ritual, comforting in a situation where they were making up the rules as they went along.

When her reluctant knock brought a brusque reply, the page pushed open the morning room door and blushed a brilliant scarlet to find both king and consort staring at her, their expressions neutral at best. "Begging your pardon, Majesties, but the chancellor asks if *His* Majesty could find a moment to speak with her. She says it's urgent."

Theron, King of Shkoder, pushed his chair away from the table with something very like relief. "Nadia, isn't it?"

The blush darkened. "Yes, Majesty."

"And it's urgent, you say?"

"Yes, Majesty. The chancellor awaits your pleasure in the small audience chamber."

"Tell her I'll be with her in a moment."

"Yes, Majesty."

As the paneled door closed behind the girl, Lilyana shook her head. "What can be so urgent it can't wait until after you finish your breakfast?" she asked with a sigh.

Theron glanced down at his food. Melon slices, bread with only a thin scraping of butter, a small amount of cold beef, and mint tea; not a sausage, not an egg, not a mug of ale in sight. He'd rather have the chest pains. It was difficult not to regard the chancellor's request as a kind of reprieve although, for Lilyana's sake, he tried not to let that show. "I'm sure Rozele has a good reason to call me away from my meal," he said as he stood, burying his plate under the snowy folds of his discarded linen napkin. "She's never abused her privilege."

"True." While the chancellor had the right to claim the ear of the king at any time, usually the times she claimed were more convenient. Lilyana frowned. "Perhaps I should . . ."

"Stay right here and eat." Coming around the corner of the table, Theron bent and kissed her lightly. "There's no point in both of us having our morning disrupted." He smiled down at her and, suddenly struck by how worried she looked, added, only half jokingly, "If it's trouble, you'll need to keep up your strength."

Rozele i'Natalia, chancellor to the King of Shkoder, turned as Theron entered the small audience chamber and bowed deeply, one hand clutching the dark purple skirt of her robe, the other sketching an apology in the air. "Please forgive me for disturbing you at your meal, Majesty, but I have just been given news I thought you should know immediately."

"I trust your judgment, Chancellor." Theron settled onto the tapestry cushion his younger daughter had worked to soften the uncompromising seat of the carved rosewood throne and indicated that the page following him should set her tray on the round table by his elbow.

Under other circumstances, fully aware that neither sausage rolls nor ale were on the diet the healers had drawn up for the king, Rozele would have faced royal disapproval and pointed it out. This morning, she was far too distracted. She fidgeted until the heavily paneled door closed behind the page, then stepped forward and began.

"Majesty, this morning I met for breakfast with Imrich i'Iduska a'Krisus, a diplomatic courier from your ambassador in the Havakeen Empire."

The king wiped grease off his fingertips. "You met him for breakfast?" he asked, brows lifting slightly.

"Yes, Sire. I thought as we both had to eat we might as well combine the meeting with food and save time."

"The day isn't long enough?"

The chancellor looked confused. It was midway through Second Quarter; of course the days were long. "Majesty?"

"Never mind." Years of practice hid his sigh. While Shkoder appreciated the zeal with which Rozele fulfilled the duties of her position, Shkoder's king occasionally thought she ought to get a life. "Please, continue."

"Yes, Majesty. The report out of the Empire will be on your desk this afternoon, but Lord Imrich gained additional information during the journey home." She paused, gathering her thoughts.

Theron put down his mug and straightened. In the seven years they'd worked together, the chancellor had never needed to gather her thoughts. In seven years, she'd always known exactly what she'd intended to say. This didn't look good. . . .

"Majesty, the Empire has sent an assassin into Shkoder."

"Majesty, the Empire has *not* sent an assassin into Shkoder."

Eyes narrowed, Theron tapped an index finger against the arm of the throne. "Then perhaps you would be good enough to tell me just *what* is going on."

The Bardic Captain shifted position slightly, the hem of her robe whispering caution against the polished parquet floor. In her younger days, she'd walked through blizzards warmer than the king's tone. "Chancellor Rozele has upset you unnecessarily, Majesty. Vireyda Magaly is an ex-assassin . . ."

"As I understand their training," the chancellor interrupted indignantly from her position to the right of the throne, "there is no such thing as an ex-assassin. Or did your bard in Pitesti not inform you of the pirate she killed?"

"She killed the pirate, Majesty," Liene made it very clear to whom she spoke, "to protect the ship she traveled on."

"She killed the pirate, Captain, by leaping between two moving vessels, making her way through an armed and bloodthirsty crew, and slitting the woman's throat." Theron leaned forward. "This does not indicate ex-anything to me."

Liene spread her hands. "Should she not use her skills to protect herself, Majesty? If we had thought she was a danger to the realm, we would not have allowed her to enter the country."

"*You* would not have allowed her to enter the country?" the king repeated incredulously, half rising.

"Since when do the bards make those decisions? You gather the information," he snarled as he sat down again. "I decide what to do with it."

"Yes, Sire. However, if you received every detail the bards gather without some sort of filtering process, you'd have no time to deal with anything else, and as this was a bardic matter ..."

"A bardic matter? An Imperial assassin entering Shkoder is a bardic matter?" Theron leaned back and smiled tightly. "I think I'd like to hear your reasoning."

I think I should have retired a year ago. Liene considered and discarded the option of telling the king only that Vree had acquired a second kigh and leaving it at that. Unfortunately, filtering out trivial information and deliberately misleading a sovereign lord were two entirely different pieces of music. Shooting the chancellor a withering glance, Liene began with Karlene's recall, a sizable document she'd spent half the night reading, and finished with both her and Kovar's personal impressions.

The tight smile remained. "Why didn't the younger bard—what's her name?"

"Karlene, Majesty."

"Yes, Karlene. Why didn't Karlene inform His Imperial Majesty, the Havakeen Emperor, that this Gyhard continued to exist in the assassin's body?"

That was the first easy answer of the morning. "As Gyhard was in some manner responsible for a number of crimes against the Empire, formulating rebellion as Governor Aralt, not to mention intending to murder an Imperial Prince and take over his body ..."

"Not to mention," Rozele repeated dryly.

Liene ignored the interruption. "... Karlene assumed that if the Emperor knew of his continued existence, he would order Gyhard's death. This would be impossible without destroying Vree, and His Majesty must admit she personally has done nothing to merit destruction."

"Except perhaps saving the abomination," Theron growled, but his gesture conceded her point. "So," he leaned back and steepled his fingers, "you are suggesting that for the sake of one ex-assassin, I harbor a traitor to the Imperial Throne. I had thought that his Imperial Majesty required those bards who served in the Empire to swear on their music that they would not act contrary to the needs of the Empire while living there."

"That is true, Majesty. However, those oaths specifically state that earlier oaths take precedence; oaths to Shkoder, oaths to the Bardic Hall."

"And this was bardic business?"

"Precisely, Majesty." Liene's voice deliberately left no room for doubt. "And it continues to be bardic business. It is an excellent opportunity for us to study the fifth kigh, Majesty."

"Oh, yes, the fifth kigh." The king's words took on a distinct edge. "I'm glad you reminded me of that." He jabbed at the air with an emphatic finger. "This assassin is not, do you hear me, *not* to come in contact with my niece!"

Magda sighed and wished that both the Bardic Captain and the chancellor—who bracketed the throne like a pair of scowling old buzzards—were somewhere else. Theron-her-uncle could be got around; not as easily as her father, perhaps, but the principle was the same. Theron-the-king was another matter entirely. "Majesty, I promise you I'm in no danger."

He shook his head. "Child, you have no idea what this assassin is capable of."

"But I *do,* Sire. I read every available reference in the Bardic Library and I'm probably safer with her than I am with anyone. Assassins kill for only two reasons." She held up a finger for each point. "Because they've been ordered to and because they're in mortal danger. That's why she killed the pirate, to save her life. You'd have done the same yourself."

Magda's tone implied that he *could* have done the same himself and Liene hid a smile at a mental picture of Theron leaping from ship to ship with a knife in his teeth. Sixteen years in constant company with bards had taught the girl a trick or two—or perhaps it was those same sixteen years spent wrapping her father around her little finger.

"They're very predictable," Magda continued, leaning forward, practically quivering with intensity. "And besides, she *needs* me. I'm the *only* person in the whole *world* who has any chance of finding Gyhard a body."

The name chased away any amusement Theron might have been feeling at her emphasis. "And what of the abomination?"

"Gyhard doesn't want to hurt me. He needs me, too. Without me, he'll never hold her or love her or . . ."

"Maggi." Theron lifted a hand and cut off the list. "You can't know what an abomination needs."

Yes, I can. But she didn't say it; even though the whole thing was really very simple, true love wasn't the argument that would convince her uncle, the king. She held out both hands and said instead, trying to make it sound as if there could be no question, "I can handle him."

Before the king could speak, Liene leaned forward. "Majesty, she might very well be the *only* person in the *whole* world who can handle him."

"I'm ..."

Surprised.

"... surprised they let you be alone with us."

Magda grinned. "We aren't exactly alone."

"I know." Her tone low and matter-of-fact, Vree kept her eyes on the flagstone path beneath her feet lest she provoke a reaction. "Two people watch us from the middle window on the second floor, one from the roof of the building on the east side of this courtyard, and a guard with a crossbow who believes the ivy at the end of the ..."

Cloister.

"... cloister is hiding him." She lifted her head and glanced at the girl circling the courtyard with her. "But still, I expected ..." A wave over the empty herb gardens indicated the hordes not present.

Her brows drawn into an indignant ebony vee above her nose, Magda glared at the places Vree'd listed. "I *told* them you weren't dangerous," she muttered.

"If I were targeted on you," Vree told her softly, "even the crossbow wouldn't be fast enough."

"Really?" Magda's eyes widened. "Wow." Then she smiled. "But you aren't targeted on me, and you won't be, so you're no danger to me. Right? And besides, you need me. Actually, they're more worried about Gyhard."

"Then the crossbow is less than useless."

"I've always thought so. You should see my father

with a mountain bow. Or even my brother." She dropped onto a weathered plank bench with careless grace and patted the place beside her. "But that wasn't what I meant when I said we aren't exactly alone."

Vree turned her face into the breeze, and the breeze moved away to dance across the tops of the flowering mint. "Kigh."

"Uh-huh."

"Can you . . ."

"Sing them? Nope. I thought you *knew*; I'm not a bard, I'm a healer. Well, I will be a healer. Eventually. They keep saying that I Sing the fifth kigh, but I don't, not *really*. It's more like I *know* the fifth kigh." Her right fist thumped into her chest. "In *here* and when I reach out, I can touch it. I can't do much with it yet, but I'm learning. My mother says she can hear me Sing while I do it, but I'm not so sure that it's me she's hearing." Kicking off a sandal, she brushed the bottom of her bare foot over the thyme growing between stones of the path. "Why did you expect there'd be more people around?"

Wrinkling her nose against the smell of the crushed herb, Vree sank down onto the bench. If she sat facing Magda, she could keep an eye on the guard with the crossbow. "Everyone thinks you're special."

"Really?" Magda looked pleased, then shifted uneasily. "They weren't supposed to tell you."

"I already knew about the fifth kigh."

"Oh. That."

Vree waited patiently. She was good at waiting, most people weren't. Most people had to do something or say something to fill the time.

After a few moments, the tips of her ears bright red,

Magda murmured, "My mother's the king's youngest sister, but you're not supposed to know, so please don't tell them I told you."

That explains a lot they didn't say, Gyhard murmured thoughtfully.

Doesn't it. "They said your mother is a bard."

"They didn't go on about her, did they? I mean, that's *so* embarrassing."

"No, mostly they *hummed* at me."

Her giggle held as much relief as amusement. "Was it Petrelis? He always hums when he's concentrating. He's leaving on a Long Walk this afternoon, and he wanted to get the shape of a kigh before he left." Pulling a damp curl out of the corner of her mouth, she tucked it behind her ear and grinned. "You don't understand, do you? That's okay. You see," her fingers sketched patterns in the air, "a fifth kigh is usually an intricate part of the body it wears, everything all mixed up together, and it's really hard to tell where the kigh ends and the body begins. But if you want to do anything with the kigh, it's *really* important to know where the boundaries are. *I* know, but it's hard to explain it to other people. With you—well, with you and Gyhard—the boundaries are really clear. His kigh is almost completely distinct from you."

"Almost!"

Magda blinked, a little stunned by the near panic in that one word. Her voice gentled. "It's all right." Needing to heal, she reached out to touch Vree's kigh and found herself pushed back.

"No. It isn't all right." Vree turned and stared down at the stone between her feet. "My brother and I nearly lost ourselves in each other. Gyhard and I have to stay separate. I can't go through that again."

"Ah." Magda nodded slowly, understanding dawning. "So *that's* why you're afraid to love him. Nothing tangles two kigh as tightly as love."

"I'm not ..." but there wasn't any point in saying it because the girl knew and she'd already made it clear that she thought it was the most romantic thing she'd ever heard of.

Vree, she's our only chance.

For what? Never mind. Getting angry wouldn't solve anything. Walking away would solve even less. Vree pleated a fold in her wide-legged trousers, her fingers leaving damp prints behind on the fabric. "Look, can we just leave it?"

"Sure, we can leave it. But I want you to know that I only want to help. Really."

"I know." And to her surprise, she did.

You trust her? Gyhard sounded as surprised as she felt. *I don't want to discourage this, Vree, but why?*

Because she isn't afraid of us. Of either of us.

The Imperial Ambassador to the Court of Shkoder stared at the Imperial sunburst on the packet delivered the night before by the mate of the *Gilded Fancy* and sighed deeply. He hated opening packets that bore the Imperial seal as they invariably contained something unpleasant, but he'd delayed opening this one as long as possible. Taking a last, slow swallow of the orange juice he imported from his sister's estates in the Seventh Province, he pushed the dishes from a late lunch aside and picked at the golden wax with one gleaming fingernail.

"I hate unpleasantness," he murmured. There had been trade difficulties of late between Shkoder and the Empire. Shkoder had been complaining for some time that the much larger country to their south had been flooding their market with cheap iron. The complaints had become more forceful, and something was going to have to be done—the Empire had no desire to cut exports. The very nature of the Empire insisted it had to keep expanding, one way or another.

"I hate trade." The ambassador sighed deeply as he broke the seal. "It's such a lousy reason to start a war. If I'm really lucky, this will be nothing more than another Imperial kidnapping."

The details of Prince Otavas' abduction had been under the last golden sunburst he'd received. He'd been informed only because a Shkoden bard had been involved.

He read the thick parchment packet twice.

The Empire had sent an assassin into Shkoder and not just any assassin, but one of the two who'd recently rescued His Imperial Highness and been released from her oaths as a result.

Technically, she was no longer an assassin.

Nor did she think she'd been sent.

She was staying with the bards.

"And just what exactly am I supposed to do with this information?" he asked himself, wondering why everything in Shkoder always seemed to come back to the bards.

When Bannon had shared her head, it had been difficult to find where her thoughts ended and her brother's thoughts began. Their shared lives had created a tangle of hers and his and theirs. Thinking about it afterward, she'd been surprised that Bannon had been able to pull free so easily when the chance came to return to his body. Thinking about *that* later still, during the long days she'd spent wandering the confines of the bardic suite in the Imperial Palace, she realized Bannon had always known which parts were him. Why shouldn't he? She'd defined him all their lives.

Gyhard was different. He was always there, but he never tried to be where she was. She could think around him and be reasonably certain he wouldn't become tangled in the thoughts.

Tucked into the thick window embrasure, Vree stared out over the Citadel wall and down at the city, her hands busy with a dagger and whetstone, needing no guidance after so many edges. If she wanted to leave, they couldn't keep her. She was small enough to fit out of the window, and the jump to the top of the wall—her lip curled—would be less than challenging. The wall itself would be ridiculously easy to descend.

And then what?

Until Gyhard, Bannon had been the one person in her life. There was the army—a living, breathing, single creature—there were targets, and there was Bannon. Occasionally, bits of the army would become more separate than other bits—Emo had almost become a person—but it never lasted. Anyone outside the army was lumped under "other" and forgotten.

She'd had to notice Gyhard; he'd been wearing Bannon's body. Then there'd suddenly been Karlene, just when she needed a hand and Bannon's no longer reached for her. Now, there was Magda, who so desperately wanted to help she was next to impossible not to trust. Three people to take the place of Bannon and an army. . . .

From a room higher in the four-story building, Vree could hear a voice lifted in song. From the other end of her floor, two instruments clashed, sorted themselves out, and began to make music. A breeze lifted her hair off her forehead, and Vree slipped down off the windowsill and inside. If the bards were going to watch her with the kigh, she wasn't going to make it easy for them.

Slipping the dagger into its sheath, Vree caught sight of her reflection in the blade and suddenly wondered if the sifting of her past originated with her or with Gyhard. Was it the situation that drove her to self-discovery or was it him?

Hey.

Hey, what? he answered and her awareness of his presence grew.

Are you messing around in my head?

I wouldn't think of it. She saw the memory of his smile as he spoke. Bannon's smile. No. Bannon's face. Gyhard's smile. *I'm leaving everything exactly as I found it.*

Liar.

The bittersweet sense of inevitability accompanying that single word closed off further conversation.

There were a number of things Gyhard wanted to say, but he couldn't, not without letting Vree know that he had access to more of her thoughts than she realized. Perhaps her need to consolidate her identity did come from him, he had no way of being sure.

He'd seen a man once who'd fallen from a bridge and broken his neck. Against all odds he'd lived, even though the closest thing around to a healer was the village midwife. The man could see and hear and speak, but he couldn't move or do anything with the body he wore. Gyhard had wondered at the time how he'd kept from going mad.

He found himself wondering it again.

The bardic touching, the tracing of his boundaries, had left him restless. Strengthening his sense of self was quite probably the most dangerous thing they could do. He wanted . . .

He wanted Vree. To hold her. To love her. To be held by her. To be loved by her. He wanted them to be able to make a future together. Whether death would eventually have a part in that future, he wasn't sure.

It had been enough just to be with her.

Had been. Now, he wanted a body of his own.

And this is after only one day of poking about at us. Carefully, he reached out and touched Vree's memory of the moment she dragged him back from oblivion. She'd been willing at that instant to do anything rather than lose him. He was trying very hard to do the same.

"Well, can you do it?"

Magda carefully anchored the scroll she'd been studying, one hand resting lightly on a faded line drawing of a caraway plant. Talent made up only a very small part of being a healer and healer's apprentices spent a lot of their evenings in the library. She twisted lithely until she could look the Bardic Captain in the face. "I'm not even sure I know what it is I'm supposed to do."

"Find the abom . . . Gyhard a body with no one dying to provide it."

"Uh-huh. And how am I supposed to do that?"

Liene scowled, drummed her fingers against the head of her cane, and finally stomped away.

Magda shook her head and went back to her reading. It was a good thing both her mother and Stasya had warned her that the old woman's bark was worse than her bite. Although Stasya *had* pointed out that Liene still had all her teeth.

They'd warned her about a number of other things as well, but she'd happily disregarded most of them.

Sighing, Magda brushed a curl away from her face. "A body without a kigh is a dead body and I can't just shove his kigh into a dead body." She made a disgusted moue at the thought. From the mice the cats used to leave on the steps of the keep to those the healers had not been able to save, dead bodies were *not* among her favorite things.

The pass between Shkoder and the Empire looked as though a giant had carved it out of the Smitts Mountains with a knife. Sheer rock walls rose up on either side of a broad passage years of use had made as easy to travel as any lowland road. Long before the current king's grandmother had convinced their duc to join the kingdom, the miners of the mountain principality of Somes had traded iron ore with the First Province of the Empire through that pass, picks and shovels amending what nature began.

As Jazep approached the guard tower on the Shkoder side, he could just barely make out through the early morning haze the Empire's sunburst flying next to the crowned ship at the midpoint of the pass.

Two of the three guards came hurrying out to meet him.

"Jazep? Is that you?"

A huge smile split the bard's grizzled beard. "Nastka! I was wondering why I hadn't seen you in town!"

"Now you know." Tossing her helm to her companion, she returned his hug with equal enthusiasm, leather armor creaking. "What brings you up here? Not crossing surely? We had two of those Imperial fledglings up here during my last shift. Who was with them? I know, Tesia. She took them to the halfway point and said she was letting them feel the difference you get in earth kigh when you're standing on your own soil. She wasn't kidding me, was she?"

"No. The kigh can always tell when you've come home." He shifted his feet and his smile faded. "I backtracked a disturbance in the kigh to the pass."

"Do tell." Nastka retrieved her helm. "Trouble?"

Jazep shrugged. "I don't know. Troubling. It's almost as if they're afraid."

"The kigh? Afraid? I don't like the sound of that."

"No, neither do I." He turned and looked toward the Empire. "Can you remember what and who came through five days ago?"

"I can do better than that. Mila—oh, this is Mila, by the way." The second guard nodded shyly. "It's her first shift at the pass. Jakub's up at the beacon. You remember him, skinny guy with too much red hair?"

"I remember."

"Of course you do. Mila, go get the lists." As the younger woman ran back to the tower, Nastka grinned proudly. "Duc's seeing to it that everyone in the guard can read and write."

Jazep had actually heard that from the Duc of Somes herself, but the disturbance in the kigh had driven it right out of his mind. "Her Grace has a lot of good ideas."

"Her Grace is going to put this place in a song."

"I saw Jelena when I went through town."

Nastka's grin softened and her dark eyes shone. "She's grown into a beautiful woman, hasn't she?"

"She has." Jazep reached out and gripped the guard's shoulder. "Just like her mother."

A few moments later, he frowned down at the rough sheet of paper and shook his head. "Two wagons and a single traveler. Not exactly a busy day. Do any of them stand out?"

"Well, the old man ..." Mila began, then lapsed into an embarrassed silence when both Jazep and Nastka turned to look at her.

"Go on," Jazep urged, using just enough charm to put the girl at ease.

"It's just he was so old. I couldn't believe he was able to walk at all, let alone cross the mountains from the Empire into Somes. He said he was looking for his family."

"Is that all?" It was difficult to imagine how one old man could so upset the kigh.

"No." Mila shook her head, frowning as she remembered. "As he walked away, he said, 'Come, Kait.' But he was all alone."

Chapter Four

"His Imperial Majesty desires your presence in his private audience chamber."

On his way out of the palace to an assignation with a very obliging young wine merchant, Bannon stared in disbelief at the guard blocking his path. "The Emperor wants to see *me*? Why?"

"I did not presume to inquire." She managed to sound simultaneously sanctimonious and disapproving.

"But I bet you know." the ex-assassin grinned, his tone evoking the shared camaraderie of uniform.

For a moment, he thought she was going to tell him, then, after a barely perceivable shake of her head, she snapped, "I know only that His Imperial Majesty desires your presence in his private audience chamber."

It's trouble and she's keeping her distance. Imperial assassins were trained to recognize danger in all its unexpected forms and, while his mind raced, trying to work out what he'd done to merit the personal attention of the Emperor, Bannon fought to calm the pounding of his heart. Whatever the danger, he wasn't going to get out of it on the edge of a blade. He needed information. "Have I time to change into a clean tunic?"

"No." Her eyes remained focused on the wall just behind his left shoulder.

"Prince Otavas is with the Empress; I should let him know where I am in case he sends for me." Considering he was the prince's personal bodyguard, it was a reasonable request.

"If His Majesty decides His Highness should know your location, His Majesty will have His Highness informed."

Big trouble. She turned, beckoned with her pike, and Bannon fell into step beside her, still with no idea of what he'd done. His unease grew as they walked through a palace complex crawling with courtiers and servants and the less easily defined classes between and passed no one he knew. By the time they reached the narrow flight of stairs leading up to the section of the palace reserved exclusively for the Emperor, sweat stained his tunic. Not even the tight muscles of the guard's butt moving under her uniform kilt as she led the way up the stairs distracted him for more than a moment or two and, as he climbed, he became increasingly conscious of the empty space at his back. *Vree, where are you when I need you!*

The half-dozen soldiers of the First Army waiting in the antechamber ignored him until he reached the small, iron-bound door. Then the corporal stepped forward and demanded his weapons. Bannon had been at the palace long enough to know that no one approached the Emperor armed but something in the corporal's tone lifted the hair on the back of his neck.

Slowly and deliberately, he drew the long dagger off his belt, unbuckled the two wrist sheaths, slid the extra throwing dagger out of the sheath strapped to his left shoulder, and removed the slender blades from the ornate leather tongues of his high sandals. Under other circumstances, he would've found the corporal's expression hilarious as he reached under his kilt and drew the three throwing stars out of their strap on the front of his sling. As it was, he merely added them to the pile and waited for the door to be opened.

When it closed behind him, habit scanned the room for avenues of escape—there were none. Marshal Usef, commander of the First Army, stood rigid behind the throne, his face below his crested helm twisted with rage, both hands crushing his heavy belt as though that grip alone kept his hands from Bannon's throat. Seated on the throne, his calm a stark and frightening contrast to the marshal's agitation, the Emperor lifted a hand and beckoned him forward, rings flashing in the lamplight.

With his mind shrieking, "Danger!" loud enough to drown out the pounding of his heart, Bannon dropped to one knee at the edge of the dais, needing Vree beside him so badly he almost saw her there.

"Is the tale you told my son the truth?" the Emperor asked. In spite of the gentle tone, each word emerged as a separate and distinct threat.

Startled, Bannon looked up. What could he have told the prince that would ...? Then, all at once, he understood. Part of the story had slipped out when Otavas asked him why he was so angry with his sister and, once started, the rest just seemed to follow.

Silk whispered against silk as His Imperial Majesty leaned forward. "There are no secrets from me in this Empire," he said. "Did your sister save the spirit of the man who led a rebellion against me? A man who intended to take the life of an Imperial Prince? And did you lie to me about it, telling me that this man was dead?"

His mouth gone too dry for speech, the stink of his own fear in his nose, Bannon nodded.

"Treason," Usef hissed, and his hand moved from his belt to close around the jeweled hilt of his sword.

Even weaponless, Bannon knew he could defeat the marshal. But then what? His mind raced. There were guards outside the small door to the antechamber and undoubtedly guards outside the larger door leading to a less private audience hall. One word from the Emperor and a good part of the first army would be in the room. He couldn't fight them all. Not alone. But if he silenced the Emperor? A fist closed around his throat, and he couldn't breathe. Lay hands on the Emperor? He didn't think he could. He didn't want to die. "Majesty, I . . ."

"You lied to protect your sister," the Emperor cut him off. "I understand that."

Bannon's eyes widened as he suddenly realized that the treason Usef referred to was not the treason he'd committed in presenting Prince Otavas' body for Gyhard's use—a direct breaking of his vow to protect the Imperial Family. The Emperor only knew that Gyhard was alive, and he understood about the lesser treason of the lie. Bannon's relief was so great, he had to fight to keep himself from trembling and at that moment he'd have walked through fire had the Emperor commanded.

"Why the bards lied, I do not yet understand." For a moment, the Imperial voice evoked shadowed rooms and heated iron. "But I will. Unfortunately, as they are both away from the Capital training our native-born bards, answers will have to wait." Bannon found himself caught in a dark gaze that seemed to strip away skin and muscle and bones and stare straight into his heart. "For now, we will have no further lies between us." the Emperor leaned back. "Marshal, relax. This young man is not a danger to me. He wants to help. Don't you?"

"Yes, Majesty." His voice sounded hoarse, barely under his command. "Yes, Majesty," he repeated; clearer, firmer. "I want to help."

"Good." Imperial approval touched him like a benediction, filled for a moment the empty space where Vree had been, then disappeared. "I want this Gyhard back in the Empire. I want him to pay for his crimes. I want you to go to Shkoder and bring him back to me because, after the great wrong he did you, I believe *you* have the right to bring him to justice."

Bannon ground his teeth at the thought of Gyhard paying for what he'd done, paying for every instant he'd spent usurping Bannon's body. And then, through the hate, he remembered. "But, Majesty, my sister . . ."

"The sister he took from you? The sister he controls?"

"Controls?"

The Emperor spread his hands. "How else would you explain her denying her training? Her denying everything she lived for? Her denying you?"

How else?

Back at last in his own body, Bannon felt Gyhard turn his head to stare at Vree, felt the surge of the other man's emotion, and heard his voice say, "I love you."

Then he pushed, viciously throwing the intruder from his body, and was alone.

"NO!" Vree's denial held as much pain as rage.

Because he'd shared her mind for so long, he knew

*what she was going to do and why and he was power-
less to stop her.*

How else could he explain her choosing Gyhard
over him? Bannon's hands opened and closed as
though they held the other man's life and slowly
crushed it.

"I give you your sister's life. I want only the one
who was Aralt."

Not as much as Bannon did. "But, Majesty, the
bards said they couldn't remove Gyhard without hurting Vree." It was, he told himself, the only reason
he'd supported the lie. He even half believed it.

"If you return your sister to the Empire, I will see
to it that the bards will be able to do exactly as I
command them. We are no longer dependent on
Shkoden bards."

It might work. Vree would hesitate, unable to raise
her blade against him. He would capture her, blindfold
her, and contain Gyhard until they returned to the
Empire. Rubbing his palms together, Bannon frowned.
"Majesty, if the bards are protecting him, I won't be
able to get close to Vree. The moment those kigh
things tell them I'm coming, they'll hide her."

"Which is why I am sending the Prince Otavas to
Shkoder to visit his uncle, the king." The Emperor's
voice softened as he spoke of his son. "The boy has
had a distressing experience and needs his mind
turned to other things. As Otavas' personal bodyguard, you will go to Shkoder with my son's household. The palace is very close to the hall of the bards.
It will be natural for you to seek out and spend time
with your sister. I will speak with Otavas tonight and
you will leave as soon as possible." He pointed at the
assassin kneeling before him, and Bannon could feel

the weight of his commission. "I am loosing you at a
target. A target only the very best could hope to
strike. Bring me justice for the Empire; justice for
yourself."

"I will not fail you, Majesty."

"I know that you won't."

Recognizing a dismissal, Bannon stood, bowed, and
backed to the door. Soon, the empty space in his life
would be filled. Soon, the person responsible for emp-
tying it would pay.

As the door to the antechamber closed, the Emperor nearly smiled. "He never looked; did you notice,
Usef? He backed straight to the door, absolutely positive he knew where it was. Can you imagine having
that certain a sense of place?"

"He is dangerous, Majesty." Stepping forward into
the Emperor's line of sight, Usef was nearly purple
under the force of his emotion. "The blades of Jiir
should not exist outside the sheath of the army."

"But you forget. Neither he nor his sister are assassins any longer."

The marshal bit back a reply that would have
stretched Imperial indulgence. His Majesty himself
had said training did not permit an ex-assassin, but if
His Majesty wished to be facetious, there was nothing
he could do about it.

"It seems, Usef, that you were right; it was a mistake to send the woman to Shkoder. But it seems also
that I was right; we have found a use for her brother."

"Begging Your Majesty's pardon, but why manipulate this, this fool into bringing her back? They are
both guilty of treason, Majesty. Treason! They lied to
you. You should have them killed!" Then he realized

what he'd said. "Not *should*, Majesty, I would never
so presume. It is merely my belief that they should
not be permitted to live."

The Emperor lifted a forgiving hand. "Perhaps they
won't be, but first I desire to speak with this Gyhard
and I need Bannon to bring him to me. He's the only
person in the Empire with the slightest chance of actually capturing the body Gyhard wears."

"But you can't trust Bannon, Majesty. He's
proved that."

"Did you know that I've never lost a hawk, Marshal? Every single hawk I have ever flown has come
back to me." He studied the scars on his left wrist,
the marks of talons made in spite of gloves and padding. "That's something very few can say. Young Bannon has proved only that he's unwilling to see his
sister hurt. *I'm* willing to allow him to believe in her
safety in exchange."

"In exchange for what, Majesty?"

"Think about it, Marshal. What does this Gyhard
have that any sane person would desire?"

Usef frowned as he attempted to follow his Emper-
or's line of thought. "Control of an Imperial
assassin?"

"Immortality, Marshal. Immortality."

*. . . first time was an accident. When the brigand
speared me, I only knew that I didn't want to die.
When oblivion began to close around me, I fought
it—fought my way through it and out the other side.
The next thing I knew, I was in the brigand's body
and he was in mine. When I tried to go home, they
only saw the body I wore.*

Perched on the edge of the bench, forcing herself

to remain still, Vree repeated Gyhard's story. Not until she finished, did she turn and look at Magda.

The apprentice healer sat, bare feet up beside her, legs tucked into the circle of her arms, chin resting on her knees. Her dark eyes were locked on Vree's face. "What about the second time?" she said softly.

The second time? Vree felt Gyhard move restlessly within the limits he'd set on himself. *The second time,* he repeated, *was no accident. . . .*

He'd been Hinrich for seven years and that was seven years too long. In the beginning, hunted away from his home because of the body he wore, he'd thrown himself into his new identity. If his own family would treat him as a brigand, than a brigand he would be. He suspected that he hadn't been entirely sane those first few years although as he could remember every excess, every disgusting or violent act, insanity didn't seem like much of a defense.

Later, after thieving and whoring had lost its appeal, he'd made a living of sorts from an ability to brutalize those smaller and weaker than himself. Finally, he'd ended up as a caravan guard for traders too poor or too stupid to hire anyone better. He'd crossed the mountains into Cemandia with two ramshackle wagons full of junk and after drinking away his pay, such as it was, in a Cemandian tavern, he found himself heading back into the mountains again. He didn't know why. He only knew he didn't want to be Hinrich any longer.

Three nights later, sober, cold, and hungry, he followed a stream to a shadowed pool, drawn by the smell of woodsmoke and roasting fish.

"Lord and Lady!" The young man behind the fire snatched up a staff. "Where did you come from?"

He turned and pointed back along the stream. "From Artis Falls." He thought that was the name of the town, but he was so hungry he wasn't sure.

"Are you lost?"

Was he lost? Clamping his teeth around a bitter laugh, he nodded, then, drawn by the smell of the food, he staggered forward another two steps.

"Are you hungry? No, wait." A luminescent smile flashed in the dusk. "That's a stupid question. You're obviously starving. Well, the dogs caught their own dinner earlier on, so there's plenty for two." The crooked staff pointed across the fire. "Sit. It's almost done."

Sitting turned into a barely controlled fall and a few moments later he was stuffing fish into his mouth too fast to taste it. Some kind of roasted roots followed— their Cemandian name meant nothing to him—and by the time he finished all he was offered, his brain had started working again. "Shepherd?" he asked as the sounds drifting in from the night began to make sense.

"That's right." Again the smile. "Tomas."

"Hinrich." But not for much longer.

Tomas stirred the embers, a shock of dark hair falling forward over brilliant eyes. "You talk funny. You're not Cemandian, are you."

"From Shkoder."

The shepherd laughed. "If you're heading home, you've missed the pass."

"I have no home."

"Oh. I'm sorry." Tomas shifted about, then launched into a long story about his own home to cover his embarrassment.

He didn't want to know about the shepherd's home. Or his past. Or his life. Knowing he was a shepherd was almost too much. He stood.

Tomas paused and looked a question at him.

"I need to wash." That was undeniable. He stepped toward the pool.

"Be careful, it's deep."

That would make it easier. Heart pounding, he knelt and stared at the water. The surface was bright with reflected starlight, but when he slid his hand beneath the surface, it disappeared into darkness. *This has to work,* he thought as he let himself fall forward. *I can't be Hinrich anymore.*

He'd known all along what he had to do, but he'd never been able to find the courage. He still hadn't. Desperation would have to serve.

Terror nearly flung him back to the surface, but he added the weight of those seven years to the weight of his sodden clothes and he drew in a lungful of water.

Except for the panic trying to claw its way free, it was almost peaceful.

He felt a hand close around his arm. Felt himself dragged upward. He twisted. And released the panic.

He was dying!

No!

Drowning!

No!

There was a shape above him, a patch of darkness with no stars.

A face.

Time stopped as he launched himself toward a pair of brilliant eyes. He fought for room, shoving everything that got in his way—images of sheep, dogs, parents, friends—viciously back behind him.

Then he was staring down through an inch of water at a sandy-haired man with a bristling red beard and a face contorted in unbelieving horror. Shifting his grip, he held him under until the struggling stopped, then he let the body float away.

He wasn't Hinrich anymore.

He was Tomas.

Tomas, Gyhard repeated. He felt Magda touch Vree gently on the shoulder, felt Vree turn to face her, and lost himself in a wave of pity. In seven lives over a hundred and thirty years, no one had ever pitied him. He wanted to hide. He wanted to scream. In the end, with an image of Vree standing guard at his back, he did neither.

"It took a long time for Gyhard to heal," Magda murmured.

That's no excuse. But he was surprised by how much he wanted it to be. *I'll tell you what I told Vree, don't make me a tragic hero. I knew exactly what I was doing.*

"I know. But I don't think you can ignore why you were doing it."

"Wait a minute." Vree held up both hands and scowled at the girl. "You heard him?"

Magda nodded, eyes wide.

Can you hear me now? When it became obvious she didn't, he repeated the question, much louder.

Vree winced and Magda lightly laid a hand on her knee. "Are you okay?"

"I'm fine."

Sorry. He knew the apology sounded terse, but his isolation had been broken for an instant and now it seemed that instant was over.

"I heard him." Magda looked down at her hand, still resting on Vree's knee. "I heard you. You said sorry. Say something else."

You must need physical contact.

She lifted her hand. "There's only one way to find out."

A moment later Vree muttered, "He wants you to touch me again."

Why is this happening? Gyhard demanded, when Magda's fingers lay against Vree's palm.

All three of them considered it for a moment. Finally, Magda shrugged. "I think it's because I touched your kigh."

Vree fought down a completely irrational flash of jealousy. "And?"

"And I think it's sad that a man so terribly afraid of dying thought he had to keep dying to live."

When Jazep saw the cluster of villagers hurrying out of Bartek Springs to meet him, he knew it had to do with the disturbance he'd been following in the kigh. The path led right by the village; too close not to have affected the people who lived in the cluster of half-timbered houses.

"Jazep!"

He dipped lightly into recall for the name of the woman who hailed him. Memory had Celestin's braid more brown than gray, but there could be no mistaking either the strong beauty of her face or the focused determination in her movements. As the only priest for at least three days in any direction, she took responsibility for the spiritual well-being of an extended Circle. Drawing closer, he was surprised to see her expression held equal parts fear and relief and his worry about what he followed grew.

When she reached him, she gripped his arm as though she gripped a lifeline. "Thank all the gods enclosed by the Circle that you've come. Did Brencis meet you on the way?" She leaned a little to the right in order to see beyond his bulk. "Where is he?"

"I'm afraid I haven't seen Brencis." Jazep closed his hand lightly around the priest's as the clump of villagers murmured behind her. In spite of the Second Quarter heat, her fingers were freezing. "What's wrong?"

Celestin took a deep breath and let go of his arm. "We sent Brencis out to find us a bard. Something . . . something has disturbed our dead."

"Scavengers?"

"No." A younger woman Jazep didn't know made an emphatic denial. "Not scavengers. Scavengers don't . . ."

Celestin cut her off. "I think you'd better see for yourself."

As they hurried through the village, she refused to elaborate, saying only, "I want your opinion unclouded by our fear."

In the graveyard, a young man stood protectively over a blanket-covered mound that lay a short distance from a disturbed grave. Jazep frowned. There was something wrong about the way the earth had been piled. *Almost as if . . . No.* He shook his head. *Impossible.*

The young man watched warily as the bard approached. His eyes were red and swollen, and he looked as though a gentle breeze could push him over whatever edge it was he tottered on.

"Dymek," Celestin called. "This is Jazep. He's a bard. Let him see."

"Bard?" Dymek repeated hoarsely. Hope skirted around grief. "Can you tell me what happened? Can you help Filip rest?"

"I'll do what I can," Jazep assured him gently. He gestured at the blanket. "May I?"

Dymek nodded, his head jerking up and down as though he had little control over its movement.

The young man under the blanket had been dead for only six or seven days. Unfortunately, six or seven days in Second Quarter was five or six days too long to be out of the ground. Jazep waved a cloud of flies away, swallowed hard, and breathed shallowly through his mouth. Filip had obviously died of massive trauma to his lower body. His legs within the unbleached linen burial clothes seemed strangely flat and the single foot hung unnaturally from a crushed ankle. But the position of the body . . .

Jazep stood, thankfully took a deeper breath, and looked back toward the open grave. He moved closer, squatted, and Sang.

No kigh responded.

They were there. He could feel them. Could feel the same disturbance he'd followed from the border. Still Singing, he slid out of his pack, unhooked his tambour, and added a compelling beat to the Song. A lone kigh rose partway out of the ground, squat body radiating distress. Jazep Sang it comfort for a moment, then changed the Song to ask it what had happened. It disappeared and refused to return.

The Song slid into silence. Gnawing at his lower lip, Jazep stood, drum dangling from one hand.

"Jazep?" Celestin prodded.

He looked at the grave, at the body, at the priest, at the villagers, and realized he'd come to the same conclusion they had. "It seems," he said slowly, "that something or someone partially unburied Filip and he dragged himself the rest of the way out. That he pulled himself over there on his hands and then he collapsed."

"He was dead when we buried him," Dymek whispered. "He was *dead.* I swear it."

"I believe you," Jazep told him, using enough Voice to be believed in turn and catching him barely in time when he fainted.

"Dymek found him two mornings ago." Together, bard and priest watched as those villagers able to overcome their fear took turns redigging Filip's grave. "His scream dragged me out of a sunrise service and up here at a run. He was kneeling, just over an arm's length away from the body, reaching out but too terrified to touch." Celestin turned enough to see Dymek sobbing within the circle of his parents' arms. "He'd only just begun to accept Filip was dead; now this."

"He loved Filip very much," Jazep murmured.

Celestin nodded. "He did. He does." She looked at Jazep, her cheeks ashen. "This thing you've been following, this thing that's frightening the kigh and hurting my people, what precisely is it doing? I mean, besides reanimating the dead."

"I don't know."

"What are you going to do when you catch up to it?"

Jazep shook his head, one hand lightly stroking the bellows of his pipes. "Stop it."

When all the loose dirt had been dug out, Filip,

wrapped again in a linen winding cloth, was lowered back into the earth. Standing at the head of the grave, Celestin traced the Circle on her breast with a fistful of dirt. "We give back to the earth as we have taken from it," she said as she scattered the dirt on the body.

"The Circle encloses us all," Jazep answered with the villagers. In the prayers that followed, he could hear an undertone of uncertainty; hardly surprising as this was the second time the prayers had been said. When they were finished, he stepped into the priest's place, settled the drones on his shoulder, and began to play.

He played grief that a young man was dead, anger at the disinterment, comfort to Dymek, to the rest of Filip's family and friends, and then he called the kigh. They came this time with an enthusiasm that suggested they were as interested in making this right as he was. The pile of dirt slid down into the hole, spread itself, and enfolded Filip back into the earth's embrace.

That should've been enough, but when Jazep tried to leave the graveside, he found he couldn't move. The kigh held him in place.

Tucking the pipes back under his arm, he Sang. Reluctantly, the kigh moved away.

"What is it?" Celestin asked, hurrying to his side.

"I don't know."

Dymek jerked forward, eyes wide, his hand stretched out toward the bard. "Is it about Filip?"

"No, not about Filip," Jazep told him gently, catching hold of the younger man's fingers for a brief moment of reassurance. "They want me to help a lost kigh."

"I can feel him, you know. It's like I can reach out and he's there."

Celestin moved to put an arm around his shoulder. "He'll always be in your heart."

Dymek shook his head, tears spilling down his cheeks. "No. It's like he's still *here*!"

As Dymek's parents led their son from the grave-yard, their own faces twisted with grieving, bard and priest exchanged a helpless glance. Time would have to heal what they could not.

"Will you stay for a while?" Celestin asked when they were alone beside the grave.

"No. I have to catch up to whatever's causing this before it can reach another village."

"And do the same thing."

Jazep nodded grimly. "Or worse." He stepped toward his pack and found the kigh had anchored his feet once again. When he asked them why, he got the same answer he had before. They wanted him to Sing home a lost kigh.

"How can a kigh be lost?" Celestin wondered when he told her.

"They can't. At least, I never knew they could." Brow furrowed, he Sang a different question. He changed the phrasing. He changed the pitch of the Song. Finally he gave up. "I don't know what they're talking about," he admitted, pulling at his beard in bewildered frustration. "They just keep repeating the same thing, over and over." It almost tore him in two, but he couldn't take the time to learn what they wanted—not when past experience said it could take days.

They made him Sing his feet free every step across

the graveyard. When he had to Sing the kigh away from his pack, Celestin lightly touched his shoulder.

"Perhaps you should stay."

"I can't." The words ripped great holes in his heart.

"Have you told them why?" She gestured at the ground.

"They don't *understand*." The final word became a plea for understanding from the priest. When she nodded, he swung the pack up onto his shoulders. "Look, Brencis is still out there trying to contact a bard. Sooner or later, he'll come home with one. If they can Sing air, have them send your recall to the Bardic Hall—everyone should know about this. If they can Sing earth ..." For a moment he was unable to go on. "If they can Sing earth, ask them to help the kigh."

The earth tugged at his shoes as Jazep hurried away from the village. Voice tight in his throat, he sang to the breezes as he walked, hoping one of them would carry the news to a bard who could hear it.

Head cocked, one hand lifted to stroke the air, Annice frowned. "Something's wrong."

"At the keep?"

"No." The bard squinted up the length of the valley to bring the distant stone bulk of the keep into better focus. "It's definitely not Stasya. In fact ..." Her frown deepened as she slowly pivoted, trying to pinpoint the source. "... it's not really a Song, it's more a ... feeling."

Pjerin, Duc of Ohrid, stepped back from the stooked corn, swept an approving gaze over the work continuing in the rest of the field, and finally turned to face Annice. While he'd come to appreciate bardic abilities over the last seventeen years, he'd spent a lifetime learning that good weather seldom lasted so close to Third Quarter Festival. He wanted the field stacked by dark, and that wasn't going to happen if *something* was wrong.

"A feeling?" he repeated irritably. "Annice . . ." An imperious wave of her hand cut him off and he folded his arms across his chest with a scowl. The scowl lightened as he realized the extent of her concern and, watching the play of emotions across her face while she Called the kigh, he began, himself, to feel a faint sense of unease.

Although the kigh seemed skittish, they couldn't answer Annice's questions. "Too far," she muttered at last, having Sung an unhappy gratitude.

Ohrid stood on the border between Shkoder and Cemandia, the farthest of the five mountain principalities from Elbasan. The farthest from the Healers' Hall. Pjerin stepped forward, as though to close the distance. "Is it about Magda?"

"No, I don't think so."

He turned on her, violet eyes narrowed. "You don't think so? If you're not *certain*, check."

His tone left no room for disagreement. Under other circumstances, Annice would have disagreed anyway, on principle—growing older had only intensified Pjerin's fondness for having his own way—but not this time. Hearing the fear behind the arrogance, she called the kigh back and Sang the four notes of their daughter's name. She didn't believe the wrongness had anything to do with Magda but, now that the possibility had occurred to Pjerin, she knew he'd not let it rest until he was convinced their child was safe.

"Shall I have them check up on Gerek as well?" she wondered. Although Gerek was not her son by birth, she had long since come to consider him hers, much the same way she'd come to consider all of Ohrid hers.

"Gerek," Pjerin growled, "is a grown man and does not need you peering over his shoulder!"

"Magda is . . ."

"A child," her father declared.

And that was that.

Over half the crop had been stacked by the time the kigh returned with the unmistakable message that all was well at the Healers' Hall. Magda was in no danger the kigh could discover.

The wrongness remained, a shadow over the Circle; faint and undefined, impossible to ignore.

"If not Magda," Annice asked herself, growing increasingly concerned, "then who?"

"Tadeus!" Magda flung herself past Vree, across the courtyard, and into the arms of a slight man standing just at the edge of the cloister. He laughed as the force of her greeting rocked him back on his heels and Vree, who'd spun around into a defensive position at the sound of footsteps behind her, relaxed slightly.

I think she knows him, Gyhard observed dryly as Magda dragged him forward.

When Tadeus stepped out into the late afternoon sun, Vree realized that the shadow covering his eyes was a narrow black leather band cut to perch on his nose and loop back over his ears. *He's blind.*

So it seems.

He's also not alone. Tadeus' companion moved hesitantly out of the cloisters and Vree was astounded to see he was Southern. In fact, if she had to place him more precisely, she'd say Sixth or Seventh Province based on the cinnamon-brown of his skin.

"Vree, Gyhard, this is Tadeus." Tucked in the semicircle of his right arm, Magda smiled proudly at the bard as though he were something she'd thought up on her own. "He's one of my name-fathers. Tadeus, this is . . ."

"The young Imperial citizen who carries the two kigh." His smile held a warmth Vree felt herself responding to. "It's actually you I've come to see."

"Tadeus!"

Ignoring Magda's exaggerated protest, he half-turned toward the Southerner and beckoned him forward. "Ullious here is one of the four remaining Imperial fledglings, and when he heard you were in the country, he expressed a very natural desire to meet you." A breeze ruffled silver-shot curls as he reached out an unerring hand and pulled the fledgling to his side. "Ullious, this is Vree and Gyhard who are sharing a body. Vree, Gyhard, this is Ullious who has an astonishing command of air and a truly amazing tenor."

"Better than yours?" Magda dug an elbow into his ribs.

"Don't be impudent, brat, or I'll tell your mother you've quit your studies, taken up hayla dancing, and are living with a drunk who beats you."

"She'd never believe that."

"You're right." Garnets glittered in his ears as he cocked his head to grin down at her. "But I could always tell her you were looking pale and I didn't think you were eating properly."

Magda winced. "She'd be here the next day."

"Or sooner," Tadeus agreed. He pinched her chin.

"So why don't you tell me what you *have* been doing, I'll pass on what I think Annice should know, and the rest can be a secret between us."

"But Vree ..."

"Can spend a few moments with Ullious who I'm sure would love to speak his own language with someone who doesn't confuse verb tenses." Tadeus turned and Vree had the strangest feeling he was smiling directly at her although he couldn't possibly see anything through the leather band. "You don't mind me stolen my name-daughter away for a little while, do you?" he asked in Imperial.

"Stealing," Ullious murmured. "Not stolen; stealing."

Tadeus winced. "Verb tenses," he muttered. "Hate 'em. Come along, Maggi, we'll sit over here and you can tell me all about the hearts you've broken while I was gone."

"I'd rather hear about the hearts *you've* broken," Magda declared as they walked toward a bench set into the far wall of the courtyard.

Vree thought she'd never heard anything quite so engaging as Tadeus' laugh. "When you're older, child," she heard him say. "When you're older."

"He's still friends with every lover he ever had," Ullious observed quietly. "And he has a lot of friends."

I'll bet. Gyhard sounded so appreciative, Vree couldn't help but smile. The expression seemed to reassure Ullious.

"You're not what I expected," he said, nervously brushing at his narrow mustache.

The smile faded. "Because I'm an assassin?"

"No, I've met assassins. I spent four years in the

Seventh Army—Third Division, Second Company, Second Unit, First Squad." He looked a little startled at the involuntary completion of the list, then he went on. "It's just that you're you, and Gyhard's himself, and there's so obviously two of you in one body. When the kigh brought us the news about you, I guess I expected things would be mixed up a little more."

"Does *everyone* know about us?" Vree growled.

Ullious shook his head. "Oh, no. Only the bards who Sing air."

"And there're how many of those?"

"Actually," he shrugged a bit sheepishly, "most of the bards Sing air."

Vree couldn't keep from glancing up into the square of sky framed by the courtyard. A shadow flickered on the west roof of the Healers' Hall as an archer moved back out of sight. *I wonder how many of them are watching us now.*

You could ask.

Think he'd tell me?

"You were talking to him, weren't you?" Ullious leaned a little forward, eyes shining.

"Yes."

The blunt monosyllable stopped conversation cold. In the distance, Vree could hear Magda filling the older bard in on the details of her life. As usual, she didn't appear to be bothering to breathe.

"You're not what I expected either," Vree admitted at last. "I thought fledglings were supposed to be young."

Oh, that's tactful.

"Younger," she corrected hurriedly.

Ullious ran a self-conscious hand over his thinning hair. "The Emperor has only allowed citizens to be tested over the last four years," he explained. "When I heard, two years ago—news travels slowly to the South . . ."

Unless it comes with a tax collector, Gyhard added and Vree remembered he'd been, as Aralt, governor of a Southern region.

"I sold my carting business and went to the Capital. The bard Karlene met me at the South Gate saying the kigh told her I was coming." He flushed with pleasure at the memory. "She didn't have to test me. She spoke of you."

Vree blinked. "Two years ago?"

"No. Twelve days ago. Tadeus had me practice Singing the kigh over long distances and from up the coast to Karlene was the longest distance we had. She said I was to see that you weren't lonely." He spread his hands. "Can you be lonely? I mean under the circumstances?"

She could feel Gyhard waiting for her answer. "Homesick," she said at last, "but not lonely." All at once, as though they'd been waiting for her to admit it, the pale gray stone of the buildings, the scent of the surrounding herbs, even the clothes Ullious wore seemed strange and unsettling. Hurriedly, she focused on his face, which could have been any of a hundred faces from home. "And you?"

"I am learning to be a bard, with bards. Lines drawn on a map mean nothing to that. But still . . ." he reached out and, fleetingly, touched the back of her hand. "It's good to see someone from home." Then he grinned, lightening the moment. "If only because everyone in Shkoder is so slaughtering tall."

Vree laughed, as much at the army curse coming from the fledgling bard as at the observation. *"I'm* small even for a Southerner. Magda is the first person I've met since I arrived that I can look in the eye."

As though she'd heard her name, Magda's voice rose momentarily over the background drone of the bees. ". . . realized when I touched her kigh that she still blamed herself for the death of her baby. Once we knew that . . ."

"She's very special," Ullious murmured as they both turned to look. "She'll be able to heal a lot of people who would otherwise have no hope at all."

Like us.

Like us, Vree agreed. Then she thought of Gyhard in a body of his own, and heard Ullious ask again, *"Can you be lonely?"* She'd already lost Bannon.

By nightfall it was obvious that the thing disturbing the kigh was moving east along the mountains. It crossed from Somes to Bicaz at a ford in the Spotted Fish River and Jazep would've given his left leg to have been able to Sing to the water kigh at the crossing. He still had no way of knowing if more than the earth was upset.

As he drew closer, the kigh became more and more agitated and harder to reach. If he hadn't known better, he'd have sworn they were afraid. Certain he was only a short distance behind, he walked until he nearly put out an eye on an overhanging branch, then reluctantly made a quick, cold supper and rolled up in his blanket for what remained of the night. Although cloud cover made the dark impenetrable, he didn't think it would rain.

He was wrong.

By dawn, he was wet and miserable and hoping he'd

run into his quarry soon so he could make the most use of his mood. Grinding up a mouthful of dried fruit, he swung his pack up onto his back and turned toward the rising sun.

"With any luck," he muttered, "this thing'll keep going all the way to Ohrid and Annice can help deal with it."

Then he frowned and put down his pack.

There was something he was forgetting.

Something important.

Something to do with Annice.

No, Annice's daughter.

Magda. A year ago, Maggi had gone to the Healers' Hall in Elbasan for training. She not only had an incredible talent for healing, but she also Sang—or did something as near to Singing as made no difference— what they were calling a fifth kigh.

His legs folded under him, and he found himself suddenly on the ground, mud soaking through his trousers. It took him three tries to find the pitch, but when he finally regained control of his voice, the kigh appeared as a seemingly solid barrier between him and the way he'd been traveling. This time, he knew what questions to ask.

Dymek said he could feel Filip's presence.

The lost kigh was not an earth kigh.

You have to Sing it home.

Jazep felt physically sick. He knew why it had looked as though Filip's body had climbed out of the grave. It had.

But if he went back, he risked losing his chance to catch the thing he followed.

But if he didn't go back . . .

His hands were shaking so badly he could barely

trace the sign of the Circle on his chest. If he didn't go back, Filip's kigh would remain lost between life and death, lost outside the Circle.

Brencis might have already returned with another bard.

But no, he couldn't have, for the kigh were still desperate that he return.

He had to choose. Had to weigh what could happen against what already had. He hoped he'd never have to make another choice like that again because he doubted that the scars from this choice would ever heal.

Sunset turned the lower margin of the clouds a sullen orange when Jazep reached Bartek Springs. He wasted no time entering the village but went directly to the graveyard. A trio of curious dogs followed him for a while but would not approach Filip's grave.

His heart lurched when he saw a body sprawled at the edge of the loose earth—he'd half-expected to see that the dead man had dug himself free once again—and began beating normally when he realized it was Dymek.

The young man lifted his head and peered at Jazep through a tangled curtain of dripping hair. "He's here," he said, his voice hoarse from crying. "I can feel him. He's here."

"Yes." Jazep slid out of his pack and untied the padded oilskin bag that held his drum. "He is."

Dymek pushed himself up onto muddy knees and stared at the bard. "You mean that."

It wasn't a question, but Jazep answered it anyway. "Yes," he said again. "Filip is the lost kigh they want me to Sing home."

"How?"

"I don't know." He only knew that it *had* to be done. "Will you help?"

Turning to look at the dirt piled over his lover's body, Dymek whispered, "I'd die for him if it would help."

Jazep took hold of his shoulder and shook him gently but said nothing because there was nothing to say that wouldn't sound like a meaningless platitude. He sank cross-legged to the ground and settled his drum on his lap. If a fifth kigh existed, which it did, then it could be Sung. The earth kigh believed he could Sing it, so he had to believe them. "Tell me about Filip."

"He had hazel eyes," Dymek told him, his own eyes locked on the past. "But he always said they were green. I used to tease him about it sometimes. He was a little shorter than me and . ."

As Dymek spoke, his voice growing stronger with every memory, Jazep stroked a heartbeat out of the drum and listened past the words. Gradually, he became aware of a presence matching the undertones of Dymek's detailing of Filip and he opened himself to contact.

Terror so intense it bordered on insanity slammed into him. His spine bowed backward, muscles spasmed, and he screamed.

"Filip, stop it! He's trying to help!"

Jazep felt the terror turn. Tried to warn Dymek. Couldn't find his voice. Found himself lying on his back, staring at a darkening sky, blinking rain out of his eyes.

"Bard?"

Either Filip could touch only those with bardic talents or love had kept him from hurting Dymek. Which, at this moment, Jazep neither knew nor cared.

Shaking, as much with rage that someone would dare to so abuse a kigh as in reaction, he forced himself into a sitting position and picked up his drum.

"Bard? He didn't mean it."

Startled, Jazep peered at Dymek through the dusk. The younger man's face was a pale blur against the approaching night but his expression clearly matched the worry in his voice. The sudden realization he was grinding his teeth gave Jazep the clue he needed. "I'm not angry at Filip," he explained. "I'm angry that such a thing was done to him." Drawing in a deep breath, he forced himself to find a measure of calm before he continued, "But I know how to help him now."

There were very few bards who Sang only earth. And there were very few bards who knew the Circle as well as Jazep did. He followed the turning of the seasons from the inside—birth, life, death, out of death a rebirth and Circle comes around once again. Filip's kigh had been ripped out of the cycle. Jazep Sang it back onto the path.

He felt a surge of joy, as strong and all encompassing as the terror had been, then he and Dymek were alone by the grave. He could just barely see new tears cutting channels through the dirt on Dymek's cheeks.

"The Circle," Jazep said softly, laying aside his drum, "encloses us *all*."

"I think that was supposed to be my line."

The two men turned as Celestin materialized out of the darkness. With a strangled cry, Dymek leaped to his feet and threw himself into her arms. Jazep stood a little more slowly.

"I heard your Song," the priest told him. "I had to

come. What . . .?" She paused, reconsidered the question and settled for, "What happened?"

"Dymek can tell you." Jazep heaved his pack up onto his shoulders. The rain had stopped and if the kigh were willing to help him hold the path, he might make it back to the river by midnight.

"Surely, you're not . . ."

"When Brencis returns with the bard," he interrupted, "have Dymek put under recall. Whoever it is will know what to do."

"But Jazep, it's dark. It's wet. Can't you stay until morning?"

He moved close enough to see her face clearly. "There are other villages in its path." When understanding dawned, he stepped back and turned. There were other villages in its path, and he had lost a full day from the hunt. The ground smoothed beneath his feet as the kigh guided him out of the graveyard. Trusting their touch, he started to run.

Chapter Five

The closed lamp hanging by the head of the bunk swung back and forth with the motion of the ship. Leaning against the cabin wall just past the shifting edge of light and shadow, Bannon watched Prince Otavas sleep and wondered if he dreamed and, if he dreamed, what about.

Held captive for seven days by an insane old man, surrounded by the living dead, the seventeen-year-old prince had seen more horror in that short amount of time than many saw in their entire lives. In Bannon's opinion, this trip to Shkoder would be good for him. Too many things in the Imperial Palace—including Her Imperial Majesty, his mother—kept reminding him of his kidnapping. Although outwardly His Highness still appeared to be the carefree darling of the court, Bannon—who saw so much more of him—could see memory lying over the superficial gaiety like an oily scum, and not even the lamp that burned all night by the prince's bed could keep the darkness from haunting him.

"But could any of it have been as bad as looking up from a dying body and seeing your own face laughing down at you?" Bannon silently asked the sleeping prince. *"Or watching another live in your body and be helpless to stop it?*

"Or realizing that the one person you trusted completely had betrayed you?"

A sound up on deck shifted his weight forward onto the balls of his feet, a dagger appearing in his hand. When he became certain it was only one of the many creaks and groans of a ship at sea, he relaxed again.

Vree had no right to save Gyhard's life, not when justice owed it to him. Even the Emperor had seen it. If he couldn't convince her of that with Gyhard in her head, he'd carry her blindfolded back to the Empire and convince her after Gyhard had been destroyed by the Imperial bards. It shouldn't, wouldn't take much for her to realize she'd made a mistake—Bannon had seen how much their separation had hurt her—and they'd be together again, just like they used to be.

Otavas moaned.

A heartbeat later, Bannon stood at his prince's side, gently pushing him back against the thin mattress and pulling the heavily embroidered coverlet up over cold shoulders. "It's all right, Highness," he murmured. "I'm here."

Soon, someone would be there for him. Just like she always had been.

This is Ghoti.

The Gyhard outside the dream identified the rounded walls of orange stucco even while the Gyhard participating walked the empty streets toward the Governor's stronghold. It was quiet, as if the city had emptied, and the knowledge that death waited around every corner ate its way through his composure. He had lived his long life by repeatedly opening death's door and, at the last moment, pushing someone else over the threshold. Death could not love him for it.

He heard a footstep behind him and forced himself to turn. Three soldiers of the Sixth Army blocked his retreat. All three carried crossbows that tracked him unerringly despite the black leather bands that covered their eyes and prevented him from jumping to another body. His heart began to pound. As he couldn't go back, he went on.

The remainder of the army, similarly shielded, waited in the area he'd cleared around the tower wall. He couldn't count the number of crossbows aimed at his heart. He tried, then decided it didn't matter when one would be enough. A slight figure dressed in black beckoned to him from the top of the wall.

Suddenly, he stared down at where he'd been and, from that exact place, Vree stared up at him.

"Time to die," announced a familiar voice.

No. Before he finished turning, a noose settled around his neck.

Vree smiled and pulled it tighter. "Long past time to die."

He fought the hands that shoved him to the edge of the battlements but for every one he pried off his flesh, two returned. Some, he thought he recognized. His pleas, his curses, neither made any difference. Tottering over oblivion, he turned to ask why and saw it was Bannon not Vree who held the other end of the rope, his eyes shielded like all the rest.

Vree stood below, hands outstretched to him, eyes uncovered.

She was too far away.

He screamed her name as he fell.

And jerked awake in her head.

It was her heart he could feel pounding. Her blood roaring in her ears. His own terror . . .

His fear of dying slammed into the barriers so carefully maintained between them, and they fell. His kigh surged out into Vree's body, shoving hers aside in a panicked need for the control so long denied him. Arms. Hands. Fingers.

Then he remembered. Her eyes had been the only eyes uncovered. With a strength he thought he'd long since abandoned, he stopped, lightly touched his/her cheek with his/her hand, and forced himself back to the space she allowed him.

He felt her tremble—in reaction, not fear—and suddenly realized . . . *Why didn't you try to stop me?*

I'd just woke up.

You wake up instantly, he snapped, tipping the terror that continued to sizzle through him over into anger. She was hiding something. He didn't know what. The urge to shake her sent his kigh racing down into her hands and it took almost all he had left to yank it back. *Did you want me to kill you? I shove you out of your body and then the bards Sing me into oblivion? Have you had enough? Is that it? Is it?*

Her anger rose to meet his. *If I've had enough of you, I'll deal with you myself.* She threw herself out of the bed, bare feet slapping against the floor. *And what the slaughter makes you think that I would even consider killing myself over you? You think I can't live without you?*

What *had* he been thinking? He hadn't. Terrified by the dream, further terrified by what he'd nearly done, he'd reacted by striking out and that kind of a reaction, he realized now, could get one or both of them killed. *Vree, I . . .*

*You what? Maybe you wanted me to kill *you*.* She stomped into the sitting room, flung open the shutters on the single window and gulped in desperate lungfuls of the night air. *Maybe you think oblivion's a better idea than spending more slaughtering time with me.*

The emotions raging about inside her head had cut him off so completely, it took him a moment to realize what was wrong with her voice. *Vree, are you crying?*

No!

Gyhard didn't bother confronting her with the lie, not when they both knew it for what it was. *Vree . . .* Uncertain what he'd intended to say, he paused. In a very short time they'd gone through fear, anger, and into an emotional storm he couldn't understand. *Why didn't you stop me when you knew I could've killed you?*

At first, he thought she wasn't going to answer him. She stood silently staring out the window, searching the sky for familiar stars and not finding any. He could feel the cool air against her skin—cooler against lines of moisture on each cheek.

"I didn't believe you would," she whispered at last to the night and, for an instant, her fear slipped out from behind the confusion.

Fear not of him but of the feelings that had defied training and kept her from defending herself.

He wanted to accept the gift. He wanted to assure her that he'd never hurt her more than he'd ever wanted anything over the course of a very long life. But he couldn't. *Vree, I love you, but I can't guarantee that will always be enough to protect you. This time I stopped, the next time I might not be able to.*

So I have to be strong enough for both of us? Her mental voice had picked up a bitter flavor. Both the fear, and the emotion behind the fear, might never have existed.

Until he'd met her, Gyhard had thought he was dead to shame. It irritated him to discover he wasn't. *Vree, I . . .*

It's okay. Her eyes were dry and he had the feeling he'd just missed accepting something very important. Their kigh were more separate than they'd been in a long time. *I'm used to it.*

"You don't look so good." Magda folded her arms, cocked her head, and studied Vree clinically. "In fact, you look like you're *significantly* short of sleep. You're not coming down with something, are you? I mean, this *is* a different country with different sicknesses and stuff, so I suppose we *should've* expected you to catch things."

Vree shrugged. "Gyhard had a nightmare."

"If he wakes up, you wake up?"

"Something like that." She'd woken up with him because she'd been dreaming with him, but if she hadn't told that to Gyhard, she certainly wasn't going to tell it to Magda.

What are you hiding, Vree?

None of your slaughtering business. Her dreams merging with Bannon's had led to a terrifying loss of self and she'd lost as much self to Gyhard as she intended to.

"I expect it's colder at night than you're used to," Magda observed, turning and walking backward down the corridor so she could see Vree's face. "It *is* almost Third Quarter but you're *probably* feeling the damp more than the cold. *I* did when I first got to Elbasan because the air's a lot damper here than it is in Ohrid.

Of course we don't have an ocean right outside the keep. I know!" She stopped so suddenly that Vree nearly ran her down. "We'll go out and get you some warmer clothes. You haven't been outside the Citadel since you got here." Her eyes gleamed. "A little shopping'll be a great break for you."

Shopping. Vree couldn't think of anything she'd rather do less. Then she caught sight of a familiar shadow at the end of the corridor as a guard ducked back out of sight. Outside the Citadel. She smiled. "Why not. The security arrangements alone ought to be worth a laugh."

"Tadeus has a cousin who's a draper; we'll go there first. I got some *beautiful* wool cloth from him back in First Quarter that I had made into a *gorgeous* cloak. Uri was *so* jealous; he said it was the exact color he'd been looking for and now he couldn't use it."

"Did you buy all of it?" Vree asked as she mapped all visible exits from the street.

"Well, no, but he could hardly have a cloak made that looked exactly like mine. That would be *so* scrubby."

"Scrubby?"

"You know, less than fine." Magda laughed and tucked Vree's hand into the crook of her elbow. "I guess you don't know, do you? Do you mind if we walk like this?" As Vree twitched, she added, "That way Gyhard won't be excluded. I'd hold onto you, but you're wearing long sleeves."

If it upsets you . . .

A muscle jumped in Vree's jaw. "I don't mind."

"Good. So what's the problem?"

Vree made note of a cistern pipe that would probably hold her weight. "Problem?"

"Between you and Gyhard." Maintaining contact, she laced her fingers together. "Yesterday your kigh were like this. Today ..." Her fingers folded into fists butting against each other.

Lovers' quarrel, Gyhard said shortly.

"If you're telling me it's none of my business," Magda began.

Vree cut her off. "Gyhard thinks I shouldn't trust him. That I should always be on guard in case he can't control the urge to take over my body."

It's not that simple!

It was last night, she snarled.

I don't want to hurt you.

Then you take the responsibility for not hurting me! I'm tired of always holding the knife. "What's so funny?" she demanded as Magda smiled.

"Just that Gyhard was right; it *is* a lovers' quarrel because love can't exist without trust. You two really are so ..."

Vree cut her off a second time. "*Don't* say we're so romantic."

"But ..."

"No."

The draper, the tailor, and the cobbler took most of the afternoon. A life spent in the army had equipped Vree with neither the skills nor attention span Magda considered necessary for picking out clothes, so for the most part she merely endured the younger woman's opinions. When Gyhard suggested high boots instead of low, she ignored him.

"You'll need oilskins if you want to go outside in

Third Quarter," Magda reflected, piling packages into the arms of the cobbler's senior apprentice who seemed more than willing to quit the shop for the remainder of the afternoon. "But I think we've done enough for one day."

More than, Gyhard agreed.

"No. There's something else." Vree twisted her left wrist and her remaining throwing dagger dropped into her hand. "I lost the other one at sea. I want to replace it."

"I guess you'll need a blacksmith . . ."

Gyhard translated; Vree shook her head. "Blacksmiths shoe horses and beat swords into plows. I need a weapons crafter."

"Izak a'Edvard." Finding himself suddenly under close scrutiny, the bits of the boy's ears visible under an untidy shock of light brown hair turned bright red. "He's the best." His eyes widened while Vree balanced the dagger on the callused tip of one finger before she flipped it back up her sleeve.

"Who says he's the best?" she asked. "Besides you."

"Alise i'Dumin."

"Who is?"

"W—weapons master for the city guard. She's my Aunt Dasa's partner," he added when it seemed like more explanation might be demanded.

Vree, that's an assassin's weapon . . .

If I'm not an assassin, then I'm not dangerous, and that trio of palace guards who've been trying to keep up with us all afternoon have been wasting their time. If I'm not an assassin, what am I? Nothing.

Frowning slightly, Magda reached out to touch Vree's hand.

She jerked it back. "I still have some of the coins the Emperor gave me." Pulling a purse out of her belt-pouch, she passed it over. "Is it enough?"

"I have no idea what a dagger like that would cost," Magda admitted, peering into the calfskin purse at the two silver Imperial starbursts barely visible among the less valuable copper. "But you'd have to change this into Shkoden money before you could spend it anyway. If the dagger's that important to you . . ."

"It is."

". . . we'll just charge it to the Bardic Hall like the rest." Handing back the purse, she grinned. "Captain Liene told me to be sure you had *everything* you needed." She pulled a gull out of her own purse, realized the apprentice had his hands full, and stuffed the coin into his pocket. His blush deepened. "They might make you leave our stuff at the gate but that's all right because someone will come out to carry it in from there." Leaning forward so his master, cutting leather on the other side of the open shop couldn't hear, she added in a conspiratorial whisper, "We'll cover for you later if you want to tell him you were delayed at the Hall."

Muttering an inarticulate protest, the boy jerked into motion.

"Hold it," Vree snapped.

He stopped so quickly he almost lost his grip on a fleece hat.

"Where is the weapons crafter's shop?"

"Uh, Ironmonger's Street. Far end. He uses a wooden sword crossed with two wooden daggers as a signboard." When it appeared that Magda was about to move closer and say something, he insisted he knew no more and headed up the hill at a stiff-legged trot.

"What was *that* all about?" Magda muttered as they picked their way across the debris on the street and into Tether Alley.

"I think it had to do with warm breath against his ear."

"Mine?"

"Not mine," Vree told her, even as she checked the half-timbered buildings that flanked the narrow lane for routes to the roof.

"Really?" The apprentice healer paused and peered back around the corner. "I don't think so," she said after a moment. Tucking Vree's hand back into the crook of her elbow, she started them walking again. "He's too young."

"He can't be that much younger than you are, if he's younger at all," Vree pointed out.

"Yes, but women mature *earlier* than men. Healers have known that for years. I mean, when you were growing up, didn't you feel so much more adult than all the boys you knew?"

"Assassins are treated as assassins from the moment they start training."

"Well, yes, but if you were seven, you were still a child. They couldn't change that."

Vree didn't understand why Magda's innocence hurt so much. "I was an assassin," she said, and that ended the conversation.

"Lookie what we have here." One of the three young men lounging about the sunny front of Izak a'Edvard's shop pushed himself up onto his feet as Vree and Magda approached. "You two an item?" He flicked the beaded ends of his mustache with a forefinger and arched his back enough to stretch his sleeveless tunic tight against the undulating ridges of his chest. "Or does a charming, sophisticated, handsome fellow like myself stand a chance?"

"No," Vree replied before Magda could answer. Her posture clearly indicated she expected him to get out of her way.

"Vree . . ."

Magda sounded so worried, Gyhard tried to keep the amusement out of his mental voice—and failed. *People usually accept it when an assassin says no.*

"He doesn't know."

And you're not to tell him.

"We got us a grumpy one, boys." His friends grinned encouragement and shifted position on the bench to get a better view of the fun. "You the little healer's personal bodyguard, Southie?"

Vree started around him, but he grabbed her shoulder with a scarred hand and pushed her back.

Oh, oh.

"I asked you a question, Southie."

Doesn't smell like he's drunk; he must be stupid.

"Vree . . ."

"Is that your name, Southie?" He laughed. "It sounds like the noise a pig makes when you slit its throat. Vreeee!" Bowing slightly toward Magda, he purred, "Excuse me, *healer*," his emphasis indicated he was fully aware of the apprentice circle on her badge, "but I'm going to have to teach your little friend here a lesson in manners."

Clutching Vree's hand tightly, Magda glared at him. "Look, you're making a mistake."

He held his hand out from his chest, just even with the top of Vree's head. "Somehow, I doubt it."

"She looks dangerous, Jak." While the warning held

a certain amount of derision, it was a warning for all of that.

Jak spread his arms. Muscles rippled from shoulder to wrist, the pattern of scars a moving history of other fights. "She's half my size, Ziv. How *dangerous* can that be?"

One of Vree's instructors had told her that women made marginally better assassins than men because they didn't posture.

No blades!

Responding instinctively to the sound of a direct order, Vree changed the direction of her initial movement and launched herself into the air. Planting a hand on each of Jak's shoulders, she flipped over his head, smacking her knee into his chin as she passed. She slapped the cobblestones, rolled, and regained her feet an instant later.

Bellowing with pain and rage, Jak spat out a bloody tooth, whirled, and charged. A few moments later, loyalty dragged his friends into the fight. By the time the trio of palace guards arrived, short swords drawn and wondering what they were going to tell their captain if the Southern woman got killed, it was all over. They stared wide-eyed from the groaning men to Vree, who was wiping a trickle of blood from her nose on her sleeve.

I'm surprised they touched you.

It wasn't intentional. These idiots don't know how to fall.

Accidents happen?

Only once.

Feel better now?

She grinned at his tone. *Much. Thanks for reminding me not to kill them.* To Gyhard's surprise, the thanks were sincere. *I thought you never served?*

I didn't. But I spent sixty years as Governor Aralt and over the years he, I, gave a great many orders.

"You're hurt!" Magda rushed forward and patted the air in front of Vree's nose. "Let me Heal that!"

"It'll heal itself in a minute." All at once, she became aware of the dozen or so people who'd been drawn out of the surrounding buildings at the sound of battle. Most wore singed leather aprons, the rest wore the weapons they'd come to this street to buy. None of them looked happy.

"No one can move like that," muttered a smith, her hands wrapped around the shaft of a heavy hammer.

"She doesn't look Shkoden,"

"She doesn't move like she's human."

"Demon. I'm tellin' ya, she must be a demon."

Magda whirled on them, hands on her hips. "Don't be ridiculous. She's from the Havakeen Empire. And if these three braggarts couldn't finish what they started, it's *hardly* her fault."

It might've worked had the three members of the palace guard not suddenly decided to make up for arriving late. As they moved into a defensive position around the two women, the rumbles from the crowd grew ugly.

Her breathing back to normal, Vree studied patterns and planned her attack, just in case. *This is stupid.*

Granted. But it doesn't make it any less dangerous.

Granted.

Don't tell them what you are. Were. You'd stand a better chance with them believing you a demon.

"No one her size could take down three people their size," the smith declared. "It's impossible!"

Magda sighed. "You've always been the strongest, haven't you? You hate the thought of anyone so much smaller than you being able to defeat you."

"What're you talkin' about?" the smith snarled. She shifted her grip on the hammer. "This ain't about me. It's about her." Raising a beefy arm, she stepped forward. "Now git out of my . . ."

Whether she intended a blow or merely a shove became irrelevant as a pair of strong hands grabbed her from behind and threw her to the ground. The hammer bounced out of her reach, striking sparks off the cobblestones. When she tried to rise, the point of a sword at her throat changed her mind.

The tall young man holding the sword, tossed a straying strand of ebony hair back over his shoulder and slowly swept an arrogant violet gaze over the area. His looks and his bearing as much as the sword, silenced the crowd. "Maggi," he sighed at last, "what is going on here?"

Everyone started talking at once.

"I was speaking to my sister." The gentle admonishment had steel behind it. A bard couldn't have done it better.

"It wasn't my *fault,* Gerek," Magda told him. "Vree and I just wanted to go into this shop and these three buffoons wouldn't let us."

"And?"

"And so Vree fought them."

"And?"

"And she won."

"And?"

"And now these people think she's a demon!"

"Maggi, demons don't really exist. They're stories told to frighten children."

Magda glared at her older brother. She didn't know what he was doing in Elbasan and while she appreciated him dropping out of the Circle to save her, if indeed he had saved her, she didn't appreciate his tone. "Don't tell me," she snapped. "Tell *them*."

"These are adults," Gerek pointed out facetiously. "They know that."

So fascinated was everyone by this exchange that they forgot about the men who'd started it and had Jak not bellowed as he surged to his feet, he might've had a slim chance of success. As it was, Vree's dagger caught the loose fabric where the wide legs of his trousers joined and buried itself guard deep in the wall behind him. Jak stared down at the pommel, just visible at his crotch, and fainted.

"Hope he tucks left," someone murmured.

One of the palace guards snickered. The tension dissolved in shouts of raucous laughter.

About to demand an explanation, Magda caught the expression on Gerek's face and stopped cold. She'd seen that expression before. Frequently. It was the last thing she wanted to see in this time and this place.

Gerek was in love.

"All right. Let me see if I understand this." Gerek paced across one of the small rooms in the suite set aside for the Duc of Ohrid at the palace and stared over at the lights of the Bardic Hall. "Not only does Vree have two kigh, but they're in love with each other."

"That's right."

He sighed, turned, and propped one leg on the polished marble window sill. "That's not love, Maggot. That's masturbation."

"Gerek!"

His teeth were very white against the shadow of whiskers on his chin. "You've been studying here for almost two years. You must've run into the word."

"Of course I've run into the word and stop grinning at me in that stupid way!" Magda spat a curl out of the corner of her mouth and glared at her brother. "You haven't been listening to anything I've said! Vree and Gyhard are two separate people!"

"In one body."

"Yes!"

"In one beautiful, desirable, very sexy body."

"No!" She snatched a tapestry cushion up off a padded chair and threw it at him.

Stretching out a languid arm, he lazily plucked it out of the air before impact and tossed it back onto the chair. "Are you saying she's *not* beautiful?"

"Of *course* she's beautiful. I'm not *blind*."

A single ebony brow swept upward in an interrogative gesture Magda'd hated all her life. The only way she could get a single brow to rise was if she tied the other one down.

"Gerek! She's my patient!"

He spread his hands, the gesture as elegant as everything he did. "Not mine."

"Look, Gerek, Vree's *really* vulnerable right now and she hates feeling vulnerable and that makes things even worse." Gathering up her robe in one hand, Magda crossed to his side and stared earnestly up at him. "She truly loves Gyhard, but she's afraid of her feelings because assassins are taught only to love the army. And being assassins. If it hadn't been for Bannon, Vree'd *never* have been able to do what she did."

"I thought you said his name was Gyhard?"

"Bannon's her brother. For some reason I'm not *entirely* clear on, mostly because I haven't wanted to ask, they were trained together, against all tradition, and she loved him. That made it possible for her to love Gyhard even though she's having trouble handling the emotions. This entire experience has *completely* messed up her whole identity. Her kigh is so *confused* all the time ..."

"All the time?" he prodded when she paused.

"Okay, it wasn't confused this afternoon. This afternoon she knew *exactly* who she was."

"And Gyhard loves her? Whoever she is?"

"Yes."

"What? No accompanying diagnosis?"

She bit her lip. "He's afraid that someday his love won't be strong enough to stop him from taking over her body."

"And what are you afraid of, little sister?" Gerek asked gently, cupping her chin with his palm.

"The same thing," Magda admitted with a sigh. "Gerek, you've got to promise me you'll stay away from her." Wrapping his hand in both of hers, she searched his face for any sign of capitulation. "The last thing Vree needs right now is you panting all over her, further confusing the issue."

He freed his hand. "I don't pant."

"You know what I mean."

"Have I ever hurt anyone?" Before she could answer, he added, "Intentionally?"

"Well, no, but ..."

"Then trust me."

* * *

Gerek fought the urge to scratch as he accompanied the page through the section of the palace that held the royal family's private apartments. It might have been more politic to shave before this visit, but having discovered upon arriving in Elbasan that beards were now the fashion, he had no time to waste. He clasped his hands behind his back to keep them from his chin. *Because it's too late to do anything about it now.*

When the page pulled open a gleaming section of paneling carved with the crowned ship of Shkoder, he tugged at his tunic and followed her into the room.

"Gerek a'Pjerin, Majesties."

He bowed extravagantly, sweeping the thick carpet with an imaginary hat—the way Tadeus had taught him when he was seven—and straightened to see the Queen approaching him with outstretched hands and a fond smile.

"It's good to see you, Gerek, and a little surprising to see you so soon after your arrival. I'd have thought Elbasan had more interesting claims on your time."

"How can you say that when I have thought of nothing but Your Majesty's beauty . . ." He laid a gentle kiss on the back of each of her offered hands. ". . . and grace from the moment I left my father's keep."

"You've been spending too much time with the bards, Gerek," the king called from his chair by the empty hearth. "You're starting to sound like one."

"Nonsense, Theron." Llyana returned to her own chair, her cheeks lightly pink. "I've never had a bard say anything half so pretty to me."

"Then you ought to spend more time with Tadeus if you're feeling the lack. Give that one half a chance and he'd say pretty things to me."

"Yes, dear, but not to me."

Theron grunted and laced his hands over his stomach. "Sit, Gerek," he commanded, nodding at a third chair. "I can't stand the way you and your father insist on towering over people."

Gerek grinned as he sat. "I'll try to be shorter, Majesty, but I'm afraid I can't speak for my father."

"Who can," the king agreed dryly. "How is he?"

"He sent his respects, Sire, and his deepest regret that he would be unable to attend the Full Council. He only hopes that my humble attempt to take his place will meet with your approval."

"Well, you're more of a diplomat than he ever was, but you can stop forking it off the manure pile, boy; I've known you most of your life. How is he really?"

"When I left, he was furious about a ram that'd been pulled out of a breeding program without his approval."

"Of course he was. And how is my sister?"

"Equally furious, sir. Nees was the one who removed the ram."

The king shook his head and exchanged a speaking glance with his consort. "Of course she was," he said. "And how are you? Besides having unfortunately lost your shaving kit."

"Theron, he's obviously growing a beard," Llyana declared as Gerek's ears reddened. "Before you say any more," she reached over and tugged at the gray-brown curls adorning His Majesty's chin, "you should remember how you looked when your beard was growing in."

Family matters took a certain amount of time to cover as Annice had entrusted Gerek with a number of messages to her brother that she didn't think needed to be sent through the Bardic Hall. Servers were setting out wine as they discussed the lack of action on the Cemandian border and the slow but steady growth of trade.

When the servers had left and the three were alone again, Theron stared down into his goblet as if he might read answers in the wine. "So, Gerek, why *did* you come to see us so soon after your arrival?"

Half smiling at the emphasis, Gerek admitted he was concerned about his sister.

"Ah. She's told you about the assassin."

"Yes, Majesty."

"We have them under constant surveillance. Besides the kigh, there are always guards within crossbow range."

"Begging Your Majesty's pardon, but that didn't do much good this afternoon."

"How fortunate that you arrived when you did then."

Gerek's jaw dropped. "How did you know . . . ?"

"Don't be ridiculous," Theron advised gently, setting the goblet on the small marble table by his elbow. "I'm the king. When those close to me are involved in a street brawl, I'm informed. So, what's your suggestion?"

"Majesty?" The abrupt question had taken him completely by surprise.

The king smiled. "I know the two who raised you, Gerek. Given that, given them, I can't believe you don't have a better way of dealing with the situation in mind."

Not entirely certain he liked being read so easily, Gerek spread his hands. "I had thought that perhaps

I could be used as an additional guard, one who could stay much closer than those now assigned."

"Magda was very insistent that there be no guard at all. What we have now is an attempt at a compromise. The guards are discreet and she pretends they aren't there."

"But she can hardly object to me, Majesty. I'm her brother."

Brow furrowed, Theron considered the offer from a number of angles; unfortunately, with no idea of the only relevant one.

If she realizes she's a healer with a healer's privileges instead of just my little sister, she won't ask me to stay away from Vree, she'll order it. She's like that. Stubborn. Certain she knows what's right. Gerek couldn't let that happen. He had to get closer to the Southern beauty who'd stolen his heart.

"I have to admit I didn't like Maggi being so far from the guards," the king allowed at last. "If you think you can get closer, go ahead, and if she gives you any trouble with it, tell her you're there on my order."

"Yes, Sire." He stood. "Thank you, Majesty, I . . ."

"Father?" The Heir paused in the open door and looked slightly embarrassed. "My apologies, Majesty, I didn't realize you were . . . Gerek! How nice to see you back in Elbasan."

"Your Highness." His bow to the Princess Onele was significantly less flamboyant than to her parents. The odds were good that when he became duc, she'd be Queen—his direct liege.

"What brings you down from Ohrid?" she asked, her gaze frankly appreciative.

Having attracted that kind of response his entire adult life, Gerek had long since learned to ignore it.

"I'm here to sit as my father's proxy on the Full Council, Highness."

"I'll be looking forward to your participation." She smiled and reached behind her, pulling her oldest daughter out from her shadow and into the room. While her relationship with her consort had grown to be distant at best, she doted on both her daughters. "Look who's here, Jelena."

Jelena took one panicked look at Gerek, turned bright red, dropped her gaze to the embroidered toes of her slippers, and murmured something unintelligible.

Gerek smiled kindly down at the girl. "But the princess Jelena was a child when I saw her last; this is a young woman."

"I was twelve then." Jelena glanced up, met his gaze for an instant, and returned her attention back to her slippers. "I'm over fourteen now."

"What was it you wanted, Onele?" Theron asked, taking pity on his granddaughter.

"It's not important, Father. It can wait until tomorrow." The Heir herded her daughter back out into the hall. "As I said, I didn't realize you had a guest. Good night, Gerek."

He bowed again. "Good night, Highness."

"I think we can take it as read that Jelena still has that crush on you," the king mused. "I had hoped she'd outgrown it in the interim."

"I would never take advantage, Majesty."

"Don't be an idiot. Of course you wouldn't."

When he was gone, Theron shook his head. "I'm getting old, my dear. I forgot to warn him about looking into the assassin's eyes. Suppose this Gyhard decides to leap into his body?"

"I'm sure Magda will warn him. And if not, Gerek's obviously made himself familiar with the situation. He's a smart young man. He'll be fine."

I don't like him.

Why not?

Isn't it obvious? He likes you too well.

Vree turned to look at Gerek, who stood smiling down at his sister as she told him for the eighth time that afternoon just how much she didn't want him around. *Obvious?*

He's continually staring longingly into your eyes. When you look like he does, you know how effective that can be. If he'd had teeth, he'd have ground them. As it was, Vree felt a muscle tighten in her jaw. *Remember, I can feel your response.*

Look at him; a corpse would respond. Which was as much reassurance as she was going to give. Bannon had needed to be told constantly he was the center of her world and she had no intention of setting that up again. Either Gyhard trusted her, or he didn't. *It seems like he's getting to you more than he's getting to me.*

Watching Gerek through Vree's eyes, Gyhard wished he could jump across one of those longing looks and throw the arrogant little shit right out of his body. *You just pray,* he thought, shielding it carefully, *that I never manage to convince Vree just how perfectly your body would fit me because all it would take is one little shove.*

Chapter Six

The Imperial Ambassador stared down at the golden sunburst sealing the parchment package that had, moments before, been placed on his desk. "Didn't I just receive one of these?" he asked the empty office. When no answer was forthcoming, he sighed and rubbed at throbbing temples with his fingertips. Two messages directly from His Imperial Majesty during the same quarter were unprecedented during his tenure as ambassador. That it had been sent up the coast on one of the sleek little ships kept for moments of extreme diplomacy did not reassure him in the least.

Muttering "Fear, fire, flood," under his breath, he reached for a horn letter opener and slid the blade beneath the seal.

His Royal Highness Prince Otavas will be arriving in Elbasan shortly on the Imperial Navy vessel, Deliverance.

The rest of the package primarily contained lists of the prince's preferences in food and drink and accommodation.

"Will be arriving *shortly?* Oh, that's useful." Shaking his head, he stood, scooped up the papers, and headed for the door. One of his attaches—a career civil servant as opposed to the distant Imperial cousins who made up most of the rest of his staff—fell into step beside him as he left the room.

"His Royal Highness Prince Otavas will be arriving in Elbasan shortly," he said as they moved together down the hall. The attaché turned enough to see the ambassador's face. "Shortly?" she asked.

"Funny, that was my response. I'm on my way to inform Their Majesties—if I change quickly, I can catch the end of the morning audience. You take care of things here and see about the status of our suite at the palace—I'll need to be accessible to him. And find a reasonably responsible translator close to his own age. I don't imagine he speaks much Shkoden. He's traveling by sea, but I'll let King Theron's people deal with the Harbor Master. The last time I tried, I very nearly disrupted trade all up and down the coast."

"Hardly that bad, sir."

"You weren't there, Tysia." He threw her a smile as he turned down the corridor leading to his private apartments. "You weren't there."

A few moments later, as his valet hurriedly dressed him in official robes, he pondered the implications of the sudden visit and began to work out how best to use it to the Empire's advantage. If he were very lucky, when the prince arrived, he might be informed exactly *why* His Imperial Majesty had decided to so abruptly send his youngest son to Shkoder.

And if not, he sighed silently, lifting his arms so that the folds of the saffron undertunic could be adjusted, *it might be best to keep King Theron's sentiments in mind and remember that nothing coming out of the Empire is ever exactly what it seems.*

* * *

On one knee, both hands pressed against the earth, Jazep stared through the trees at the cluster of buildings. The extended families who made up the settlement called it Fortune, after what they hoped to take out of the silver mine they jointly worked. He hadn't been here for about six years but, by risking a light trance, he could touch the recall and compare it with what he could see.

Although a few small cottages had been built, it appeared that most of the people continued to live communally—a sensible way to conserve heat during the long, hard mountain winters. The kitchens should have been busy with the preparation of the evening meal, but no smoke rose from any chimney. The only sound he could hear was the high, thin crying of an unhappy baby.

Jazep closed his eyes for a heartbeat and fought with the still, small voice in his head that told him to leave as quickly as he could, to not face this thing alone. He'd been walking without kigh since dawn; the earth had been as empty of their presence as the settlement was of visible life. Without their guidance, he'd spent the day feeling crippled and lost but kept continually moving in the direction all his senses told him to stay away from. Whatever it was he followed, it had to be stopped.

Now, it seemed he'd finally caught up to it. Until this moment, his greatest horror had been the thought of another emptied grave and a kigh brutalized as Filip's had been, but as he lifted his eyes to a flock of buzzards circling the buildings, he began to realize the terrifying possibilities.

Had there been kigh, they would have warned him he was no longer alone.

A strong arm wrapped around Jazep's chest and callused hand clamped tightly over his mouth. After the initial, involuntary jerk, he twisted enough to find himself staring into the frightened face of a pale young man.

Bard? The young man mouthed, hope beginning to dawn.

Jazep nodded.

Be quiet. When Jazep nodded again, he removed both hand and arm and stood. He stared, wide-eyed, as Jazep rose and shrugged back into his pack, then he motioned for the bard to follow.

The woman waiting at the makeshift shelter lowered her club and sagged against a tree as the two men came out of the underbrush. "I thought they had you," she whispered, relief not quite enough to banish the fear. "I thought they had you."

"Evicka, he's a bard." The young man crossed the clearing and took hold of her shoulders. "A bard!"

Evicka straightened and looked past him to Jazep. Her face began to lighten with a sudden incredulous joy; then, just as quickly, the shadows returned. "A bard," she repeated. "What is *one* bard going to do?"

"What does he have to do?" Jazep asked quietly.

"The old man wandered in yesterday morning. I never thought anything that old could be alive." She pushed her hair back off her face and laughed bitterly. "Maybe it can't. Anyway, he came and we fed him and sat him in the sun because, well, we're all enclosed in the Circle, aren't we?" Again the bitter laugh. The young man reached out and closed his hand around her arm. She covered it with her own and went on. "Johan had taken down one of the deer that's been stripping our gardens, a big buck, so tough they practically needed the picks to take it apart, but after long enough in the pot, well, anything tenders up and it was venison stew for last night's meal. Everyone ate in the big hall—stupid to let that kind of bounty go to waste and with a dozen cousins off to Bicaz with a load of ore there was lots to go around—but me and Krisus had just been joined a few days and well, we were in one of the cottages. We didn't eat any of the stew.

"About full dark, they woke us up. Everyone was sick. First the old and the young, then everyone else. By the turn of the night, six people were dead. A couple hours later . . ." She paused and swiped at her eyes. ". . . everyone."

"We thought at first the meat had been diseased." Krisus took up the tale when Evicka fell silent. "The only ones in the whole place who weren't sick were us and Amalia's baby—she's still on the tit. Even Great-grandfather had a bowl of the broth. There wasn't anything we could do. We don't have a healer."

Evicka spread her hands. "We just watched them die. Then . . ." She shook her head and tried again. "Then . . ."

Jazep thought he understood the terror that kept her from going on. "Then you watched them live again?"

Two pairs of shadowed eyes locked onto his face. "How did you know?"

He couldn't tell which of them had spoken. Maybe they both had. "I've been following the thing that did it, trying to stop it before . . ."

"Too late." Hysteria hovered around the edges of

Evicka's interruption. "And it isn't a thing, it's the old man. And he Sings. We heard him."

"*Sings?*"

"Yeah, like a bard. He took hold of my brother's hand, my brother's dead hand, 'cause I'm telling you I watched Justyn die, and he Sang, and my brother came back. Or at least part of him did."

. . . and he Sang . . .

Jazep scrambled to his feet and made it to the edge of the clearing before expelling the contents of his knotted stomach all over a bush. He retched until there was nothing left and then he retched some more. When he finally straightened, they were both watching him blankly; their concern had been used up on greater things and nothing remained for a bard who'd just realized he'd been following not a thing, but an old man—an old bard.

Wiping his beard on the back of his hand, Jazep turned and murmured, "How many?"

"Don't know. We ran. You couldn't stay around them."

As far as we know," Evicka said, shoulders hunched against a chill only she could feel, "we're the only survivors. Us and Amalia's baby—and we're not going nowhere without her."

"Except we can't go back. We've tried, but we always end up going around, finding ourselves on the other side without knowing how we got there. It's like your head was pushing you aside from something, something it doesn't want you to see."

Jazep stared at them in amazement. At the moment, they were the bravest people he'd ever met. "You tried to go back?"

"We aren't going nowhere without Amalia's baby,"

Evicka repeated, then her lower lip started to tremble and her eyes filled with tears. "But she's been alone all night and all day and we can't get to her and she's just three months old and she's probably dead by now, too."

"She's alive." Jazep used just enough Voice to leave no room for doubt. Evicka, wrapped in Krisus' arms, looked up. "I heard her crying. She's not happy, but she's alive."

"But we can't get to her."

"I can." Trembling with anger and fear combined, he knelt and began unbuckling his instrument case.

"This is as close as you can get before your head starts pushing you away." Evicka's fingers dug into Jazep's arm. "What are you going to do?"

He settled the drones on his shoulder. "First I'm going to get their attention, then I'm going to Sing the dead to rest."

"All of them? All at once?"

"Yes." There were times when Jazep felt limited Singing only a single quarter, but this wasn't one of those times. All his life, he'd followed where the earth had led, and the earth kigh were tied to the turning of the Circle in unmistakable ways. When the old man had Sung the kigh back into the dead of Fortune, he'd ripped them out of the Circle. They were lost, like Filip's kigh had been, and like Filip's kigh they needed to be shown the way home.

And then; then he'd deal with the old man.

"Deal how?" asked a little voice in his head.

He didn't have an answer, so he ignored it. "I want you two to stay out here until I stop Singing. We know

the old man is dangerous so let me take care of him
before you move in."

Krisus shifted in place defensively, wanting to be
the one who rode to the rescue and, in spite of himself, resenting the bard for being able to do what he
couldn't. "What are you going to do? Sing to him?"

Sing to him ... The old man was as much out of
the Circle as the dead he abused. Perhaps ... Jazep
reached out, took hold of the idea, and gathered it
close. Perhaps the old man, too, was lost.

"Yes," he said gently, as fear and anger fled to be
replaced by sorrow so overwhelming his knees nearly
buckled beneath its weight. "That's exactly what I'm
going to do. I'm going to Sing to him."

The late afternoon sun threw long shadows through
Fortune as Jazep walked out from under the cover of
the trees and onto the rutted track. He felt as though
he were pushing against an invisible wall; each step
requiring more effort than the one before.

I know the path, he told the wall, fingers moving
purposefully up and down the chanter, blowpipe
clamped between his lips. *You cannot keep me from
following it. The walking dead are to be pitied, not
feared.*

The resistance ceased so suddenly, he stumbled and
nearly fell. Both Krisus and Evicka had described their
failure to approach the settlement as having had their
heads push them aside. It was personal horror and
disbelief that had to be overcome, Jazep realized, living kigh simply preferred not to deal with the dead
returned.

He would have preferred not to deal with it himself,
preferred that whatever it was that had driven the old

man so far out of the Circle had never occurred but, as it had, he had no choice.

The call of the pipes rose up into the unnaturally quiet air and, as the bard followed the track between the first two outbuildings, the dead began to answer.

Filip had been crushed in a rock fall and buried three long days in the heat of Second Quarter. The people of Fortune had been poisoned and so it was harder to see the seven drawn, one by one, through the door of the largest building as dead. They moved with a careful deliberation, as though they'd had to relearn the use of arms and legs and they wore identical blank expressions that would, Jazep assumed, grow more identical as death began to wipe away physical differences.

Why these seven had been chosen out of all the poisoned dead, he had no idea.

He could feel their kigh, confused and frightened. Although they hadn't wanted to die, neither had they wanted to return, thrust back into shells of lifeless flesh. Jazep felt no terror, only the pity he'd earlier assumed. The thought of the desperate loneliness that would allow the old man to commit such an injustice, to drag other lives so brutally out of the Circle, nearly broke his heart.

Spitting out the blowpipe, he took a deep breath and began to Sing. His voice, deep and resonant, filled the spaces between the buildings and gently covered the dead. He Sang of their life the way it had been, drawing on the recall of his last visit, adding to it the story Krisus and Evicka had told. He redefined the individual paths of their lives and then he walked them to the one path all life followed around the Circle and he Sang them home. It was so very simple, it was the most powerful Song he'd ever Sung.

One by one the bodies began to fall as each kigh took up its journey, once again.

As the afternoon deepened into dusk, the last of the walking dead remained standing above the empty husks of her companions. Jazep could feel her kigh being torn, needing to go, needing to stay, and he paused in his Song to better listen to hers.

Had he not been a bard, he might have missed the baby's cry; it had grown so weak and faint it barely made it out of the building. The woman turned toward the cry, stretching out a graying hand. When she turned back to Jazep, her face as expressionless as before but her pain impossible to mistake, he Sang of how Evicka and Krisus had overcome their fear for her baby's sake, that although she couldn't stay, her baby would never lack for love or protection.

The dead cannot cry, but her kigh wailed its sorrow as it fled and her body faced her baby when it fell.

Tears streaming down his face and into his beard, Jazep Sang the Circle's welcome. He could feel its comfort enclosing him and had to force himself to put that comfort aside. Shaking himself vigorously, feeling as though he'd just emerged from a trance state deeper than any he'd ever reached before, he let the Song trail off to silence.

There were still no earth kigh about, but he could deal with the implications of that later. Before he did anything else, he had to get to that baby.

He'd taken only a single step when he saw the bent and ancient figure emerge from the shadows. He'd thought, when Evicka had said she hadn't believed anything so old could live, it was merely youth defining the parameters of old. He was wrong. Although the old man was alive, his kigh was somehow as trapped as the kigh of those he'd killed to hold.

Their eyes met over the distance. The old man's face was wet and twisted with longing. Much as the young woman had reached for her child, Jazep stretched out his hand toward him and opened his mouth to Sing again.

NO! NO! NO!

It slammed into his awareness, a kigh too far gone in insanity to reach.

Not the old man's kigh.

Then who?

Jazep screamed, felt muscles tear as his back arched impossibly far. He clawed at the air as the attacking kigh clawed his spirit. Red and black waves of pain ripped through his head. Worse than his pain was the pain of the other kigh. He could feel every tortured nuance tearing through him again and again and again.

He heard the old man call out a name and had barely enough self remaining to realize that if he'd known Kait's name sooner, he might have been able to find her Song.

Too late.

The pain became more than even he could bear.

Holding tightly to the only Song he could remember, his kigh fled and his body fell to lie beside the other seven.

"Annice!" Drawn by the long, low moan of pain, Stasya raced across the garden, dropped onto the wet dirt beside the kneeling woman and gathered her into the circle of her arms. "What is it, dearling? What's wrong?"

"I don't know." Her body rigid, her face wet with tears, Annice slowly opened the fingers of one hand. Nestled in her palm lay a clump of earth, compacted by the pressure of her fist. "I don't know," she repeated. "But it just got worse."

"So, Vree." Kovar smiled kindly across the desk at her, the waxed ends of his mustache rising. "How are you finding your stay with us?"

Finding? What does he mean, finding? I haven't lost anything.

Vree felt her lungs expand and contract as Gyhard sighed. *I'm going to assume you don't know enough Shkoden to make puns. Our Bardic-Captain-in-waiting here, wants to know how you are, relative to where you are.*

Oh, that makes just as much sense. She nodded at Kovar, her expression carefully unreadable, and said, "Fine." Since arriving in Shkoder, she'd discovered it was a good, all-purpose answer for those times she didn't quite understand the question. Unless, of course, she was talking to Magda, who'd be all over it, like fire ants in a bedroll.

"The food's all right? The room? The bards aren't pestering you too much?"

The bards didn't actually see her. Most often, they saw two kigh and reacted accordingly. Occasionally, they saw some sort of romantic nonsense she didn't understand. Of all the bards who'd Sung at, around, and to her since she'd arrived, only the Bardic Captain had actually responded to her, as herself, and Gyhard, as himself, instead of treating them like some strange new piece of music to be learned.

What about Tadeus? Gyhard asked. Since his return, Tadeus had used his age and position to co-opt more than his fair share of their time.

He does it, too, although he's so slaughtering charming about it, it's hard to mind.

And Kovar? He seems worried about you.

He's not worried about me. He's worried about someone he thinks is me. Realizing that Kovar was waiting for an answer, Vree shrugged. "The food is good. The room is more than I've ever had. The bards have been very interested."

Kovar frowned and lightly drummed his fingers on the desktop in unconscious imitation of Captain Liene. He suspected there was more to Vree's response than an imperfect command of Shkoden, but as he also suspected that the cause of her unhappiness was a perpetual eavesdropper on her life, he didn't dare ask for further explanation lest she suffer for it later.

"Interested," he repeated. "That's one word for it. You've been a great help to us, Vree. I don't know if she mentioned it to you, but Karlene believed that part of being a bard involved an ability to Sing the fifth kigh. That we've all always done it without realizing it. That every time we touch an audience, one listener or one hundred, we're Singing the fifth kigh. Thanks to you . . ." His pause was so short that anyone but another bard would have missed it. Another bard or an assassin trained to notice the smallest detail connected to survival. ". . . and Gyhard, we're discovering that Karlene was right. We're beginning to find out why some Songs work, why some don't. If we can learn to consciously Sing the fifth kigh, we could reach so many more people."

Or they could fine-tune the way they manipulate emotions. All for the greater good, of course.

Karlene said bards aren't like that.

Karlene's a bard, Vree. She's not exactly unbiased.

Noticing Vree's blank stare, Kovar shook his head. "I'm sorry; I'm lecturing, aren't I? Bad habit of mine, I'm afraid. Have you heard the songs the fledglings are writing about you?"

"Songs? There's more than *one?*" Vree's cheeks grew hot at the memory of the lengthy and overly tragic ballad she was already aware of. Hearing it sung in front of Magda and her brother had been the most embarrassing moment of her entire life. When the young bard had left, Gerek had summed up her feelings pretty much exactly.

"Don't you wish you were still an assassin?" he'd caroled, surrendering to the laughter he'd charitably suppressed while the fledgling was within earshot. *"I bet you wish you could use your daggers right about now."*

"On me or on him?" she'd asked miserably. Gyhard's amusement hadn't helped.

And now she'd been told there was more than one. "Are the rest as bad?"

Kovar hid an involuntary smile at her tone. "Very likely. Never mind, Vree, the pressure'll be off you in a little while. The bards will be too busy to drown you in their creative juices and there'll be more Southerners around, so the Citadel, at least, shouldn't look so strange." When he saw he had her full attention, he went on. "According to the Imperial Ambassador, your young Prince Otavas is coming to Shkoder for a visit. His ship will be arriving sometime tomorrow." The panic that flashed in her eyes disappeared so quickly he thought he might have imagined it. "Vree?"

She stared at him but saw another face—a younger face; Bannon's face.

Vree?

Why is he coming here?

You don't know that Bannon is still with the prince.

Rising, Kovar came around the desk and stood, outstretched hand not quite touching Vree's rigid shoulder. "Are you all right, child?"

Before she could answer, or not answer, the door to the office burst open and Captain Liene threw herself into the room. "Open the window, Kovar! Quickly!"

Propelled across the room by Liene's voice, Kovar flipped up the latch that held the multipaned window closed. It flew open with such force that he lost his grip and it slammed back against the wall. The howl of the wind drowned out the crash of breaking glass.

The two bards tried to calm the half-dozen agitated kigh that spun around them, drenching them both with the rain the window had been closed to keep out. It wasn't until they raised their voices in harmony that the kigh's message began to make any sense.

A young bard named Marija had been intercepted by a hysterical teenager and taken to the small town of Bartek Springs where she'd found that something had caused the dead to walk. Fortunately, Jazep had arrived before her and Sung the dead to rest—her relief at the older bard's intervention was the strongest part of the message. Unfortunately, before she'd arrived, he'd then gone hunting the abomination that had done such a horrible and hideous thing—here the kigh grew agitated again and had to be soothed. Marija had Sung the notes of Jazep's name to an air kigh and sent it to find him. When it returned, it told her that Jazep no longer was. She'd sent another, and another, and another. The answer didn't change.

The final part of the message was less a Song than a wail. *What should I do?*

Liene groped her way to a chair and sat heavily, fingers white around the head of her cane. Kovar stared out the window as though he could find an answer in the blowing sheets of rain. Neither noticed that Vree was no longer in the room.

"Jazep." The Bardic Captain fought for breath, feeling as though she'd just been hit in the chest. "Marija has no ability in earth and that's the only quarter Jazep Sings. I need to get out of the city and hear what the earth kigh have to say."

Kovar shook his head slowly, as though even that limited motion was almost beyond him. "She didn't say that the air kigh couldn't find him, Liene. They told her he no longer was."

"That's impossible!"

"No. It isn't." His shoulders sagged. "You *know* the only reason they would have told her that."

"But Jazep . . ."

"Is dead. And we'll mourn him later." He lost his voice in grief, swallowed, and found it again. "Right now, we have a living bard who needs our help. What is Marija to do?"

Liene closed her eyes, feeling her age tighten around her. She touched a recall of Jazep as a fledgling. The only one in his year unable to Sing air, he'd never resented the others' easy communication with bards in other parts of the country; he'd just smiled his slow smile and been their anchor. The breadth of his shoulders and the heavy muscles in his arms made his legs seem short and out of proportion to the rest of his body, but everyone who met him saw his kindness and *then* his great strength. He had a tendency to fuss. She'd taught him the tambour and he'd soaked up the knowledge as effortlessly as the earth soaked up rain.

She'd mourn him later.

Straightening, Liene opened her eyes to meet Kovar's concerned gaze. "It seems," she said, "that if the dead are walking, the abomination of Karlene's recall has crossed the border from the Empire. Who else is in that area?"

"It's almost to the border, Captain. There's no one close. Jeremias is near the south end of the Coast Road, but he's only got two quarters—air and water, I believe . . ."

"All right." An upraised hand that trembled only a little cut him off. "Marija needs the description of the old man from Karlene's recall. We need the recall she's carrying about what happened at Bartek Springs. The Duc of Somes needs to be warned what's walking her province. We can't do anything with bits of information scattered all over the country so we have to consolidate, and we have to get a bard who Sings earth into those mountains. Jazep must have left a Song."

"With Jazep walking that way, we've spread the others with earth over the rest of the kingdom and with this opportunity to study the fifth kigh, we've shortened a number of walks . . ." His face went blank as he worked out the rough locations of the bards they could use. Suddenly, animation returned. "I'll go. And we needn't send the courier. I can ride with the recall myself."

In spite of everything, the corners of Liene's mouth quirked up. "Kovar, when was the last time you were on a horse?"

He frowned. "Ten, twelve years ago, why?"

Bards walked. It kept them connected to the land and the people. The few times it became necessary for a bard to ride, younger bards, those closest to their lives before the Bardic Hall, were invariably chosen.

"I think," Liene told him kindly, "we'd best leave this to those who ride for a living." When it looked as though he were going to protest, she added, "You wouldn't ask a courier to Sing the Fourth Quarter service, would you?"

"No." He sighed. "No, I wouldn't." His chin rose. "All right, then what?"

"That depends on His Majesty's orders." Liene stood and smoothed down her robe, her palm lingering over the brown quarter. "I'll request an immediate audience. But, no matter what His Majesty says, this much is definite: Marija is not to try and find Jazep's body until she knows what she may be facing. We have few enough bards to risk their lives so foolishly." She could see a pair of kigh just outside the window, waiting for an answer to Marija's final question, their presence a reminder of the message they'd brought, a reminder of Jazep's death. All at once, she wanted to smack their pointy little ethereal faces. "Could you send her my decision please, Kovar. I don't think . . ." She shook her head and blinked away tears. "I don't think I could Sing right now."

By the time the Bardic Captain had slammed the door all the way open, Vree had been out of her chair reaching for the daggers she didn't wear within the

Bardic Hall. When the winds blew into the room, she'd kept her back to the wall and slid toward the door. While the two bards were trying to calm the air spirits, she'd slipped out of the room.

This was bardic business, not hers. If they wanted her to know later, they'd tell her. A quick glance showed she hadn't been missed.

Aren't you the least bit curious about what the kigh are telling them? Gyhard asked.

No. Whenever the air spirits . . .

The kigh.

She rolled her eyes. *Fine. The kigh. Whenever *the kigh* blew around Karlene that violently, it was always bad news.*

Gyhard tried to remember every time the kigh had come to Karlene and decided, after a moment, that Vree was right. *I'd still like to know what they had to say.*

You know what we used to call people who always had to know what was going on? Jiir's targets—and then we'd bury them.

But this message might have been about us, he argued. He let her feel his desire to turn her around, back toward Kovar's office.

That, she declared, ignoring the feeling with the ease of much practice, *is all the more reason to make ourselves scarce. If they want us, they can find us when they calm down.*

After a moment's consideration, Gyhard muttered, *That's not a bad idea.*

Yeah, well, a lifetime in the army teaches a number of useful survival skills.

Halfway up the stairs, a bard Vree'd forgotten the

name of rushed past, eyes streaming tears. The ex-assassin froze in place, head cocked.

What is it? Gyhard demanded.

A breeze touched Vree's cheek and moved on. "There's a lot of air moving around in here," she murmured.

What?

Something's wrong. Can't you feel it? Silently, she sped down the stairs to the first floor and headed for an exit. Although she had no reason for believing it, she was convinced that the arrival of the air spirits and the weeping bard were connected. *This building suddenly seems too small for what it has to hold.*

Fully aware that Vree's instincts had been developed by years of brutal training, Gyhard examined that statement from every possible angle. *I think you've been spending too much time with the bards,* he concluded as they stepped out into the rain.

Maybe. But listen.

From one of the upper windows came the same four notes, repeated over and over and over. The raw emotion lifted the hair off the back of her neck and made it impossible to tell if the voice was male or female. Eddies of wind, given definition by the rain, spun around the building.

Unwilling to leave the Citadel, Vree made her way to the cloister where she and Magda most often spent their afternoons. With a minimum of effort—more for practice than anything—she slipped unseen into the Healers' Hall and then out into the cloister. Choosing a bench that gave her a clear line of sight on both doors leading back into the building, she sat and stared out at the herb garden, deserted because of the rain.

What are we doing here? Gyhard demanded, moving restlessly within the confines of Vree's mind. *If we're hiding, we're not doing a very good job.*

We're waiting for something to happen.

Like what?

If I knew, we wouldn't have to wait. We could go looking for it.

She reminded him of a cat, sitting by a hole gnawed in the wall, certain that, in time, a mouse would appear. It wasn't that she was focused—he could almost feel her concentration spreading out to cover all possibilities—it was that *all* she was doing was waiting. It made him very uncomfortable although he wasn't entirely certain why. *Did they train you to do this?* When she nodded, he wondered if maybe that was it; that perhaps she was, in a way, training him, and he didn't want to learn to be an assassin. He wanted to fidget, to pace, to twiddle his thumbs—except that he didn't have thumbs of his own to twiddle. *Shouldn't we be doing something?*

Like what? she demanded in turn.

When Gyhard couldn't find an answer, he decided it might be time to change the subject. *Vree, about Bannon; I'm sure if you don't think you can face him, it can be arranged so that you don't have to.*

First of all, she snapped, * what makes you think I don't want to see him? And second, what makes you think anyone here could stop him if he wanted to see me?*

Her mental voice suggested she'd be equally unaffected by either scenario, but she couldn't block the chaotic mix of emotions churning just below the surface of her thoughts. Though it was far from that simple, guilt, longing, and fear seemed to predominate.

What are you more afraid of, Vree? Gyhard asked quietly. *That he won't want to see you or that he will?*

Maybe I'm afraid that the moment you see him, you'll jump back to his body. It suited you well enough before.

He couldn't be angry, not when he could feel her frightened uncertainty and knew she lashed out at him only because he was there. He could, however, be irritated by her desire to pick a fight rather than face an emotion or two. *I can't jump unless your body is dying or you push me out. So if I end up back in Bannon's body, it won't have been *my* choice.*

Just for a moment, he caught the memory of her thigh brushing his with nothing between them but scented water. Before he figured out whether it was his memory or hers, it was so strongly suppressed it took other, less heated memories, with it.

There's just so slaughtering much between us. Gyhard recognized Bannon in the plural rather than himself. *Or maybe,* she continued as she remembered a strained good-bye on the docks of the Capital, *it's that there's nothing between us anymore at all. That we used it all up. Besides . . .* she flicked one finger at a dead leaf back of the bench, the closest Gyhard could ever remember her coming to fidgeting. *He probably still hates you and you're still with me.*

A lot of people don't get along with their sibling's partners.

Vree snorted. *You're not exactly a partner. You're more like a . . .*

A parasite.

The lengthy silence became agreement.

She stared out at the rain, watching it bead on the

broad leaves of the boneset, listening to it run down the cistern pipes, tasting it with every breath. Finally, she sighed. *We have to find you a body. Soon.*

Gyhard fought the urge to nod her head. *No argument here.*

The main door into the cloister flew open and Gerek charged through, momentum taking him right out into the garden.

That boy is too good-looking, Gyhard grumbled as Vree straightened out of her defensive crouch.

Murmuring a distracted affirmation, Vree stepped forward enough to be seen.

For a heartbeat, Gerek's worried frown disappeared, returning when he saw she was alone. Ignoring both the rain and the herbs crushed under his feet, he jerked forward. "Have you seen Maggi? I can't find her anywhere!"

"What's wrong?"

"The kigh are saying that Jazep is dead—it's all over the Citadel. He was one of Maggi's name-fathers. She's going to need me."

"Name-fathers," Vree repeated.

Gyhard made the connection first. *Didn't Magda tell us that Tadeus was one of her name-fathers?*

"Tadeus!" The name cast a deeper shadow over Gerek's face when Vree asked Gyhard's question aloud. "Of course! He's going to be in pieces. She'd have headed right for him!" Spinning on one heel, he ran back into the building with Vree close behind.

No one got in their way.

They raced into an ominously quiet Bardic Hall, took the stairs to the third floor two at a time, and pounded down the corridor. As they neared the end of the hall and began to slow, a door opened.

Magda staggered from the room, pushed out by the hoarse sound of crying. When she saw her brother, her face crumpled, as though, seeing refuge at last, she'd let go of an artificial strength. She threw herself at him and burst into tears.

"Jazep . . ."

"I know, Maggi. I've heard." Enclosing her in the circle of his arms, he rested his cheek on her curls.

"I felt it when Tadeus found out," she sobbed. "I was on my way to a lesson and his pain, it just *hit* me and *hit* me and *hit* me. When I got here, he was Singing Jazep's name, over and over. It was like there was a whirlwind in the room with him—the kigh wouldn't let me get close to him. Then that Imperial fledgling he has, Ullious, he showed up and he Sang the kigh enough away that I could touch him and Tadeus just *looked* at me like his heart was broken and he stopping Singing and he started to cry and, oh Ger, I couldn't. I just couldn't."

"Couldn't what, Maggi?" Although his own face was wet, Gerek's voice was gentle and calm.

She twisted the loose folds of his shirt up in both fists. "I couldn't handle his pain and mine. He was . . . I was . . . It just *hurts* so much."

"Is Ullious still with him?"

"He is, but I'm *not*. I should be in there, Gerek. I'm *supposed* to be a healer!"

Trembling a little at the sudden rush of emotion, wishing there was a target she could hit to make it all better, Vree reached out and gently gripped Magda's hand where it was tangled in her brother's shirt. "Wounded healers need bandages themselves. You can't save anyone if you bleed to death."

"I'm not *bleeding*." Her protest emerged damp and muffled from Gerek's chest.

"Your heart is bleeding. You've done what you can for Tadeus. Now you need to heal yourself."

"But . . ."

"No buts," Vree interrupted. She gave the younger woman's hand a final squeeze, released it, and stepped back, holding tightly to her own control.

Gerek swung his little sister up into his arms where she clung to him, her face pressed into the angle of his shoulder, the curve of her neck below the tangle of dark curls looking vulnerable and lost. "I'll take her to her room and stay with her," he said. "Where will you be if she needs you?"

Startled, Vree stared at him. "Needs me?" she repeated.

Settling Magda more securely in his arms, Gerek rested an expression on Vree that held too many variables for her to understand. "Yes, needs you. Where will you be?"

"I guess my room, but . . ."

"No buts."

She watched him carry his sister down the hall and moved only when they disappeared into a stairwell.

Where to now? Gyhard asked, the tone of his voice reminding her of Gerek's expression.

I guess to my room. Wondering how much pain a blind man had to be in to *look* at someone as though his heart were broken, she turned on one heel and walked silently back to the room she'd been given.

Kovar arrived just as she did. His eyes were red and his lashes clung together in clumps. "Have you heard?" When she nodded, he swallowed and visibly squared his shoulders under the quartered robe. "How much?"

"Only that a bard named Jazep is dead."

There's more, Gyhard murmured.

No slaughtering shit. She opened the door and gestured for Kovar to enter. "You look like you need to sit down," she said abruptly. "I can make tea."

"No, no tea, thank you." But he accepted the offer of a place to sit, lowering himself into a chair as though he'd broken ribs and not taken the time to have them bound. Lacing long, ink-stained fingers in his lap, he looked up at her and said, "We need your help."

Vree cocked her head to one side and moved her weight forward onto the balls of her feet. Not quite a fighting stance but ready for the eventuality. "You want me to kill the person or persons who killed Jazep."

The Bardic Second was so surprised his mouth opened and closed, but no sound emerged. Finally, he managed a strangled, "Not that. No."

"Then what?" Vree relaxed slightly, refusing to acknowledge the relief his answer gave.

"We need your knowledge of the abomination who was Kars."

Kars?

She couldn't entirely prevent Gyhard's cry from leaving her mouth. It burst past her lips as a truncated, wordless wail. Regaining control, she wrapped herself around him, protecting him as she would have protected Bannon had he been hit from ambush.

Kovar misunderstood. "I know. You're shocked. You thought that part of your life was over. But something is in Shkoder causing the dead to walk, and we can't think of who or what else it could be." He drew a shaking hand across his forehead. "We have Karlene's recall, of course, but if we are to defeat this thing, we need to add your knowledge as well."

Vree waited. Silently.

"Yours and Gyhard's."

Gyhard stirred out of his shock. *They want to put *me* under recall?* When Vree repeated his questions and the bard nodded, he asked, his mental voice incredulous, *Do they know what that means?*

They should by now. "Sorry," she said, spreading her hands. "I can't risk that."

Looking as though he'd expected her response, Kovar nodded, somehow managing to sound both disappointed and relieved. "I understand, but I had to ask."

Vree, what are you doing? He could sense the lie but not what it was about, memories of Kars—as a young man, as an old man—kept getting in the way.

Before she could answer, Kovar continued, his tone so incredibly reassuring Vree suspected he was using some sort of bardic trick and she steeled herself against it. "We still need your memories, though, and I personally assure you there'll be no danger of Gyhard trying to take control while you're in recall."

Why that suspicious, son of a . . .

Shut up! Vree snapped and added aloud, "All right. When?"

"It'll have to be tomorrow morning. There isn't a bard in the hall who could do it tonight." His face folded along lines drawn by grief and he looked ten years older as he slowly pulled himself out of the chair and back onto his feet. He paused at the door. "Thank you for helping, Vree. We'll be Singing for Jazep at the Center tonight; you're welcome to attend."

As the sound of his footsteps faded down the hall, Vree closed the shutters, lit a lamp, and pulled her pack out from under the bed.

Vree, what are you doing?

Kars is our business, not theirs.

I can't . . .

Can't what? she interrupted. *Can't face him? You've said you failed him twice.* Gyhard jerked as her intentional blow hit home and, making no effort to block out the pain she'd caused him, she forced herself to go on. *I say that third time pays for all.*

We don't even know where he is!

Then we eavesdrop a little and find out where the message came from. I can track him from there. One of the bulky knit sweater things took up more room than she liked, but if it was about to get as cold as everyone said, she supposed she'd better take it.

Vree.

What? You started this, Gyhard, don't you want to finish it?

Not exactly. I want it to be finished. He could feel the memory of the ancient throat between his hands—Bannon's hands—could see behind the rheumy eyes the young man he'd pushed over the edge into insanity then abandoned an impossible number of years before. He could have—would have—killed him then, but one of the walking dead had intervened. He wasn't sure he could bring himself to that point again.

You were alone last time. This time, you've got me.

Stop reading my mind.

He felt her almost smile. *Strong emotions, remember?*

But if you're afraid I'll take control . . .

The almost smile disappeared. *Is that why you think I refused to let them recall you? You think I'm stupid enough to believe you'd try to take over with half a dozen slaughtering bards marching through our minds?*

No, but . . .

What happened between you and Kars is private. You shouldn't have to share it with everyone who can carry a tune. She bent over to fight with a stiff buckle and Gyhard suddenly realized she was embarrassed, that she was trying to distance herself from her words.

I'm sorry.

She shrugged. *It's all right.*

And thank you.

Look, I said it's all right!

He drew back before she could push him away, willing to give her what little space he could, maintaining too tenuous a hold on his own emotions to deal with hers.

Vree laid her daggers out on the bed and lightly touched the empty wrist sheath. Allowing for slight differences in weight, Bannon had an identical set—except, of course, that Bannon still had a *set*.

For the moment, memories of Kars had wrapped Gyhard in an emotional soup too thick to see through. It hadn't yet occurred to him that in going after his past, they'd be avoiding hers.

Chapter Seven

Twisted up in memories of Kars, Gyhard had been paying little attention to Vree's preparations. He'd roused briefly when she'd discovered that the dead were walking in Bartek Springs and then allowed himself to be sucked back down into a roiling mix of emotions. As he hadn't noticed her turn off the lamp or open the shutters, it came as a bit of a shock to realize they were perched on the window ledge outside her room and he hastily quelled an urge to propel her body back inside. *Vree, why are we going out the window?*

So no one sees us. We're going to need as large a lead as we can get.

But . . . He refused to look as she pushed off the narrow ledge, dropped, and caught herself on fingers and toes. The pack pulled at her shoulders and she compensated for its extra weight. *But we're heading down into an enclosed courtyard. We're going to have to go back into the Hall or over the . . .*

Wall? she finished for him, dropping onto the worn flagstones. They were still damp from the day's rain, but the sky was clear overhead, the bowl of night filled with stars. After an unhappy glance up at the unfamiliar constellations, she followed the shadow path along the foundations of the building.

Vree.

Look, since you're new at this, I'll explain. The windows overlooking the courtyard held no signs of life. Based on their evidence, the Bardic Hall might well have been empty. *We can't go out the gate—there's always a bard on it and we can't exactly pretend to be someone else. Nothing overlooks this piece of wall except the Bardic Hall. The bards are at the center, Singing for Jazep. If we go over the wall here, no one will see us.*

It very nearly made sense. *The kigh can see us.*

So slaughtering what? By the time the bards ask them where we've gone, we'll be a good six or seven hours closer to Kars. Splaying both hands out against the huge, squared stones used to build the wall around the Citadel, she smiled. Although the outside rose perpendicular from the street, the inside, in the interests of strength and stability, angled gently in from the base to the crown. *We're not hiding, this is a race,* she continued as she started to climb. *We have to get to Kars first.*

And when they use the kigh to send messages ahead?

To stop us? Lying flat, she rolled across the top of the wall and started down the other side. *I don't think so.*

About to protest further, Gyhard remembered that Vree had been a military assassin for five years. Two years longer than assassins usually managed to outwit the odds. She'd never gone after a target that hadn't known she was coming, and they'd never been able to stop her. What chance would the bards of Shkoder, who really had no idea of her capabilities, have against her? He only hoped that would occur to the bards of Shkoder.

He briefly noted how fast Vree was moving and how tiny the edges of stone she gripped were, then quickly turned his attention elsewhere. It wouldn't take much of a twitch to send them plummeting to the ground. The trouble was, elsewhere almost immediately became thoughts of Kars.

Gyhard had wondered once if new love had called back the old, if the gods or the fates or the Circle or whatever anyone of a dozen different religions wanted to call it had set Kars in his path in order for him to close the door on the past and open it on the future. He didn't believe in coincidence, especially not when he'd had his nose rubbed in the past with a thoroughness that had made it impossible to ignore.

That he'd failed Kars a second time had been no fault of his. He'd done everything he could.

Apparently, it wasn't enough.

The knowledge that Kars continued to live, somewhere, could be ignored. He'd had lifetimes of practice ignoring it. But something had propelled Kars across the border into Shkoder. And something had seen to it that he got the news.

He was being given another chance.

Vree was right. He had to take it.

Staying in Elbasan and letting the bards deal with the situation would release Kars from the trap but leave him in it. If he and Vree were to ever have a life together—even as strange a life as they were living now—he had to be the one who finally laid Kars to rest.

As Vree dropped to the street and checked to make sure they'd been unobserved, Gyhard gave himself a mental shake and decided it was probably a good thing they were leaving the bards behind. Melodrama appeared to be catching.

They taken maybe six steps on level ground when they heard horses approaching from behind, shod hooves chiming against the cobblestones.

Vree?

The wide road encircling the Citadel wall provided no cover and the night was too bright to hide them.

Vree refused to turn although she could feel how much Gyhard wanted to. *Ignore it. It has nothing to do with us. Even if someone saw us going over the wall, they wouldn't have sent out the cavalry.*

The horses drew closer. Close enough to hear the creak of harness, to catch a whiff of the stable, to feel the warm bulk of the animals looming up behind them.

"We'll get there a lot faster if we ride."

"We?" Vree demanded before she finished turning.

Magda let the hooded cloak fall back. An afternoon of crying had left her face blotchy, but her eyes were dry and she carried her chin at a determined angle. "I knew you were going as soon as I worked past Jazep being dead and actually thought about how he ... how he died. Gyhard has responsibilities to Kars he *has* to honor or they'll eat at him, at both of you, all the rest of your lives. I have responsibilities to you. I *can't* let you go alone."

"You can't go with us."

The younger woman held out the extra set of reins. "You can't stop me. I won't go back willingly and if you take me back, you know you won't get out again. This is your only chance to get to Kars first, and I'm afraid I'm a part of it."

Vree's eyes narrowed. "I could knock you out and leave you here. Take both horses. It might be a couple of hours until you're found."

"You won't."

"You're very sure of yourself."

"No." Magda shook her head and half-smiled. "I'm very sure of you."

The generous curves of her mouth pressed into a thin, irritated line, Vree secured her pack behind the saddle and mounted. "The king, your uncle, is not going to allow this."

"The king, my uncle, will have to catch us." Magda flicked a wet curl out of the corner of her mouth. "These are the same horses our couriers ride—the same horses Imperial couriers have been riding since His majesty got the idea and the stock from the Empire, so you *know* how fast they move. By tomorrow morning when they notice we're gone, we'll be three or four stations down the Coast Road and even if the bards get a message ahead of us, we'll have a huge lead."

"If the bards get a message ahead of us," Vree pointed out acerbically, "they'll try to stop us."

The pale oval of Magda's face tilted to one side. "Stop *you?*" she asked.

As Vree had said almost the same thing to Gyhard, she had little room left for argument. "This is going to get you into a lot of trouble."

"Why? I'm not a prisoner here." Her chin rose in a motion Gyhard recognized from days and nights of watching Vree. "I can leave if I like."

"What about studying to be a healer?" Vree leaned forward and stroked a silken neck. "What about stealing these horses?"

"I'm not *stealing* anything," Magda protested indignantly. "Healers are *allowed* to use the couriers' stables so they can get to emergencies as fast as possible. Now I may only be an apprentice healer, but I think that the dead walking in Shkoder qualifies as an *emergency*. As for the rest, you're my patient. I can't abandon you. That's covered under Healers' Oaths. Besides . . ." She sighed and her tone gentled. "I heal the fifth kigh, and healing Kars is part of healing you."

She has a slaughtering answer for everything.

Vree, she can't come. It's going to be hard enough dealing with Kars. If she's there . . . Gyhard's voice got lost in the painful prospect of once more seeing the ruin the years and his interference had made of Kars. *Dying has to be easier than having your heart ripped out over and over.* The ancient image grew younger; the chin pointed; the hair grew thick and brown and curly; the skin darkened; the brows lifted to a sardonic angle. Not Kars. Bannon. Which was when he realized that neither the pain nor the thought accompanying it was his alone

The second realization seeped around the edges of the first. Bannon would be arriving shortly with Prince Otavas. If they went after Kars, Vree wouldn't have to face him. His rush of anger at having his personal demons used as an excuse to avoid hers smashed apart the barriers between them, crashed into her fear, and ground to a halt, its momentum destroyed.

Vree stiffened. The horse, who'd been standing quietly while she'd been adjusting the stirrups, began to move forward. *Bannon can wait. Kars can't.* She yanked back on the reins. *If the bards get to him first, you'll have lost your chance.*

You were hoping I wouldn't notice. You didn't want me to know how afraid you were.

Her teeth were clenched so tightly together both temples throbbed. *Assassins are trained to face their fears. I . . .* The barriers were down. She had no self-image left to save. *I can't face him. Not yet.*

Then it's a good thing you're not an assassin any more, isn't it?

I'm sorry. She didn't know what exactly she was sorry for, so she hoped he did.

"It would be a healthy thing, a distinct step forward if you two managed to resolve *something* in your lives. At least you both know what has to be done in order to deal with Kars."

Breathing heavily, Vree looked down at Magda's fingers lying across her wrist. Until the young healer had spoken, she hadn't even felt the touch. If she needed proof she was no longer an assassin, there it was.

This was a private conversation, child, Gyhard told her shortly.

Magda snatched her hand back as though the fingers had been burned. Her lower lip started to tremble. "I only wanted to help. Vree was looking so . . . I mean, I'm a healer, and I have to do *something!*"

Gyhard used Vree's lungs to sigh. *You know, her wanting to go along probably has as much to do with a response to Jazep's death as with us.*

No shit. As Magda sniffed, Vree reached between the horses and gently grabbed her shoulder. "He's . . ." *How do you say pissed off in Shkoden?*

I don't need you to explain me to her, Vree.

"He's upset because we have so little privacy and so every bit we lose seems too large." She tightened her grip for a moment then let go. "But it's a good thing you're going with us."

"Really?"

"Yeah."

Vree!

*Maybe healing Kars *is* a part of healing you. Us. Besides, she's right. We don't have a choice. We have a saying in the army; don't waste your strength trying to push a dagger through armor. It only dulls the blade and irritates the enemy.*

Very profound.

Thank you.

The moist sound of horseshit hitting cobblestones echoed against the Citadel wall. Magda giggled, just a little hysterically. "We'd better get moving before we're caught by a garden-wagon and escorted home at pitchfork point."

As Vree settled into the rhythm of her horse's gait, she revised travel plans. If they managed to avoid bardic entanglements, Magda's presence had cut their time on the road at least in half. Which had to be weighed against Magda's presence complicating things rather significantly.

Then let's look at the bright side, Gyhard put in wearily. *If the king's niece, the only healer they've got who can heal the fifth kigh, *has* to go tearing around the country, at least there's no one she's safer doing it with than you.*

Vree grinned, thinking of the omnipresent trio of guards, and of Gerek who shadowed every moment she and Magda spent together. *You really think His Majesty and her brother are going to believe that?*

About as much as I think His Majesty and her brother are likely to sprout wings and fly.

*   *   *

"I assure you, Your Majesty, that Magda is completely safe."

"You also assured me," Theron growled, both hands pressed white-knuckled against his desk, "that the assassin would remain under bardic control. Now you tell me she's galloping down the South Coast Road with my niece." He held the Bardic Captain in a basilisk glare. "Which am I to believe?"

Projecting a calm she wasn't entirely feeling, Liene spread her hands. "The kigh are watching them, Majesty. They're not trying to hide."

"That's very helpful." The words squeezed out from between clenched teeth. "But I don't care about the kigh. What are *you* going to do?"

Liene blinked. "Do, Majesty?" They hadn't realized until they'd sent a fledgling to her room after breakfast that Vree was gone—they'd thought she'd merely missed the meal and had been concerned that she might be ill. When she wasn't in her room, they'd assumed she was with Magda and sent the fledgling to the Healers' Hall only to find Magda missing as well and an irritated Captain of Couriers demanding to know why an apprentice had signed for two horses.

Kovar had immediately Called a kigh—his summons so peremptory four of them appeared and nearly blew him over—and sent them searching for the missing assassin. The two senior bards then began to put the pieces together and by the time the kigh reappeared, their answer came as no surprise. Liene had headed immediately for the palace. She hadn't actually thought of much beyond getting to the king before he heard his niece was missing from a non-bardic source.

"Do," she repeated. "Majesty, as I said, Magda is

in no danger. She was, according to Cecilie, the bard on the gate, under no compulsion when she left the Citadel. We believe that the three of them—Vree, Gyhard, and Magda—are heading into Somes in order to deal with Kars."

"Who is—if I remember Karlene's recall correctly, which I assure you, Captain, I do—an insane Cemandian who Sings the dead to life and has recently killed a bard." Theron's face began to darken. "Not to mention, he was once Gyhard's lover and was not killed by this same assassin although she had every opportunity to do so and had apparently been trained never to miss. You'll have to explain to me, Captain, how you can possibly stand there and say that Magda is in no danger!"

Considerably more worried about the vein throbbing on Theron's temple than she was about Magda, Liene stepped toward the desk. "Majesty, please believe me when I say that both Vree and Gyhard view Magda as the only person who might possibly be able to help them. They would never, ever hurt her and will, in fact, do everything they can to protect her. There is no one in Shkoder, Majesty," she continued soothingly, "who would be able to get past Vree to Magda."

Unfortunately, the king was past being soothed. "No one except this bardic abomination!" His left hand curled into a fist. "The very thing she's rushing off to face! I want her stopped, do you hear me! Send a kigh to every bard between her and Somes!" He paused and his left shoulder flexed forward, but before the Bardic Captain could explain that they'd already begun to move the only bard in the area, he went on. "And *then*, you throw everything you've got at this thing that is killing my people!" His expression changed between one heartbeat and the next, pain wiping out anger.

"Majesty?"

Beads of sweat suddenly appeared on his forehead, combining and trickling down both temples. He opened his mouth, but no sound emerged. Right hand clutching at his tunic front, he slumped forward, his face smacking into the desk.

"Majesty!" Liene raced to his side just as a tentative knock sounded against the office door. "What!" she snapped, one hand pressed on a pulse point in the king's throat, relief that he still lived overwhelming fifty years of vocal training.

A section of paneling swung open and a page stepped into the room. "Majesty, the ..." Her jaw dropped.

"Get the king's healer! Now!"

The page whirled around and raced away, leaving the door ajar behind her.

As Liene eased Theron back against the leather padding of his chair, the second page on duty poked his head into the room. Eyes impossibly wide under ginger brows and every freckle standing out against pale skin, he crept forward, shoes making no noise against the thick carpet. "Majesty?"

Liene jerked around. "Don't do that!" she snarled.

The page ignored the old woman, his gaze locked on the king. "What's wrong with him?"

"Do I look like a healer?" When the boy seemed about to cry, she clutched at control and managed to gentle her voice. "I don't know what's wrong, but he needs your help."

"My help?"

"That's right. Go get Her Majesty and bring her here as quickly as you can. Be careful not to frighten her."

He sniffed. "What about the Heir? Should I get Princess Onele?"

Her hand on Theron's shoulder, Liene nodded, grateful that the boy had thought of it. *He's ten years younger than I am. This shouldn't be happening.* "Yes. Get her, too."

"Where you headed, Healer?"

"Somes." Magda covered a yawn with the back of her hand then scrawled her name across the bottom of the form that would get them fresh horses. She began to make the apprentice symbol, realized what she was doing, and flushed.

The stablemaster only laughed. "Haven't been a healer too long, have you?"

"No, in fact, I . . ." Exhaustion wiped out the rest of the thought and she stared blankly up at him, unable to remember the lie she'd been about to tell.

"Never mind." He looked as though he were about to pat her on the head. "I'll just check this against the list the Healers' Hall sends me out from Elbasan." Yanking open the single drawer under the scarred table, he pulled out a folded sheet, swept aside some straw and spread it out. "Can't just have anyone riding off on the King's horses," he explained as he ran a thick finger down the first column of names.

Vree shifted her weigh forward and wished she had her second throwing dagger.

Gyhard quickly shifted her weight back. *You're not going to have to kill him.*

How do you know?

Magda would never put us in a situation where that was the only option.

She's tired. Tired people make mistakes.

Not one that so completely contravenes everything she believes in..

Big words. What the slaughter do they mean?

She wouldn't make a mistake that big.

"Ah, here you are. See that loopy bit there? Unmistakable." He turned frowning slightly. "I see you're still an apprentice on the Second Quarter list. Funny you should make full healer before Third Quarter Festival."

Magda shrugged, making no effort to hide how exhausted she was. "*I'd* have waited, but they need my specialty as soon as possible in Somes and they couldn't spare a healer to travel all that way with me. If I was going to go, and I had to, I had to go as a healer."

"Poor thing. Missed your ceremony, then tossed on a horse and pounded against a saddle for days on end." Clucking his tongue, he looked over at Vree. "If you're her helper, Southerner, you ought to be helping her up to bed. She's nearly dead on her feet."

Startled, Vree took a closer look at the younger woman. They'd been on the move since just after full dark and it was now well into morning. Stops had been infrequent and the two previous times they'd changed horses, Vree hadn't bothered going inside. There were purple-gray shadows under Magda's eyes, her mouth was slack, her shoulders slumped, and she carried her head as if it were too heavy for her neck.

You're used to your own rather remarkable endurance, Gyhard reminded her, feeling her guilt. *You're not used to traveling with someone who doesn't share it.* He well remembered how Bannon's body had effortlessly done everything he'd asked of it.

Vree shoved aside a memory of Gyhard/Bannon riding beside her, laughing, eating, bathing ... and lightly touched Magda on the arm. "He's right. You need to rest."

"We need to keep moving." But it was almost a question.

"You'll do no one no good if you fall off the horse and break your neck, Healer," the stablemaster pointed out, kindly. "I got a nice quiet corner of the mow for just this kind of situation. You two head up there and lie down and I'll see that you're woke in three hours."

"Three hours," Magda repeated.

Vree met the stablemaster's eyes. There appeared to be nothing behind his smile but an honest desire to help. "Come on." She put her arm around the younger woman's shoulders. "We can spare three hours."

A horse blanket spread over the straw was a better bed than many Vree had slept in. Taking a deep breath, she allowed her muscles to relax and was nearly asleep when an unfamiliar sound snapped her fully alert. Unfamiliar to her; Gyhard obviously knew what it was.

Imperial Army service starts at fifteen, he murmured. *Don't soldiers ever get homesick?*

Not around assassins, she told him shortly, rolling up on one elbow. Rays of sunlight, glittering with dust, slanted through cracks and knotholes, providing more than enough light to see thin shoulders shaking. "Magda? what's wrong?"

"Jazep's dead." Nearly lost against the crook of her elbow, the childlike wail took years off Magda's age.

Vree reached out a hand, but left it hovering in midair, uncertain of what to do.

Hold her.

Are you sure?

Trust me.

I don't know how. She'd meant it as a bald statement of fact, but it came out more like a desperate apology.

Yes, you do. He didn't want to say it, didn't want to remind her, but he couldn't allow her to believe she was unable to give comfort, couldn't allow jealousy to cause her such pain. *Just pretend that Magda is Bannon.*

Bannon? Slowly, hesitantly, ready to pull back if it were the wrong thing to do, Vree reached out and drew Magda into the circle of her arms.

Magda pressed herself against Vree's side. Her sobs turned to ragged breathing, evened out, and in a few moments she was asleep, too tired to grieve further.

Resting her cheek on the soft cap of dark curls, Vree shifted to settle herself more comfortably beneath the warm weight and tried to work out how long it had been since she'd held another person; if she'd *ever* been granted the kind of trust that allowed sleep in such a position. Breathing in the scent of sweat and hay and horses, she forced herself to relax and grant that trust in return.

Just before sleep claimed them both, Gyhard realized that Vree hadn't reacted to his instinctive control of her body down in the stable and he found himself suddenly unsure if that was a good thing or a bad.

*   *   *

Her Royal Highness, the Princess Onele, Heir to the crown of Shkoder, looked grim as she left her parents' bedchamber and entered the solar where the Bardic Captain and the Chancellor were waiting, their mutual animosity lost in shared worry. She nodded at Liene. "He wants to see you." Her lips twisted up in a humorless smile. "And he says you're not to start composing any eulogies."

"Highness, is he . . ."

"In a very bad mood," Onele interrupted. "Use as much Voice as you have to to keep him from losing his temper."

"Yes, Highness."

Neither of them meant it, but the exchange lightened the tensions in the room just a little.

"When His Majesty is finished with you, come and see me. We have things to discuss."

"Yes, Highness."

As the Bardic Captain left the solar, leaning heavily on her cane, Onele took a deep breath and squared her shoulders under the faded shirt she'd been wearing when summoned from the stables. Unlike most children, she'd been raised with the full knowledge that one day her father would die. *"When you are Queen, Highness . . . "* had begun every lesson, the implication clear, and she had to admit that increasingly over the last few years she'd been impatient to get on with the job she'd been trained to do. She was thirty-four years old. Long past time to finish her apprenticeship. Now that the job was almost hers, she found that she wouldn't mind putting it off for a little while yet.

"When you are Queen, Highness . . ."

When my father dies . . .

"Highness?"

The Heir gave herself a shake and focused on the Chancellor.

"Highness, Prince Otavas' ship has passed the outer harbor and will be mooring shortly. Everything is in readiness, but ..." Chancellor Rozele spread her hands.

Onele nodded. "But obviously I can't go down to greet my Imperial cousin as planned. I don't suppose Aunt Milena's boy is still here?"

"No, Highness, he went home." And, good riddance, her expression added. "I had thought perhaps His Grace, Heir of Ohrid ..."

"Perfect. It'll keep him from worrying about his sister and there's only what, five years between them?"

"Four, Highness. Unfortunately, we haven't been able to find His Grace." Her lips pursed. "He didn't spend the night in the Citadel and has not yet returned."

Onele briefly closed her eyes. It was just like Gerek not to be around when he was needed. "Who's left?"

The Chancellor glanced down at the floor, as though looking for inspiration in the polished wood. "Princess Jelena is barely three years younger than Prince Otavas, Highness and, as Heir Apparent, would bring a certain diplomatic sense of rank to the meeting."

Jelena's mother frowned. "But she's so shy."

"The pressure on her will be slight, Highness. Although an official duty, it is also a family duty." The shared knowledge that Princess Jelena would, given her position, have to overcome that shyness, lingered behind the Chancellor's words. "If one of the older bards took the duty, she'd feel like she had someone to depend on."

Olena sighed. It seemed her father's illness would

also force her daughter forward into new responsibility. "Have her sent to my quarters. I'll tell her myself while I change." Her hand on the door, she paused. "I want to see His Grace when he returns to the palace."

"I'll have him informed, Highness."

Uncertain of what to expect when she entered the royal bedchamber, Liene swept her gaze over healer, consort, and king.

The Healer, Jokubas i'Brigita a'Jokubas, looked too young for the critical position he held—although honesty forced Liene to admit that, of late, everyone looked too young. Standing by the head of the bed, one thin hand resting lightly on Theron's shoulder so that he could constantly monitor the king's condition, his expression was far too serene to give anything away.

Light diagnostic trance, Liene noted as she approached.

Llyana, sitting close against the bed and holding one of Theron's hands in hers, could not maintain a mask over her emotions. Fear, grief, fear, love, fear—they chased each other around her face. Her grip suggested that if the turning of the Circle intended to take the king from her, it would have to pry him loose one finger at a time.

The king himself was a pleasant surprise. Propped up on a pile of pillows, his face had regained its normal color, and, although he looked very tired, his eyes were clear.

"You're to tell Annice she's to stay right where she is."

Not entirely finished bowing, Liene frowned. "Majesty?"

Theron snorted. "I know my sister, Captain. Her daughter is racing toward an insane bard in the company of an assassin and I've been confined to my bed. One such incident alone would have been enough to bring her here, the two together surely will." Theron sipped at the mug he held and grimaced. "Willow bark tea. Apparently, I've got to drink a cup of this swill every day for the rest of my life."

"It will help you live a good long time, Majesty," Jokubas murmured.

Theron swallowed and his upper lip curled. "I'm so thrilled."

Llyana leaned forward—fear, grief, fear, love, fear making another circuit. "The Bardic Captain will have to leave if you grow excited," she warned.

He pulled his fingers free and patted her hand. "You want to see excited? Dealing with Annice, that would excite me. Captain, see that she stays right where she is. King Rajmund's not quite as ambitious as his mother but I don't trust him not to try and take advantage of the situation when he hears I'm laid up. The last thing we need is a war with Cemandia, so Annice must stay on top of the situation at the pass. Tell her that and make sure she listens."

"Majesty," Liene sighed, thankful she was no longer strong enough to Sing a kigh all the way to the border and that the Song would fall to Kovar, "if you have a way to make Annice listen, I'd love to hear it."

"Nees?" Sitting on a stump at the edge of the creek, Stasya watched Annice pace, more than a little worried by how quiet she'd grown. They'd spent the night Singing for Jazep at the small Center in the village, had shared memories of him with Pjerin and the others who'd been touched by his Song, and had been walking alone together with their grief when the kigh carrying Kovar's message had found them. "Nees, are you all right?"

Annice started, pulled out of her reverie. Her eyes were red and puffy and she moved back and forth along the path as though movement kept dark possibilities at bay. "I will be when we hear that Maggi's safe," she said, although she didn't sound convinced.

"We should tell Pjerin ..."

That stopped the pacing. "We tell Pjerin nothing until we know Maggi's okay. We don't want him charging off after her like a hero out of a bad ballad."

Stasya, who considered Magda to be hers as much as Annice's or Pjerin's, and who'd Sung a kigh in pursuit immediately upon hearing Kovar's message while Annice still stared openmouthed and disbelieving into the air, dropped her gaze to the muddy toes of her boots and forced herself to ask, "And if Maggi isn't okay?"

"She is." Annice lifted her head and a muscle jumped in her jaw. "She has to be. Kovar wouldn't lie to us about something like that." Her tone made the words very nearly a warning.

"And His Majesty?"

"He seems to want me to stay here."

"Are you going to?"

"I don't know." Ignoring the damp, she sank crosslegged to the ground and picked up a double handful of earth. "First Jazep's killed, then Maggi runs off, then Theron's heart tries to quit—I feel as if someone's been smashing at my head with a ... with a ..."

"Nees?"

Eyes locked on the soil dribbling out from between her fingers, Annice murmured, "Stas, something's wrong."

"Center it, Annice! Stop saying that!" Exhausted by a night of grieving and the morning's news, Stasya had reached her limit. She leaped to her feet and, breathing heavily, glared down at Annice. "Either tell me exactly what's wrong, or shut up about it!"

"The dead are walking, Stas. I can feel the earth recoil from their tread. Life flees before them. Sorrow travels by their side."

"Annice, stop it!" Arms wrapped around her body, Stasya shivered as the sun disappeared behind the tattered edges of a gray cloudbank. "You're scaring me!"

Blinking in the dull light, feeling as though she'd just been granted a glimpse of the horror that existed in shadows beyond the safe enclosure of the Circle, Annice wiped her shaking hands against her thighs. "I'm not surprised; I'm scaring me." She drew in a long breath and let it out slowly, searching for strength. "There's more."

"More? More what? More dead?"

"Jazep . . ."

Stasya squatted down and brushed a strand of hair back off Annice's face. "Nees, we know Jazep is dead," she said gently. "Don't you remember? The kigh brought the news last night."

"An air kigh brought the news." Annice caught up the other woman's hand in hers and stared up into the dark eyes. "But Jazep Sang only earth. I have to *do* something, Stas. I can't just sit here and let this go on."

"But His Majesty said . . ."

"His Majesty said what?" Annice snapped sounding more like herself. "That I wasn't to go to Elbasan?" She stood, hauling Stasya up with her. "He doesn't want me by his sickbed, fine." Her tone suggested it wasn't fine at all. Stasya winced. "As it happens, I have no intention of going to *Elbasan*."

Wakened by the clash and clatter of a procession going up Hill Street toward the Citadel, Gerek dragged himself out of bed and stumbled naked to the window, cracking the shutter just enough to peer outside. The flags and pennants flying above the crowd told him everything he needed to know.

Looks like Prince Otavas arrived safely. Realizing that his mouth tasted like the inside of a boot, he turned and tried to remember what he was doing in what was obviously the best room in a less than quality inn.

He'd left Maggi at the Healers' Hall and gone to the service the bards were holding for Jazep at the Center—where it had finally hit him that the man who'd brought him an orphaned fox cub tucked down inside his vest, was dead. He'd gone out and gotten drunk. Very drunk. After that, things became a little less clear.

Crossing over to the washstand, he sniffed the water in the chipped pitcher and drank the lot, ignoring the handleless mug.

"Better," he husked, wincing as the cheering outside momentarily increased in volume. He didn't see why the prince couldn't travel through the city just a little more quietly.

His pants were under the bed and as he dragged them out, a brass button spun across the floor. Teeth gritted, he bent and picked it up. Stamped with the crowned ship of Shkoder, it seemed to have been torn from the uniform of His Majesty's navy.

Gerek sighed as the memories returned. He didn't

feel any better about Jazep being dead but, all things being enclosed, he'd gained new respect for the navy. As the young woman he'd spent the latter part of the night with had long since left—he vaguely remembered her explaining she had to be back on board ship at dawn—he dressed and headed downstairs to pay the reckoning.

Not feeling up to either the crowd on the street or the chaos Prince Otavas would be causing at the Citadel, he spent an hour in the common room remembering Jazep over biscuits and sausage gravy. When he finally stepped outside, a wind blew up in the harbor and nearly knocked him over.

He recognized Annice's touch. For the last seventeen years, ever since Maggi's mother had come to live in Ohrid, breezes that blew where breezes had no business blowing had pushed him around.

Fear quickly took the place of his initial irritation. As far as he knew, Annice was still in Ohrid—as far from Elbasan as possible while remaining in Shkoder. In order for her to be sending the kigh after him instead of just sending a message through one of the bards at the Hall, something had to be wrong. Very wrong. More wrong than Jazep's death alone could account for.

Breathing Magda's name like a prayer, he raced up the hill, wishing he'd picked an inn a little farther from the harbor. When his heels hit the cobblestones, painful reverberations bounced about his skull. Breezes continued to swirl around him, completely oblivious to the direction of the actual wind. He wasn't surprised when the bard on the gate was waiting for him.

"What's she want?" he panted. "What's she trying to tell me?"

Ziven frowned and Sang the notes that made up Annice's name. Half a dozen kigh expanded their circle to include him then, message finally delivered, sped off in different directions—one of them twisting its ethereal body around so that it appeared to blow in one of Gerek's ears and out the other as it left. "She says that you're to go after your sister and then find Jazep."

"You mean, find Jazep's body?"

"That's what I mean, but that's not what Nees said." Ziven blinked back tears and half shrugged. "She probably doesn't believe it's true. She probably doesn't believe he's really dead."

"I find it hard to believe myself," Gerek admitted. "And what does she mean 'go after my sister'?" He wiped the sweat off his brow with the sleeve of his shirt and scowled. "What's she talking about? When I left last night, Maggi was safely tucked in her room. Where's she gone?"

Glancing pointedly at the pair of guards also on duty at the gate, Ziven said, "Princess Onele wants to see you."

No answer could only be a bad answer. Heart pounding, Gerek stepped forward, anxiety and frustration warring against a lifetime of training. He was younger, bigger, stronger—his fingers curled to grab the bard's tunic—he'd find out what happened to Maggi if he had to shake Ziven so hard his teeth shattered.

Ziven made no attempt to move away. "Princess Onele," he repeated calmly, his tone adding a quiet counterpoint of both sympathy and warning, "wants to see you."

"I asked you here to arrange for you to spend some time with His Highness."

Ullious, who'd met the Imperial Ambassador twice in the three years he'd been studying at the Bardic Hall—just after he'd arrived and at a court function he'd been Witnessing under supervision—stared at the man in astonishment. "Me, sir?"

The ambassador bit back a sigh. Having been informed at the last possible moment that the king was under a healer's care, he'd had an exhausting morning tiptoeing around the wide-eyed self-consciousness of the *child* they'd sent to welcome the prince. He'd been as diplomatic as he knew how, but Princess Jelena had not responded well to the formal phrasing. The highlight of his morning had involved Prince Otavas telling him to stop being such a bully and then moving to stand between him and the grateful young princess in a blatant breach of protocol.

"Yes, you," he said shortly. "His Highness likes bards. You're studying to be one. It is the duty of all Imperial citizens in Shkoder to make His Highness welcome. You're an Imperial citizen. I don't see where there's a problem."

Ullious flushed and tried to explain, using the most formal of the ambassador's titles in order to stress the seriousness of his objection. "Imperial Voice, I was only a carter before I began training to be a bard. I'd have no idea of how to behave around an Imperial Prince."

This time, the ambassador allowed the sigh to expand. The people of Shkoder were raised with very clear ideas of the liberties afforded to bards. The citizens of the Empire were not. He'd always believed that this would be the hardest adjustment that the Imperial bards would have to make. "Just behave like a bard. His Highness will accept that."

"I beg your pardon, Imperial Voice . . ." There was no trace of actual apology in Ullious' voice. ". . . but His Imperial Highness accepts such behavior from foreigners. Will he accept that kind of behavior from one of his own?"

"A very good point," the ambassador admitted, studying the ex-carter/almost-bard with increased respect. "I guess we'll have to find that out together."

A cursory knock brought Tysia in from the outer office. "Begging your indulgence, Ambassador," she murmured. "But there's someone here I think you'd better see." Her hand signal indicated that the matter was extremely urgent and, if he hadn't known better, the ambassador would have sworn she was afraid.

He stood and motioned for Ullious to remain where he was. "Wait here," he said. "We still have a schedule to arrange." Sweeping Tysia out of the inner office before him, he closed the door between the crisis and the bard. "What is it?"

Silently, she handed him a square of leather stamped with a black sunburst.

The ambassador's gaze slid off the assassin's calling card, traveled across the room, and locked on the slight young man standing by the window. *How . . . interesting,* he thought. *Two Imperial assassins in Shkoder when assassins have never previously been allowed out of the Empire.* His hand began to rise toward his throat. He forced it back to his side.

*   *   *

Ullious would never have considered eavesdropping had the ambassador's assistant not sounded so frightened. *An Imperial citizen,* he told himself as he made his way to the window, *even one who's spent years in Shkoder, would never think of asking a bard for help.* Whistling softly, he sent one of the multitude of kigh that hung about the Citadel to peer into the next room and asked it to repeat everything it heard.

"Unfortunately, Bannon, your sister is no longer at the Bardic Hall."

Bannon's easy smile disappeared. "Where is she?"

Rubbing his thumb over yet another gold Imperial seal, the ambassador reflected on how this was all becoming absurdly complicated. First one of the assassins that helped to rescue the kidnapped Prince Otavas, then the prince himself, and now, apparently the second of the assassins. *Who's next?* "I have been informed that she disappeared some time last night."

"Informed by who?"

"A reliable and discreet source whose anonymity I would prefer to maintain." *None of your business* didn't seem like the politic thing to say to an assassin looking for his sister. The hem of the ambassador's official court robes whispered against the floor as he walked over to a high-backed chair and lowered himself into it.

"His Imperial Majesty," Bannon reiterated, a minor change of posture making him look imminently dangerous, "wants me to bring my sister back to the Empire."

"And I obey His Imperial Majesty in all things." Steepling his fingers together, the ambassador refused to surrender to the subtle intimidation. "I will offer you every assistance I can, but destroying a contact it has taken me years to establish will not help you and will certainly not advance the Emperor's interests in Shkoder. Your sister has left Elbasan with the king's niece, a young healer of some rare talent. I have no idea where they are heading, but my source seems to think it has something to do with the bard who died."

"What bard?"

"A man named Jazep." Anticipating the next question, he added, "In Bartek Springs, a small town in the principality of Somes. Tysia, if you would be so kind as to find our guest a map?"

Tysia jerked into motion. Her attempt to walk toward a multidrawered cabinet while continuing to stare at the assassin—the attractive, dangerous, deadly assassin—was not notably successful. When, fully aware of her interest, he flashed her a charming smile, she cracked her knee on the cabinet's corner and grunted in pain.

Bannon made a graceful gesture of sympathy that only flustered her further, then turned his attention back to the ambassador. "If this Jazep is dead, what good's a healer going to do?"

"An excellent question. The young woman apparently heals the fifth kigh." To his surprise, the assassin nodded in understanding. "There was something said about the dead walking ..." Under the full force of the young man's stare, his voice trailed off. "What is it?"

"Is this Bartek Springs near the border? Near a pass?"

"It's the principal trading town by the Giant's Cleft, the pass between Somes and the First Province. Why?"

Shaking his head, Bannon propped a thigh on the windowsill and ran a hand through thick curls. The gold rings he wore in both ears gleamed in the sunlight, matching the gleam in gold-flecked eyes. "Do you know about what happened to the prince? To Vree and me?"

"Essentially. Something took over your body, your sister saved you, together the three of you and a bard saved the prince. Although, to be honest, I am unable to understand any motivation but yours and your sister's."

Bannon snorted. "You don't understand hers either. The thing that took over my body didn't die. It's still alive and it's in Vree. That's why the Emperor wants her back, to destroy it."

"In the report, everyone involved swore it was dead." Eyes narrowed, he studied the assassin. "Swore to the Emperor."

"Yeah, well I was *convinced* by the bards. They wanted to study it."

Of course they did. And the ambassador had never yet met a bard—Shkoden or Imperial—who didn't, deep down, believe that he or she knew best.

"From what the Emperor told me ..." Bannon leaned forward as a breeze ruffled the hair on the back of his head. "... those bards, Gabris and Karlene, are going to be in for a nasty surprise when they get back to the Capital."

"I think you'll find that the Empress has Gabris sufficiently under her protection."

"Him maybe, but not Karlene," he said with satisfaction. He'd never liked the possessive way the Shkoden bard had looked at Vree.

The ambassador slowly shook his head. "I'm not sure you should be spreading that around."

"No one ever repeats what they're told by an assassin," Bannon told him with a feral smile.

"A very good point." As Tysia, having gotten a grip on her reactions, presented the deadly young man with the maps, the ambassador silently considered how, once again, everything had come around to the bards. "You realize that the Shkoden authorities are not going to be happy about having you careening about the country after your sister."

"How are they going to stop me?"

Wincing slightly, the ambassador raised a cautioning hand. "Please, allow me to attempt to arrange an approach less likely to pitch us all into an unpleasant situation."

Ullious whistled a quiet gratitude, dismissing the kigh. He'd heard enough.

He was an Imperial citizen and interfering with the Emperor's justice would be treason. Nervously, he ran his thumb over the narrow edge of his mustache and desperately searched for a solution that would keep not only Karlene and Gabris but himself alive.

"Her Royal Highness considers Kars to be a bardic problem, and we're to deal with it." Ignoring Kovar, who'd moved out from behind the desk, Liene lowered herself onto the pile of faded tapestry cushions heaped in her favorite chair. "I am far too old to deal with a third Sovereign Head of Shkoder. Far too old. You were right. I should have retired at Second Quarter Festival. If I had, I'd be sitting in my garden right now with nothing more to worry about than worms in the apples. Bardic problem. Hmmph."

"It is essentially what Karlene concluded in her recall. She did point out that we'd have to deal with him eventually."

Liene glared up at her second. "I know that." She pounded the tip of her cane against the floor. "But I should have been the one to tell Her Highness, not the other way around. *It's a bardic problem, Captain,* she said. *When you've worked out a plan for dealing with it, come back and see me.* Of course, it's a bardic problem. It's destroyed one of our own."

"So, what shall we do?" Kovar asked calmly, resting one leg over the corner of the desk and using as much Voice as he thought he could get away with.

"Stop trying to calm me," Liene snarled. "I'm not angry at Her Highness. I'm angry because Jazep was thirty-three years younger than I am, and he's dead and I'm not. And stop looking at me like that! I don't want to be dead, I want *him* to be alive. Her Highness would also like us to send a message to Marija at Bartek Springs and arrange to have Magda and Vree stopped."

"Stopped?"

"Apparently the how and why is a Bartek Springs problem. I suppose she'd best stay and not go on to the Duc of Somes. Once Jeremias is there, and the recall's there, they'll have to Sing each other the particulars." A tentative knock on the door jerked her head around. "What!"

A little startled by his reception, Ullious stepped into the office. "Captain, Kovar, I believe I have at least a partial solution to the problem in Somes."

"You mean a solution to Kars?" Kovar asked.

"Yes, sir."

Kovar shook his head. "I doubt you have all the information necessary to ..."

"Oh, let him talk," Liene interrupted, leaning forward, gnarled hands clasped over the head of her cane. "It's not like the Circle's been spitting out great ideas at us. Besides, anyone who can run a successful business under the weight of the Emperor's taxes deserves to be listened to."

Ullious bowed in the Imperial fashion at the Bardic Captain—and then, to be politic, at Kovar. "Recently," he began, falling into a storytelling cadence, "in order to test my range, Tadeus had me Sing to Karlene in the Empire. Both she and Gabris were out Walking with the first group of Imperial fledglings to return home and were, at the time, quite close to the border. If they remained on their intended route, they're closer to the border now. Very near, in fact, to the pass into Somes." He paused. Singing Karlene into Shkoder would betray the Emperor's plans. As an Imperial citizen, suggesting it would be treason. However as a bard, if he were told to send a message across the border, he'd only be following orders.

"If she's that close to the border, she's the closest bard we've got," Kovar mused. "And having recently dealt with Kars, she's already familiar with at least part of the situation."

"Doesn't Sing earth though," Liene put in thoughtfully.

"Granted. But she Sings a strong three quarters and has proven ability in Singing the fifth kigh. She's also proved she can track this enclosed abomination." Kovar turned to face the Imperial fledgling, even the waxed curls of his mustache looking more hopeful than they had a moment before. "Can you find her again?"

"Yes, sir."

"Good. We'll work out a message to send her that can't be misinterpreted. Gabris can explain things to the Emperor."

Ullious prayed to Kattinni, god of cartage and the personal deity he'd brought with him into Shkoder, that Gabris was as protected as the ambassador believed. "There is one other thing. You are aware that Vireyda Magaly's brother Bannon is Prince Otavas' bodyguard?"

"Of course we're aware of it," Liene snapped, then her head jerked back and she stared, wide-eyed, up at Kovar. "Center it! Jazep's death pushed Bannon completely out of my head. All things being enclosed, I imagine *he'll* have an opinion to express about this as well."

"Your Grace, with the lead your sister and the ..." Onele paused and frowned. "... and the other young woman have, you won't catch up to them before they reach Bartek Springs where they'll be stopped and then returned here. I neither want my cousin with her unique and irreplaceable talents endangering herself by confronting this bardic abomination, nor do I want an assassin with two not entirely stable kigh wandering around Shkoder."

"Then allow me to go to Bartek Springs," Gerek pleaded. "I can escort them back to Elbasan."

The Heir leaned forward and rested her chin on her fist, her father's signet on her index finger. There were shadows under her eyes that had not been there earlier. "Tell me why," she instructed. "Do you believe she's in danger from her companion?"

"No, Highness! Vree would never hurt her."

"What about Gyhard? He may not be able to jump to another body without Vree's help, but suppose he pushes her out and takes over the body he already has?"

Gerek shook his head. "It wouldn't happen, Highness."

"Why not? Because he allegedly loves her?"

"Your Highness is very well informed . . ."

Onele straightened. "There's an unstable Imperial assassin staying at the Bardic Hall. You're unenclosed right I'm very well informed and I haven't got time for your vague petitions. Why is it so important that you go after your sister?"

Gerek felt his cheeks grow hot. He glanced down at the carpet, noticed the toes of his boots were filthy with street grime and wished he'd taken the opportunity to clean up while he was waiting for Her Royal Highness to have time to see him. Finally, he murmured, "It isn't entirely my idea, Highness."

"Annice sent the kigh after you?" Onele smiled for the first time since she'd been summoned to the king's side. "I thought she took an oath not to use the kigh as weapons?"

"She doesn't exactly use them as weapons, Highness. If she feel the situation merits it, she sends messages it's difficult . . . no . . ." He reconsidered, scratching at his beard. ". . . impossible, to ignore."

"While I'm inclined to say that this is your problem, not mine, I'll speak with the Bardic Captain. You're twenty-two years old, it's time Annice stopped trying to run your life. The Circle knows your father and Stasya should be enough for anyone."

Under normal circumstances, Gerek would have jumped at the chance to have Annice's interference pared back. Under these specific circumstances, however, he'd just realized she was his strongest argument for going after Maggi. "Highness, please, for a moment, put yourself in her position. Your only child is galloping toward the insane thing that just killed one of your oldest friends. Duty prevents you from intervening personally. Wouldn't you do everything you could?" He spread his hands. "And I assure you it isn't just for Annice's sake that I want to go. Maggi is entirely too trusting. Vree is in a foreign land and I'm one of her only friends. And, if you think that once Maggi's set her mind on facing this thing you can get her back to Elbasan in anything short of chains, think again. I'm one of four people she actually listens to and the only one close enough to get to her in time."

Leaning back in her chair, Onele exhaled noisily. "I can't decide, Your Grace, whether you've become an excellent politician or you've just spent too many of your formative years among bards."

Gerek bowed, recognizing capitulation. "You won't regret it, Highness."

"At the risk of sounding clichéd, I already regret it." She rolled her eyes at yet another knock on the door; there hadn't been less than three things at a time claiming her attention all day. "Come."

"We have a solution, Highness," Liene declared as she came into the office. "Oh. Hello, Your Grace. I heard about your message from Ziven. Hiding inside?"

"Actually, Captain, I'm just about to leave. I'll be catching up to my sister and her companion in Bartek Springs and escorting them back to Elbasan."

"Will you? Well, I wish you luck, but I don't think you've thought the thing through."

"What do you mean?"

"Your sister's companion is an Imperial assassin. If she decides not to return to Elbasan with you, there's no way you can make her."

"Captain," Onele interrupted, "if I give orders that this person is returning to Elbasan, she *will* return."

"I don't doubt it, Highness, but before you go making an enemy of someone whose business it is to sneak past armed guards and slit throats, I have a suggestion. Perhaps Gerek could take his own companion along. Vireyda Magaly is not the only assassin in Elbasan."

Onele and Gerek both stared at the Bardic Captain.

"And that's supposed to be good news?" the Heir demanded.

Liene shrugged. "From what I hear, he's likely to go off on his own. I merely thought that it might be a good idea for us to maintain some control over his actions."

"Why would he want to travel with me?" Gerek wondered.

"Charm and good looks aside, Bannon's in a strange country where he speaks almost none of the language. Even an Imperial assassin will need a translator."

Both Onele's brows rose, her expression suddenly making her look very much like the king. "I wasn't aware you spoke Imperial, Your Grace," she said dryly.

"Tadeus had him learning under deep trance," Liene explained before Gerek decided on his best response. "The two of them had some stupid romantic notion it would make him more attractive to Vree. Normally, I'd suggest we send young Bannon off with a bard, but I doubt he'd go for that. I understand he doesn't care much for bards."

"Why not?"

The Bardic Captain glanced pointedly at Gerek. "One of them cared a bit too much for his sister."

Chapter Eight

"I'm not so sure you should go back to the Capital," Karlene muttered as she fastened the straps of her instrument case to her pack. "Ullious' message had undertones I didn't much like."

"I can't say as I cared much for the message itself," Gabris told her, morosely scraping his thumbnail along his jaw. "Jazep Sang the strongest earth I'd ever heard."

"A grave loss to Shkoder."

Gabris sighed. "I wasn't actually thinking of Shkoder. You probably didn't know him very well, but he was only six years younger than me. We were good friends."

Karlene straightened. "I'm sorry, I didn't know."

"We used to Sing the Fire and Earth duets together whenever we managed to be at the same Center at Festival. After I came south with the Princess, he'd send long letters with diplomatic couriers, traders, the new bards ..." He raised an eyebrow at the younger bard. "You brought one with you. I came because Her Highness—Her Imperial Majesty—asked me to, but I think I was only able to stay because of Jazep's letters."

"There were always the kigh ..."

"The kigh are not usually interested in carrying a wealth of personal detail. Nor," he added, scowling at the sky, "are they infallible. They should have told us when Jazep died. A bard does not die unremarked even if he only Sings earth."

"He does if Kars killed him. The kigh couldn't bring the news because there were no kigh around; they'd all fled." She tucked a strand of pale hair back into her braid and whistled a terse **Stop that!** as long, ethereal fingers tugged it forward again. "Frankly," she admitted, acknowledging the sick feeling in the pit of her stomach, "I'm more worried about what happened after he died."

"You think that Kars could have . . ." Gabris let his voice trail off, as if putting the fear into words made it more possible.

"I don't know." Shoving her arms through the straps, Karlene heaved her pack up onto her shoulders. "There's only one way to find out."

Gabris pulled her into a quick and awkward embrace—awkward both because of the pack and because neither was, by nature, overtly demonstrative. "Be careful."

"You, too." At his protest she added, "At least I know what I'm facing. You don't. I found what Ullious didn't say in that message to be very disconcerting."

"Her Imperial Majesty's protection will, I'm certain be sufficient."

Karlene studied him for a moment, brows drawn in, then she shrugged, allowing him his belief that in any contest between Their Imperial Majesties involving him, the Emperor would lose. She'd asked him once, just after she'd first arrived from Shkoder, what exactly his relationship with the Empress was.

"I'm Her Majesty's lifeline to home," he'd told her.

"That's all?"

"Anything else is not your song to sing."

And that had been that.

"Do you think you can get this lot back to the Capital on your own?" she asked, turning enough to gesture at the four Imperial fledglings sprawled out in the shade of a giant cottonwood tree.

Gabris snorted. "I think I'm up to it."

As though she'd been waiting for Karlene's signal, Virine rose gracefully to her feet and stepped forward. In her late twenties, barely a full Quarter younger than Karlene, she'd been an acolyte in the temple of Eddam, the three-headed, androgynous god of music. When Gabris and Aurel had reminded the priests of her temples that technically speaking she would still be an acolyte—the sphere of her devotion having merely grown larger—they'd voted four to three in favor of allowing her to become a bard. Of the ten Imperial fledglings, she was the only one to Sing all four quarters.

"I think I should go with you," she said.

"Why?"

"Two reasons. The first, you don't Sing earth. I do. And the second, Jazep taught me recall. He was ..." Virine frowned as she searched for the exact word then spread her hands expressively. "He was kind. I want to help."

Karlene shook her head. "First, Singing earth didn't help Jazep and he had a lot more years' experience than you do. Second ..." Her second objection got lost in memories of Jazep teaching *her* recall. As his

single quarter had kept him at the Bardic Hall in Elbasan almost every Fourth Quarter since he'd been
fledged, there couldn't be a bard under thirty he
hadn't taught. She remembered his gentle smile, his
joy in life, his kindness. "Third," she went on, her
voice rough-edged, "this is going to be dangerous and
frankly, Virine, you are just too precious a resource
to risk."

"But . . ."

"No buts. You're the only Imperial bard who Sings
all four quarters and you may remain alone in this
ability for some time."

"Gabris?" Virine's face fell as the older bard shook
his head. Her sigh brought a kigh in to lightly brush
her cheek. Although the gaze that met Karlene's was
steady, her eyes were bright. "Then, when you find
his body, will you Sing my good-byes?"

"And mine," said one of the three fledglings behind
her. The other two murmured a quiet agreement.

Not trusting her voice, Karlene nodded. She
scrubbed the back of her hand across her cheeks and
started along the road toward the border.

"Karlene!"

When she turned, she saw that the four fledglings
had moved up to stand by Gabris' side.

"You were right," he called, tears glistening silver
in the gray of his beard. "Jazep's death *is* a grave loss
to Shkoder."

"You will be traveling with His Grace, the Heir
of Ohrid." The Imperial Ambassador's voice held a
warning that narrowed Bannon's eyes to speculative
slits. "His Grace's sister is traveling with your sister,
and he is as anxious as you are to return them to

Elbasan." As Gerek stepped forward, he added, "His Grace speaks some Imperial."

Bannon touched his heels together and nodded. His gaze flickered down the length of Gerek's body, noting and dismissing both sword and dagger. *Too big and too slow,* said the lift in his lip. *I don't need you.*

Gerek smiled and made an obvious point of looking down at the much shorter man. "Your sister told me so *little* about you," he said.

Layers upon layers and practically a bardic emphasis. Liene made a silent note to have a word with Tadeus about the tenor of his linguistic lessons when grief allowed.

"My sister is not for you to discuss."

"Your sister makes her own choices."

"My sister . . ."

"Is probably halfway to Bartek Springs by now," the ambassador broke in, stepping forward—although not quite *between* the two. "I think it would be best if you wasted very little time in beginning your pursuit."

A few moments later he dropped onto a bench and sighed deeply. "Frankly, Captain, you weren't much help."

Liene grinned. "You seemed to be doing fine on your own. I suspect they're going to have an interesting trip."

"Interesting?" The ambassador rolled his eyes. "You bards have such a way with words." He supposed he should be thankful that it would be interesting some distance away from him.

"Of course you have my permission to go after your sister." Prince Otavas clasped his hands together behind his back, hiding the way his fingers had begun to

tremble. "She's in danger the closer she gets to that
. . . that . . . to Kars. Stop her. Bring her and my cousin
back to safety. And if this Gyhard has other ideas,
well, do what you have to."

"Thank you, Highness." Bannon frowned slightly as
he studied the prince. It was evident to the trained eye
that the younger man was very afraid. "Highness, you'll
be perfectly safe. There's no one here who wishes to
harm you, and Kars is not only far away but they say the
bards . . ." With an effort, he kept the distaste from his
voice. ". . . are preparing to deal with him."

Otavas tossed his head. "Of course I'll be safe," he
snapped, irritated that Bannon had recognized his
fear. "Why wouldn't I be?"

"No reason, Highness." The Emperor had ordered
him to return Vree and Gyhard and the Capital. Gyhard
had to pay for what he'd done; for his treason, for
Vree's betrayal. But the prince . . . Bannon shook his
head, confused. He had a target and the target should
be everything. But the prince's safety was his responsibility. If the prince was afraid, then he'd failed. *And
who will guard his dreams while I'm gone?*

"Is there something else?"

"No, Highness." Bannon bowed. "I'll return as
quickly as I can."

"Take the time you need," Otavas told him. He
managed a shaky smile. "I'll try to stay out of trouble
while you're gone."

"Thank you, Highness." If Bannon's answering
smile was steadier, it was only because he was a much
better liar.

"Don't trust him."

"Why not?" Gerek jerked the strap tight on the

bulging saddlebag. "Because he's an arrogant, amoral, little shit?"

Kovar snorted. "Because he's an Imperial assassin."

"So's Vree."

"Exactly. And as Vree has proven herself capable of killing without orders, it's very likely that Bannon can, too. Vree, however, needs our good will; her brother does not and therefore has no external controls on his actions."

"So you want me to control him?"

"Don't be ridiculous." Kovar paced across the bedchamber and back, his agitation sounding through the slap of his soles against the polished wooden floor. Only the Duc of Ohrid had refused carpet in his palace suite. "You couldn't control him if you wanted to. If it comes to a fight, you'll lose—don't ever forget that."

Gerek's lip curled, the expression making him look remarkably like his father. "Anything else?" he snarled.

"Yes. Don't trust Gyhard either. And don't forget that according to Karlene, Bannon hates him."

"Vree seems to be the only one who doesn't." Throwing open the trunk at the foot of his bed, Gerek waved away the smell of cedar and began to rummage through his clothing. "Oh, and Maggi," he added, without looking up. She feels sorry for him."

Kovar snorted again, the waxed curls of his mustache trembling. "Your sister is very young and I believe that Vree is afraid."

"Afraid?" Gerek straightened to stare indignantly across his bedchamber at the bard. "Vree isn't afraid of anything."

"I think I have been a slightly more impartial observer than you, Your Grace, and I have seen this fear."

"I didn't think anyone's impartial observing Vree, she's carrying too much history. However," Gerek held up a surrendering hand as Kovar opened his mouth to protest, "I suppose I may be more partial than most. So, what's she afraid of?"

Kovar drew in a deep breath and let it out slowly, wondering if the younger man was being deliberately obtuse. "Gyhard. She's afraid of Gyhard."

"I don't think so." He threw a sweater up onto the bed with unnecessary force. "As much as I wish she weren't, she's in love with Gyhard."

"Is she? Is it logical that she would be? This man, this abomination, destroyed her life, drove a wedge between herself and her brother, and now sits like a parasite in her mind. Why would she love him? Isn't it more logical to believe that she does what he wants because she is afraid of him but, unable because of her training to admit fear, she calls it love instead?"

Both Gerek's brows went up. "I think you've been listening to too many fledgling ballads, Kovar. Even by bardic standards that doesn't make any sense."

"Doesn't it?"

Unfortunately, it did. "Maggi says . . ."

"Magda is little more than a child." It was Kovar's turn to raise a cautioning hand. "This whole situation is much more complex than a simple love story. I'm not asking that you believe me, Gerek, just keep it in mind. Please."

"Yeah. Sure." He shook his head as if trying to settle unsettling information. "Anything else?"

"Yes. Be careful." Kovar used enough Voice to make his concern plain. Due to the circumstances of

Gerek's upbringing, the bards considered the Heir of Ohrid to be one of theirs. "I'd hate to have to tell your father that he'd lost you."

"You're the entire country away from my father," Gerek reminded him with a not entirely successful laugh. "If I were you, I'd worry more about telling Annice."

"My mother's death was what made me an assassin." So strange to say *my mother* and *made me* when it had been *our mother* and *made us* for so long.

Magda paled under the color the sun had laid across her cheeks. "You didn't ... I mean, you were only seven, you couldn't have ..."

"No. I didn't." Unable to decide if she were amused or hurt by the assumption, Vree's voice held no expression at all.

"I'm sorry, Vree." The younger woman reached between the horses and laid her hand lightly on Vree's arm. "That was a stupid thing to say. I forgot the most important lesson the Healers' Hall tried to bang into my head." When Vree lifted a questioning brow, she lifted her hand and explained. "Brain first. Mouth second."

She was so contrite, it was impossible not to smile. "I always thought I hid my reactions better than that."

"Not from me. I've been learning your kigh, remember "

"And when you've learned it, you'll know me better than anyone?"

Magda grinned and tucked a curl of hair into the corner of her mouth. "Not quite anyone."

About to say, *Bannon,* Vree felt Gyhard's kigh stir and realized that her brother hadn't really known her at all. "And will I know you better than anyone," she asked.

"That depends on you."

If they hadn't been riding down a public road, she might have surrendered to the unexpected lack of barriers between them. Might have. As it was, she had no real desire to fall off the horse.

She felt Gyhard withdraw enough to keep them separate. *There'll be other times,* he promised.

The reins gripped between damp fingers, Vree suddenly needed to fill the silence. "*My* teachers always said, throat first, eye second."

"Eye?" Magda asked uncertainly.

"Through the socket and into the brain. Takes a more specialized dagger, though. Longer, narrower blade. You can slit someone's throat with your teeth if you have to."

"Vree, that's really gross."

"Only if you forget and swallow."

Magda swiveled in the saddle and stared at her, aghast.

As far as Vree could remember, she'd never seen anyone look so disgusted. Although she tried to keep a straight face, she couldn't stop herself from laughing. "It's a joke, Maggi, a joke."

Is it? Gyhard wondered, and then wished he hadn't because it stopped the laughter.

Mostly.

Two days' travel into the mountains, a pair of ravens led Karlene to the scattered remains of a body by the side of the road. A shallow indentation scratched into the dry soil and an oblong pile of fist-sized rocks indicated an attempt at burial, but such pitiful protection had been no protection at all against the local scavengers.

Wrinkling her nose, Karlene squatted by a piece of bone and was astonished to see that desiccated tissue still clung to it. Although the body had been torn apart, none of the flesh appeared to have been eaten.

"That's very odd," she muttered as she stood.

Cocking an ebony head, one of the ravens fixed her with an amber eye, its cry sounding very much like loud and raucous laughter.

"Easy for you to say," Karlene told it derisively, then she stopped and took a closer look at its perch. Cracked and faded, the leather collar that had held Kait's head erect on her broken neck was unmistakable. Needing no further confirmation, she turned away before she chanced to spot Kait's head.

While her right hand sketched the sign of the Circle over her breast, Karlene Sang the kigh a question. Considering what had happened when Kars' other companions had fallen, the answer surprised her.

Kait's kigh was nowhere around.

It was very strange.

The timber-holding stood at one end of a narrow valley close by where the river broadened into a natural basin to hold the logs sent down from the cutting crew upstream. Although a high wooden stockade surrounded the buildings, the gate was open and a small herd of shaggy cattle were grazing around the stumps in a cleared pasture.

Had he come out onto the lip of the valley anywhere else, the trees would have blocked his view and he very likely would have missed the holding entirely. Sinking down onto his haunches so that the necklace of bone he wore tucked under his robe clattered against the ground, Kars stared at the cattle, at the buildings, at the stockade, and wondered where he'd seen them all before.

"In a dream," he murmured. "Or in the memory of a dream?"

Perhaps the shadow of familiarity that lay over the valley was an omen. He didn't think he believed in omens, but as he couldn't remember exactly what he believed in, he supposed it didn't matter.

"There are people there, Kait." She brushed the back of her hand against his cheek and he smiled, teeth still surprisingly whole and white between cracked and bleeding lips. "Our family. Yours and mine." There had been a family before the Song ... before the Song ... the Song ...

NO! NO! NO! NO! NO!

Trembling, tears spilling over into wrinkles so deep the moisture disappeared within the crease, Kars held up a placating hand.

"I won't leave you," he said softly. "I promise." How could he leave her? She'd given him reason to live when he'd lost his heart for the second time. She'd stayed with him even after her own Song had ended. She was all he had. "We'll be a family again. Like we were." When she nodded, he smiled again. "Your legs are younger than mine, child. Go down there and look around. See if they'll welcome us."

He watched her move down into the valley, skimming the ground, swirling around rocks and trees like pale smoke. She looked so much better without the brace. He remembered how pleased he'd been when she'd put it aside.

As she passed, the cattle rushed to the far side of

their pasture and stood, shaggy orange rumps against the fence, heads turned toward the open gate of the stockade.

Trouble coming.

How can you tell?

Shoulders hunched against the driving rain, Vree tossed her head to clear the water from her eyes and said, *There's a horse galloping hard toward us. In this weather, you don't ride like that unless there's trouble.*

I can't see anything. He could see the rump end of Magda's horse and Magda slumped forward in the saddle. Past her, he could see another horse-length, maybe two, of the ribbon of mud that Shkodens referred to as a road—the Empire spent considerably more tax dollars on road building than on music and, at the moment, Gyhard wholeheartedly approved—but then the translucent curtain of rain became opaque.

Listen.

Rain. Creak of wet leather. Hooves lifting out of and falling back into wet earth. *I don't hear anything.*

Listen for what doesn't belong.

He heard it then, the low pounding like an angry drum roll, held against the ground by the weather. From the way Magda straightened, he suspected it had now come too close to ignore.

Head cocked, wet hair plastered tight to her skull, Magda tried to figure out not only what the sound was, but where it was coming from. The rhythmic pounding seemed to bounce off the individual drops of rain and surround her. "Which is ridiculous," she told herself, pulling her mount's reluctant head around.

Diagonal across the road and turned toward Vree, she didn't see the rider burst suddenly into view. Her horse slammed back onto its haunches, Magda fought to keep her seat. And lost.

A moment later, Vree knelt on the shoulders of a very wet young man. Gasping for breath, he stared up at her, unable to understand how he'd been on the back of a galloping horse one instant and on his back in the mud the next.

"You should watch where you're going," she said, her voice devoid of inflection.

Gyhard had a sudden memory—it had to be one of Vree's—of Avor lying in the same position. The only difference had been, the Sixth Army Messenger knew how he'd ended up flat out on the road and how long he had left to live.

"Vree?"

Rising lithely, Vree moved to where Magda sat pulling mud out of her hair. "Are you hurt?"

"I don't think so." Her confused expression was, in most ways, identical to that of the young man.

"Can you stand?"

"I don't know."

Grasping Magda's left wrist, Vree slowly pulled her up onto her feet, ready to stop if she gave any indication of pain. "Does anything hurt?"

"No. No," she repeated, her voice growing stronger as she looked down at the imprint of her body in the mud. 'I guess I was lucky I didn't land on a rock." She spotted her horse and Vree's, bulky shadows cropping grass by the side of the road, noticed a third horse a little way off, then noticed the rider carefully getting to his feet. "Who's he?"

"The idiot who ran into you."

"What happened to him?"

The corners of Vree's mouth curled up into what was only peripherally a smile. "He stopped to make sure you weren't hurt."

Magda glanced from Vree to the filthy young man and came to the correct conclusion. Rolling her eyes, she stepped toward him. "Are you all . . ."

He charged past her, fists raised.

". . . right?" she finished as he hit the ground again.

When he grabbed for his dagger, Vree stepped on his wrist. "I wouldn't," she said quietly.

He stiffened, then saw his own mortality in the dark eyes looking down into his. The fight went out of him so completely, its absence left him trembling.

Gyhard was pleased to see that the boy wasn't a total fool.

"Dusty?"

"Your horse?" Magda asked as she squatted beside him. "It's right over there. It didn't go far after you . . ." She paused.

"Fell off?" Vree offered.

". . . parted company. *Are* you all right?" Licking rain off her lips, she rested her palm lightly on his chest. "It's just that I'm a healer and . . ."

"A healer!" He jerked up out of the mud and clutched at her hand. "I was riding for a healer!"

The village had been built just above the high tide mark down on the flats where a broad creek spilled fresh water into the sea. Small boats were pulled up on the gravel beach and empty drying racks made skeletal outlines against the gray on gray of sea and sky.

"Why is it all fishing villages look the same?" Vree wondered. "Put this on the coast anywhere in the Sixth Province and it wouldn't look out of place."

Maybe it's because all fish look the same.

They didn't stop at the village but pounded right up to the crowd of people standing on the clifftop overlooking the bay. The young man was off his horse before it had actually stopped moving.

"I didn't have to bring Raulas, Mother! I found a younger healer just up coast!"

Magda dismounted almost as quickly.

Younger healer? Gyhard wondered as a thin woman with pale hair hurried toward them.

"Thank all the gods in the Circle and then some!" She grabbed Magda's hand and pulled her toward an oiled canvas tarp propped tentlike over two still forms and the bent figure of her son. "We've kept them as dry as we can, but we didn't want to move them any farther!"

"What happened?"

"Didn't Dumi tell you?" She broke off as Dumi moaned and ran out from under the tarp toward the edge of the cliff. "Dumi! Stop! It's gotten worse! Don't go past the ropes!"

Dumi ignored her. A few of the villagers began moving to intercept him, but they seemed to be carrying the weight of the world on their shoulders and were obviously not going to get to him in time.

Vree slammed her heels into her horse's ribs and when the astonished animal leaped forward, she slipped free of the stirrups and drew her feet up under her on the saddle. As they drew level with her quarry, she yanked back hard on the reins. The sudden stop catapulted her forward. She flipped in the air and landed with knees bent, palms against the ground, facing a still running Dumi. Straightening her legs, she drove her shoulder into his stomach and, a heartbeat later, knelt on his shoulders for the second time that afternoon.

The only sound on the clifftop was the angry pounding of waves against rock.

Impressive, Gyhard murmured, feeling as though he hadn't quite caught up.

Thank you.

You know, people would pay good coin to see something like that.

Yeah? Well, maybe we'll let them; the bards aren't going to feed us forever.

"You don't understand!" Dumi wailed, tears running back into his hair. "Celja's still down there."

Vree twisted as she stood. The edge of the cliff had the raw look of a fresh wound. "Down there?"

"Stupid, stupid place to build a house. Stupid."

Nice view, though.

Maybe yesterday. Grabbing onto Dumi's wrist, Vree hauled him to his feet. "Celja's house fell off the cliff?"

"Her father's house." He rubbed the back of his hand under his nose, but before he could continue, another voice cut in.

"It'd be more accurate to say the cliff fell out from under the house." A heavyset woman, wet gray hair plastered against a round head, exhaustion turning her face a slightly paler shade of gray, closed her fingers around Dumi's arm and stared tiredly at Vree. "It's all sandstone around here. Stuff gets wet enough, it starts to slide. The boy's right though, it's a stupid place to build. You're with the healer, Southerner?"

"I am."

"When we sent him . . ." *To get him out of the way,* her tone added. ". . . we thought he'd have to go up coast to old Raulus i'Ilka at Eel Cove. He's been retired for years and he's older than spit, but he's the closest healer around."

Dumi twisted in her grip. "Gran, I have to get to Celja!"

"You can't get to her, boy. Things are worse than when you left. The rest of it's going to go any minute."

"NO!" Dumi jerked free, but before Vree could knock him down for the third time, one of the village men got him in a secure hold and dragged him back from the sagging rope barrier.

His grandmother sighed. "She passed up her little brother and got the ropes around her father before the house slipped right off. We dragged him out through a wall. Didn't mean to, but the wall ended up where he was. Now Celja's tangled in the wreckage, can't climb out and we can't get a rope to her, because every time someone steps over that line, the whole enclosed mess starts to slip."

Vree studied the area, well aware that the villagers were studying her. "Are you sure she's still alive?"

"She was a few minutes ago."

"If someone goes over to get her, the house will fall and both girl and rescuer will die?"

The heavyset woman shrugged. "That's about it."

"If no one goes over to get her, the house will fall and the girl will die?"

The silence was answer enough.

"There's no chance she'd survive the fall?"

Vree.

Calm down. I'm just asking.

"You don't know what's down there, Southerner." Vree allowed herself to be led about thirty feet along the cliff. "If you're careful, you can crawl out there and look over." The old woman pointed at a rain-slick patch of grass that extended out to where land met sky.

Taking the reference to crawling literally, Vree dropped to her belly and crept forward. When she got her first view of the wreckage, she sucked air through her teeth. The upper third of the cliff had collapsed. The house—the remains of the house—balanced between a steep slope of loose rock and a nearly perpendicular drop fifty feet into a churning sea. While she watched, a wave lifted a tabletop and smashed it into kindling against the cliff.

She crept a little farther forward and allowed the upper half of her body to drop over the rim. "Someone could climb down here and work their way over level with the house."

Someone?

Behind her, Dumi's grandmother snorted. "Don't be ridiculous. There's no holds on that face big enough to support an adult, and I'll not send a child down."

"There's holds," Vree said, still scanning the rock.

"We haven't time to anchor a safety line way over here." But the protest held less force than it had.

"Don't need one. Just drop two lines down by the house."

"It can't be done." Colored by hope, it was almost a question.

Vree rolled over and looked up at her. The rain

had stopped, but the sky was still a sullen gray. "Yes, it can."

Why, Vree? Gyhard's thoughts paced the confines of Vree's mind as though looking for a way to escape. *Why risk both our lives for a girl you don't know? Her own people have given up!*

I don't leave people to die.

He bit back a protest as he realized that emotionless statement made a warped sort of sense. Death and Imperial Assassins were active partners. Besides, from his position inside her head, he could see that it would be no use trying to talk her out of it. *Are you *sure* you can do this?*

I could do this in the dark under the noses of guards who would desperately like to kill me. As Dumi's grandmother shouted orders, Vree began stripping off her sodden clothes.

Yeah, but can you do it in daylight under the noses of people who desperately want you to succeed?

First time for everything. Naked, she began to limber up.

Uh, Vree . . .

What? Gyhard's unease drew her attention to the various reactions of the watching villagers. *They look like they've never seen skin before.*

Well aware that Vree had no nudity taboos—they were impossible to maintain in the army and, as most Imperial citizens spent at least two years in uniform, they'd disappeared almost entirely throughout the Empire—Gyhard could only assume the embarrassment he felt was his own. The problem was, they weren't in the Empire. *Is this really necessary?*

Before she could answer, Dumi's grandmother asked much the same thing.

Vree flexed the muscles across her shoulders. "Wet clothes are heavy. They also get in the way."

"But protection . . ."

"From what?"

"Scrapes. The rock."

Is she kidding?

You're a new experience for them, Vree.

Spitting on her palms for luck, she dropped over the edge of the cliff. She could hear Dumi calling and a faint answer rising up from the ruin of the house. *The tricky part's going to be remembering not to kill her when I get there.*

Another joke?

Mostly. Now shut up, I need to concentrate.

Drawn back into himself as much as possible, Gyhard felt her attention shift to the cliff face. Her thoughts cleared until they focused on nothing but moving down and across, fingers and toes. The world became rock.

The rock under her right foot crumbled. Her left foot, already in the air, could find no purchase.

She dangled, her entire weight on fingertips alone.

Then the toes of her left foot found a crack; the side of her right foot, a crevasse.

Breathing heavily, she rested her forehead against the wet stone, unable to tell if the roaring she heard was her blood in her ears or the sea, waiting hungrily below.

A few moments later, still some distance from the slide, she felt a shiver deep in the rock. *If it goes now, we'll go with it.* Her thought. Gyhard's. It wasn't important.

Knees and elbows were bleeding when she finally reached the house. The area was remarkably con-

tained, loose debris having already fallen into the
water. She was reaching for one of the two waiting
ropes when the world shifted.

One chance. Everything risked on it. Lips pulled
back in a vicious parody of a grin, Vree launched herself off crumbling holds at the wildly swaying rope.
Rock careened off the cliff around her. Wood shrieked
as timber framing twisted like taffy. She closed her
fingers. The rough hemp cut into her palm. Something
slammed into her shoulder. She snarled and hung on.
The noise pounded at her.

Flung back and forth on the end of the rope like a
rag doll, she fought to get her other arm up. To double
her chance of survival.

Then it was over.

Her first thought was for Bannon. The sight of the
second rope, hanging empty, nearly accomplished
what the rock fall had been unable to do. Then she
remembered and her heart started beating again.

Miraculously, the house had not yet gone all the
way over.

Climbing back up to the lower edge of the slide as
quickly as she could, Vree tied the ends of both ropes
around her waist and then dropped back down even
with the canted wall now the bottom of the building.

"I need more line," she yelled. "Play it out slowly.
Keep the .."

Tension, Gyhard offered.

". . . tension the same!"

Cries from the clifftop seemed to indicate they'd
thought she'd fallen.

"Talk it over later!" she screamed. "Just give me
some slaughtering rope!"

She'd yelled in Imperial, Gyhard noted. It didn't

seem to matter. Her tone appeared to be enough for results.

Muttering under her breath, she moved sideways toward the smashed remains of a window that appeared to open out of a floor. When she reached it, she was astounded to see a young woman her own age peering out. "Celja?"

Celja smiled and brushed at the line of blood dribbling into her eyes. "Hello. Do I know you?"

Shock?

Good guess. "Celja, can you move toward me?"

"Sure. My legs are free now. They weren't before, you know." She crept forward on her elbows, looked down, and added. "I don't think I could swim right now. Maybe I'd better stay here."

"Come a little farther," Vree told her, ducking as a splintered chunk of wood dropped past her ear. "Just a little."

"I don't think so."

"Dumi's waiting for you up top," she said, untying the second rope.

Her face brightening, Celja pulled herself another few feet closer to rescue. "Do you know Dumi?"

"Not very well." Her toes gripping the rock, Vree leaned out, slid the free end of the rope under the young woman's arms and tied it off.

"You're not from around here, are you?"

"No." Easing back, she began to slide Celja out of the window.

The world shifted again.

One hand gripping the front of Celja's tunic, Vree flung them both away from the slide, hoping the arc of the rope would be long enough.

It was.

Just.

Celja was unconscious but alive when they pulled her up.

Half a dozen hands reached for Vree as she came over the rim, most of her weight on the rope. Someone untied the knots, someone else threw a rough wool blanket over her shoulders. The scene had taken on a clarity she recognized and her blood sizzled the way it did after a target had been taken out. All that was missing was Bannon. And a body.

The villagers were shouting things, but she didn't understand most of them. Everything seemed to be happening some distance away from herself.

Then she saw Magda kneel by Celja's side. The healer looked up, caught her gaze, and nodded.

It's funny, she murmured.

What is?

If I hadn't been so thoroughly trained to kill people, that girl would have died.

Her need overwhelming caution, Gyhard extended his awareness and pulled the blanket more tightly around her, leaving his/her arms wrapped around her/his body.

She shivered.

You're cold.

No ...

"One double pallet or two singles, my lord?"

Scowling, Gerek pushed wet hair back off his face. "What?"

The innkeeper sighed. The Circle enclose her away from nobility determined to rough it. "One double pallet," she repeated, "or two singles? The double'll cost you half an anchor; the singles, a gull each. You two sleeping alone or together?"

"Alone," Gerek told her indignantly, reaching for his purse.

"Very well, my lord. There's stew in the pot if you and your .." She took a good look at Bannon, reassessed both her first and second opinion and decided she didn't want to know. ". . . companion want a late supper. Quarter-gull each, bowl of stew, bread, and beer. Bowl of fruit's another quarter-gull."

"Fine." Gerek laid a half-gull beside the two copper coins already on the scarred counter. Until he'd spent the last few days in the saddle pounding at a full gallop down the South Coast Road, he'd thought he was in good shape, but every time they'd changed horses he'd mounted a little more slowly. The short walk from the stable to the inn—an establishment chosen purely on the basis of proximity—had nearly crippled him. All he wanted was to sit for a few minutes on something that wasn't moving, shove some food into his abused body, then fall over. That Bannon appeared to be completely unaffected by the punishing ride irritated him more than he could say, and he strongly suspected that had it not been raining so hard, the southerner would have expected them to reach the next station before stopping for the night.

The public room was nearly empty. Although the three trestle tables could probably hold close to thirty people if they were willing to be friendly, this evening there were only six other customers. Two old men sat by the empty hearth pushing tricolored game pieces around a strategy board, and four young women sitting in the seats closest to the door giggled over mugs of beer.

Shoving his saddlebags under the table with the side of his foot, Gerek began to drop onto the end of the bench nearest the counter.

Bannon lightly touched his arm. "No," he said. "You sit on the other side of the table."

Gerek felt his lip curl—about the only protest he had the energy for. "Why?"

"Because this the only seat in the room where you can see all four entrances."

"Four?"

"Door to the outside; door to the kitchen; stairs to the second floor, chimney."

"Chimney? That's not an entrance!"

"It is when there's no fire lit."

Grinding his teeth, Gerek shuffled around the table. "Fine," he snarled. "Sit there. And I wouldn't be surprised if someone came down the chimney and tried to kill you."

Bannon bowed mockingly. "*Tried* to kill me, Your Grace. This way, I can protect *your* back."

The giggling grew louder. Although they didn't understand the language, they understood the tone.

As much as he resented both the implication that he would be unable to provide a similar protection and the reaction it had evoked, Gerek let it go. His father was fond of saying, *Never fight with a man trying to pick a fight with you. Even if you win, you'll lose.* When Annice demanded to know what he meant, he'd add, *The boy understands.* It drove her crazy. Sometimes, Gerek thought that was why his father said it, except that he *did* understand.

"Suit yourself," he said, slowly lowering his aching body down onto the bench.

Bannon bowed again, playing to his audience. When

one of the girls called out something, he frowned—not because of what had been said, but because he suddenly remembered who'd have to translate it for him.

As the realization showed in Bannon's expression, Gerek smiled guilelessly. "Did you want something?" he asked.

The young woman added a longer statement along with a lecherous waggle of pale brows. Her friends continued to giggle and one of them shrieked, "Kasya!" in exaggerated horror.

The gist was unmistakable and Bannon couldn't stand not knowing the particulars any longer. "If you could tell me what she said, Your Grace?"

Gerek dropped his chin onto the heel of his left hand. "You know," he drawled, "that's the first time you've used my title and haven't made it sound like an insult."

"And it could easily be the last, *Your Grace.*"

All at once, he was tired of the posturing. Maintaining it took more energy than he had to spare. "She said you had a nice *bow,* emphasis obvious, then she said it was too bad the table blocked so much of the view."

"Did she?" Gerek forgotten in the possibilities, Bannon took two running steps, leaped lightly onto the table, flipped in the air, and landed on the far side. He bowed a third time, then made his way back to his seat by the more conventional route.

The giggling stopped and after a moment's stunned silence, a low-voiced argument ensued.

"End of round one?" Gerek asked as Bannon sat down, impressed in spite of himself.

Bannon smiled, his expression for the first time

since Gerek had met him, free of anything but the moment. "The advance, as we say in the army, is on her front."

The innkeeper put a heavily laden tray down between them. "You break anything," she growled, with a pointed look at Bannon's damp footprint on the tabletop, "and you pay for it."

The food was surprisingly good; the stew no more than two days on the fire and the bread soft enough to dip into the gravy without breaking.

Bannon took a cautious sip of the beer and set it aside.

"Too strong for you?" Gerek asked facetiously.

"A strong beer slows your reaction time." Bannon moved his gaze deliberately from Gerek to Gerek's half-empty mug.

Gerek ignored him. He wasn't in the mood.

They were almost finished when the door slammed open. The flames flickered in the half-dozen flax-oil lanterns and one of the old men muttered a curse without looking up from his game. The five men who stomped in, rain dripping from grimy clothes, wore an assortment of scars and identical scowls.

The innkeeper laid a metal-headed club on the counter. "Get out," she said. "I've told you before Jonakus a'Vasil, I don't want you and your boys in here."

The eldest, lamplight reflected in the beads of water on his greasy bald head, held up a purse in a three-fingered hand. "We got money."

Weighing the nearly empty room against her expenses, the innkeeper's eyes narrowed. "One drink each."

"Just one." Jonakus smiled. Under the mashed remains of his nose, most of his teeth were missing. "Sit, boys. I told you she'd do right by us."

Five heavily-muscled bodies dropped onto the benches at the far end of Gerek's and Bannon's table. The old men ignored them, all their attention on the game. The young women nervously shifted positions in order to keep them in sight.

"Hey, Pa!" A sausagelike finger pointed down the table at Bannon. "Look at the pretty little man."

Five heads swiveled on bull necks.

"I hear that in the South they cut off their balls to make'em that pretty."

"What did he say?" Bannon asked.

Gerek shook his head. "You don't want to know."

"I heard," offered one of the others through scabbed lips, "that if you stroke a Southerner just right, they squeal like a pig."

"You squeal, Southerner?"

Teeth clenched, Gerek began to rise.

A viselike grip around his wrist stopped him. "It's me they insult," Bannon said quietly. "So it's my slaughtering fight. Tell me what they said."

Two of them squealed. Three of them laughed.

Gerek told him. Bannon's fingers tightened around his wrist. "I don't need your help," he growled.

"There're five of them."

"I *can* count, Your Grace."

Scowling, Gerek sat back down. *Fine,* he snarled silently. *He thinks he's such hot shit, he can prove it. I'll be here to pull his butt out of trouble when he gets in over his head.*

Over his head seemed an apt observation when the four younger men stood.

"Jonakus!"

He waved a placating hand at the innkeeper. "Don't worry. The boys won't bust nothin' but the pretty little Southerner."

"I'm warning you . . ."

Her warning came too late. Bannon somehow managed to spit in three out of four faces.

Over the next few moments bellows of rage turned to shrieks of pain that didn't quite drown out the wet crack of more than one joint separating.

Gyhard watched with his mouth open and barely managed to get it shut in time to yell "Don't kill anyone!" before it was all over.

Eyes glittering, Bannon stroked one of his daggers across Jonakus' throat. "Squeal," he said in heavily accented Shkoden.

Sweat beading the dome of his head, Jonakus stared in horror at the broken, bleeding bodies of his sons and squealed.

Bannon moved the point of the blade to the stubbled chin and lifted Jonakus' head until their eyes locked. "I see again," he told the older man quietly, "I kill."

The sudden smell of urine and a spreading stain indicated just how much Jonakus believed the threat.

Stepping back, Bannon gestured at the door. "Go."

Three of them carrying two of them, they went.

The innkeeper picked the abandoned purse up out of a puddle of beer. "This oughta cover the damages."

Wondering why he was the one panting when Bannon had been in the fight, Gerek stared at her. "That's a pretty minor reaction! Does this sort of thing happen often?"

She snorted. "Not usually until they've had a bit more to drink. Then they get ugly."

"What did she say?" Bannon asked, cleaning off his daggers.

When Gerek translated, the ex-assassin laughed, his eyes still gleaming. "I'd hate to see them any uglier."

"No one's ever beaten them before," the innkeeper added. "I'm impressed."

"Only impressed?" Gerek shook his head. "As much as it pains me to admit it, I'm amazed!"

Shrugging, she started to clean up. "Keep an inn long enough and nothing amazes you, my lord. We had a two-headed calf in here once. Still alive it was, too."

"What did she say?"

By the time Gerek finished translating the information about the calf, both men were laughing so hard they had to sit down. A soft touch on Bannon's arm drew him around.

Kasya stood looking down at him, eyes half-lidded, cheeks flushed, moist lips slightly parted. "I think," she sighed, drawing one finger lightly along Bannon's jaw, "that I'm in love."

Bannon didn't bother asking for a translation.

Far to the south, at the Sixth Army garrison, the corporal of the watch stood over the huge brass drums and pounded out the pattern that began the day. A soldier for fifteen of his twenty-one years, Bannon obeyed the command and woke. He lay testing his surroundings for threat then rose silently to his feet. In the pale gray, predawn light, he scanned the loft, not moving, barely breathing, until he was certain he and Gerek were alone.

He'd returned to the inn when Kasya had fallen asleep, slipping away from the warm comfort of her embrace and back to the security of a companion he knew was no threat. While he regretted leaving, and doubted the necessity, he couldn't break the caution of his training. Assassins had died of warm comfort before. For all Gerek a'Pjerin was an arrogant millstone hung around his neck, he was also an ally.

And an attractive ally, too, Bannon admitted, his gaze tracing the line of dark curls running over ridged muscle and disappearing behind a loosened waistband. Had circumstances been different ... He put desire aside with little difficulty, Kasya having taken the edge off.

Wearing only breeches and wrist daggers, he slipped down to the inn yard. In the Empire, inns even smaller than this one would have a bathhouse. "Well, what can you expect from barbarians?" he sighed, glancing disdainfully at the hand-pump and trough by the door.

Back to the rising sun, he began his morning exercises. As he moved through the increasingly complicated pattern, he couldn't help but imagine he was no longer alone. Every now and then, out of the corner of his eye, he'd actually see Vree in her accustomed place and it hurt every time when he turned to face her and she wasn't there.

She should be there. Beside him.

This was the time of day when he missed her the most; missed the sound of her, the smell of her, the mirror image as they moved together in the assassin's deadly dance that promised an eternal partnership. He'd get her back. He had to get her back.

And what then? asked a little voice in his head. *Do you return to the army?*

No. Not the army.

What about the prince?

The prince needed him. He needed Vree. But some-how he couldn't seem to bring those two needs together.

The prince is mine. Not Vree's. Not the army's. Not our-slaughtering-father-the-dead-commander Neegan's. Mine. In his whole life, the only other thing he'd ever had of his own had been Vree. Until Gyhard had taken her.

Gyhard.

He twisted in the air, his heel slamming into an imaginary throat, a dagger suddenly in each hand. Once Gyhard was dead, everything would be like it used to be between him and Vree.

Rolling up off one shoulder, he saw Gerek cross the yard to the privy and his lip curled. *He's hobbling like a slaughtering old man.* When he emerged, a moment later, Bannon was as far from the privy as he could be without leaving the yard. He wanted to be alone with his memories of Vree. He didn't want to put up with the facetious comments of the slaughtering use-less noble foisted on him by a ball-less ambassador.

Ignoring the hint, Gerek crossed the yard and stood just outside the danger zone. He had a good eye, Ban-non reluctantly acknowledged. One of the more com-mon scars in the Imperial Armies came as a result of standing too close to an assassin's morning exercises.

He went on a little longer and a little more strenu-ously than he would've without this particular audi-ence, but finally, torso shining with sweat, he had to stop.

"What?" he demanded.

"Nothing." Gerek spread his hands, determined not to be provoked. Maybe the Southerner could be a pain in the ass all the way to Bartek Springs, but he had better things to do with his energy than reply in kind. "I watched Vree exercise one morning back in the Citadel and you two move exactly the same way." Uncomfortably the same way, actually. Although not usually attracted to men, he thanked the Circle for loose trousers.

Unbuckling his wrist sheaths, eyes locked on the sweaty leather, Bannon scowled. "And why were you up that early, Your Grace. Because she was?"

His implication colored the question. "We didn't sleep together, if that's what you're asking." Making an obvious point of considering it, Gerek added, "I guess I'm not Gyhard's type."

Bannon's head jerked up. "My sister makes her own choices!"

That was more, much more than Gerek could resist. "Funny, that's what Gyhard said. You may have a greater amount in common than you think."

Even half-expecting the attack, it still came faster than he was able to react. He survived only because Bannon ignored a lifetime of training and tried to throttle him bare-handed. Fighting for air, Gerek threw himself forward. The impact with the ground broke the smaller man's hold. He managed to get in two good blows before something that felt like a steel bar drove up under the center of his ribs and he found himself flat on his back, gasping for breath, staring up at a dagger point suspended terrifyingly close over his left eye.

Oh, shit. The moment he could speak, determined to hide the fear even if it killed him, he gasped, "Your nose ... is bleeding."

Startled, Bannon touched his upper lip with the

fingers of his free hand and gazed in astonishment at the crimson smear.

Gerek tried very hard to look past the dagger. "The four guys last night ... didn't even touch you."

Rolling his weight back off Gerek's shoulders, Bannon stood, shaking his head as though to settle in unsettling information. He picked up his wrist sheaths, and walked, still shaking his head, toward the inn.

With his left arm clamped against his chest, Gerek got to his feet. "Well, I hope that shook up your worldview," he muttered at the closing door. "You arrogant little prick." Then, with the memory of that dagger poised to take out his eye sending him limping back to the privy, he added, "Remind me never to do that again."

Chapter Nine

On his hands and knees in a stand of larch, Kars gently picked another mushroom. He examined the pale yellow cap for blemishes, ran a finger lightly over the white warts, turned it over to check that the gills were open and free of insect damage, and, satisfied, placed it with the others in a fold of his robe.

"We're very lucky," he said softly. "In a few weeks, it will be too late. Do you see, Kait? This little veil here, it becomes a collar when they're old."

Kait whispered something, but he couldn't hear it over the gentle patter of dead larch needles falling from the trees. He didn't ask her to repeat herself; he knew how frustrated she was that she couldn't help. He wished she'd believe him when he said it didn't matter, that he loved her for what she did and loved her no less for what she could no longer do. But she was young and the young always felt they had to prove themselves. Being dead wouldn't change that.

The inner flesh of the mushrooms was firm and white. He tested each with the point of a ridged fingernail to be certain they hadn't lost their moisture to age. It was late afternoon before he found enough. When he'd finally filled the fold in his robe, he straightened, ancient joints protesting the damp, and carried the fungus carefully back to the hollow where he slept.

He had the rocks ready—one with a hollow and one with a curve—and his small, fire-blackened pot, and a green glass flask that had once held ... once held ... He couldn't remember. It had last held the same promise he would pour into it today.

Who had told him about the mushrooms? Who had shown him how to crush them for their juices? It had to have been the dead, but there had been so many dead.

So many.

One hand rose to stroke the necklace of bone; a remembrance from each of them as they'd left him. He had lost them all. All but Kait.

"Now we've found a new family," he told the shadow of the girl hovering protectively around him. "A family the stockade will help us to protect."

Kait knew where they kept their beer. They took all their water from a single well.

He hummed as he poured the cloudy liquid from the pot to the flask. Kait moved closer to listen. He could only remember one Song.

Eyes narrowed, Karlene rocked back on her heels and watched a guard wearing the double sunburst of the Second Army efficiently search her packs. He'd obviously been on border duty long enough, or often enough that he didn't have to actually think about what he was doing. His bored expression never changed as he rummaged through her meager possessions.

"Please ..." When he looked up from her instrument case, she added, **"Be careful with that."**

A few minutes later, she was back out in the drizzle

and moving up the gentle slope to the pass. She'd been prepared to use Command to get across the border, but no one in the customs house seemed to think it strange she was going back to Shkoder—after all, the Empire now had bards of its own. Shoulders hunched against the wet, she walked quickly through the Giant's Cleft.

The moment she passed the midpoint, the world felt different. It shouldn't have, as she didn't Sing earth, but it did and in a multitude of ways she couldn't define, she knew she was home. Her step lightened as she hurried toward the guard tower at the Shkoden end of the pass. When a helmed figure stepped forward, she Sang her name.

"Bard?" Nastka pulled off her helm and peered across the border, as though she were checking to be sure that this unexpected bard was alone. "What are you doing here?"

"I've been called home." Remembering why destroyed her pleasure in it. "I've been in the Empire for the last two years."

"Well, since you're not Gabris, you must be Karlene. I'm Nastka i'Milena." Holding out her fist, Nastka laughed at the other woman's expression. "This is the easiest pass through these mountains. We make it a point to know about any prominent Shkodens on the other side." Her other fist lightly pounded her leather armor. "If the Empire tries anything, we'll be ready."

She seemed so proud that Karlene didn't have the heart to tell her the Empire barely thought about Shkoder at all and that its most likely venue for "trying something" would be dumping surplus production and not an armed invasion. Shkoder's natural defenses were too good to attempt the latter and the trade imbalance too great to ignore the former.

"So, what do you Sing?"

"Air, fire, and water."

"You going to be in the area for Third Quarter Festival? Jazep's around somewhere and if the two of you could get together in the next couple of days, you'd have all four quarters. You might even get *me* into a Center to hear that."

"Jazep's a friend of yours?"

"Oh, yeah, we go way back. We thought my eldest girl, Jelena, was his. Turned out she wasn't, so he stood as her name-father." As Karlene's expression changed, she frowned. "What is it?"

There were a hundred ways to tell her, but they all came down to the same thing. "Jazep's been killed. That's why I've been called home."

Nastka stood perfectly still for a long moment, her complete and utter lack of reaction speaking of a greater loss than weeping and wailing would have. She blinked once, silent tears cutting a warm path through the rain on her face. "Was it the thing he was following? The thing that scared the kigh?"

"Yes."

"And you're going after it." Not a question; but then, it didn't need to be. "Do you know what it is?"

Karlene sighed and nodded. "It's a Cemandian bard."

"I thought the Cemandians hated bards."

"They do." Remembering the abomination Kars had become, she added, "They tortured him because he could Sing the kigh. They made him insane."

The information elicited no sympathy. "Him? It isn't an old man, is it? Looks too old to live?" When

Karlene's eyes widened, she explained about Jazep's visit and about the old man who'd come into Shkoder at around the right time. She didn't mention that he'd called out a name as he crossed the border. He was crazy, after all. "If we'd known," she growled, grinding the knuckles of her right hand into her left palm, "we could've stopped him. Jazep might still be alive."

"Or you might be dead."

A jerky rise and fall of armored shoulders was her only response. "Two days and I'm finished this shift. I've got free time coming. I want to help."

"Thank you, but **no**." Karlene used just enough Voice to push the last word over into Command. "I've faced him before, and I think I know his Song. He doesn't seem to have any protection against bards."

"Tell that to Jazep," Nastka reminded her grimly.

Just down from the pass, Karlene sat under the umbrella of a huge old pine and listened in astonishment to the message the kigh brought from Marija at Bartek Springs. Her Royal Highness wanted Vree and the healer she was traveling with held? Captain Liene had told Marija to deal with it? It would've been laughable had the potential for disaster not been so great. She Sang back a single word.

"How?"

While she waited for an answer, she reflected that Vree's imminent arrival—or perhaps more accurately, Gyhard's—came as no surprise. Gyhard had unfinished business with Kars. His past seemed determined to interfere with whatever future he and Vree could cobble together.

"Her Highness leaves how *up to us. We don't have to hold her long, her brother is close behind."*

"Bannon?" Karlene whistled away a kigh unbraiding her hair, and frowned. "What's Bannon doing in Shkoder?" Then she remembered, the fledglings and Jazep had driven Prince Otavas' trip to Elbasan right out of her head. Given that Bannon was in the country, sending him after Vree made sense. He was probably the only living person with a chance of stopping her.

It wasn't going to be pleasant. Bannon hated Gyhard and the last she'd seen them, he wasn't getting along that well with his sister either.

Had she a way to do it, she might have warned Vree. "All things being enclosed, probably a good thing I can't." Neither Her Highness nor the Bardic Captain would be very happy about it. "On the other hand, I'd better warn Marija.

"Remember that Vree has two kigh. Neither Charm nor Command will hold her long."

When it came right down to it, Karlene would've welcomed Vree's company, but she wanted Gyhard stopped. He'd had his hands around Kars' throat once before and Kars had gotten away. Now, Jazep was dead. She didn't trust him. Didn't trust the bond between the two men. She'd deal with this herself.

There was no reason for her to go to Bartek Springs. It was far more important that she catch up with Kars; the sooner she got to him, the sooner people would stop dying.

The reaction of the kigh told her Kars was east, up in the mountains. She heaved her pack up onto her shoulders and started off cross-country, the kigh choosing her path.

"A woman trained to kill, who's immune to Command and Charm because she has two kigh." Marija sighed deeply and ate another butter cookie. "Why me?"

Celestin smiled. "Think of what a great song this will make."

"Yeah, wonderful." The priest had proved to be a valuable ally when the Bartek Springs town council had decided, much as Her Highness had, that this was a bardic problem. Imperial assassins were not for them to deal with. Marija brushed crumbs off her shirtfront. "I knew I should've walked north this quarter, but, oh, no, I wanted to be in the mountains when the high berries ripened. Are you sure that shed will hold her?"

"It held the bear."

"I get the distinct impression that this Vireyda Magaly is more dangerous than a bear."

"Are you all right?"

Slumped in the saddle, a breeze pushing her curls first over one eye and then the other, Magda forced a close approximation of a smile. "I'm fine. Why?"

Vree swept a critical gaze over the younger woman. "You look like you've been riding under the horse, not on it."

"So I'm a little tired." She tried to straighten, then sighed and sagged again. "They keep saying that healing energies have to come from somewhere."

"You told us that the sugar-water you drank would take care of it."

"I lied."

We should've left her in the village. Gyhard's tone had a distinct *I told you* flavor.

Granted. Vree guided her mount around a low branch—Magda merely sagged lower, the yellowing leaves that announced the coming Third Quarter brushing her head. *But since we didn't, what do we do now?*

Go on without her.

And just leave her like this?

*Vree, she's slowing us down. We already lost a day in the village while she dealt with the accident. Pursuit *can't* be far behind. If they catch us before we get to Kars ...*

I won't let that happen.

How are you going to stop it? Suppose His Majesty sent a whole troop of guards? It's not unlikely, considering that Magda's not only his niece but a valuable healer and he doesn't trust us. Even you can't kill that many people! He felt her wince. *Vree, I'm sorry but ...*

No. You're right. I can't. She twisted around and looked back the way they'd come. Unfortunately, although some of the leaves had turned brilliant shades of orange and yellow, very few had actually fallen. She couldn't see a thing even though their path had been rising all morning. Similar geography back in the Sixth Province would've left everything below them exposed. *This country has too many trees.*

Homesick?

Closing her eyes, she saw the village spread out around the garrison wall; pots of flowers bloomed on red slate roofs, olive groves lifted silver-green leaves to a brilliant blue sky and, in the distance, the heat shimmered over plateaus of orange stone. Behind her, she could hear the soldiers of the Sixth Army; the metal on metal of a practice bout, a corporal calling cadence, dice rattling in a cup, men and women laughing, lying, belonging. Breathing in, she could smell the omnipresent odor of cooking onions. And at her back . . .

Vree?

She opened her eyes and stared at the trees. *I have no home.*

"See anything?" Magda asked.

"No." Turning to face forward once again, she left the past lying where it had fallen. *I can't gallop off and leave her behind.*

*Why not? I guarantee that whoever is after us poses no danger to *her*.*

I've never left a wounded comrade behind, and I'm slaughtering well not going to start now.

She's not wounded.

She's not well! End of argument. "Magda, can you canter?"

"No, but I've been told I have an attractive trot." When Vree's eyes narrowed, Magda raised a hand and cut off the response. "Joke." She sighed deeply and, her voice wistful, added, "I thought we were sparing the horses?"

Although they were still riding courier horses, they were no longer galloping wildly down the Coast Road. They'd left the line of stables—extending from Elbasan to Somesford where the Duc of Somes had her principal residence—when they'd turned toward Bartek Springs.

"No, not now. We wouldn't ask except . . ."

"That you think we're going to be stopped. That whoever His Majesty, my uncle, has sent after us is breathing right down our necks because of me." Magda's chin rose. "Was I supposed to just let those people die?"

Vree stared at her in some confusion. "We never . . ."

"I told you right at the beginning I wouldn't slow you down. I can do *anything* I have to do!" She slammed her heels into her horse's ribs and, clutching the saddlehorn with both hands, pounded away up the track.

Where did that come from? Gyhard wondered.

Exhaustion. We'd better catch up before she bounces off and breaks her neck.

Which would certainly not be what we were hoping for when we wanted her to find us a body.

As they raced after the young healer, Vree realized it had been days since she'd thought of Gyhard in a body of his own.

"Yer less than a day behind. See, that's the problem. They come pounding in just after dawn this mornin'. My boy gets me up and I checked the healer's mark against the list—she's an apprentice on the list, but that don't mean squat—and I mount them, see?"

It took an effort, but Gerek managed to keep his expression pleasant. "So what you're saying is that the only horses you have are the two my sister and her companion rode in on this morning?"

The stablemaster beamed at him. "That's it Yer Grace. That's it exactly. And you see, the problem is, the horses, they don't go out again unless they got a full day's rest." She shrugged apologetically. "I ain't never had four riders in so close together before, being at the end of the line as it were 'cepting for the Duc's stable at Somesford."

"Is she refusing to mount us?" Bannon asked quietly from his place behind Gerek's left shoulder.

"Essentially. The horses require a day's rest and they haven't had it."

Bannon turned and stared into the corral where a bay and a black were standing nose to tail in a patch of late afternoon sun, lazily swatting at the last, hardy flies of the season. "They don't look tired."

"She says Vree and Maggie rode in just after dawn."

"Dawn? Then they rode all night? I don't think so, there was no slaughtering moon."

Gerek nodded. "You're right." They'd spent dark till dawn on opposite sides of a haymow for that very reason. "Do you know how far they'd come?" he asked the stablemaster, who'd been staring at Bannon in rapt fascination.

She shifted her slightly protruding gaze back onto Gerek. "Oh, yeah, they just come from Three Rock Cove, see? Just up the coast a fish, skip, and a jump. Terrible accident there day 'fore yesterday. Healer saved three lives. Southern girl— This one's sister is she? Thought as much. Look right alike. —She rescued young Celja right off the side of the cliff. Plucked her out as handy as a kid stealing eggs from a gull. My Gerri, he was there doin' what he could, he says everyone was some impressed." She nodded sagely. "Did it with no clothes on, too."

"What's she babbling about now?" Bannon muttered.

The stablemaster sighed happily. "I do love to hear him talk Southern. Sounds so pretty."

Gerek just barely managed to stop himself from saying something very rude. He sighed and squared his shoulders, his voice dropping into an almost bardic cadence. "Stablemaster, these horses have been ridden a very short distance by two very light riders. At most, we have only a couple of hours until dark. The track to Bartek Springs is not one you can go galloping down even in full daylight without risking your neck. We have no desire to risk either our necks or the horses'. I give you my word that if you mount us now, we will treat these animals as if they were my own."

"Yer own?"

As assorted breezes lifted ebony curls, he spread his hands and turned the full force of his smile on her, teeth gleaming in the dark depths of his beard. "As if they were my father's."

She blinked and flushed. "Yeah, that's more like it. You gots a tongue like a bard, Yer Grace. And if I gots yer word, you gots the horses."

"What the slaughter was *that* all about?" Bannon demanded as she led the animals from the corral.

"We have a saying in Ohrid: you can get more flies with honey than you can with vinegar."

"We've got one like it," Bannon admitted suspiciously.

I just bet you do, Gerek thought, remembering how charming the southerner could become when he wanted something. He gestured at the stablemaster saddling the bay. "I got us a pair of flies."

"So we'll catch them tonight?"

"No. Probably not until tomorrow. But the less time they have to be held in Bartek Springs before we arrive, the better the odds are they'll still be there. I don't imagine Vree's going to like being held."

"You *can't* imagine." Bannon's chin lifted. "You know nothing about my sister."

"I know enough not to refer to her like she was some kind of possession. You say 'my sister' like you say, 'my knives' or 'my boots'."

"I don't . . ."

"You do." Gerek turned away, took a single step, then turned back. "And I'll tell you something else," he added, catching the shorter man's gaze and holding it, "if anyone talked about *my* sister the way you talk about Vree, I'd beat the living shit out of him."

Bannon's right hand curled into a fist, but his left touched his nose, still slightly swollen.

Splintered finger ends clattered together as Kars lifted the necklace of bone over his head and hung it carefully on a broken spur of branch. While he hated to leave the mementos of his old family behind, they had, in the past, made it difficult for him to acquire a new family and this time he was taking no chances.

"I will return for you," he murmured, lightly stroking the memories of those who'd been his companions over the years, "when things are settled down below."

He checked that the green glass flask—now full of cloudy liquid—was safely tucked into a corner of his worn, leather pouch then settled the broad strap on his shoulder. As he looked down into the valley, he had the feeling that this was what he'd been searching for all along.

"Come, Kait. Let's go home."

Standing in the open gate of the stockade, Kiril a'Edko i'Amalia shielded his eyes against the late afternoon sun and squinted in the direction his youngest son was pointing. "You've got eyes like a hawk, boy, if you can tell that's an old man from this distance."

"A very old man, Papa." His stance identical to his father's, Edko narrowed his eyes a little more. "Older even than Granduncle was before he died."

"Older than Grandmother?"

The boy snorted. "No one's older than Grandmother."

"Can't argue with that," Kiril laughed. "Not when she says it herself." Folding his arms over a barrel chest, he leaned against the huge peeled log that anchored the gate. "Wonder what he's doing way out here."

"Wandering?"

"From where to where, that's the question. And why?"

Edko shrugged. "Why does he have to have a reason?"

"Everyone has a reason, lad, even if they don't know it themselves."

"There's something kind of funny around his head."

"Funny?"

"Yeah like, uh . . ." He cocked his own head, but it didn't help. "I dunno; funny."

Kiril straightened and stared searchingly at his son. Of late there'd been indications he'd be a bard once his voice changed. "Kigh?"

"No, Papa, not kigh." His voice held all the weary disdain of a twelve-year-old who was tired of hearing adults plan his future.

"Probably just the light being behind him, then."

"Yeah, I guess." But he didn't sound convinced. "Are we gonna take him in?"

"Well, we're not going to leave him standing at the gate. Frankly, I'm amazed he hasn't been eaten by something before now."

"Maybe he's too old and tough?"

"Show some respect for your elders, boy." He swung a three-fingered hand in the general direction of his son. Grinning broadly, the boy danced back.

"Day after tomorrow being Third Quarter Festival and all, I'd just as soon we stayed on the good side of the gods. No point in moving farther from the Center of the Circle than you have to. I'd better go tell your Aunt Ales there'll be company for supper."

Edko wrinkled his nose. "Better tell someone to heat up the bathwater, too."

Kiril took another long look and nodded. "Good idea."

As his father turned and ambled inside, Edko trotted toward the fenced pasture and the waiting cattle. He sang as he ran, his pure soprano wrapped incongruously around a disgusting ditty involving cow patties in the spring. Because he was moving, he didn't realize that, for the first time in his life, no breeze answered his song.

"Bartek Springs?"

"Uh-huh." Magda pulled a damp curl from the corner of her mouth. "Kind of pretty, isn't it? Pity we're not going in."

Vree turned her gaze from the town—they'd arrived at dusk, just as lamps were being lit in the windows of half-timbered houses—and looked at the healer. "We're not?"

"If they're going to stop us anywhere, they're going to stop us here. You know that as well as I do. If you planned on going in, you planned on getting caught and then leaving without me."

I thought she didn't read minds, Gyhard grumbled.

Magda smiled sweetly at them. "I have an older brother. I'm harder to ditch than that."

"And you're exhausted," Vree told her bluntly, not bothering to deny the accusation. "You need to rest."

"Have I slowed you down?"

Vree sighed. "No."

"Then I think it should be my choice, whether I go on or not. Don't you?" She rested her elbow on the saddle horn and her chin on her cupped hand. "Well?"

"Yes. It should be your choice ..."

Vree.

"... but I think you should stay here."

"No. Everything I said back at the Citadel still stands. You're my patient and I won't abandon you. Kars needs healing, and I won't abandon him either."

Vree!

You're the one who said she has an answer for everything. You want her to stay here so badly, you come up with a good reason. "So where do the good people of Bartek Springs put their dead?" she continued aloud when Gyhard remained silent.

Looking worried, Magda straightened. "Their dead?"

"Tombs or graves or something. If Kars is making the dead walk, he needs fresh bodies."

The younger woman winced at the matter-of-fact reference. "According to the bardic maps I studied back in Elbasan, there's a cemetery on the far side of town."

"Then let's get going." Guiding her reluctant horse off the main track, that would very shortly become the town's main street, Vree nudged him with her heels until he lengthened his walk.

"But it'll be dark by the time we get there," Magda protested.

"So we'll get an early start tomorrow morning."

"We're spending the night in the cemetery?"

"It's okay. The bards said that Jazep took care of what Kars did here."

Magda urged her horse after Vree's. "Yeah, but ..."

"Unless you'd rather go into town?" When Magda muttered something Vree couldn't quite catch, the ex-assassin almost smiled.

You're mean.

She's a healer, Gyhard. She's going to have to learn to deal with dead bodies.

Try to see it from her side. A dead body means she failed. For you, dead bodies meant success.

And for you?

She felt herself sigh; knew it was his reaction. *Only that I was still alive,* he said softly.

Wishing that there was a little more light, Vree dismounted and stretched. She could just barely make out the dark on dark slabs of gravestones on the other side of the low stone wall and she wondered just what it was the Shkodens did for their dead. In the Empire, army dead were most frequently buried in mass graves with the rites performed once for the lot and their only memorial in the memories of their surviving comrades. The rich stacked their dead in stone tombs along the Great Roads. She didn't know what the poor did.

"It's spooky," Magda whispered, pressed tightly against the comforting bulk of her horse.

"Without the kigh, there's nothing left but meat."

"I know."

"Meat can't hurt you."

"I *know*."

You have such a comforting way with a metaphor, Gyhard noted as Vree unbuckled the saddle girth.

Hobbling the horses—fortunately, they'd been able to water them on the way around town—the two women ate quickly and settled down for the night, wrapped together in their blankets to conserve warmth.

"You know, this close to Third Quarter this far up in the mountains, we could *easily* have a touch of light frost before morning."

Vree tucked her chin closer to her chest. "I'm so thrilled."

As sleep claimed them, the night seemed to take on the rhythm of their breathing. Leaves danced with the breeze to the same slow time; the thousand and one noises of the creatures who made the darkness their own became a gentle harmony. At first, the music was only an extension of the breathing, the breeze, the creatures, but then it took on a definition all its own. Promising security, it lay over the sleepers like another blanket.

When it finally trailed off, the other sounds went with it and the night was, for a moment, perfectly still.

On the far side of the graveyard, Celestin pulled her fingers from her ears and yawned. "Is that it, then?"

"That's it." Marija Sang a quick four notes and a kigh danced on the wick of the lantern she held. "I can't guarantee it'll hold them until morning, but we'll have time enough to lock them safely away."

The priest shook her head as she beckoned her nephew and three other men forward into the light. "I don't much like this."

Marija shrugged and rummaged a bit of hard candy out of a pocket. "You won't have to not like it for long. According to the kigh, they'll only be our problem until noon tomorrow."

Clean and fed, dressed in a borrowed robe better than any he could remember wearing, Kars lay on a pallet by the hearth and listened to the sounds of people sleeping. Tomorrow, they'd told him—speaking slowly and loudly for he understood very little of the language—the cutters would be coming in and everyone would be home for the festival.

Everyone would be home.

He would wait.

Eyes still closed. Breathing regular. If anyone was watching, they'd think she remained asleep. She was in a building. A small building. She was alone—or at least Magda was no longer with her—and her weapons had been removed.

Vree?

Quiet.

The urgency in the command and the surge of adrenaline accompanying it penetrated Gyhard's usual waking fog and he found himself completely attuned to Vree's senses.

It wasn't a stable, although it had held an animal. She could smell a faint hint of musk behind an overlay of soap. The pallet beneath her was clean. The blanket, the one she'd fallen asleep under.

She could hear dogs barking. A rooster crow. Farther away, a baby cried fretfully. She could hear only her own breathing.

She opened her eyes. Before her lids were all the way up, she stood, hands out from her sides, in the center of the shed.

Logs as big around as her thigh had been sunk into the ground to make a square, each wall a little longer than the pallet they'd laid her on. Light and air came through a multitude of tiny chinks. Something large and angry had gouged lines of parallel claw marks into the wood. The roof had been built of more logs with sod laid on top. The door dragged open outward on bullhide hinges and had been braced or barred. The dirt floor showed signs of having been recently re-packed around the base of the walls. There was a jug of water by the bed and an empty, covered pot in the opposite corner.

A cautious look outside showed a field, a dirt yard and a fence, the back of a building, and the side of what smelled like a cow stable.

Moving back to the center of the floor, she drew in a deep breath and let it out slowly through her nose, teeth clenched too tightly to allow even the passage of air. "What happened?"

Offhand, I'd say there's a bard in Bartek Springs.

A bard did this?

Probably Sang us a lullaby.

Vree flexed her fingers around an invisible throat. "I'm beginning to understand the Cemandian attitude."

"So you stuck her in a shed that used to hold a bear? You locked her up like an *animal?*"

Marija was beginning to regret ever having mentioned the shed's previous occupant. "She's an Imperial assassin; I doubt very much Celestin's house would hold her."

Eyes blazing, Magda stomped across the room and jabbed her finger at the bard. "You have no business holding her at all! For that matter, you have no business holding me!"

"Her Highness commanded . . ."

"What? That you break your vows and use the kigh against an innocent pair of travelers!"

"I haven't broken anything!" Astonished to find herself shouting, Marija took a deep breath and regained a measure of control. "You know as well as I do that Singing a lullaby involves no kigh."

Magda smiled triumphantly. "Does, too. Fifth kigh. And you can't argue with that because *I* know."

"I was just following orders . . ."

"Oh, sure, convenient excuse. If they'd ordered you cover us in honey and stake us over an anthill, would you have done *that*, too?"

Marija sighed. "Maybe not yesterday."

"What's *that* supposed to mean!"

Raising both hands, palm out, the bard stood. "Look, Magda, as much as I personally find it difficult to understand, the powers that be want you back in Elbasan. They also want your companion, an Imperial assassin with two not entirely stable kigh, back where she's under some kind of supervision."

"And they don't consider *me* sufficient supervision?"

"Apparently not." With one hand on the door, she cautioned the young healer against approaching any closer. "I've done what I was told to do and in a very short while you won't be my problem. The kigh say your brother and her brother are a very short distance from town."

"Her brother?"

"His name is Bannon. He came into Shkoder with Prince Otavas and was recruited to help out. That's all I know." Nodding at the table she added, "Try a little jam on the oatcakes, they're really good." Then she left.

"Oh, sure." Magda slapped a spoonful of jam on an oatcake with one hand and dashed away angry tears with the other. "*I'm* not sufficient supervision for an Imperial assassin, but Gerek *is*? Like *that's* fair."

"Magda is locked in the priest's spare room, Your Grace. We felt her companion . . ." Under the intensity of Bannon's stare, Marija cleared her throat and began again. "That is, under the circumstances and considering everything we'd heard about her ability, we felt her companion should be put someplace a little more secure.

As Gerek translated, Bannon shifted his weight forward and flexed the muscles across his back. Although he looked ready for a fight, all he said when Gerek finished was, "Where?"

Someone's coming. Vree rolled up onto her feet and held her breath as she sifted the quiet sound of approaching footsteps from the sounds she'd been listening to all morning. Whoever it was, was walking softly. Not furtively, as though expecting to reach the shed unnoticed but with a sure and quiet tread that kept the weight balanced and the noise to a minimum.

Whoever it was . . .

Vree! Are you all right?

No . . .

Vree, breathe!

She jerked and sucked in a frantic lungful of air just in time to expel it as a name when the footsteps stopped. "Bannon."

"He's made you weak, Vree. These people should never have been able to catch you." His voice dripped disdain; for Gyhard, for her, for the people who'd caught her.

"Their bards don't exactly fight fair."

"What was it Commander Neegan used to say? The survivors determine what's fair?"

"Things are more complicated now," she said, turning to follow the sound of his movement as he circled the shed. "Survival isn't everything."

"Does *he* think so, too, sister-mine?" He used to say it like an endearment. Now, it was more of a reminder. "Remember what he's done in the past to survive."

"We remember."

"We?" His voice picked up an edge, just as arrogant but a little less certain. "You'll never share his memories the way you shared mine, Vree, because you'll never share his life the way you shared mine."

"What makes you think I want to?" She watched his shadow flicker silently past the chinks between the logs.

Finally, it stopped, a hand's span to the right of the door. "So it's like that, is it? I might have known. Do you let him use your body? Does he touch you with your hands?"

Vree rolled her eyes. "Is that all you *ever* think about?" she demanded. "Bannon, what are you doing here?"

"I've come to take you back to Elbasan."

"By whose command?"

"As a favor to the crown of Shkoder."

"Then as a favor to me, let me go."

Bannon laughed. "That'd be a favor to *him,* not to

you. It isn't you that's running after Kars, it's him. It isn't you that needs to be stopped, it's him." His voice grew slightly shrill. "It isn't you who left me, it's him!"

"I chose."

"NO!"

His pain ripping great holes in her heart, Vree took a step toward the wall. He was the younger brother she'd loved and protected her entire life, and she wanted to destroy the thing hurting him so.

Vree.

Not you; me.

I know. He gave her his strength and was surprised when she used it.

"Bannon, even if I'd let Gyhard die, things could never have been the same between us. We can't go back into the past."

"I know that. I'm not stupid, Vree. But why can't we go into the future together?"

She laid her hand against the logs. Saw bits of him mirror the movement on the other side. "Because we'd drag the past with us and it would drag us down. I'm not going back to Elbasan with you."

"Yes, you are." His hand fell away. "If I have to knock you out and tie you to the slaughtering horse."

Can he? Gyhard asked as they listened to the footsteps move away.

Trying to remember if her palms used to sweat, she dried them on her thighs. *No. If it came to a fight, I'd know every move he'd make before he made it.*

Wouldn't he know yours the same way?

My life revolved around him. So did his.

Vree, if it came to a fight . . .

As the sound of Bannon's footsteps blended with

the sounds of Bartek Springs, she shook her head. *He can't kill me. He wants me for something.*

What? Besides the obvious.

Settling back cross-legged on the edge of the pallet, she snorted, the sound more sad than indignant. *Don't *you* start. I don't know what he wants but, trust me, I know when he's hiding something.*

Vree?

Don't . . .

*Can *you* kill *him*?*

She closed her eyes and touched the memories of her brother. *I hate you sometimes, you know.*

He let his control move down into her arms. Once again, she allowed his embrace. *I know.*

"Gerek, things are happening here that you don't understand!"

He dropped his head into his hands and sighed. It'd been a long hard ride and this accusation was not what he needed at the end of it. "What don't I understand, Maggi?"

"If you force us to go back to Elbasan with you, you'll have completely *ruined* Vree's life. Destroyed *any* chance that she and Gyhard might be able to create some kind of a future together."

"How?" Suddenly suspicious, he studied her through narrowed eyes. "You're not thinking of putting Gyhard into Kars' body are you?"

Magda made a disgusted face. "Yuk, no."

"Then explain how I'd be destroying anything."

"Sometimes the past is like, like a millstone around your neck and it keeps dragging you back whenever you try to go forward. Kars is that kind of a millstone for Gyhard. As long as Gyhard was just killing time . . ."

"Not to mention assorted young men."

Magda ignored him. ". . . then he didn't have to deal with all the feelings of betrayal and guilt, but the moment he fell in love with Vree, then it all came to the surface like, like a festering boil that has to be lanced."

"Lovely imagery, Maggot," Gerek muttered, curling his lip. "Don't tell me—you're the healer to lance the boil?"

"Yes!" Throwing herself to her knees at his feet, she gazed up at him, using an expression that had, in the past, softened his resistance. "Singing the kigh back into the dead for all these years, Kars has taken his *own* kigh out of the Circle. Gyhard and I *together* are the only hope of stopping him." Grabbing his wrists, she shook him as hard as she could—unfortunately, it made little impression. "If you can't help us for Vree's sake—who, I'd like to remind you, you were so *infatuated* with such a short while ago—then do help us for Shkoder. Who *knows* what terrible things will happen if Kars isn't stopped!"

Shaking free of her grip, Gerek captured her hands in his. "Listen, Maggi, I know you're used to being the only one who can do certain things, but Captain Liene has called Karlene from the Empire to deal with Kars. She's faced him before. She knows what to do."

Magda shook her head, her dark eyes suddenly bright with tears. "She'll die, Ger. She'll die like Jazep did."

"Jazep only Sang earth, Maggi." His voice gentled, he wiped tears from her cheeks with his thumbs.

She sniffed and pulled away. "Karlene's a bard. Kars needs to be *healed*. She won't be able to reach him and she'll die. Vree and Gyhard need to be healed, and I need *Kars* to do that." Rising, she walked to the window and stared in the direction of the shed. "This is *a lot* more important than keeping me safe or keeping Vree under some sort of supervision."

"Maggi, it wasn't only Her Highness. Annice sent me after you as well."

"*Mother* wants me back in Elbasan?"

"She sent me to find you."

"But did she tell you to take me back to the Capital?"

Gerek frowned. "Well, no, but . . ."

"Then *maybe* she wanted you to help me." Hands on her hips, she turned and glared at him. "Did you even *consider* that?"

"Help you?" There were times . . . "Maggi, when she sent the kigh to me, she had no idea of what you were going to do. She still doesn't."

"Are you sure?"

"What?"

"If you think, under these circumstances . . ." Waving arms emphasized the circumstances. ". . . Mother hasn't had the kigh watching both of us, you're not half as smart as you think you are."

"Look, even if Annice does want me to help you," he sighed, his tone suggesting it was highly unlikely, "I've been given a direct order from Her Highness to bring you back."

Lips pressed into a thin line, Magda pivoted on one heel and stared out the window once again.

"Maggi . . ."

She shook her head.

Gerek sighed and left the room. It had seemed so simple when he'd left the capital. Stepping out the

back door he saw Bannon approaching across the
yard. Something in the Southerner's face, or his posture, or the way that he moved, made Gerek frown.

All at once, he suspected that his little sister was
right.

Things were happening here that he didn't
understand.

Chapter Ten

Singing softly, Karlene tried to work out what was wrong with the kigh. They weren't frightened, although the air trembled still with the faint reverberations of Kars' passing. They weren't trying to warn her of danger; if anything, they seemed sad. Even after she Sang a gratitude, three or four hovered about her head not, as they would usually, in order to make mischief but almost as though they thought she might need the support.

She began to get a very bad feeling about walking into Fortune.

From where she stood, the mining settlement seemed normal enough. A little quiet perhaps, but as it was barely noon, it seemed logical to assume that most of the activity should be going on out of sight at the mine. The breeze shifted and from one of the cottages she could hear the faint wail of an angry baby.

As one, the kigh around her head spun up and out of sight.

"Fickle," she muttered. Squaring her shoulders under the weight of her pack, she walked slowly along the track. At the point where it spread out and became the central square of the settlement, a trio of huge, rough-coated dogs bounded out to meet her. Their greeting seemed subdued. Two of them were strangely submissive, the third sniffed her outstretched hand, then turned and ran barking back the way it had come.

Karlene stayed where she was, waiting for someone to respond to the barking and taking a closer look around. In spite of a Third Quarter chill in the air, all the doors and windows were open in the two, large, communal buildings fronting the square. Except for the dogs, the place seemed deserted. Even the baby had stopped crying.

Then a young woman stepped out of one of the small cottages, pulling the door closed behind her. The way she moved spoke of both fear and suspicion. Karlene thought she saw a shape stir at the window and the fine hairs lifted off the back of her neck as she felt herself watched.

"What do you want?" the young woman called, one hand resting lightly on the dog's broad head.

Karlene Sang her name.

To her surprise, the young woman started, raised both hands to her mouth, and burst into tears.

"Why didn't you send word to the duc? Or even down to Bartek Springs?"

"How?" Krisus demanded, bouncing a now smiling baby on his lap. "We had so many people to bury and Ilka to take care of—she's not even weaned yet—and . . ."

Karlene laid her hand lightly on his shoulder and cut off the flow of bitter words. "I wasn't criticizing," she explained gently. "It's just that you've been through so much, I'm amazed that you managed without sending for help."

"We couldn't leave them," Evicka declared defensively. She poured warm milk into a glass flask and deftly tied a cloth nipple to the top. "What if the others had come home while we were gone and found only bodies?"

"You're right." Astounded by the strength these two just barely out of their teens had shown, Karlene didn't bother being subtle with her voice. She let all her admiration and her sympathy and her sorrow show.

Krisus sniffed. "After what happened ..." No need to actually say what had happened; the memory lay like an oily film over the settlement. "... it was almost a relief that they were dead." He jerked and stared at the bard, horrified by what he'd said. "Except for Jazep, I mean. I wasn't ... I didn't .. when he Sang ... If it wasn't for Jazep, they'd still be walking around and Ilka would have starved and I didn't mean we were relieved that he was dead."

"I know." And they had to believe her.

Only the baby, feeding with the single-minded intensity of the very young, remained unaffected. After a moment Evicka cleared her throat. "Could you Sing over the grave? We said what we thought we should, but the nearest priest is in Bartek Springs and it feels unfinished."

The mound of stone at the edge of the forest was larger than Karlene expected, larger and sadder.

"There's rock close to the surface up here," Krisus told her. "I had to dig near the trees to get down far enough that they wouldn't get dug up again by scavengers." He looked at the dirt ground into the creases of callused hands. "I—we, haven't been back to the mine since it happened. I grab onto a pick and all I can think of is . . ." Words failed him, and he waved toward the mound.

Evicka shifted the baby from right arm to left. "We put Jazep's body in with the others. We didn't know what else to do. If the bards want him . . ."

"No. Let him lie where he is." The body without the kigh was an empty shell. Karlene knew that, had seen the proof of it, but it was harder, far harder, to believe it when the body belonged to a friend. "He liked to have people around him."

"We didn't get to know him very well."

Blinking back tears, Karlene remembered what Virine had said. If Jazep had to have an epitaph, she couldn't find one better. "He was kind."

"And brave," Krisus added.

"And one of many." Karlene straightened and drew in a deep, cleansing breath. "Tell me about the others."

"Just the seven that walked?"

"No, all of them."

It was one of the longest Songs, she'd ever Sung, but when it was over, she felt curiously clear-headed as though more than just the dead had been Sung to rest.

Evicka smiled tentatively, then looked guilty when she'd realized what she'd done. Krisus pressed his lips against the top of the baby's head, who woke up and started to fuss.

"One thing I still don't understand," Karlene murmured as they walked back to the cottage. "In the

Empire, when Kars did what he did, babies died. How did Ilka survive?"

"Her mother was one of the dead?"

"A possible reason, but I doubt that's it."

"Our babies are tougher?"

Karlene shook her head. "Nice to believe, but I don't think so." Turning and walking backward, she tickled Ilka's nose with the end of her braid. "What is it about you, baby? Why are you still here?"

Ilka shrieked with laughter and stretched out chubby fists. To Karlene's surprise, she wasn't reaching for the braid.

The kigh slid its elongated body through the infant's grasp and, twisting back on itself, stroked both her cheeks with ethereal fingers.

Too stunned to notice where she was putting her feet, Karlene tripped over a rock and sat down. Hard. To her companions' astonishment, she stayed where she was, and Sang a question to the kigh. When they answered, she bounced up, took Ilka, and swung her in the air.

"All four quarters! You little music box, you!"

"What are you talking about?" Krisus asked, his hands extended to retrieve the baby but unwilling to insult the bard as long as Ilka herself seemed to be happy with the situation.

Eyes gleaming, mouth stretched out in so large a smile her cheeks hurt, Karlene handed the laughing child back to her anxious guardian. "She's a bard. Or she will be in time. *And* all four quarters. This is incredible. This is absolutely incredible! I've got to tell the Captain!" Opening her mouth, she noticed the expressions on the two people facing her and closed it again. "What's the matter?"

Evicka stroked a rounded cheek, much as the kigh had. "Will she have to go away?"

Suddenly understanding, Karlene shook her head. "Not for fourteen or fifteen years, and not even then unless she wants to."

Relief came off them in waves. "So she doesn't *have* to be a bard?"

"No. She doesn't have to be anything she doesn't want to be." There was no need to mention that the odds of any person who could attract such attention from the kigh as an infant deciding *not* to be a bard were so small as to be essentially nonexistent. They'd dealt with enough for one day.

One day . . .

"By the Center of the Circle, Third Quarter Festival starts tonight!"

Frowning, Evicka began to count on her fingers. "That's im .. Oh, my heart, you're right."

"It doesn't matter," Krisus sighed. "Not this year."

"It matters this year more than any," Karlene told them gently. "Grieving is a needful thing and it's enclosed by the Circle, but it can't be allowed to stop the Circle from turning."

"We don't have much to give thanks for."

"I realize you've lost a great deal." Her voice slid from sympathy into wonder. "But you have the strength that a loving family gave you and you have Ilka and you have each other and isn't that something to be grateful for?"

The young partners looked at each other over the baby's head.

"If I hadn't had you," Krisus murmured.

Evicka took his hand and together they turned to

face the bard. "All thing beings enclosed, we think that we'd like to keep the festival."

Karlene smiled and taking each of them by an elbow, she pushed them toward the cottage. "Come on, we've got to get some kind of a harvest in, there's festival cakes to bake, and, if I'm going to Sing the Quarter around, I'm going to need some honey for my throat."

"Here, if you're going to be sitting around in my way, you can make yourself useful." When Kars stared at her in confusion, Ales closed his fist about the shaft of the wooden paddle. "Stir," she said, moving his arm around in a circle.

He looked down into the tub, smiled, and nodded. Using both hands he swirled the perforated paddle around and around in the batter. As grandmother had taken to her bed to rest up for the festival, his age entitled him to her place by the hearth. He'd spent the morning sitting and watching the bustle of festival preparations—trying to make sense out of the chaos. He didn't understand much of what was said, but he'd have time to learn the language later.

"What is?" he asked after a moment.

"Festival cake," Ales told him without looking up from the pot she was seasoning. "Enough for everyone in the settlement to have themselves a good healthy piece." Cuffing the shoulder of the boy chopping vegetables at one end of the heavy plank table, she sent him to the garden for a horseradish root. "Cake'll go in the Circle to be blessed at sunset, then cut and served and frankly, I think it needs more raisins. Keep stirring." Lifting a crock down off an upper shelf, she worked the stopper free and shook more dried fruit into the tub.

Kars frowned and worked his way through her somewhat disjointed speech. "Everyone eats?"

"That's right. Moment the service is over they descend on it like bears on berries. Nobody has to fake eating my festival cake, I'll tell you—I save spices all year for this. By the time this crew is done, there's never enough left over to bring in a mouse. Not that we need more mice after what they did to my bellflowers." She gave Kars a quick pat on the arm and a friendly smile. "Don't worry, there'll be enough for you. Jorin, hurry on out and see if those chickens have ..." Turning, Ales remembered she'd already sent Jorin to the garden, and bustled out to check the chickens herself, throwing a not to be argued with "Keep stirring" back over one plump shoulder.

Everyone eats. Retrieving his pouch from its place under a bench, Kars worked the stopper out of the flask and poured the contents into the batter. When Jorin trotted back in, a plump root born triumphantly in grubby hands, he was stirring again as instructed.

"Mama?" Jorin asked, looking around.

Kars searched for the word. "Chickens!" he announced at last.

"All right!" Tossing his root on the table, he rubbed his hands against his shirtfront and extended a curved finger toward the batter.

"No ..."

"It's okay." He grinned up at Kars. "I'm allowed to taste. Really."

"Jorin! You get your filthy hands away from that tub."

The boy whirled, saw his mother had both hands

full of eggs, and, with a relieved grin, began briskly chopping vegetables once again.

"Kids," Ales snorted depositing the eggs safely in a bowl. "More trouble than they're worth." But she smiled fondly at her son. "Do you have family, Kars?"

"No more."

"I'm sorry."

"Have again."

She studied him skeptically, but in the end only shrugged and said, "Sure you will. Keep stirring." If he wanted to believe he was still capable of creating children, it was no skin off her teeth.

Outside the open door, Kiril took his son by the shoulder and the two moved with exaggerated silence toward the gate. "I see she's got our guest working," he said when he thought they were safely out of earshot.

"I don't like him, Papa."

"No? Why not?"

"He makes me feel funny."

Brows drawn in until they met over his nose, Kiril turned Edko around to face him, a hand on each shoulder. "Has he *done* anything to you, boy? Don't be afraid to tell me."

Edko sighed and shook his head. "It's nothing like that. It's just that when I'm near him ..." He stretched out one bare arm. "It feels like there're ants climbing on my skin. He feels wrong."

Visibly relieved, Kiril ruffled the boy's hair. "It's probably just because we didn't think anyone older than Grandmother could exist."

"Well, yeah, but ..."

"Cutters coming in!"

At the sound of the cry drifting up from the riv-

erbank, Edko twisted out of his father's grip and raced
for the gate, whooping with joy. Kiril took a step to
follow and was nearly run down by Jorin charging
after his cousin. The next few moments were chaotic
as the family who remained in the stockade greeted
those who were returning from cutting trees in the
forest.

"Where's Enrik?" Edko demanded, clutching at the
bronzed forearm of his older sister.

She laughed and shook herself free. "He spotted a
hawk's nest halfway up a cliff and decided to go after
one of the nestlings. We didn't want to wait, so he
said he'd follow us down later."

"But the festival starts at sunset!"

"Listen, Sapling, I know the rest of us aren't worth
much next to the glorious cousin Enrik, but you know
what he's like. Once he gets an idea in his head, you
couldn't shift it with an ax."

Edko sighed and turned away, searching the edge
of the forest for any sign of his favorite cousin. His
sister just didn't understand. Enrik was special. He
was always willing to climb to release a deadfall, even
when an uncle or aunt said it wasn't safe. He was the
first into the river in First Quarter and the last out in
Third. He could throw his ax up into the air and catch
it behind his back. Sometimes maybe he took chances
even Edko realized weren't too smart, but he cut the
best willow whistles and he told the *best* stories.

Standing apart from the rest, released from his stirring duties by the pouring of the batter into greased
and floured pans, Kars watched Edko watching the
forest and slowly shook his head. The boy was demon-
marked. He remembered other children lost to the
demons. He remembered a boy not much older than

this taken from his home. His throat tightened as he remembered the screaming that he'd tried for a very, very long time to forget.

Pushing one of the dogs aside, Karlene finished tracing a circle in the packed dirt of the square. Pulling the stake from the center, she coiled the four-strand measuring rope—each strand dyed to represent a quarter—and stepped over the line. A quick search of the communal buildings had found all the festival trappings recently gathered and made ready for use. Tears had flowed freely as they'd carried everything they needed over to the cottage.

Karlene laid the measure aside and squatted, a little dubiously, to lift the huge clay bowl of water. It was as heavy as it looked. Glazed the exact shade of green used in bardic robes, and etched inside and out with stylized water kigh, it had obviously been bought just for this purpose and transported carefully up into the mountains. It went over the hole where the stake had been and Karlene considered it a small miracle that none of the water spilled.

The four thick beeswax candles, set on each of the four compass points, were a lot easier on her back. Checking the position of the sun, she turned toward the cottage, but before she could call, Krisus hurried out with a basket.

"They're still really hot," he said, laying the steaming cakes in position. "Vicka's sure they're not cooked through."

"They smell great."

He smacked her hand away. "Oh, no, not until after the blessing."

Karlene sighed and began to pile vegetables. "I love festival cakes."

Krisus grinned at her. "Like my mother used to say, since you have to eat them, you might as well decide to like them." He half turned toward the communal kitchen. "Vicka! What about the . ."

"Cheese," she finished, appearing with a round in her arms. "You haven't left the baby alone?"

"She's asleep." But he set the last cake down and hurried into the cottage.

The last thing to be laid in the circle was the silver. From a dull nugget to a beautiful filigree representation of the four quarters, the individual pieces made a small circle of their own just outside the candles. Although it felt wrong when so many others had died, Karlene found herself thankful that the artisan who'd created the final piece of filigree had gone to Bicaz with the load of ore and lived to create again.

The sky had just begun to turn when they finished.

Krisus put the basket holding the sleeping baby in position, then moved to stand across the circle from Evicka. Behind each of them were a pair of lamps ready to be lit when it grew dark. The lamps were an addition to the service, the need for their light Kars' last legacy to Fortune.

Karlene draped her tricolored stole around her neck—a bard walking couldn't be expected to carry robes—and took a deep, calming breath. Gabris and the fledglings would be back in the Capital by now, Singing at the Empress' Center. Silently she wished them a happy festival and prepared to Sing.

Together, as the sky to the west became a glorious, streaked pinky-orange and the sky over the mountains to the east deepened into sapphire blue, the three adults sang the choral that gave thanks for the long, hot days of Second Quarter, and welcomed the cooler days and longer nights of the Third. Just as the sun set, Evicka and Krisus fell silent.

Fire kigh danced on the candles and in each of the lanterns, throwing more light than was possible for their size. Karlene Sang thanks for heat and light.

The Song changed, and the water in the bowl rippled although there was, as yet, no breeze to move it. Karlene Sang thanks for thirst quenched and cleanliness, for the power of the moving stream.

Ilka laughed and clapped her hands as the Song changed again and air kigh danced within the circle. Karlene Sang thanks for breath and the power given to the windmills.

The Song changed a third time.

Karlene turned in place, searching for the voice. There were chorals to be used if the bard Singing the service had less than four full quarters, and she'd just been about to begin one, expecting Krisus and Evicka to join in.

Somewhere, somewhere close, there was a bard Singing thanks to earth.

The dirt in the circle began to move and a kigh emerged. Karlene stared, her heart pounding so loudly she was sure its beat must throw off the rhythm of the Song. Without the ability to Sing earth, she'd never seen an earth kigh before but everyone knew that, where the other three quarters were essentially sexless, the earth kigh always appeared to be female.

This kigh did not.

Its shape seemed somehow familiar.

It was six, maybe eight inches high, broad-shouldered, short-legged, barrel-chested.

The earth Song ended, the last notes rumbling away into the gathering dusk, and the kigh began the Blessing. It was amazing that such a pure bass tone could come from such a tiny figure.

Instinct overcame shock and a half measure into the Blessing, Karlene added her voice. The harmony grew and rose until it touched the stars just appearing over the mountaintops. The sky seemed close enough to touch, the earth small enough to enclose in a protective embrace. For one glorious moment, the Singers became the Song and Karlene felt a presence she had thought never to feel again. Somehow, Jazep's kigh had not gone on when he'd died; it had, instead, gone to earth.

She Sang the gratitudes alone.

The earth kigh was the last to leave. It looked once around the circle, its calm gaze resting longest on the baby, then, arms spread in benediction, it sank out of sight.

Her own small festival service ended, Annice settled the straps of her pack on her shoulders and set her feet on the path the kigh created. She had too far still to go to allow the night to stop her.

As she walked, she listened to a familiar voice Sing answers to her questions.

Gerek stood in an open window of Celestin's house and listened to the sounds of Third Quarter Festival spilling out of the Center. Marija only Sang fire and air, but the Bartek Springs choir cheerfully filled in the other two quarters, making up in volume what it lacked in bardic abilities. If he listened closely, he could hear the rhythmic counterpoint of Magda's footsteps sounding against the ceiling as she paced back and forth across the room directly overhead.

Because Magda had emphatically refused to give her word that she wouldn't attempt an escape during the service, bard and priest had decided she'd best stay right where she was. Gerek had remained with her out of loyalty; or possibly guilt, he wasn't entirely sure.

They'd be leaving in the morning.

Although he still wasn't exactly certain sure how they were going to accomplish it, he and Bannon would be taking an unwilling Magda and Vree back to Elbasan. It wasn't likely to be a pleasant trip.

Things were happening here that he didn't understand.

Digging his fingers into his beard, he scratched along the edge of his jaw and wished there was someone around he could talk to, someone who didn't already have their mind made up. Scowling, he began to pace as well, falling into the cadence still being drummed out up above. Apparently, he was going to have to talk this over with himself.

"All right, Maggi's positive Vree and Gyhard can only be healed by confronting Kars. Do I believe her? Do I have any reason not to believe her?" If he accepted that his little sister was a new and powerful kind of healer—and considering that he'd been her first patient he'd be a fool if he didn't—then he also had to accept that she knew what she was talking about.

Next point.

"Do I want Vree to be healthy and whole? Of course I do." Perhaps he wasn't as much in love with the lovely, dangerous Southerner as he had been, but he still wanted only the best for her.

Gyhard was a thornier question. Gerek, as much as he hated to agree with Bannon, would've preferred Vree had let Gyhard float off into the great beyond back when they'd found themselves a body short. As she hadn't, and as Gyhard was now a very important part of Vree's life, Gerek supposed it would be best for Vree if Gyhard were healthy and whole as well.

"If a bard, say Karlene, gets to Kars first, then according to Maggi, Vree will never be whole." He didn't much like where this was heading.

Holding out his hands, palm up, Gerek lifted first one, then the other. "So I weigh Her Royal Highness' desire to have Vree and Magda returned to Elbasan against two lives." He sighed. "Three if Maggi thinks she's going to heal Kars as well."

While he stood there, staring at his makeshift scale, searching for an answer, a breeze from the open window brushed a chill across the back of his neck. Lifting a hand to rub at the gooseflesh, he wondered if it was from Annice. "Under the circumstances, she'd be more likely to send a full blown gale."

Find your sister. He chewed over her original message. It wasn't like Annice to be so unspecific.

"I've found her, Nees." His mouth twisted up into a wry grin. "Now what am I supposed to do?"

Believe in her.

The answer came from his heart.

Gerek nodded slowly, remembering. "All things being enclosed, that sounds like good advice," he said at last. Grinning broadly, he bounded up the stairs two steps at a time.

When he threw open the door to the priest's spare room, he found his sister tying the last knot in a rope made of torn bedsheets. "Good, you're ready to go," he said matter-of-factly. "Although this is very ingenious, we'll make better time if we take the stairs."

She glared at him, backing toward the tiny dormer window. "What do you mean, we? Is this some kind of a trick? Because if you think I'm going to go quietly back to Elbasan with you, you're *wrong*."

"Trust me, Maggot, I don't think you'll go *quietly* anywhere. But as it happens ..." He paused and spread his hands, the giddy feeling of relief that had come with making what he knew to be the right decision suddenly leaving him. "As it happens, Maggi, I think you're right. I think you and Vree and Gyhard need to get to Kars before the bards Sing him into or out of or all around the Circle. It's the only way to end this thing once and for all."

With a crow of joy, Magda scooped her bulging saddlebag up off the floor, launched herself into his arms, squeezed him once, and ran for the door. "Come on! We've got to get Vree and get well away from here before the service ends."

"The kigh will still be able to find us," Gyhard reminded her as together they raced down the stairs.

"It doesn't matter if they know where we are," Magda told him, "as long as they don't catch us."

"You mean, catch you *again?*"

She punched him on the arm. "You looked just like Father when you said that. What have you done with Bannon?"

"Nothing at all. Bannon found someone willing to spend the festival giving thanks for getting laid."

"With a stranger?"

"He makes friends fast when he has to. Do you know what they've done with Vree's weapons?"

"All her stuff's in the kitchen."

"Good. I'll get *my* stuff and meet you there. See if you can find some journey food; if the bards stay here, there has to be some around."

A few moments later, saddlebags abandoned for a pack with shoulder straps, Gerek carrying Vree's weapons as well as his own, the two of them ran out the back door of the priest's house and toward the shed at the edge of town. Neither them looked back to see a shadow move away from the building and follow them.

. . . actually, Second Quarter Festival is the fertility festival because that's when things are blooming and, well, ready to be fertilized. First Quarter Festival celebrates new beginnings.

*Don't new beginnings usually come after *fertilizing*?*

She felt him smile—felt herself smile, knew it was him. *I'm just explaining how it is, Vree. I didn't make it up.*

So what are they singing about now?

He listened for a moment. *Right now, they're giving thanks for colley.*

For what?

It's a vegetable. I don't think you grow it in the Empire.

You're putting me on.

Afraid not.

They're giving thanks for a slaughtering vegetable?

Uh-huh.

People in this place have too much slaughtering time on their hands. Fingers laced behind her head, Vree lay on the pallet and stared up into the darkness. The priest had brought her food twice, the bard and

Bannon standing by in case she tried something. All three of them had obviously wanted to talk but just as obviously couldn't with the others around. She had no idea what the priest wanted to talk about—who ever knew with priests? The bard wore an expression she'd grown used to during her time at the Hall and had there not been an audience would no doubt have blurted out the familiar, *"You really do have two kigh!"* Bannon had stared at her with an intensity that evoked unwelcome memories of the heat that used to burn between them.

He needs me, she'd said when they were gone.

So do I, Gyhard reminded her. *The question is, which of us do you need?*

I've made my choice, she'd snarled and stopped herself just in time from adding, *leave me alone.* Because that was the one thing she didn't want.

The distant singing changed and Vree wondered if they'd moved on to more important things, like maybe sausage and onions. *Gyhard, if you weren't locked up here, would you be there?*

You mean at the Center, for the festival? He hadn't been to a Quarter Festival since the brigand had murdered his first body and he'd murdered the brigand in turn. A long time. A very long time. *I don't know.*

Nothing to be thankful for?

It's not that. It's just the festivals are a part of a past I never expected to re ...

Be quiet.

A sudden flash of insight and he understood what her question actually meant. *I didn't mean that I'm not thankful for you and—*

*Shut *up*, Gyhard! There's someone coming.* Rising to her feet in one swift motion, she faced the door, head cocked slightly to one side. *It's Magda and Gerek. They're coming to let us out!*

You can tell that from their footsteps?

No, I can hear Magda talking.

I can hear exactly what you hear and I don't hear . . . oh.

Relief at their approaching freedom making her feel a little light-headed, Vree grinned. *Given enough time, you may learn to listen.*

"Vree?" A familiar voice whispered her name through a crack between two logs. "Gerek came to his senses and decided to help. We'll have you out in a minute." The voice shifted direction. "What's taking so long?"

"It's dark, and I can't see well enough to undo the tie down."

Madga snorted, and Vree knew exactly what expression she'd be wearing. "So cut it! Honestly, Ger!"

Although there was only a crescent moon riding low in the sky, the almost total lack of light in the shed made the yard seem bright in comparison. With Gyhard's help, Vree managed to prevent a defensive response to Magda's enthusiastic hug.

"Where are my knives?" she asked urgently, putting the younger woman to one side.

She could see the flash of Gerek's teeth in his beard. "Don't I get thanked first?"

The slam of a throwing dagger sinking into the shed answered his question.

"You knew he was there." Gerek moved to stand in front of Vree and found himself shoved firmly out of the way.

Hands empty and held out from his sides, Bannon faced his sister across the yard.

Gerek reached for his sword. A slim brown hand clamped around his wrist like a vise, and the bit of blade he'd managed to draw was forced back into the scabbard.

"Not your fight," Vree told him in Imperial, so Bannon could understand. "This is just between the two of us."

"Don't you mean the *three* of us," Bannon sneered.

"Gyhard isn't involved in this."

"Oh, he slaughtering well is, but how much is my sister involved, that's the question!"

She stepped forward, away from the shed, away from Gerek and Magda. "Don't be an ass, Bannon. I'm in control, not Gyhard."

"Sure you are," Bannon scoffed. "That's why you walked away from everything you've ever known. Why you walked away from me."

"Things change."

"Not that much. Not all at once."

If he couldn't remember the choices he'd made while in her body, she couldn't forget. "It didn't happen all at once," she said softly. "What do you want, Bannon?"

"I told you. I'm taking you back to Elbasan with me."

Gerek shook off Magda's cautioning grip and, hands carefully away from his weapons, moved to stand by Vree's side. "Bannon, I think they're right. I've listened to what Magda has to say and I think they have to get to Kars before Karlene does."

"I don't give a rat's ass about Kars, or Karlene, or

your sister, or you," Bannon told him with a pleasant
and entirely false smile. "I want my sister back."

"Taking her to Elbasan won't change anything. In
fact, it could make things worse. It could mean she'll
never get rid of Gyhard."

Nice to be wanted.

He sounded so insulted, Vree fought a completely
inappropriate urge to giggle—then scowled when she
realized what she was doing.

"I thought Her Royal Highness ordered you to
bring your sister back to Elbasan, Your Grace," Bannon reminded Gerek, although his eyes never left
Vree's face. "Or does duty and honor mean nothing
in this slaughtering country?"

"You let me worry about that," Gerek snarled. The
hand that had begun to drop to his sword hilt suddenly
jerked up as Magda grabbed the back of his jacket
and nearly yanked him right off his feet.

"Have you got a *death* wish?" she demanded, using
her whole body to shove him up against the rough
logs of the shed. "Or are you so stupid you actually
think you could survive a fight with *either* of them?"

Gerek's mouth opened, then closed again as he took
a good look. Neither Vree nor Bannon had drawn
a weapon. There was no need. They were weapons.
Although they stood perfectly still, mirror images of
each other, something about them screamed of an incredible, deadly potential for movement. They were
like bowstrings, pulled taut and waiting to be released.

The skies had cleared. Moon and stars gave light
enough to throw Bannon's shadow almost to Vree's
feet and to spill hers back into the deeper shadow of
the shed. The songs of the festival seemed to be coming from a very long way away.

"What do you want, Bannon?"

You asked him that already.

I know. He didn't answer.

What are you talking about? He wants to take you back to Elbasan!

That's not the answer.

"What do I want?" he whispered mockingly. "I want you back."

With his face in shadow and his voice so low, he might have been Commander Neegan; he might have been their father. Whom she'd killed. "And what *I* want?"

"You can tell me what you want once that slaughtering parasite is out of your head." As he charged, Vree flung herself into the air. They hit the ground together with her legs wrapped around his neck, his eyes wide in disbelief. Half a dozen heartbeats later, she rose to one knee and checked to see that he was still breathing.

"That's it?" Gerek asked, peering from one to the other as though he were searching for an answer. "It's over?"

Breathing heavily, Vree stood and stared down at her brother, arms crossed tightly under her breasts. "The thing to remember when fighting an assassin," she told him bleakly, "is that you only get one chance. It's either over very quickly, or you've lost."

Gerek shook his head, still finding it hard to believe that anyone could move so quickly. "He never really thought you'd fight him."

"Yes, he did." Vree stepped back as Magda dropped to her knees by Bannon's body. "He just thought he'd win."

"You do realize that it's the next thing to *impossible*

to shut off the blood to his brain without crushing his windpipe," Magda muttered, fingertips dancing over Bannon's throat.

"The *next* thing to impossible," Vree repeated changing the emphasis. "The first four people I tried it on died instantly, the next two choked to death slowly . . ."

Gerek, who'd been reaching out to comfort her, let his hand drop slowly back to his side.

". . . the seventh survived the first attempt but not the . . ."

Vree. That's enough.

I'm cold. She reached for him, and he came. *I don't know who I am anymore.*

Most of us never do.

How do you stand it?

By holding on tightly to anything you're sure of. *Don't leave me.*

This time, Gyhard realized, she might have acknowledged the plea, but Magda stood and pressed two fingers against the back of Vree's wrist and they both fell silent.

"He won't stay unconscious for very long, you know. What do we do now?"

Gerek pushed past them and stuck his hands in Bannon's armpits. "We lock him in the shed," he grunted, dragging the smaller man backward into the building, "then we get out of here."

"He'll follow us."

"Not until someone lets him out." Gerek took one last look at Bannon's face, the pale oval just barely visible in the spill of light through the open door. He frowned, sighed, and pulled the door closed. Any questions would have to wait. "He has a plan for getting rid of Gyhard."

"What?"

What?

"Did he *tell* you that, Ger?"

"He told all of us. He said Vree could tell him what she wanted once that slaughtering parasite was out of her head."

Magda rolled her eyes. "That just means he wants Gyhard gone, not that he has a plan to get rid of him."

"No." Vree shook her head, the motion so minimal only Gyhard was sure of it. "Gerek's right. He was hiding something, and that's probably it."

"But in order to separate you and Gyhard, he'd need someone who can Sing the fifth kigh," Magda protested. "And *none* of the bards, even though they consider Gyhard an *abomination*, would risk it."

"None of the bards in Shkoder," Vree said slowly. "But now, there are bards in the Empire."

"No. Even Imperial bards wouldn't do that. You just don't understand bards."

Vree lightly caressed Bannon's throwing dagger still buried hilt deep in a log just to the right of the shed door. It was heavier than the one she'd lost; weighted for her brother's hand, not hers. "You don't understand the Empire," she said quietly.

Magda and Gerek stared at each other in silence for a long moment, a breeze stroking the hair back from their faces.

Finally, Vree turned, her expression unreadable. "Let's move. We still have to get to Kars before Karlene." Leaving Bannon's dagger where it was, she began buckling on her weapons.

"What about . . ." Gerek gestured at the shed.

"Maybe when he wakes up, he'll realize I've made my choice."

Maybe pigs'll fly, but I doubt it.

They're changing each other, Magda thought, watching Vree respond to Gyhard. She could feel the edges of their kigh, not so much overlapping as meshing, creating a new, shared area that was a part of them both. If this combining of kigh was a result of their feelings for one another—much the way echoes of her mother's kigh appeared in Stasya and Stasya's in her mother—then that was good. If, however, it was a result of their situation, then that wasn't good. But how could Vree talk about her feelings for Gyhard when he could hear every word? How could Gyhard speak of Vree? *I wish I could talk to them one at a time.*

"So how do we find Kars?" Gerek asked, shrugging the pack up onto his shoulders. "Where do we start?"

"We go east." Magda pointed along the bulk of the mountains, her finger indicating the heart of the star cluster Shkodens called the Sun's Herald. "I overheard Marija and Celestin talking. Jazep died . . ." She swallowed and tried again. "Jazep died in a mining settlement called Fortune that's due east of here."

Her night sight by far the best, Vree led the way across the graveyard, chance returning them to almost the exact place they'd been captured. At the edge of the trees, she threw aside a lifetime of training and looked back—although she had no idea of what she was looking for.

I think you do.

He's locked in a shed, Gyhard. If I couldn't get out of the slaughtering thing, neither can he.

So?

So he can't be following us yet. The festival service spilled out of the Center and filled the whole valley with song. *What are they giving thanks for now?*

He considered lying, decided against it. *Family.*

After the Blessing, the festival cakes were divided into generous portions and everyone ate. Some of them died quickly, cleanly. Some of them went into convulsions, soiling themselves as they thrashed and moaned. Ales screamed—a short shrill cry that forced Kars to clap his hands over his ears and hum to block the sound—then she ran at a wall over and over until she died in a bloody heap. Kiril had time to gather his dying daughter up into his arms. With her head lolling slack against his shoulder, he collapsed and died searching for his son.

The musty taste of decay coating the inside of his mouth, his back arched and his heels drumming the floor, Edko stared up into the dark gaze of a girl who seemed made of smoke. *If I knew who she was,* he thought, desperately trying to push death away, *I'd understand. If I knew who she was* ... The darkness in the strange girl's eyes spread. It was too heavy. He couldn't breathe. When he understood, it was too late.

"Is he dead, Kait?"

Yes.

They were all dead. He could feel their kigh filling the hall; confused, crying, wanting to return. "Soon," he told them soothingly. "Soon."

Slowly, painfully, he stood and walked past the young and the old and the very young and the very old. There were too many dead. He would not have strength enough for everyone. As he had before, he must choose those who would be part of his new family. It would not be an easy choice but it was never an easy choice. He wanted to save them all.

All but one.

Kneeling by Edko's side, Kars straightened the boy's contorted limbs and lovingly kissed the pale cheeks. "The demons cannot get you now," he murmured. "I have done for you what no one would do for me." The memory of the rod rose and fell. He hunched thin shoulders and endured.

When it was over, he straightened and smiled. They would never have the boy.

Enrik heard the Singing as he approached the stockade and moved a little faster. "At least I haven't missed the entire festival," he told the half-fledged hawk wrapped securely in his shirt and carried close against his chest. He realized his coming down out of the forest after dark would be considered both dangerous and stupid by most of his extended family, but he personally figured it was only stupid if he didn't make it. Since he had, it wasn't. No one knew the forest better than he did. He'd just proven that.

Feeling more than a little pleased with himself, he picked up his pace, his feet sure on the path between the river and the stockade. "They better have saved me a piece of festival cake, or I'm going to stick my finger down someone's throat."

Then the dogs began to howl.

The fledgling stirred in his grip and he paused. Except for the dogs—and the Song he could still hear faintly behind their howling—the night seemed ominously still. "Something's wrong." A sinuous black shape appeared suddenly out of the darkness. He cried out and leaped back as it brushed against his legs. A moment later, when his heart began beating again, he called himself several kinds of idiot as he realized it was just one of the cats.

Running *away* from the stockade?

Tucking shirt and bird both up into the broad crotch of an ancient willow, Edko ran toward the gate. The large cattle-gate was closed and barred, but when he lifted the latch on the narrow door cut into it, it opened under his hand. He stepped into the yard. The Song ended. Heavy bodies almost knocked him over as the family's dogs raced past him, flinging themselves through the open door and into the night.

He pursed his lips to whistle them back but made no sound, suddenly convinced it wouldn't be a good idea to announce his return.

In the spill of light from the hall, he could see the cattle crammed tightly against the near end of their pen. He'd seen the bull take on a mountain cat once, lowering its great shaggy head with its huge spread of horns and charging, bellowing in fury at the intruder. Until this moment, he'd thought nothing frightened them.

The Song began again. The hair lifted off the back of his neck, and although the night air was cool on his bare torso, he began to sweat. It wasn't a festival Song.

Every instinct screamed at him to run, to follow the dogs away.

Something had happened to his family.

He had to know what it was.

The Song had ended and begun again before he managed to force his protesting body across the yard. Through the slats in the shutters he could see Uncle Kiril standing with his back to the window, his daughter Anca by his side. Breathing heavily, his weight pressed against the outside wall, Enrik worked his way around to the door.

It took him four tries to grasp the latch and lift it. RUN! RUN! RUN!

The urge was so great, he half-turned. The small door was still open. The night beckoned from beyond, promising safety.

He had to know what was wrong.

Teeth clenched, blood roaring in his ears, he stepped over the threshold and into the hall.

The toes of his boots pushed into something soft and yielding.

He looked down.

His mother stared sightlessly up at him, dried blood around her mouth from where she'd chewed through her lips. The dead were scattered all over the hall. Feeling as though he were dreaming, that none of this could possibly be real, he stepped over his mother's body and walked toward the place where his uncle and his cousin stood.

The Song grew louder.

An old man crouched over the body of his brother Ondro.

It was the old man who was Singing, Enrik realized suddenly—although how such an incredible Song could come from such a frail form he had no idea. *He's older even than Grandmother.* Except that Grandmother was dead, one arm smoldering in the hearth where she'd fallen.

Ondro twitched. His hand rose to clutch at the air.

Looking for an explanation, any kind of explanation, Enrik turned to Kiril.

Both his uncle and his cousin were dead.

They were standing.

They were looking at him.

They were trying to speak.

But they were dead.

The belief he was dreaming washed away in a horror so overwhelming it had to be truth. Enrik could smell the stink of flesh burning, of bowels voided, of vomit, of death. Everyone he loved was dead in this room. He began to shake as a scream built behind his ribs, pressing against the bone that confined it.

But worst of all, somehow, the old man's Song had made Kiril and Anca dead-not-dead.

Enrik charged forward screaming as Ondro, his dead brother Ondro, opened his eyes.

Kait, lost in the Song, reacted too slowly.

The old man looked up and saw death approaching. He pulled the living kigh from the charging body, held it within the Song until it stopped wailing and Sang it back in again.

Enrik's body dropped, knees slamming into the floor. It swayed back and forth and finally fell.

Kars crawled to its side and, with an effort, managed to turn it over. The chest rose and fell. The heart continued to beat. But a dead man looked up out of the hazel eyes.

Too far gone in madness to understand the unease he felt, Kars forced himself to pat Enrik's hand and murmur, "It'll be all right. You'll see."

The kigh rose up under Annice and dropped her forward onto her knees. Hands braced against the ground, gulping in desperate lungfuls of air, she fought to free herself from an overwhelming feeling of horror.

The basic tenet of her faith promised that all things were enclosed within the Circle.

But some things were not.

"Maggi! What is it? What's wrong?" Gerek grabbed his sister by the shoulders and shook her until she looked at him. Her eyes focused and high-pitched shrieks turned to frightened whimpering. He wrapped his arms around her and pulled her against his chest. "I have you. You're safe. Tell me what's wrong."

"Something horrible," she managed, then shook her head and started to cry.

Gerek looked over at Vree, who stood ready for a fight, a dagger in her hand. They'd stopped to catch a few hours of sleep before dawn brought pursuit, and although Gerek had insisted on standing watch, Magda's terror had woken them both. "She has nightmares sometimes," he explained. "Always has, ever since she was little."

"No." Magda pushed herself out of his embrace and wiped her nose on the back of her hand. "Not a nightmare. Something'd *happened*. Something so horribly wrong it woke me."

"What?"

"I don't know." She sank back on her heels, swallowing bile, suddenly very glad her stomach was empty. "But I can find it." A deep breath, intended to steady her voice, had no noticeable effect. "And when I do, we'll find Kars."

Chapter Eleven

Eyes wide, heart pounding so loudly it nearly drowned out the sound of steel-clad wheels rolling over dressed stone, Prince Otavas stared around him in horror at the high sides of the cart and the old man who held him prisoner.

"I have lost my heart," the old man said quietly. "I only want to find it again."

"I am *not* who you think I am!" Otavas cried as he had a hundred times before. "*They* know me!" He gestured toward the dead who sat silently watching, but they looked at him with no sign of recognition on decaying faces and, all at once, the prince knew that he'd never seen these people before.

Rising, he searched among the motionless men and women for a familiar face and found only strangers.

This is wrong, he thought. *There're too many.* There had only ever been two in the cart at a time and now he pushed past row after row of the dead/undead.

When he finally struggled through to the back of the cart, he found a tall, brown-haired man dressed in rough work clothes standing at the tailgate and gazing back the way they'd come. This man, too, was a stranger but, Otavas realized with a surge of joy, he was alive. His broad chest rose and fell in a steady rhythm and a vein pulsed in his throat at the edge of a day's stubble.

"I'm so glad I'm not alone," he sighed and took hold of the other man's arm. "Sometimes I think I'm the only living person left in the world."

Slowly, jerkily, as though he were not entirely comfortable in his body, the man turned.

"No ..." Otavas tried to back up a step but was held in place by the unyielding press of bodies behind him.

"I live, but I am dead. I am dead, but I live. I live, but I am dead. I am dead, but ..."

"NO!" Dripping with sweat, Otavas jerked up in the bed and fumbled with the lamp. He turned up the wick until the flame danced over the edge of the glass chimney and the shadows withdrew far enough to be endured.

Heart pounding, the prince lay back and stared at an unfamiliar ceiling. The dream had been so real, so terrifying and the worst he'd had for weeks. It left him feeling as though the life he'd lived since his rescue was the dream and his return to terror was the reality. He could see the old man's face, feel the rumble of the cart, see the countless pairs of endlessly staring gray and filmy eyes, hear a trapped and despairing voice say, *"I live, but I am dead."*

The words resonated, echoing forlornly over and over inside his head. Every time he closed his eyes, he saw, not the dead/undead but the living/undead, and that was infinitely more horrible still. It soon became apparent when the terror refused to recede, he'd be sleeping no more that night.

With trembling fingers, he pulled on a robe and picked up the lamp. He needed air; needed to stand under the stars and know he was no longer the captive of an insane—and an insanely lonely—old man. There was a terrace off one of the corridors in the royal wing that he thought he could find his way back to.

Ashamed of the control the past still seemed to hold over him, the prince moved silently by the door to his valet's tiny chamber. Of all his household, only Bannon understood. Had Bannon been guarding his sleep, there would have been a quiet voice and a strong hand to help chase the terror away. Without Bannon, he would have to exorcise the dark memory of the old man and the cart on his own.

The halls of the Palace were deserted. No guards stood outside the heavy wooden doors of individual suites, for only the most trusted of retainers came this far into the heart of the Citadel. Safe within his small circle of light, Otavas traced a path he struggled to remember, marble floors cold beneath bare feet.

To his astonishment, the terrace door was open and, through it, he saw a slender figure bending over a pipe pointed at the sky. When the figure straightened and stepped back, Otavas recognized the profile silhouetted against the night.

"Please put out that lamp, whoever you are. I don't want my eyes to have to adjust all over again."

He understood just enough of the language to lick thumb and forefinger and quickly pinch off the end of the wick. The darkness jumped in at him and lest it show him memories he didn't want to see, he hurried out to stand by his cousin. "What are you doing out here in the middle of the night?"

Without any sign of the shyness she'd worn like armor during the three unending banquets they'd spent sitting side by side, Princess Jelena switched to Imperial and said, "Watching for falling stars. There're always a lot out toward the Broken Islands around Third Quarter Festival."

As his sight adjusted, he saw that she was bending over the eyepiece of a distance viewer—a much larger one than the sailors used and much, much larger than the collapsible leather cylinders used by the marshals of the Seven Armies. "Don't you have to be up before dawn for the sunrise part of the festival?" he wondered.

"Uh-huh."

He smiled at her preoccupied agreement. "Won't you be tired?"

"I'll stay up until after it's over. I've found it's easier that way." Apparently satisfied with what she saw, she straightened again and turned to face him. "What are *you* doing out here in the middle of the night?"

"I had ... that is ..." Something in the pale oval of her face, so nearly at a level with his own, made him think she'd understand. "I had a nightmare about ... about what happened and I couldn't sleep."

"About the kidnapping?"

Otavas nodded and waited for her to tell him that he had to forget about it.

Her hand closed cool around his wrist—he could feel the sympathy in the touch—and after a moment, she tugged him forward. "Would you like to look through my starviewer?"

The sky held more stars than he'd ever suspected, and he backed away a little overwhelmed.

"I know." Jelena nodded. "It was like that for me at first, too."

"How did you get interested in ..." Mere words didn't seem enough. Otavas waved a hand at the night.

She shrugged. "When I was younger . . ."

His grin flashed white. "Younger?"

"I'm fourteen, almost fifteen. And you needn't sound so superior, Your Imperial Highness who's barely three years older." But she smiled back at him before continuing. "When I was younger, I was afraid of the dark—I had to sleep with a lantern lit and everything. It was so bad that they even had me checked out by healers, and everyone started worrying that I'd never outgrow it."

"But you did."

"When I was ten, Jazep went to my grandfather and asked if he could try. His Majesty agreed and Jazep started teaching me about how the night is more than an absence of light. He taught me about the animals that live in it. About the flowers that bloom in it. And he showed me the stars. I haven't been afraid since."

"Jazep?"

She drew in a long breath and slowly let it out. "He was a bard."

Now Otavas knew why the name sounded so familiar. "The one who died?" When she nodded, he was surprised to feel a sense of loss, even though he'd never met the man. "He sounds like he was a really nice person."

"He was. He told me, well, he sang me a song, about falling stars being the lamps that light the way for babies being born." After a moment, she sighed and tossed her head, the dreamy tone—suitable for fables—gone from her voice. "There's a scroll in the Bardic Library from a stargazer in the south, the Sixth Province of your Empire, I think, and he says that the stars are suns, like ours and that the world isn't flat, it's round."

"That's ridiculous."

"Maybe. I had the bards ask the kigh. Air and fire and water seemed to think it was a stupid question and wouldn't answer. Earth said, *The world is.*" Thumbs tucked behind her belt, she rocked back on her heels and stared out toward the harbor. "When I'm Queen, I'm going to send ships out into the ocean as far west as they can go and see if they end up in the east again."

Otavas tended to agree with the kigh. It was the stupidest thing he'd ever heard—but somehow, it didn't seem so stupid when Jelena said it. "When you are Queen," he murmured, wondering where his tongue-tied little cousin had gone.

A wind, smelling of the sea, whipped around the edge of the terrace and he shivered.

"Well, no wonder you're cold," Jelena declared, tugging at the billowing sleeve of his robe. "Look at all you're wearing. You'd better go in before you freeze."

That, he wholeheartedly agreed with.

"Tavas."

He paused, one hand on the terrace door, and turned.

"If the night gets too dark, and the dreams come back, remember the stars."

The Emperor had been wrong. Lying back on the pallet, mapping the graduations of dark on dark within the confines of a prison he couldn't escape, Bannon turned that truth over and over in his mind. The Emperor had been wrong; Gyhard was not controlling Vree. He'd fought beside Vree for too many years not to know when he was fighting against her.

He swallowed and winced, his throat painfully bruised. He'd tried to believe in her. He'd given her the benefit of every doubt. All he wanted was for her to be a part of his life again. Was that so terrible?

"It isn't you who left me, it's him."

"I chose."

This was the second time she'd chosen Gyhard.

The Emperor wanted Gyhard back in the Empire to pay for his treason. The Emperor had bards who could rip the parasite right out of Vree's head.

Then *she'd* know what it was like to be alone.

Make the most of the night, Vree. When they let me out, I will *be after you and the next time, you'll get no warning.*

"Magda? Are you awake?" When there was no answer, Celestin sighed deeply and unbolted the spare room door. The child had sulked her way through both festival services and that, as far as the priest was concerned, was quite enough of that. Dark and disturbing dreams had interrupted what little sleep she'd had, and she was in no mood to continue excusing teenage extremes. "Magda, we have to talk. I brought you some festival ca ... Oh, my."

She stared from the crude rope braided out of torn bedsheets to the dormer window she could've sworn was too small for even someone Magda's size to climb out. *Except*, she realized, *if she went out the window, there wouldn't still be a pile of ruined sheets lying in the middle of the room.*

"Oh, my." She said it again because there didn't seem to be much else to say.

Vree's weapons were missing from their place in the kitchen.

A pack and journey food had been taken from the storeroom.

Gerek had not slept on the pallet she'd had made up for him. His kit was gone, but Bannon's was still in the stable where he'd left it.

All four horses were still in the corral.

"I don't believe this is happening," she muttered as a black gelding lipped at her hair.

"Then don't stand so close to the fence," Marija advised, coming around the corner of the building, a half-eaten apple in one hand, her instrument case in the other.

Celestin stared at the bard in complete confusion. "What are you talking about?"

"The horse eating your hair. Why, what were you talking about?"

All things being enclosed, Celestin figured there was one more thing she had to know before she jumped to any conclusions. "I think you should send a kigh to find out who's locked in that shed."

A few moments later, an urgent message sped toward Elbasan.

The kigh found Liene resting on a bench set into the curved stone wall of the Center. She hadn't slept well. Dragging old bones out of bed for the sunrise service had left her feeling her age, and all she wanted to do for the next few moments was sit and listen to the cheerful babble of voices as those of the Bardic Hall, the Healers' Hall, and the palace who'd remained in the Citadel for the Third Quarter Festival milled about in the courtyard, chatting happily.

His Majesty stood joking with his treasurer about how the realm would soon have to strike new gold coins whether he dropped dead or not. "After twenty-seven years," he laughed, "the old ones are wearing out." It was obvious that both Her Majesty on his right and Healer Jonakus on his left, thought the humor in bad taste. Liene frowned and tried to remember the treasurer's name. She could remember his mother—Denyse i'Janina a'Albinek; a great body, a brilliant grasp of economics, and a tendency to giggle in bed—but the son, even though he was standing right in front of her, she couldn't recall.

I hate getting old, she grumbled to herself, tucking her hands into the wide sleeves of her quartered robe.

Her Highness, Princess Jelena, and her cousin, His Imperial Highness Prince Otavas were having what appeared to be a spirited argument off to one side of the semicircular yard. Watching with a critical eye, Liene wondered how the boy had gotten past Jelena's shyness. She seemed unusually animated. *Well, he's a good-looking lad. I suppose there's always the obvious reason.*

Its pointed features twisted in pique, the kigh stuck a long finger in Liene's ear to get her attention.

"Not my problem ..." she grumbled when she finally worked out just what it was trying to tell her. Weight on her cane, she rose and Sang a gratitude before calling for Kovar.

"To be honest, I'm not surprised that His Grace went over to the other side, as it were. Magda's always been able to wrap her brother around her little finger, and he's infatuated with Vree."

Liene watched Kovar pace the length of the office and back again before she said mildly. "*Why* Gerek suddenly decided to join forces with Magda and Vree isn't the immediate problem. Marija needs to know what to do with Bannon. Should she keep him in Bartek Springs? Should she stop him from following?"

"Could she stop him from following?" Then he answered his own question. "Of course she could, he's only got one kigh." Still pacing, he dragged at the ends of his mustache, realized what he was doing, and held out waxy fingers to Liene. "You're enjoying this, aren't you?"

"You bet. You became Bardic Captain at midnight and this is your problem. I'm retired."

"So you're not going to get involved?"

The old bard grinned at him. "Don't be ridiculous." The grin faded when she saw Kovar's expression suddenly change. "Look, you're conducting, I just thought I'd . . ."

He raised a hand and cut her off. "What if Gerek didn't decide to join forces with Magda and Vree? What if Gyhard jumped to Gerek's body?"

"No. Vree would have had to push him."

"We only have Gyhard's word for that." His lip curled. "We only have Gyhard's word for a lot of things."

"True," Liene acknowledged, "but then you're forgetting Magda. She'd never allow it!"

"Could she stop it? Would she even know it was happening before it was over?" Kovar sat on the edge of the desk, brows drawn in as he worked out possibilities. "Or maybe that's why they're going to meet up with Kars. We've been assuming Magda can Sing Gyhard into another body—how much do you want to bet Kars can? And he won't have her scruples."

"Now, you're forgetting Vree."

"Vree is afraid of Gyhard." Kovar remembered that

first evening in the Bardic Hall—the rage that had belonged to a second intelligence flashing for a heartbeat in Vree's eyes, the fear he'd felt rolling off her like smoke. "I've seen it."

"I haven't," Liene snapped, then her face fell as she remembered her trouble with the treasurer's name. "I suppose I might not have noticed. No." She reconsidered. "You're wrong about that. She's not afraid of him although I'll grant you she may be afraid of what she feels *for* him."

"We don't have enough information."

"We could believe the story Magda told Marija; that Gyhard needs to put his past to rest before he can build a future."

Kovar snorted. "Magda is a romantic child."

"Magda is a healer of the fifth kigh."

"That doesn't matter. None of this matters." The new Bardic Captain began pacing again. "We have to allow Bannon to go after them. People are dying out there at the hands of a crazed Cemandian bard and it's our responsibility ..." He thumped both fists against his chest. "... to put a stop to it. Vree and Gyhard can't be allowed to interfere with Karlene stopping this maniac."

"And if Magda's right?"

"If Magda's right," Kovar repeated sharply, then he stopped and sighed. "It doesn't matter if Magda's right. As much as I dislike Gyhard, I like Vree, and I wish we could give her a happy ending. However, a happy ending for one person cannot outweigh the deaths of countless others. In the final chorus, we can't trust Gyhard. By his own admission, he is responsible for what Kars has become. We can't allow them to get together again. As long as Gyhard remains in

Vree's body, Bannon is still the only chance we have of stopping her."

"You don't trust Bannon either," Liene reminded him. Both hands folded over the top of her cane, she leaned forward. "So your answer to Marija?"

"My answer to Marija . . ." The new Bardic Captain stood in the open window and watched a pair of kigh chase each other around a snapping pennant on the gatehouse tower. He frowned. "We're just whistling into the wind, you know. Kars is a bardic problem; stretching a point, Vree and Gyhard may be a bardic problem as well, but the other three are not. We have no right to stop Bannon from following anyone he chooses. He's broken no laws. We're not at war with the Empire."

"Her Royal Highness did make it clear that she wanted Magda back in Elbasan and she didn't want an unstable assassin roaming about the country."

Chin up and eyes flashing, Kovar spun around to face Liene. "The bards have not become the royal police force!" When he saw her expression, his brows drew in. "That was where you wanted me to arrive, wasn't it? Why didn't you just come right out and say so?"

The old Bardic Captain smiled up at the new. "Because now, you'll remember it."

"You're an obnoxious old woman; you know that?"

Her smile broadened. "I revel in it."

Watching Bannon quickly and efficiently stow supplies into a borrowed pack, Celestin debated with herself about offering to help. Not with his packing, he'd obviously done that countless times before, but with the other burden he carried. She didn't need to be able to read his kigh in order to feel the anger coming off him in waves, anger that went back beyond a night spent locked in a shed. This was a young man used to getting his own way and, in spite of evidence to the contrary, he seemed determined to continue.

Well aware that the young were often both angry and self-indulgent, the priest was equally aware that time was the only sure solution. Sooner or later, most discovered that they weren't the center of the Circle. On the other hand, most young people weren't angry, self-indulgent assassins.

On yet another hand, she'd seen his face when Marija—apologizing for the delay as profusely as possible with her limited Imperial vocabulary—had let him out of the shed. She could have sworn that, just for an instant, he'd hoped to see someone else and when he hadn't, he'd first looked hurt and then derisive and then there had only been a superficially charming young man, apparently more than willing to forgive.

Finally, she could stand it no longer. "Bannon?"

He turned and smiled. In a foreign land where he barely spoke the language, pleasantry was a crucial tool.

Now that she had his attention, she wasn't sure of how to begin. "Where do you go from here?"

A little surprised by a question with such an obvious answer, Bannon shrugged. "I get my sister."

"Why?"

His expression hardened. "Told to."

Celestin shook her head and laid a hand gently on his chest. "Why in here?"

Bannon met her gaze and was totally astonished to see that she seemed to really care. All at once, he was reminded of how Vree had held his face in both hands after his first target and asked him if he was all right. About to crow that the target had never touched him, he'd realized that she didn't want to know if his body had been wounded, she wanted to know how he felt. He'd turned in time to see them drag the body from the practice yard and discovered he felt nothing at all. When he'd told her, she'd nodded, like it was the answer he was supposed to give, but he'd thought, just for a moment, he saw sadness behind the patina of her training. He'd been twelve; Vree was thirteen.

But that Vree, his Vree, was gone.

For an instant, Celestin was reminded of how Dymek had looked when they'd told him Filip was dead. Confused and lost and unable to believe how such a horrible thing could have happened.

Then the instant passed. Bannon picked up a small sack of dried apples and stared down at it, as though searching it for answers. Finally, he looked up. He wasn't sure why it was important he make this woman understand; maybe because he thought she *could* understand. "Without Vree, like lost arm or leg."

"Without her you feel crippled?" When he nodded, Celestin spread her arms, her posture as nonthreatening as thirty years in the priesthood could make it. "But is it like losing an arm or leg or like losing a crutch?"

"Crutch?"

She mimed walking with a crutch then straightened as the assassin jerked toward her.

"It isn't like that!" Both hands curled into fists, Bannon shouted his protest in Imperial, using volume to replace the Shkoden words he didn't have. "She doesn't hold me up! She never held me up! We were partners, a team! The best slaughtering blades Jiir ever had! All I wanted was my body back and she betrayed me! First she saved the life of the man who tried to kill me and then she walked away. I'd leave her to rot in this slaughtering country if the Emperor didn't want her! I don't want her! He does! I don't care!" As the last word slapped against the walls of the small room, Bannon was horrified to find his eyes were wet. No one had ever looked at him with such sympathy before. He swallowed three or four times in quick succession and used the pain to find himself again.

Although she hadn't understood the words, the priest recognized the reaction. "It's frightening being alone, isn't it?"

"Alone?" The bark of laughter tore at the bruising on his throat. "His Imperial Highness Prince Otavas *need* me!"

"Good. I'm glad."

Her smile offered comfort. Terrified he might take it, Bannon grabbed up the pack and ran out the door.

"Ger, I'm fine. Honest." Pushing her hair back off her face with one hand, Magda shoved her brother away with the other. "I'm a healer, *remember?* If there was anything wrong with me, I'd know."

"You're shaking."

"I'm cold."

"It's a beautiful day."

She narrowed her eyes. "I didn't say it wasn't. If you want to do something *useful,* give me your sweater and stop fussing."

Gerek recognized her expression; she'd borrowed it from her mother and years of experience had taught him not to bother arguing. Yanking the sweater up over his head, he silently handed it to her.

"Thank you." Pulling it on, she spent a moment rolling up the cuffs, then sighed deeply and stood. Her calves ached from all the climbing, she had scratches all over both hands from pushing through prickly ash, and a low-hanging branch had left a painful welt across one cheek. "All right, let's get going."

Because he knew what Magda would say, Gerek looked to Vree.

Vree shook her head. "Karlene was closer than we were when she started, and Bannon won't have rested."

"Maggi . . ."

"Is a healer. She knows when she's ready to go on."

"She's leaving," Magda called as she reached the edge of the clearing. "And she wants to know if you two are coming?"

Gerek glared at Vree and jerked his head in the direction of his sister.

Vree moved to take up position just behind the younger woman's left shoulder. She didn't much like being between Magda and her brother, but as a marching order it made sense. Gerek could see over and around her; with their positions reversed, he was just too slaughtering big.

I don't think he loves you anymore.

Don't be an ass, Gyhard, he never did. He's a romantic. Probably falls in love every time he wants to get laid.

How exhausting for him.

Rolling her eyes, Vree reached ahead and lifted a low-hanging branch out of Magda's way. "Can you still feel the way we have to go?" she asked rubbing

at the sticky sap smeared over the scar on the back
of her hand.

Magda turned enough to show Vree a melancholy
smile. "I think I'll always be able to feel it. It's like
when someone's sick—not injured, but sick—and a
healer can *feel* the wrongness. I can feel the wrongness
in the world." She stumbled and would have fallen if
Vree hadn't grabbed her elbow. "Sorry. I guess I have
to pay more attention to where I put my feet."

"That's it, Maggi." Gerek's tone suggested he not
be argued with. "Back to the clearing. You need a
longer rest."

The two women exchanged a speaking glance.

"Don't get your bowstring in a knot, Ger," Magda
advised, starting up the tumbled end of a rocky ridge.
"I *need* to find this wrong and heal it. I *don't* need
to rest."

Bannon dropped to one knee and studied the pattern in the clearing. He'd found where they'd slept
and now he'd found where they'd rested. Shaking his
head, he straightened and moved cautiously after
them. *This pace must be driving Vree crazy.*

He caught up on the top of the ridge and froze as
Vree motioned for her companions to be quiet. They
weren't very good at it, he noted smugly; neither of
them seemed to have any idea of how to stand absolutely still. While Vree might have heard something—
he hadn't been moving as noiselessly as he could because he hadn't realized he was so slaughtering
close—he'd make sure that she wouldn't hear anything else.

Predator patient, he waited. Once, his sister might

have been able to outwait him, but that was no longer her decision to make.

"It was probably just a pinecone falling. Let's get moving."

His Grace was not a patient man. Bannon appreciated that. He let them gain some distance, then followed, watching for his chance. In the Empire, an assassin on target could kill anyone who got in the way. Two things kept him from sending a dagger into Vree's companions. The first; he was not, at present, in the Empire. The second; a good assassin seldom admitted that anyone was *in* the way. A good assassin took out the target regardless and Bannon had been the best.

One of the best, he corrected. The third reason, was that he had no intention of warning Vree he was coming. She'd beaten him once; he wouldn't let that happen again. They were going to pay for their treason— Gyhard for his against the Empire, Vree for hers against him.

"This is it," Magda declared, nodding at the river that cut through the bottom of the defile. "The river will take us right to Kars."

Gerek stepped forward, shrugging out of the pack as he moved. "Are you sure?"

Magda turned to face upstream and shivered. She could almost see the wrongness lying like a dark blot on the mountains. "I'm sure."

"Well, if we're going to follow the river, we'll have to find another place to climb down." Arm braced against his thighs, he leaned forward. "This is too loose and too steep." When he shifted his weight, a clump of dirt broke off the edge and bounced down toward the water, picking up other clumps and rocks as it went. "Maggi, step back. This whole thing's just looking for an excuse to give way."

With her eyes still locked on the evil in the distance, Gerek's voice seemed to come from very far away. Clutching her elbows, taking comfort in the familiar wool under her palms, she pivoted on her left foot until she faced him. "What did you sa . . ."

The last word became a scream.

Gerek grabbed for her, missed, and threw himself after her.

Feeling the ground roll out from under her feet, Vree leaped back.

What are you doing? Gyhard demanded.

He's going to bring the rest of that slaughtering face down on top of her. I follow, I bury them both!

We can't just stand here!

Oh, yes we can. Someone has to be standing when this is over to dig them out!

Bannon heard the scream, slid out of his pack and raced ahead. He arrived just in time to see Gerek disappear over the edge. Without slowing, he flicked a dagger down into his right hand.

Tumbling end over end, pushed along by the fall of earth and rock, Magda scrunched her eyes shut, closing out the terrifying kaleidoscope of images. Things were happening too fast for conscious thought. Her head bounced off the ground, a rock bounced off her shoulder, her arms and legs flailed about, sometimes moving with her, sometimes moving with the hill, and sometimes it seemed they were moving completely on their own.

She could hear Gerek shouting, but the roar of blood in her ears mixed with the grinding roar of the earth and drowned everything else out.

Then it was over.

Her arms slapped down on a gravel beach, her face smacked into her arms, a few final rocks slammed into her back. Half the hillside seemed to have landed on her lower body, pinning her left leg at a painful angle.

Blinking stupidly, she lifted her head and stared at the pattern a breeze was lifting the river into right under her nose. "Mama?"

Riding the crest of the fall, arms windmilling, weight back on his heels, Gerek fought to stay upright. Then an eddy sucked his right foot under. He started to fall forward.

"NO!"

He twisted, rolled, and somehow ended up on his back, head pointing downhill, one leg buried, one leg kicking futilely at the air. He felt his sword rip free, one boot tear off, and got one arm up at the last possible instant to deflect a rock big enough to do serious damage away from his head.

His first indication that he'd reached the river came when his shoulders slid into something cold and wet, his neck whipped back, and the water covered his face. Coughing and choking he jerked forward, only to have the weight of the fallen hill push him back.

The kigh were beginning to grow nervous. Karlene picked a careful path to the river's edge and glanced upstream. Although they'd still answer her Songs, this was as far upriver as they'd go. It seemed, therefore, that upriver was the direction she had to travel.

As it wasn't specifically Kars that frightened them but the trapping of the fifth kigh to create the dead/undead, he must have found more of the living to destroy. There were small two- and three-family settlements all through these mountains; sometimes they grew into villages, sometimes the resource that created them played out and they were abandoned. The last recall Karlene had heard on this area was three years old, but she seemed to remember a timber-holding, a valley, and a river.

"There's no way around it," she sighed, disgusted with her inability to remember more detail. "I'm going to have to drop into trance."

Slipping her arms out of her pack straps, she leaned backward, letting it drop a handbreadth onto a waist-high, flat-topped boulder, then she squatted, flexing the stiffness out of her shoulders, and dipped a cupped hand into the water for a drink. Even one day into Third Quarter, the river held the memory of ice that had been and the promise of ice to come. A half-formed plan for a quick bath fled shivering. She sucked the cold water off her palm and bent to scoop out another handful.

A water kigh wrapped itself around her wrist. When she tried to free herself, it refused to let go. Behind it, two others spun about so frantically they created a half-dozen tiny whirlpools. At first, she thought they were warning her about Kars—the air kigh had been trying to get her to turn all day—but then she realized that Kars had nothing to do with their message: *Two children in the water. Hurry! Hurry!*

Karlene Sang understanding and wasted a moment or two convincing the three kigh to go back downstream and push the children out of the water if they could. Racing along the bank, splashing through the shallows, she wondered where a pair of children had come from and why the kigh had made that specific distinction. Usually, they referred to all non-kigh as flesh. Stumbling over a half-submerged branch, she decided it didn't matter. Had she not been available to take care of things, the water kigh would probably have avoided the area until the current swept the bodies away and then complained bitterly about it to the next bard who could Sing their quarter. It seldom occurred to them to attempt a rescue by themselves.

Scrambling across the neck of a rocky outcrop, hoping she wouldn't break an ankle, Karlene got her first glimpse of the raw gash on the side of the defile through a break in the heavy cedar. All at once, it became obvious how the children—whoever they were—had ended up in the water. She could hear them struggling, which made her hope they weren't badly hurt.

It was strange they weren't crying.

And then she saw the body at the water's edge. With no breath to spare for questions, Karlene covered the remaining distance faster then should have been possible.

A dark-haired man lay on his back, torso buried in such a way that his head and shoulders were pressed down into the river. A roll of water beneath him indicated that the kigh were attempting to do what she asked, but as he kept fighting them, struggling wildly to get free, they were doing little more than merely raising the water level.

Singing them away, Karlene waded out into the river.

Center it, there're two of them! The girl had been hidden behind the mound of earth and rock that had nearly buried her companion, but, as only her legs were buried and she'd landed short of the water, she could wait.

Ducking under a flailing arm, Karlene grabbed the young man's head, anchoring one hand in a short curly beard, and locked her eyes on his. **"Be still!"** she Commanded.

He went limp so quickly, she almost lost her grip. Without terror contorting his face, she discovered that he wasn't very old. A quick look showed that the girl was younger still.

Well, I suppose they're someone's children, she allowed silently.

Shuffling around behind him, she gritted her teeth against the cold, dropped to her knees, and let his upper body rest against hers. With the immediate possibility of his drowning averted, she took a deep breath and reviewed the situation.

Had she been able to Sing earth, it would've been a simple matter to free them; to free them both. As she didn't, and as she didn't really have a lot of time to waste before she lost all feeling in her legs, the solution would have to be more creative. Keeping her voice low and calming, she murmured, "I'm going to have the river wash enough of the dirt off you so that I can pull you out. Please, don't be afraid, and don't move."

"My sister's . . . downstream."

"She'll be all right."

His lack of reaction seemed to indicate that he'd

dealt with bards before. Or that he was in shock. In this part of the country, the latter seemed more likely.

Her breathing deepening as she found her focus, Karlene shifted about just enough to see upstream, opened her mouth, and Sang. Gabris had often told her that she Sang the strongest water he'd ever seen. Time to prove it.

The water began to pull away from the far shore until a wave, three feet wide and four high, rolled toward them. Just before it reached her, it lifted and slammed, not into the young man's body but an inch higher, lifting the earth off him. Brown and muddy, it followed the Song back into the riverbed to avoid the girl.

When the wave ran clear, Karlene Sang a gratitude. The last kigh arced even higher into the air, twisted through itself, and sprayed them both. An instant after that, the river flowed as it always had.

The young man brushed at the remaining inch of earth on his torso with shaking hands. "Okay," he said. "I'm impressed."

A little shaky herself, Karlene shoved her hands into his armpits and pulled. "Frankly, so am I."

Protected by a thick sheath of muscle, he'd taken no real damage from his fall and it only took the two of them a few moments of silent struggle to free his legs, both of them realizing the girl had probably not been so lucky, neither wanting to be the one to say it.

The moment he could move, he scrambled over the remaining scree to the girl's side.

"Maggi? Magda? Are you okay? Are you hurt?"

Half out of the water, her teeth chattering and her toes numb, Karlene paused. Magda? The young man *had* looked vaguely familiar. "Your Grace?"

Gerek didn't bother turning. "Help me with her!"

Karlene had an uneasy suspicion she knew the only possible reason for Annice's daughter to be traveling so far from home. If Magda actually Healed the fifth kigh as the Imperial fledglings insisted, then she could only be out here looking for Kars.

When your mother finds out about this, she thought dropping to her knees and helping the heir of Ohrid scoop away dirt and gravel, *she's not going to be happy.*

Then she called herself several kinds of idiot. Annice had to know where Magda was—there could be no other explanation for the kigh telling her that *the children* were in the water.

"Ger, my knee hurts."

"I'm not surprised." He ran his hands gently over the joint before straightening it. "Is that better?"

"Little."

"Can you turn over and sit up if I bring your legs around?"

"I guess." She sniffed, wiped her nose on the back of her hand and tried to do as he asked. The world shifted and she clutched his arm. "Ger!"

"It's okay, Maggi, I've got you."

Leaning against his shoulder, she turned to where she thought Vree should be and the lines of pain were replaced by confusion. "Who are you?"

"Karlene." The bard sat back on her heels. "I was having a drink upstream. The kigh told me there was someone in the water." It didn't seem politic to mention to a grown man, and a nearly grown woman, that their mother was looking out for them—even if in this instance it had saved their lives.

Magda frowned and looked up at her brother. "Where's Vree?"

"Vree?" Karlene repeated, not entirely surprised. *I guess I was right about what they're doing here. Annice is really not going to be happy about this.*

Gerek forced his thoughts back before the water, before the fall. "She was right behind me."

As one, all three turned and looked up the slope. Gerek's boot-top protruded from the dirt about half-way up, but there was no sign of Vree.

Magda squirmed free of Gerek's grasp. "Vree! Vree!" She threw herself forward and collapsed in a slide of loose gravel.

"Maggie, stop it! Karlene's a bard! There's an easier way!" He pulled her back into his arms and turned to face the other woman. "You do Sing more than just water, don't you?"

"I Sing three quarters, but I don't Sing earth."

"So we can't find her!" Magda wailed.

"We can find out if she's under there at least." The air kigh were skittish and not inclined to help, but after a moment, Karlene managed to send one to the top of the cliff with Vree's description. It was gone longer than she expected and she could see by the growing fear on Magda's and Gerek's faces that they believed Vree had been lost in the collapse of the bank.

When the kigh returned a moment later, she had to Sing a question at it twice before she believed the news it brought.

"Vree's alive," she said at last, after Singing the indignant kigh a gratitude. "But Bannon has her."

* * *

The last time Vree had found herself bound, she'd opened her eyes to see Bannon studying her—or rather, Gyhard in Bannon's body. This time, she couldn't open her eyes as they were bound as securely as her hands and feet. This time, the rope tied wrists to knees to ankles and she was sitting in leaf litter, leaning against the trunk of a tree. This time, Gyhard and Bannon's positions were reversed.

Vree? Are you all right?

His voice drove multiple spikes of pain up through the crown of her head. *Why ask me? You're in here, too.*

I don't think he broke anything, Gyhard allowed after a moment.

Of course not. He's a professional.

He's a professional killer, Vree. That doesn't give me much faith in his ability to take us alive.

Imperial assassins try to kill only the target. It makes the Empire look bad if you leave a trail of bodies getting in and getting out.

So, where is he?

About six inches away from my right knee.

For the sake of their head, he toned down his exclamation of surprise. *How can you tell that!*

The air patterns tell me something's there, and my nose tells me who.

All I can smell are trees.

We bathe more often in the Empire than they do here.

"I know you're awake, Vree. You can stop pretending." He sounded nervous and triumphant both, as though he'd beaten her at a game but wasn't entirely positive the game was over.

She turned her head to stare directly at him, although he'd know she couldn't see anything through the cloth tied around her eyes. "Why the blindfold?"

"A precaution in case the carrion eater decides he wants to be back in my body again."

I'd make better use of it, Gyhard snarled.

Vree tested the strength of the rope, felt the knots tighten, and forced herself to relax. "He can't jump unless I push him."

"And I'm supposed to believe you won't?" Bannon snorted. "I had the same training you did, Vree. Survive at all costs."

"No." She fought her way through the memory of Commander Neegan dying on her blade. "Not at all costs."

"He's changed you."

"I've changed."

She heard him stand, felt his shadow cross her body. "It's the same thing!"

His tone suggested there was no point in arguing. It was a tone Vree had heard frequently in the past. "Now what happens?"

"Now . . ." A branch snapped, silencing the background birdsong. "Now, we go back to the Empire."

By twisting her right wrist as much as possible, the upper buckle on her wrist sheath rubbed against the rope.

Given ten or fifteen days, you could probably cut us free.

Do you have a better idea? Vree snapped, struggling to remain outwardly serene, to give Bannon no weakness to exploit. "I thought you were taking us back to Elbasan?"

Another branch snapped. "Only on the way to the

Empire. And Elbasan's a little out of the way when you consider how close we are to the border."

"You're going to take me across the border like this?" She could think of a number of alternatives, none of which she liked.

"No." He bent down and his breath lapped warm against her cheek. "I'm going to take my poor sick sister home on a travois." One hand lightly cupped her chin and turned her face toward him. "There's some pretty toxic fungus around here; I think they'll believe it."

She relaxed into his grip, softening her posture, drawing in a deep breath through a slightly opened mouth.

Bannon exhaled sharply and then backed away. "Forget it. You had your chance."

Vree! Gyhard jerked her chin up. *What are you doing!*

Trying to get him close enough to smack him in the face with my forehead.

Oh. She felt him release control. *Would that have worked?*

Probably not.

You're awfully calm!

I used to be an Imperial assassin.

Most Imperial assassins don't survive very long!

Muscles tensing and untensing, she worked the knots. *But they always believe they will.*

Vree . . .

Would you shut up! You're not helping! It was only a small crack and she hastily patched it over. Imperial assassins never left the Seven Armies. It was hard not to believe she'd have to answer for that.

"What happens when we get back to the Empire, Bannon?"

"The carrion eater pays for his treason."

Imperial bards were still bards, but as she'd pointed out to Gerek and Magda, the Empire wasn't Shkoder. "And what happens to me?"

"The Emperor's willing to blame it all on Gyhard. You made your *choice,* Vree." Thrown back at her, the words hit her like a blow. Finally forced to acknowledge that choice, he was clearly going to make her pay. "You'll have to live with it."

Without Gyhard. Alone.

"I can't believe you told His Imperial Majesty about Gyhard."

He hesitated for an instant before answering and when he finally spoke, his tone was as much petulant as it was sarcastic. "Funny, I couldn't believe you saved the carrion eater's life."

"What about your treason, Bannon? What about your willingness to give Gyhard the prince in order to get your body back."

"Only you and I know about that. And I'm certainly not going to tell."

The implication was clear. "You think I won't?"

He leaned close again. His voice, although he'd obviously intended it to sound gloating, sounded a little sad. "I know you won't."

He's right, isn't he?

It wouldn't save you.

And if it would?

That's a really shitty question!

Gyhard fought to stay close as her anger tried to slam him away. *I'm sorry.*

You slaughtering well should be!

Bannon slipped his hands under her arms and quickly flipped her over twice, face down then face up, the motion too fast for her to take advantage of. The crosspieces of the travois pressed into her back. He was really going to do it. "Why, Bannon?" she asked.

At first she thought he wasn't going to answer.

"There was a hole in my life where you used to be. I wanted you back to fill it."

"Why didn't you fill it with something else?"

"Like you did?" he snarled. "Sorry, there weren't enough parasitic carrion eaters to go around."

"And when you woke up in the shed and you knew it wouldn't happen?"

"Oh, then I thought of something to fill the hole. An Imperial command. Remember duty, Vree? And honor? Oh, no. I forgot. You gave that up for the carrion eater, too."

She spat in his face. When the return blow came, she rolled with it, curled around the ropes and kicked him in the back of the thigh with both heels. He pitched forward and she threw her body up to meet his.

The back of her head slammed into his cheek and it was over a moment later.

"You're going to pay for that," he growled. "You're going to ... to ..."

Her own head ringing, it wasn't at all hard to believe she'd hit him hard enough to scramble his thoughts.

No. Listen.

All I hear are trees and leaves. She heard Bannon stand, heard him shuffle around making no effort to hide the noise his boots made in the carpet of dried leaves. A sound stroked the edge of her hearing, too indistinct to identify.

Incredibly, she heard Bannon walk away, his footsteps hesitant as though he went reluctantly.

Then the sound of his footsteps stopped and a familiar voice said, **"Albannon Magaly, do not move until I release you."**

Chapter Twelve

"Does anyone else think that dragging him along with us is a really stupid idea, or is it just me?"

Sitting by the fire with a wet tunic of Karlene's wrapped around her knee to keep the swelling down, Magda scooped up a pebble and threw it at her brother. It had been a long day—healers were unable to Heal themselves—and she didn't need him making it a long night. "What do you *suggest* we do, Ger? Leave him tied to a tree and come back for him when we've settled things with Kars? Or should I say come back to what's left of him. There are wolves around here, you know. And bears."

Gerek glared at her, past Bannon's blindfolded, bound, and hobbled figure. "At least being eaten by bears would have some dignity!" He turned on Karlene. "Look, if holding him captive is as temporary a solution as you say it is, why can't you keep him under Command?"

"Because it isn't good for him."

"And this is?"

"He could still kill you, Your Grace." The bard waved a hand at Bannon's semi-prone body—only the slow rise and fall of his chest, barely visible in the light from the leaping flames, indicated he was alive. "Even like that."

"Yeah, except he doesn't want to kill me. As far as I can tell, he doesn't want to kill anyone." Gerek pulled his sword, swung around, and viciously beheaded a small evergreen. Vree and Bannon both turned their heads to follow the swing of the blade although Bannon couldn't actually see it. "Kidnapping, yes. Murder, no."

When the weapon remained unsheathed, Karlene moved prudently to the other side of the firepit. "You're forgetting, Your Grace, that Bannon is an Imperial assassin."

"No, he isn't." The point of the sword rose until it was on a level with Bannon's heart. "He's the personal bodyguard of His Imperial Highness, Prince Otavas. He's no more an assassin than Vree is!"

The only sounds were the crackle of the flames, the lapping of the river against the shore, and a breeze pushing through the tops of the trees.

Finally, Magda shook her head. "Bullshit," she said succinctly.

"Maggi!"

At Gerek's outraged tone, Vree found herself looking toward Bannon to share the joke—except he couldn't see her.

"We may all be what the past has made us," Magda declared, ignoring her brother, "but we are just as much what we've made of the past. Vree made a choice, a conscious decision to break with her training. Bannon hasn't. By taking over his body, Gyhard forced him away from the army. By saving Gyhard, Vree forced him away from her, by giving him an order, the Emperor forced him into this confrontation. I'll bet he never chose to tell the Emperor that Gyhard was alive, it just spilled out one day."

"Maggi . . ."

This time, she jabbed a finger toward him, the light in her eyes not entirely a reflection of the fire. "And stop saying *Maggi* in that obnoxious tone, like you're trying to sound like Father. I hate it when you do that. I've spent the last two years learning to Heal, Gerek, and I know what I'm talking about. This isn't going to end until Bannon *actually* makes a choice!"

"I think you're both forgetting that Bannon isn't *actually* the problem," Karlene said softly, poking at the fire with a stick. "Kars is. And since I can't get rid of you . . ." She swept a resigned gaze around the circle of light. ". . . any of you, and since we're probably all going to have to cope with a great deal of very unpleasant death tomorrow, I suggest we get some sleep. So that we don't inadvertently cut off Bannon's circulation, I'm going to lullaby him and untie him for the night." A raised hand cut off Gerek's protest. "First of all, Singing him to sleep is nothing like keeping him under Command and secondly, if you don't trust me, Your Grace, stick your fingers in your ears."

He sheathed his sword, sank cross-legged to the ground, and did exactly that.

Karlene continued the Song for a few minutes after Bannon sagged against his bonds and then let it trail off. "He'll sleep until I wake him," she said easing him into a more comfortable position and loosening the ropes. Her gaze met Vree's and held it while Magda and Gerek settled down for the night. She wanted to say something, but had no idea of what. Finally, she shook her head, went back to the spot she'd chosen, and rolled herself up in a blanket. *So near and yet so far.* She sighed. *Cliché, but appropriate.*

Wearing every piece of clothing she'd brought, Vree

moved closer to the fire and lay down, pillowing her head on one arm.

You know that either Gerek or Karlene would be willing to keep you warm.

Her brows drew in. *Don't start.* It had been an interesting evening; Gerek leaping to Bannon's defense, Magda standing up to him, Karlene suddenly acting like a corporal or a squad leader. *You know what I'm wondering?*

She felt him shift, as though he were settling in, getting comfortable for the night. *What?*

How much Shkoden does Bannon actually understand?

He didn't react to anything.

Vree closed her eyes and listened to the comforting sounds of people sleeping all around her. *Neither did I.*

From the far end of the valley, the timber-holding appeared peaceful enough.

"Is the gate closed?"

"I can't see from this angle, but there are some big, orange hairy things outside the stockade."

Karlene squinted but could only see gradations of brown on brown, broken by the occasional small evergreen and clumps of golden-leafed willows by the river. She hated being without the kigh; it made her feel as blind and bound as Bannon. "They're probably cows."

"Cows?" Vree shifted her grip on the branch and peered down at the bard. "Orange cows?"

"They're a mountain breed. They can live on just about anything and they don't mind the cold. Anything else."

"Someone's . . ." About to say alive, she changed it to, ". . . awake. There's smoke. I don't see anyone moving around the piles of logs, though."

Kars could easily be the one who lit the fire.

Or not. If it were Kars, it would soon be over and Bannon would no longer be an inconvenience but a problem that had to be solved—one way or another. Trouble was, she couldn't think of another. "I don't see anything else. I'm coming down."

On the ground, Bannon frowned behind the masking blindfold. They used to spend hours, sometimes days, on reconnaissance; tucked into a safe vantage point they'd watch and weigh every inconsequential movement until they found the pattern. It drove him crazy, but Vree would insist. It was the way they'd survived for five long years when the life expectancy of an Imperial assassin seldom passed three. Today, in comparison, Vree had climbed up the tree, glanced around, and come straight back down again.

She'd changed in less than obvious ways.

"He's no more an assassin than Vree is!" Gerek's declaration chased itself around and around in his head.

What a load of slaughtering louse shit. He hadn't changed, not the way she had. A twig cracked as she came back down the tree, not making a lot of noise but not moving nearly as quietly as she could.

What's the slaughtering rush? he wondered. *If Kars is there, then hurrying saves no lives and might risk ours.* Bannon wasn't looking forward to running into the crazy old man with his hands tied behind his back and his ankles hobbled. While he wasn't completely defenseless, he certainly wasn't at his best. *At least His slaughtering Grace got them to drop the slaughtering blindfold while we're moving.* Once he would have

trusted Vree to lead him blindfolded through an
enemy camp. Not anymore.

Even sitting a careful distance away, Magda could
feel the emotions rolling off Bannon like smoke. Besides the petty, self-absorbed jealousy, the "if I can't
have my own way I'm going to eat worms" petulance,
and the understandable anger at being captured, she
could sense a deep hurt. Although she couldn't tell for
certain without trance work, it seemed he honestly
didn't understand how, after everything that had happened, Vree could've chosen to save Gyhard. *At least
he's admitting she did choose.* Magda supposed that
was progress.

When she sighed, Gerek turned. "Troubles,
Maggi?" he asked, concerned.

She shrugged; Bannon's emotional state was none
of his business.

"It's that wrongness, isn't it? Maybe you shouldn't
go any closer."

Magda started. The wrongness was still there, like
a great dark weight in the back of her mind, growing
larger and heavier with every step they'd taken toward
the valley, but she hadn't actually thought about it all
morning. It frightened her how quickly she could get
used to something like that. "I have to go." Her voice
was a little too high, the words spilling out a little too
fast. "I have to heal Kars."

Karlene went down on one knee beside the young
healer. "There's only one way to heal Kars," she said
softly. "And that's by returning him to the Circle."

"*. . . and when there is nothing left but pain, I will
not deny my patients the embrace of the Circle.* It's
part of the Healers' Oath." Magda sighed again and

tucked a damp curl behind one ear. "Some pain only death can cure."

"And are you prepared for that?"

"I think so."

"Have you ever done it before?"

"No." Her chin lifted. "Have you?"

Killed someone. Taken a life. Even a life that should have ended years ago. It was the bard's turn to sigh. "No."

Magda shifted gaze and question to her brother.

He spread his hands; she already knew the answer.

When she looked at Vree, the ex-assassin shook her head and sighed. "I guess it's a good thing I came," she muttered dryly.

Bannon couldn't help it. He snickered.

Kars could feel lives approaching; five lives, moving slowly up the valley. One of them felt almost like the demon that had convinced his last family to leave him. There were differences, he would never mistake the two, but the similarities were terrifying.

Father?

"It's all right, Kait." She worried so. He was glad there were others now to keep her company. Such a young girl shouldn't have to spend all her time with ... with ... He reached for who he was, nearly touched it, and felt it slip away toward the five new lives.

They were moving closer. They were coming here. They would try to take this family away as they had taken the others.

"No." He shook his head, confused by names out of the recent past. Wheyra. Iban. Hestia. Faces half-formed in memory. Twisted fingers rose to stroke the necklace of bone that Anca and Kait had retrieved for him. He had no token from those three, from Wheyra, Iban, and Hestia, snatched from his side by the demon. Just as he had no tokens from the seven who'd been taken from him such a short time before. He hadn't even had time to learn all their names.

Gyhard.

His heart pounding, he turned toward the gate, but the approaching lives were still too far away to see. That name did not belong to one of his. Had never belonged to one of his. But it had left him, too.

They all left him.

"No. Not this time. This time I can protect you. Kiril, Ondro, close the gate."

As the two dead men shuffled forward to do as he commanded, he herded the other four together and got them moving toward the cool depths of the timber-holding's root cellar.

"If they cannot reach you," he told them happily, "they cannot hurt you." He waited by the door until Kiril and Ondro climbed down to join them, then smiled lovingly on all six, five of whom smiled involuntarily back at him, their lips already beginning to pull up off their teeth. "Wait here. When they are gone and you are safe again, I will come and get you."

He closed the door and sighed. He would miss them, but hopefully, they wouldn't have to stay there long.

Father, you need to eat.

"I do?"

Yes, Father.

Patting her cheek, completely undisturbed by his hand passing through the shadowy outlines of her face, he murmured, "You take such good care of me, Kait. What would I do without you?"

Enrik's tongue dragged across dried and cracking lips. While his kigh shrieked and fought within the confines of its prison, his body, driven by desperate need, shuffled forward until stopped by the rough wall of the cellar. Hands splayed out, he moved blindly to the right, face pressed up against a row of stone crocks. The earliest of all instincts opened his mouth and he sucked at the moisture dribbling down their sides.

"He's there." It suddenly became impossible to take another step forward. Not because she was physically exhausted, although she was. Not because the damage to her knee made walking painful, although it did. But because the dark wrongness had moved from the back of her mind to the front of her thoughts. If she squinted, Magda could almost see it, pulsing on the path they'd been following along the riverbank.

"You're sure?" Karlene asked, more for the sake of asking than because she doubted Magda's word.

The young healer nodded, swallowed once, swallowed twice, and began to shake so hard she lost her grip on the crutch Gerek had made her.

Without thinking, Gerek shoved the rope he'd been leading Bannon with into Vree's hands and raced to his sister's side. "It all right," he murmured into her hair as she flung herself into his arms. "I'm here. I've got you."

Vree stared down at the twisted hemp lying across her palm and slowly closed her fingers around it. Then she turned to look at Bannon who could have, should have, used that moment to escape. He was staring in turn at Gerek and Magda as though he'd never seen comfort offered before.

"... if anyone talked about my sister the way you talk about Vree, I'd beat the living shit out of him."

Watching Gerek, Bannon felt as though he were forcing his way to understanding through an opposing army. He kept catching glimpses of it, but every time he thought he was getting close, another sword, another shield, another soldier, slammed into his way.

Because he was so totally unaware of her, Vree allowed her gaze to linger. In spite of the stubble, he looked younger than she remembered. *I wish ...* Her mental voice trailed off.

What?

I wish that, just once, Bannon had held me while I cried.

Gyhard heard the thought so clearly he couldn't pretend he hadn't. *Did you ever give him the chance, Vree?*

Her chin rose and her mental voice maintained a bored nonchalance made completely unbelievable by the emotional turmoil surrounding it. *Don't be ridiculous. Assassins never cry; they allow the hurt to build up year after year after year until the only way they can find peace is to have their daughter kill them.*

Good thing you're not an assassin anymore. His tone matched hers, but he reached out with what comfort he could. He was no longer surprised when she accepted it.

Yeah. Good thing.

"I'm going to have to get closer."

Vree snapped her head around so quickly it seemed

for a moment she was looking in two directions at
once. *"You're* going to have to get closer?"

Karlene sighed. She didn't need this. "Look, Vree,
I said I'd give you and Gyhard a chance with Kars
but he isn't the only one behind that stockade. Before
you do anything, I need to find out how many dead
are walking in there."

"How?"

Both women turned to face Magda, who lifted a
blotchy face from Gerek's chest. "There's *no* air kigh
to send in, Karlene, and you'll *never* be able to Sing
the fifth kigh from outside the stockade, not when
they're total strangers. If you want to know what's
going on in there, *I'll* have to do it."

"Maggi!"

She looked up at her brother. "You *know* I'm
right, Ger."

He brushed at her cheeks with the palm of one
hand then bent down picked up her crutch. "Okay,"
he growled. "It stinks, but you're right. Just be careful
for a change."

"Okay. Fine." Karlene threw up her hands. "Let's
all go. Let's make it a parade!"

Vree handed the rope back to Gerek and walked
forward until she stood a hands span from the bard.
"Do you really want to do this alone?"

Karlene's shoulders sagged and she shook her head.

"Then let's get this over with."

The three women walked single file up the path.
Gerek and Bannon walked side by side.

"If anything happens to her," Gerek muttered, "I
might as well kill myself because I'll never survive
explaining it to Annice and Father. I'm going to be in

deep enough shit if they ever find out why she's using that crutch."

"But is it like losing an arm or leg or like losing a crutch?" Bannon's memory translated the priest's words to Imperial.

Like losing a crutch.

They'd shared every important memory from the time he was six and Vree was seven. He knew that; he'd seen the memories in her head. But they weren't his memories.

When he had her tied, like a parcel to take to the Emperor, he'd been punishing her for what she'd done to him. Had he been punishing himself? No. That was ridiculous.

Two bodies, one will, she used to say when they were working. Two bodies, two people; undeniable after what they'd been through.

He stared past Magda and Karlene at the familiar line of Vree's back. She'd made her choice. And he hated it.

Hated her choice.

For the first time in his life, he stumbled and would have fallen had Gerek not instinctively thrown out a hand and caught him.

"Are you okay?"

Bannon looked from Gerek to Vree then back again. "I don't know," he admitted at last.

Gerek glanced ahead at his own sister. "That makes two of us," he muttered.

About halfway up the valley, they stopped to rest and drink from the river.

"It'll be late afternoon by the time we get there." Karlene passed around the last of the dried fruit. "Do we camp a safe distance away and get a fresh start in the morning or do we go right up to the walls, assuming we can finish before dark?"

Vree shrugged. "What difference does it make if we can't? The walking dead are no more dead at night than they are in the day."

"But the dark can hide so many other things ..." The bard turned toward the stockade and her voice took on the rhythmic cadence of tales told.

"Worse things?" Vree asked pointedly.

They'd moved only a very little bit closer when Karlene had to pull out a set of multiple pipes and play them forward. Without her help, they kept veering off along water channels and animal trails, away from the river, away from the holding.

They found the half-eaten body of the young hawk at the point where the path left the riverbank. Magda gave a little moan as Vree dropped to one knee beside it. "What happened?"

"Probably a cat. Or two."

"Don't you *know*?"

"I know that no one crept up behind it and slit its throat, but more than that ..." She straightened and glared at the young healer. "... I don't know."

"Vree ..."

"Look, I was an assassin, not slaughtering Death herself! Just because it's dead, doesn't mean I know how it got that way!" She felt Bannon's gaze, met it, and saw he understood. Of course, he did. There were some things that only Bannon *could* understand.

And I can't?

It had begun to seem only natural that Gyhard could hear her thoughts. *No.*

Gerek's free hand curled into a fist and he took a

step toward Vree. "I think you owe my sister an apology," he growled.

Eyes blazing, Magda turned on him. "I don't *need* you trying to protect me all the time, Ger. I am *perfectly* capable of taking care of myself!"

With his guard distracted, Bannon dove forward, hit Gerek in the lower back with his shoulders driving him to the ground. At the moment of impact, he got his feet under him, took a deep breath, and used his weight and momentum to rip the rope out of Gerek's slackened grip, taking the brunt of the pressure across the muscles on the back of his neck. After a day's walking, he knew the exact extent of his hobble and measured his steps accordingly as he ran.

"Albannon Magaly, stop!"

He stopped, but he tottered on the bank of the river. If he could just force himself to fall forward, the current would soon sweep him out of range of Bardic Command and there were definitely no kigh in the water this close to the crazy old man. He swayed, began to fall; too late. A familiar arm dragged him back from the edge. Vree had realized exactly what he was going to do.

For a moment, they stood together side by side—the way they'd stood for most of their lives—then the moment passed. Vree shoved the rope into Gerek's hands and strode up the path toward the stockade.

"Vree!" Karlene ran to catch up, the others following. "It's not that easy!"

"Why not? Because the gate's closed?" Without slowing, she waved a derisive hand at the wall. "I could go over this in my sleep."

"Vree!"

When the bard grabbed her arm, she stopped so

quickly Karlene stumbled forward another two paces. "Kars is behind that wall. Are we agreed?"

"Well, yes, but . . ."

"Then I am going either through it or over it and Gyhard is going to do whatever it is he has to do with Kars because I want something in my life settled. Do you understand?"

"Better than you think." Karlene sighed and, greatly daring, cupped the other woman's chin in her hand. "But dearling, I'm going to ask you the question you asked me this morning; do you really want to do this alone?"

The edges of Vree's laugh had unraveled just a little. "I'm *not* alone."

"I know." Karlene turned her head so that she could see Magda and Gerek and, because it was unavoidable, Bannon. "But Gyhard isn't the only person who cares about what happens to you."

Her breathing growing fast and shallow, Vree searched for a response and couldn't find one. The only thing that came to mind was a distinct desire to run—except that she didn't think she could control her legs.

"So what do we do next?" Gyhard asked through her mouth.

Tracing Vree's jaw with her thumb, Karlene let her hand fall away. "First, I Sing. Maybe we can get someone to open the gate."

Vree nodded and stepped back. She could feel Magda's gaze pushing against her and knew that although the bard hadn't noticed Gyhard's brief exposure, the healer had.

You seemed . . . Terrified. *. . . at a loss for words. I was just trying to help.*

I know.

You're not angry.

Why should I be? The Imperial Army put a great deal of effort into training me to act as part of a team. A little light-headed, she felt complete for the first time since Aralt's tower. While Bannon had been inside her head, he'd concentrated solely on getting out—he hadn't had a thought to spare for her and the barriers between them had been as thick as possible. Now, she ended where her abilities ended and Gyhard began where his started.

No barriers?

Do we need them?

He smiled. She never ceased to amaze him. *No.*

Magda frowned. She could no longer feel a definitive separation between the two kigh. That wasn't good. That couldn't be good. Could it? It was very hard to think so close to the stockade; the wrongness kept pulling at the abilities that made her a healer, leaving no room for coherent thought about anything else. She had to do something about Vree and Gyhard, but first she had to deal with Kars.

"Karlene, wait." Passing Vree, she hurried to the bard's side. "If I drop into a healing trance, I think I can tell how many damaged kigh there are. I might even be able to tell you who they are."

"Not if it puts you in any danger," Gerek protested. He pushed Bannon up against the only tree still standing in the immediate area and quickly secured him.

Shaking off the lingering effects of the Bardic Command, Bannon managed a strangled "No!" when Gerek reached for the blindfold.

The two men locked eyes for a long moment. Finally, Gerek nodded. He didn't have time to argue,

not with Magda suggesting she open herself up to contact with the walking dead. Other reasons for giving
in to Bannon's plea, muddier reasons, he ignored.

But when he reached his sister, it was too late for further protests to do any good. She sat on a section of log
with her hands lying loose in her lap, her eyes half
closed, and her breathing deep and regular. There were
two vertical lines between her brows, and although he'd
always thought healers healing were supposed to look
serene, Magda looked distinctly unhappy.

"One living kigh," she murmured. "The dead, the
dead are so hard to tell apart. I don't understand.
They don't seem to care. How can they not ... Oh."

That single syllable was the most heartsick sound
Gerek had ever heard. "Maggi?"

"One of them cares. One of them cares very much."
Tears spilled down both cheeks. "It's so *wrong*."

"How many are there?" Karlene prodded softly, not
even noticing Gerek's scowl.

"More than three. Less than ten."

The bard glanced from the healer to the stockade.
"There had to have been more than ten people in
there."

"Kars is a very old man and these are the second
set of companions he's Sung in a short time." Vree's
gaze drifted down to rest on Karlene's face. "I doubt
he could manage to bring back ten."

They were Gyhard's words, Karlene realized, and
perhaps more than merely his words. All at once, she
remembered what Gyhard had asked Vree every
morning during their quest for the prince. *Are you still
sane?* She wondered why she felt so much like asking
it now.

"If you Sing now, Karlene ..." Magda's voice,

trembling but determined, cut off speculation. "... I can tell you if your Song has any effect."

Demons. Kars sat by the hearth and tried to control his fear for Kait's sake. The rod rose and fell once again in memory.

"Stop it! Stop it! Do you want the demons to come? Do you want them to destroy you?"

"I've been good. I've been good." He hadn't called the demons. Why were they here?

Father? Her eyes were wide and frightened, and her edges were beginning to spread.

"I'm sorry Kait. I'm so sorry." He wiped away tears and straightened as much as he was able. "Come here, child. You mustn't listen to the demons. They'll hurt you."

He wrapped his arms around her smoky image and Sang her Song to her over and over until she calmed.

No sound passed through the heavy earth insulating the root cellar.

"Karlene?"

Still Singing, the bards cocked an inquiring eyebrow at Magda.

"You might as well stop. Nothing's happening."

She Sang an ending, because the last thing they needed right now was more unfinished business, then said, "Nothing?"

"No." Magda sighed and swiped at the moisture on her cheeks. "Something started to happen, then it stopped. I think Kars was Singing, too."

Karlene snorted. "One old man is not going to be able to drown out my Song."

"Well, he has. And you needn't glare at me because I'm just telling you what was happening." She tucked a curl into the corner of her mouth and despondently examined the dusty toes of her boots. "We're going to have to deal with Kars first. Vree's going to have to go over the wall because she's the only one who can."

"But just open the gate," Karlene declared before Vree could move. She stepped in front of the ex-assassin and stared down into her face. "You are not to confront Kars until we're inside."

"You promised Gyhard could deal with him."

"And he can."

"But you want to be there."

"No." She wished she knew just what it was that felt so wrong. "I want Magda to be there."

Vree dragged the heavy sweater over her head and tossed it to one side. There'd be exercise soon enough to keep her warm and she didn't need the added weight.

"Vree!"

"I'll open the gate." She checked the release on her single throwing dagger, smiled, and flicked the bard's pale braid back behind her shoulder. "You worry too much."

Half a dozen running steps and she was her own height up on the wall, clinging to a surface never meant to keep out human climbers. An instant later, she paused on the top, balanced easily between the points on two massive logs, fought the urge to look back at Bannon, and dropped out of sight.

Gerek laid an arm across Magda's shoulders as she sighed and wiped her eyes with the back of one hand. "You okay?" When she shrugged, he lightly kissed the top of her head. "If anyone can heal this mess," he told her softly, "you can."

A short distance away, Bannon fought the ropes that held him.

"Hush, child, hush. Tell me what's wrong." When the demons quieted, Kait had gone into the yard but almost immediately returned. Something had upset her, but Kars didn't understand what.

Two. Not one, two!

"Two what, child?" When he stood, she tried to push him back away from the door, but her hands passed right through him. "Just let me look, Kait. It isn't the demon. I'd know if it was the demon."

Leaning heavily on a staff he'd found, he pulled open the door and stepped outside, eyes squinting nearly shut in the sunlight.

Kars.

I know. Vree dropped the last few feet and moved away from the wall, eyes locked on the old man. She hadn't expected this; Kars, alone, no walking dead to protect him. *What do we do now?*

Gyhard felt as though his past had him in a vise and it was closing tight around him. *Lend me your body. Let me finish this.*

She hesitated, remembering how Bannon had shoved her aside, usurped control, and refused to give it back without a fight that had nearly destroyed them both.

I'm not Bannon, Vree.

Kars raised a twisted hand to shade his eyes. "Who's there?"

* * *

Vree?

One heartbeat. Two.

*Vree, the bards consider this to be a bardic problem. If we let Karlene in, *she'll* have to do something!*

Two heartbeats. Three.

Vree!

Yes.

She felt Gyhard surge forward. One moment she was Vree. The next, Vree and Gyhard combined, a joining so intense she almost lost herself in it. For that moment, she knew everything there was to know about him—his strengths, his weaknesses, his fears—and he knew the same about her. It was terrifyingly intimate and, because of that intimacy, the most incredibly sensual experience she'd ever had. Her whole body throbbed in reaction. As they slowly began to separate again, she couldn't help but think of sweat-slicked skin, welded together by heat and passion, pulling apart, inch by sticky inch.

Vree?

Pushed back into a corner of her own mind, Vree struggled to gain enough control to form a conscious thought. She could still feel her body but from a distance, almost as though she were feeling an outer layer of clothing. *I'm here.*

That was . . .

Yes. Looking through her eyes was like looking through a window that flickered every few moments. Kars had taken a step back toward the building. He seemed older, more tired than he had.

"Go away! We don't want you here!" So desperate to protect his family from the demons, Kars had forgotten how the world could attack with other weapons. He should have kept one of them with him to keep the living away. Kait did her best, but they didn't even seem to notice her as she swirled about their . . .

He shook his head and peered around the yard. He could see only one person, but he could feel two. And one of them felt achingly familiar.

Distracted for a moment by the graceful play of muscle over bone, a grace he now controlled, Gyhard stepped forward, hands held out from his sides. "Kars?"

"I know who I am." He hadn't for a long time, but the knowledge had been given back to him. Stepping over the threshold, he struggled to close the door.

Don't let him get inside!

Gyhard raced across the yard and pushed against the planking. "Do you know who I am?"

The voice was wrong, but the kigh, he knew the kigh. "Gyhard?" Kars scowled through the wedge-shaped opening, barely visible in the deep shadows of the hall. "You went away. You came back, then you went away."

Swallowing around what felt like a dagger stuck crosswise in Vree's throat, Gyhard nodded. "I didn't have a choice." He could reach in, grab the front of what was obviously a borrowed robe, and yank the old man outside. Vree's hands were smaller than Bannon's but strong enough for what had to be done. He *should* reach in—but he couldn't.

"They always go away." The old man sighed, fingers stroking the necklace of bone. "I thought they wouldn't, you know, but they do."

"I know." In memory, Kars, young and beautiful and so dreadfully damaged, held out a cup of poisoned wine because he believed that the dead would never leave him.

"What is going on in there?" Gerek demanded, pacing back and forth on the hard packed earth in front of the gate. "Why hasn't she let us in?"

"She isn't ..." Magda dragged a wet curl from the corner of her mouth and tried again. Closing her eyes, she reached out with all her strength. "She isn't in control anymore. Gyhard is."

Bannon shrieked in wordless fury and flung himself against the ropes.

Gyhard stepped back and held out Vree's hand. "Kars, please come outside. I've come to stop the pain."

Unable to do anything herself, Kait sped toward the root cellar. She couldn't open the heavy door, but neither could it keep her out.

Five of the others stood where they'd been left. The sixth sat crumpled in a corner. It wasn't like the others. It wasn't like her. She stopped in front of it.

Get up!

It ignored her. She could feel it frantically struggling against the tormented flesh that held it.

Five would have to be enough.

Kars looked at the hand stretched out toward him. "I can't leave now."

"It's time."

Just for a moment, it seemed that the insanity left his eyes and he was only a very old and very tired man "Long past time," he said softly. "But I've promised Kait I'd stay."

*   *   *

Gerek grabbed Karlene's shoulder, fingers sinking deep into the heavy sweater, and spun her around to face him. "Do something!"

"Like what?"

"How should I know? You're the bard!" He waved his sword at the stockade. "Sing something!"

"There are *no* kigh!" she reminded him through clenched teeth.

He pushed his face toward hers, and spat each word at her with separate emphasis. "Yes. There. Are."

"She's too far away!"

"Try!"

Jerking free of his grip, Karlene faced the stockade and pitched her voice to carry. **"Vireyda Magaly!"**

Gyhard barely held on as Vree surged forward. They meshed for a heartbeat, then separated again. *What the . . .?*

Karlene's using my name, like she used it at the way station when Bannon took control.

How could she know which kigh is dominant from outside the holding?

How the slaughter should I know? I've been here with you.

She's going to ruin everything!

"Vireyda Magaly!"

The second call was harder to fight.

Head cocked to catch the sound of the distant voice, Kars slid back into insanity, his eyes growing wider with every passing second.

"Vireyda Magaly, answer me!"

"Demons! A trick! A trap!" Gibbering in terror, Kars leaped backward, slamming the door.

"Shit!" Impossible to tell which one of them spoke, which one of them was in control.

The cabbage hit them just above the left elbow, numbing the arm and knocking them sideways. They turned and saw the dead approaching, their joined *kigh* too strong to accept the false comfort of denial.

Gyhard, give way. You can't fight them.

Neither can you! But he released her body, drawing quickly back within his original boundaries as she surged forward. The brief moment of unity brought a flare of heat that lasted long enough to be a dangerous distraction. *We've got to open the gate!*

Unfortunately, in order to confront Kars, they'd come too far in the yard. An ax balanced across her palms, one of the dead moved to stand between them and reinforcements.

Vree dove forward to avoid being brained with a stone crock of honey, rolled awkwardly because of the numb arm, and felt fingers close around her ankle, the touch so cold she could feel the chill through the leather of her boots. Writhing in the dead man's grip, she kicked up with her free leg, catching him on the point of his chin.

Teeth shattered as Ondro's head whipped back, but he didn't let go. Kait had told them the father was in danger. The father must be protected. He could dimly remember a man he'd called father being set gently into a hole in the ground, but that memory had been stripped of power by the Song that held him. If Kait said the father was in danger, then Ondro would protect the father.

"Shit, shit, shit!" Narrowly avoiding a grab by the dead man's other hand, Vree curled up and drove the point of her long dagger into his waist, sawing it from side to side, severing tendons, separating the small bones. Suddenly, she could feel the air above her being pushed aside. At the perimeter of her vision, she could still see the woman guarding the gate—obviously, someone else had stopped to pick up a weapon. There was no longer time to waste on freedom. Flinging herself to the right, she dragged the dead man over with her and left a fold of her sleeve lying severed in the dirt of the yard.

"Now what's happening?"

"They're fighting."

"Who?"

Magda blinked and looked up at her brother. "The dead."

Gerek glared at the stockade then, snarling wordlessly, ran down the path to the tree where Bannon was tied. Barely pausing, he raised his sword. As it descended, Bannon twisted to present as small a target as possible.

"GEREK!" Magda rushed forward, hands outstretched, unable to believe what she was seeing.

Two more quick cuts and the ropes binding wrists and ankles were in pieces. Another and Bannon's knives spilled out of a split pack and onto the ground.

"Gerek, what are you doing!"

He grabbed his sister as she flung herself by him, but he directed his answer up the path at the bard. "Bannon's the only one who can get over the wall. Don't you dare call him back!"

Karlene's pale eyes blazed. "Are you threatening me, Your Grace."

The steel point lifted. "If I have to."

Bannon ignored them. Scooping up the two throwing daggers and the long belt knife out of the pile, he sprinted for the wall, swarming up the same imperfections Vree had used, pausing as she had at the top. A quick glance down into the enclosed area showed him five to one odds. When his gaze tried to slide away as his kigh refused to deal with the dead/undead kigh below, he forced his focus back onto the fight. Vree was down there. And she needed him.

He saw her sever a hand to free herself and grimaced, remembering the fight with the dead soldiers at the ford. The dead didn't feel pain. Unless the bard could get inside the stockade and do whatever it was she did, this lot would have to be chopped to pieces before they'd give up. Five to one odds were no longer survivable.

With his feet braced against the inside of the logs, Bannon scuttled hand over hand along the top of the wall, his weight hanging from the rough points hacked into the upper ends of the logs. His right arm throbbed just above his wrist where it had been broken while Gyhard controlled his body. Swearing under his breath, he moved a little faster. He dangled for a heartbeat over the gate, then dropped, landing behind the dead woman with the ax.

Straightening, he grabbed the bar, began to lift, and flung himself to one side as an ax head thudded into the wood where his right shoulder had been. *Almost like someone told her I was there . . .*

Twisting the blade out of the wood with practiced ease, Anca swung again. She would protect the father.

The edges split the air an inch from Bannon's back as he dove under the swing and slammed his shoulder into her stomach. They hit the ground together, but with no air to be knocked from her lungs, she continued to flail about and managed to smack him in the side of the head with the ax handle.

Grunting in pain, he rolled clear and staggered for the gate. *Could use that pig-sticker of His Grace's in here right about now.*

On the other side of the yard, the severed hand still clutching her ankle, Vree dragged herself under a split rail fence and into the cow byre. At this moment, crawling through shit was a small price to pay. As a heavyset middle-aged man with arms like small trees chopped through the rails, she lurched toward the stable. From the stable roof she could get to the wall. Once on the wall, she could get out.

Slipping in the muck, she twisted to keep from falling, and saw Bannon lifting the bar on the gate. Her left arm snapped forward.

The throwing dagger embedded itself hilt-deep in Anca's armpit, grinding in the joint. The ax missed flesh and it bit deeply into wood. One arm dangling uselessly, she fought to free it.

Cut off from the stable, Vree picked up a splintered rail and smashed it into the face of the charging dead man. It slowed him down a little. With all her strength, she drove her heel into his knee. That shook off the clinging hand and slowed him down a little more. It didn't stop him.

Bannon kicked back, catching Anca in the ribs, hurling her away from both ax and gate. The sudden appearance of the dagger told him that Vree was back in control of her own body. Whatever had happened between her and Gyhard before the dead attacked was no longer happening. *Kars kept calling Gyhard "my heart"; maybe he Sang his lost heart right back into his chest.* The thought of Gyhard trapped in an ancient ruin of a body with a crazy old man made him smile as he shoved open the gate.

Gerek's sword whistled down through the slowly widening space, deflecting the ax blow aimed at Bannon's head.

"Chop off her slaughtering arm!" he yelled scrabbling out of the way.

Momentum carried Gerek into the yard, but when it ran out, he stood frozen in horror, surrounded by the walking dead. His sword arm began to shake and the point fell until the tip dimpled the packed earth.

"Gerek!" Seeing only her brother's danger, Magda rushed forward.

NO! NO! NO!

Hands clutching her head, she screamed and fell writhing to the ground.

"Maggi!" The edge of his sword chopped through flesh and into bone. Jerking away from clutching hands, he fought to free the blade from a dead thigh.

Karlene Sang as she ran into the holding and that was all that kept her from falling as Magda had.

NO! NO! NO!

The voice shrieked denial in her head, trying to drown out the Song.

NO! NO! NO!

The pain was so intense she could hardly see, Karlene forced her voice to run up and down an eight-note scale. It was the best shield she could manage, and it wasn't nearly enough. Grabbing Magda's foot, she dragged the girl back out through the gate.

The shrieking stopped.

Wiping at a dribble of blood from a lip she didn't remember biting through, Karlene dropped to her knees and gently lifted Magda's head onto her lap.

When the girl's eyes fluttered open, her heart started beating again. "Are you all right?" It was probably a stupid question, Karlene realized, considering how *she* felt, but it was the only question that came to mind.

Magda blinked and tried to focus on the bard's face. "Her name is Kait."

"Whose name?"

"The girl who kept saying no." Tears spilled over and ran down Magda's cheeks. "She's just barely hanging on to who she is."

"I'm not surprised." Setting Magda gently on the ground, Karlene got shakily to her feet. Considering the condition Kait's body had been in when she'd found it on the other side of the pass, and how long before that Kars had Sung the girl's kigh back into a parody of life, she was amazed Kait had any sense of self remaining at all. But since she did . . .

Leaning on the gate, careful not to cross over into the yard, Karlene Sang. Although she Sang everything she'd found out about the girl after returning with Prince Otavas to the Capital, Kait's kigh stayed just out of reach of her Song.

"She's protecting her father," Magda said, waving a shaky hand at the fighting. "They all are."

"Her father?"

"Kars. I think if Kars wasn't there, they'd stop fighting." She winced as Gerek parried blows from a maul. "I think."

A living fighter recoils from pain, leaving openings to be exploited; the dead do not. Unable to disengage long enough to run for it, Vree found herself pushed back against one of the buildings, an ax blade cutting patterns in the air inches in front of her face. Instinct flipped her right arm forward, but the dagger that should have dropped into her hand lay somewhere off the coast of the Broken Islands.

"Shit!" She ducked as the ax smashed through the narrow shutter behind her and swore louder as a splinter of wood embedded itself in her cheek.

"Vree! To the right!"

She flung herself sideways as the dead man catapulted toward her. Dropping to one knee under the flailing arms, she caught a glimpse of Bannon running something into his back.

Pinned to the wall by the steel point on the log gaff, Kiril struggled to free himself. He must protect the father. Pressing his palms against the wood, he pushed and, inch by inch moved backward, passing the shaft through his body. When his arms no longer reached the wall, he dug his heels in and kept moving.

Bannon grabbed Vree's arm and shoved her toward the broken shutter. "Karlene says Gyhard has to deal with Kars. Kait won't let her into the holding, and it's the only thing that'll stop this lot."

"What?"

"I'll explain later. Just deal with Kars." He ripped off the remains of the shutter and boosted her into the narrow opening. "Hurry up, before Gerek gets his legs chopped off. His Grace doesn't like hurting people."

"But they're dead!"

He flashed her a brilliant and achingly familiar smile. "Tell him."

NO! NO! NO!

Reeling backward, Karlene threw everything she had into Kait's Song. It was barely enough to chase the tortured kigh out of her head. Panting, most of her weight on Magda's shoulder, the bard shook her head. "All that seems to do is remind her we're out here."

Squatting by the hearth, a hand resting on the partially burned body of the old woman, Kars rocked back and forth Singing softly to himself, trying to drown out the Song of the demon. It wasn't working. One after another, the demon Songs that had been beaten out of him in his childhood welled up out of memory and built piteous harmonies in his head.

Lips caught between his teeth, his Song faded to a moan. He rocked farther back, beating his head against the fieldstone wall. Beating. Beating. He could still hear the demons.

"Kars, stop it." Breathing shallowly through Vree's mouth, thankful for her nightsight, Gyhard stepped carefully over and around the corpses and broken furniture scattered down the length of the dim room. "Hurting yourself won't drive away the kigh."

"The demons." The protest came out of the old man's mouth in a young man's voice.

"They're not demons, Kars. They're just the kigh."

"I don't want them. Make them go away, Gyhard. Make them go away!"

You've had this conversation before.

A long time ago. He stepped up onto the hearth and wrapped Vree's arm around the old man's shoulders, forcing his bleeding head away from the wall.

Kars buried his face against Vree's chest. "Hold me until they go away."

Her skin crawling, even though she wasn't exactly in it, Vree stared down at the tangled mat of gray hair. *Do what you have to.*

She could feel Gyhard's grief and his guilt as he took her hand and lifted the old man's chin until their eyes met. "Kars . . ."

He frowned. "Were you always a girl?"

Gyhard blinked. "What?"

"A girl. You're a girl. You weren't always a girl."

"No, but . . ."

His smile was everything it had ever been, "I didn't think so." Then the smile disappeared. "Why do you keep leaving me?"

"I never meant . . ."

"Yes, you did." The rheumy eyes narrowed. "You got on that horse and you rode away."

Gyhard. Do it!

Her hands closed around his neck. "I'm sorry."

Ignoring the hold intended to kill him, Kars shook his head. "Sorry isn't enough for what you did." Remembering another life he'd made his own, he filled his lungs with air and shrieked out a Song.

GYHARD! She could feel his kigh being dragged from her body. Forcing her consciousness past him into her hands, she changed her grip and twisted the old man's head around in one swift motion, snapping the ancient, brittle neck.

Gyhard!

I'm here.

She threw herself into him, not sure of what parts of her body were under her control and what were under his and not caring. He needed comfort, so she gave it, finding ways to hold him.

"Gyhard."

It was a name whispered with air pushed out of dead lungs. Meshed as tightly together as was possible and still maintain separate kigh, they looked down at the body.

"Help me."

When Vree disappeared into the building, the dead tried to follow, throwing themselves futilely against the door Kars had bolted from the inside.

Forcing herself to think past the moment, Anca slowly backed away. She couldn't remember the kitchen. She couldn't remember exactly what it was for, but she remembered a door from the kitchen to the hall. The father was in the hall.

They had to protect the father. She began moving as quickly as possible toward the back of the building.

"Something tells me there's another way in!" Bannon yanked his borrowed log gaffe out of the wood, ignoring the rancid fluids smeared along its length, and ran after her. Slashing at her ankles, he brought her down. Planting the point in the center of her back, he leaped up into the air and drove it through her into the ground. It hadn't worked the last time, but it was all he could think of to do.

Jumping off the body, already rising moistly onto her hands and knees, he looked around for another target and saw Gerek leaning on his sword being noisily sick. Behind him, sunlight glinted on an ax as it descended. Even as Bannon raced forward, he knew he was going to be too late.

"Gerek!" Magda's scream echoed off the stockade walls.

Gerek straightened . . .

. . . started to turn . . .

Inches away from his shoulder, the ax fell from nerveless fingers and the blow that should have chopped through living flesh from neck to groin, skidded through the heavy muscle across the top of his shoulder on its fall to the ground.

Gerek cried out, clamped his left hand over the wound and swayed where he stood, blood pouring over his chest and arm. He would have fallen had Bannon not grabbed him around the waist and used his own momentum to get him moving toward the gate.

"Lucky we brought a healer with us, Your Grace." He dumped him into Magda's arms and turned once again to the yard. He had to stop the dead from getting to Vree.

Except that the dead had stopped.

They stood, or knelt, perfectly still, their faces blank.

Staggering back under her brother's weight, one hand clamped over the wound, Magda would have fallen had Karlene not lowered them both to the ground.

"Can you Heal him?"

Brows knit together, Magda took a quick look at the bloody gash, then clamped her hand down again, her relief so great it took her a moment to find her voice. "He doesn't need Healing," she sniffed, trying to sound unconcerned for Gerek's sake, "he needs to be sewn up and bound in clean linen packed with comfrey, but since I don't have a kit with me ..." She sent a watery smile in the bard's direction. "I Healed Gerek while still in the womb. There isn't anything about his body I don't know. Which, I might add, is a *disgusting* amount to know about your brother, in spite of what the girls in the village think." Lower lip trembling, she drew in a deep breath and let it out slowly. Her eyes unfocused as she laid both shaking hands over the wound.

Gerek screamed and nearly threw himself out from under her touch.

An instant later, Magda sagged forward over an indented line of pale pink skin.

Her own heart beating uncomfortably fast, Karlene stroked damp hair back off Magda's face. "Are you all right?"

"I *hate* hurting people," she whimpered.

"It's only one quick pain against months of pain. I think Gerek understands."

"He passed out."

"I hear that often happens."

"I think I'm going to faint."

"Not now," Bannon called softly, in his thickly accented Shkoden. "Trouble comes."

With Kars' limp body cradled in her arms—he was nothing but skin and bones, the bulky robe weighed as much as he did—Vree crossed the yard toward the gate. The dead faces turned toward her as she passed, but that was the only movement they made. Vaguely aware of a confused wailing that seemed to come from the air around her, she laid the body down and turned to Karlene.

"He's dead." That was obvious to them all. The heads of the living never rested at quite that angle. "But he's still in there."

Chapter Thirteen

"It's been too long," Karlene said, sagging down onto her knees by Kars' body and pushing damp hair back off her forehead. "With the others, I used the Song to show them where they should go, but for Kars . . ." She sighed and spread her hands. "It's just not enough."

"We have to do something," Gyhard murmured through Vree's mouth.

"I know." Kars had been responsible for dark and terrible things, but he had suffered as much torment as he'd caused and had been trapped in the darkness far longer than any of his companions. Pity had proven stronger than revulsion and anger both. "Someone has to show him the way."

"You mean that someone has to die?"

Head bowed, exhaustion dragging her shoulders forward, Karlene nodded.

Vree, I . . .

No. Her body jerked with the force of her denial. *Not you.*

I have lived as much past my time as he has. He lifted a hand to stroke her cheek.

She lowered it again. *I don't care.*

Vree . . .

Don't leave me.

He looked down at Kars, at the tortured and undying creature his love had inadvertently created, then he looked into Vree's heart and wondered how many people were given such a second chance.

Leaning on the open gate, arms folded over his chest, Bannon nodded toward the neat line of dead bodies laid out along one side of the yard. "Should've thought before sending them off then," he snorted.

Karlene glared up at him. "They were suffering, and I had no way of knowing!" He shrugged and she barely resisted the urge to smack him. Besides, considering that he poisoned their entire family, I doubt any of them would be willing to do him a favor."

"Point," Bannon admitted after a moment's consideration.

"Thank you."

"No one dies," Magda declared from her place by Gerek's side.

Dropping her gaze to the young healer, Karlene gentled her voice. "It's the only way," she insisted softly.

Eyes narrowed into obstinate slits over purple shadows, Magda raised a hand from the rise and fall of Gerek's chest and pulled a curl of hair from the corner of her mouth. "Find another."

A heavy, uncomfortable silence settled over the living. Almost certain she could hear individual heartbeats, Vree asked, "What about Kait?"

Bard and healer both instinctively clapped their hands over their ears as the background wailing only they could hear grew in volume. It rose to a painful crescendo of grief and loss, slicing back and forth through their consciousness like hot, serrated knives.

"Hush ... Kait."

The wailing stopped so suddenly its absence echoed.

Breathing heavily, Karlene nodded down at Kars' body, her gaze moving quickly enough to avoid eye contact. "Thank you." Looking up, she swayed and pushed a hand against the ground to brace herself. "Kait's as lost as Kars is," she explained when the world stopped moving.

"No one dies," Magda repeated, wiping her nose on the back of her hand. "Too many people have died already. Here, in Fortune ..."

In Fortune. Karlene started. She could hear the music—if she could only identify the Song. Her fingers closed around a handful of earth. In Fortune, where all four quarters had been Sung the night of Third Quarter Festival. "Jazep!"

"Jazep's dead!" The protest brought a sudden renewal of grief. There were so many dead ...

To Magda's astonished indignation, the bard laughed and held out a fistful of dirt. "He's dead, yes, but he's not gone. His kigh went into the earth. He Sang Third Quarter Festival with me!"

Although Magda and Gerek stared at her in bewilderment, the absolute certainty in her voice kept them from arguing.

Rocking back onto her heels, Karlene surged up onto her feet, exhaustion pushed aside, words tumbling over each other in her eagerness to be heard. "Kait has no effect on the others because they can't Sing the kigh, but she kept attacking Magda and me because we can. Suppose, after Jazep Sang the dead away in Fortune, she attacked him? Suppose she's what killed him? He knows what she needs! What

Kars needs!" She brandished the fistful of dirt. "That's why he stayed. To show them the way!"

"Even if that's true ..." Even with a limited understanding of how things worked, Vree had her doubts anyone, even a bard, would stick around to help the one who'd killed them. "... the dirt he went into is back in Fortune."

"Essentially, true; he went into the earth in Fortune *but* all kigh are part of a greater whole. There's only one earth kigh—just as there's only one air or fire or water." Exalted, Karlene threw open her arms. "Jazep's here, back in Fortune, checking out the gardens in Vidor—he's everywhere!"

"But I thought there were no kigh *here*." Vree jerked her head toward Kars without really looking at him. "Because of him."

"Jazep's a bard. Kars isn't going to be able to stop him."

"Even if you're right, Karlene ..." The young healer's subdued tone suggested she thought the possibility remote. "... we'd *still* have to Call his kigh."

"It's a fifth kigh," Karlene began, but Magda cut her off.

"I don't *feel* it. I don't feel anyone but Kars and Kait. I can barely feel *myself*." She sighed deeply, looked up and held the bard's gaze with hers. "And *you* don't Sing earth."

"I do."

One moment Magda was sitting cross-legged on the ground beside her brother, the next she was wrapped in the embrace of a not very tall woman wearing travel-stained clothes and boots marked by a long, hard journey.

"Mama! Oh, Mama." Face buried against her mother's neck, Magda couldn't stop herself from bursting into tears.

Eyes closed, Annice murmured comfort with such fierce intensity that even Kars sighed and allowed his head to sag forward on the ruin of his spine.

Vree tried not to stare. *You have to believe her when she says everything's going to be all right.*

Gyhard smiled. *It wouldn't dare not to be.*

Swallowing sobs, Magda pushed herself out to arm's length, her face blotchy and her lashes in triangular clumps. All children believe that in times of trouble their mothers will miraculously come to the rescue, but Magda not only considered herself too old for that particular bardic tale, she'd never heard of it actually happening. "Mother, what are you *doing* here?" Then she scowled, the effect somewhat ruined by the grip she maintained on Annice's hands. "You've been using the kigh to watch me, haven't you?"

"You and your brother," Annice admitted easily, throwing a quick, grateful smile at Karlene. "But, as it happens, that's not why I'm here." She sighed and suddenly looked very, very tired. "I felt the dead walking, Maggi, and when Kovar told me you'd left Elbasan, I knew what you were going to do—what you had to do. Under the circumstances, I thought you might need some help."

"Magda shook her head. "Mother, if you were in Ohrid . . . I mean, we were *riding*—there's no way you could have got here . . ."

"Jazep made sure I'd arrive in time."

"Jazep?"

"Karlene's right. When I Sang earth at Third Quarter Festival, Jazep Sang with me as well. He led me here."

"Then you *know* what's going on."

Annice swept her gaze over the others, noting the blood on Gerek's shirt and his newly healed wound, noting two kigh in one body, noting the piled bodies of the dead, and finally noting the dead man watching her with what could only be called hope. "No, dear," she said, almost smiling in spite of accumulated horrors, "I haven't the faintest idea."

The sun was setting by the time explanations were over, and the valley looked as though it had been gilded with fire.

"Lost," Annice murmured, one hand holding tightly to Magda, the other to Gerek as though keeping them from being lost as well. When Gerek had opened his eyes to see her bending over him, he'd smiled and said with very little surprise, "Hullo, Nees. Have you come to make it all better?"

"Yes." She'd kissed him on the cheek, helped him to sit up, and only then allowed Karlene to recount everything she'd missed since she came close enough to lose the kigh.

"Lost," she said again. She could feel Kars watching her from where he lay, wrapped in the gathering shadows. If he was lost, it was long past time for him to be found. She stood, and pulled both Gerek and Magda to their feet. "Well, then, let's get to it before we lose the light. Gerek, go sit over there with Vree and Bannon. All three of you, try to stay out of the way."

Brother and sister exchanged wary glances.

"Out of the way of what?" Gerek asked.

"The Song." She took Magda by the shoulders and walked her around to stand at Kars' head. Beckoning Karlene closer, she joined her left hand with Magda's right, then moved herself so that the healer stood between the two bards.

Karlene looked a question at Magda who shrugged, equally confused. As everyone's position received a last assessment, the younger bard murmured, "Annice, just what exactly are we going to *do?*"

"What has to be done. It'll all be over soon," she promised, squeezing her daughter's hand. Breathing deeply, she moistened her lips and began to Sing.

To her listeners it seemed as if the Song grew roots that reached down into the center of the earth. It thrummed through the ground and vibrated up through the soles of their boots. The Song was earth the way bards had Sung since the very first Song, but then Annice reached deeper, added the four notes of Jazep's name, and it became something more.

The kigh formed at Kars' feet. First head, then shoulders, then the barrellike torso, then finally the legs that weren't quite long enough to put the whole thing in proportion.

Magda blinked away tears and found a smile to answer the smile her name-father Sang at her.

For a moment, Jazep Sang with Annice, then the harmonies began to subtly change as he began directing the Song. They were Singing the fifth kigh, Karlene realized, but it wasn't the Song she Sang—it was more like a part of a larger Song, one she knew, although she had no idea when she'd learned it. Squeezing Magda's fingers in hers, she added her voice.

All at once, Kars' body was only that. A body. No longer a prison.

Jazep looked at Magda and nodded.

It took her a moment to understand and then she

reached out with the part of her that healed. *It's time, Kait. They're waiting for you.*

In the last of the light, three translucent figures stood hand in hand. The young man, who, had he been born in another place would have been one of the greatest bards the four quarters had ever known, looked down at the ruin of his body and then at Magda. *Would you tell Gyhard I loved him, even when I forgot what that meant.*

I will.

And would you tell Vree that trust . . . His smile was sweet and a little tentative as he broke off and shook his head. *Never mind. I think it's something she has to learn for herself.*

The girl looked up at him with a puzzled frown. *You're not my father.*

No. He took her free hand with his, completing the circle. *I'm Kars.*

Jazep smiled on them both and although Magda was sure she heard him speak, she could still hear his voice in the Song. *Come, children. It's time to go home.*

As the earth kigh lost its shape, the Song rose until it filled the valley and for a moment, the moment between one heartbeat and the next, Magda heard another voice join in. Not Kars. A silent voice. A gentle voice. A strong voice. And one she knew.

All kigh were part of a greater whole. Earth kigh. Air kigh. Water kigh. Fire kigh. The kigh they called the fifth kigh because the bards had Sung four before it. *All* kigh were part of a greater whole.

Annice and Karlene Sang the gratitude alone. As the last notes rose up into a sapphire sky, they were nearly blown over by the rush of air kigh demanding their attention. They barely noticed when Magda pulled her hands free and walked over to join the others by the stockade wall.

"You okay, Maggi?" Gerek asked, draping an arm over her shoulders and pulling her close to his side.

She nodded, then, as the euphoria began to fade, she frowned. Something still wasn't right.

Vree and Gyhard found him in the root cellar, pressed up against the earth wall. He'd obviously relieved himself where he sat, and he stank. At first they thought he'd hidden there from Kars but when they led him—not so much unresisting as uncaring—out into the yard, Magda took one look at him and began to shake.

"I think," she said through clenched teeth, "that I'm going to be sick."

"Smells bad," Bannon agreed, moving upwind.

"It's not that. He's dead. His body is alive, but he's dead."

Holding the lantern up by his face, Vree looked into his eyes and quickly looked away again. "She's right."

Gerek shook his head. "That's impossible," he began but fell silent when Vree turned toward him.

"I've seen enough of the dead to know when I'm seeing another," she snapped. "I don't give a shit if this one's breathing, he's dead."

I think, Gyhard told her slowly, trying not to remember the feeling of being dragged out into nothingness and suspecting that he'd never forget, *this is what Kars tried to do to me, just before you killed him.*

"A dead kigh in a living body." Magda chewed over the words. It should have been horrible, it was horrible, but suddenly all she could see was the answer they'd been searching for all along. "A dead kigh in a living . . . Gyhard!"

"What?" The exchange happened almost effortlessly now.

"This is *your* body!"

"What!"

"He can't *want* to stay, he's dead." Breathing shallowly through her mouth she stepped forward and took the unresponsive hand. "You *don't* want to stay, do you?"

When the body dies, I am free.

The word "free" reverberated off the inside of her skull. "Except *we* don't want the body to die. What's your name?"

Enrik.

"Okay." She released him and couldn't stop herself from scrubbing her hand against her thigh. Feeling as though she'd been stretched out by the events of the day, she gritted her teeth, determined to hold together until the end—she only hoped it would be soon. "Enrik here wants to leave. So Karlene. . ." She grabbed Karlene's arm as the two bards joined them and pulled her forward. ". . . Sings him out of his body and away."

"Maggi, this is a dead man in a living body!" Annice exclaimed just as Karlene demanded to know what she was talking about.

Magda sighed, explained, and finished with, "Once he's *out* of the body, Vree gives a little push and Gyhard moves in. Simple."

"Simple?" Gerek muttered. Bannon indicated complete agreement with the raising of both brows.

Gyhard studied Enrik in the lamplight. He was probably in his mid-twenties, brown hair bleached out by a working day spent in the sun, skin bronzed by the same. His nose had been broken at least once. His hands were rough, the nails ridged. It was hard to determine anything else under all the dirt. "The funny thing is," he said so quietly only Vree heard him, "my family owned a timber-holding. If I hadn't met up with those brigands, this might have been me."

You're going to do it?

He thought of all that it would mean. *If it can be arranged as simply as Magda thinks, yes.*

What about me? She could feel the emptiness surrounding her. Waiting. *What about us?*

Vree . . . Confused, he paused. He could feel her distress, but he didn't understand the source. *You'll still be you,* he hazarded at last. *And we'll still be us. The body's young and strong and . . .*

"No." Vree's head snapped back and her eyes narrowed. "NO!" You're not going to leave me, too!" She flung the lamp to the ground and in the sudden darkness raced for the gate.

Vree! What are you doing? Her fear pushed him into a tiny corner of her mind, blocking him from any kind of control, any kind of communication, but not from the desolate weight of her pain.

He'd asked her if she was still sane nearly every morning since Bannon had shared her body. Pummeled by the force of her emotional storm, he realized he'd hadn't asked it once since he'd taken Bannon's place. Perhaps he should have.

She'd almost reached the gate when something hit her from the right and took her to the ground.

This fight, Bannon won. He thrust his arms under hers and locked his hands behind her neck in a supposedly unbreakable hold just as Magda threw herself down beside them.

"Vree, listen to me. You haven't got time for this! Enrik says his body is dying, and he's not going to wait!"

"I don't care!" she spat. Bannon twisted so that her heel hit him only a glancing blow, got her to her knees and sat on the lower part of her legs. "I don't want it!"

"Why not? What are you afraid of? Vree, if you and Gyhard don't separate soon, you might not be able to. Your kigh are becoming so interlinked, even now you might not be able to find all of the bits of you and all the bits of him. You'll lose yourself in him and he'll lose himself in you."

"Yes."

Startled by the longing in that single syllable, Magda drew back. "But he *has* to have a body of his own!"

Vree shook her head. "He has me."

"He can't have all of you," Bannon growled.

"Not now, Bannon!" Magda snapped, "We've got to . . ."

"Maggi. Come here."

She turned to frown at her mother. "But . . ."

"No. Come here." Annice's voice took on not-to-be-argued-with tones.

Still frowning, Magda stood and slowly backed away until Vree and Bannon became a strangely shaped shadow in the night.

Annice stepped forward and put both hands on her daughter's shoulders, the grip equal parts comfort and caution. "Sometimes," she said, the past weighting her words, "people need to heal themselves."

*   *   *

"Let me go!"

"No." Bannon adjusted his hold. "Not this time. I let you go before, but I'm not doing it again."

Vree tried to smash his nose in with the back of her head but only hit a cheekbone.

"Vree, listen to me," he pleaded. "I understand what you're afraid of." Jerking back to avoid another blow, Bannon breathed in the warm familiar scent that all his life had meant he wasn't alone. "You're trying to do the same thing to Gyhard that I wanted to do to you."

"What are you talking about?" She'd intended it to be a snarl, but it emerged as more of a wail.

He knew what he meant, but he wasn't sure how to explain. Vree had changed, but so, he'd come to realize, had he. "You're not my arm or my leg, you're a separate person, with a separate life, and I have no right to try to make you into what I want. Being your brother doesn't give me that right. Loving you doesn't give me that right. The whole slaughtering Imperial Army doesn't give me that right. And you haven't the right to do it to Gyhard either."

She went limp in his arms and started to shake. It could have been a trick, but he didn't think so. As he gathered her close, she pressed her face against his shoulder in blind need. He tried to remember if she'd ever turned to him before and wasn't very surprised when memory told him their position had always been reversed. "I will always love you," he murmured into her hair. "Just because you've chosen to share your life with a carrion-eating *abomination* ..." He stumbled a little over the Shkoden word. "... well, you won't get rid of me that easily. I guess that you can love him, too."

Too. Vree fought to find her way through the maelstrom roaring around inside her head. Assassins had no family but the army. But she'd had Bannon. Had loved Bannon with a desperate intensity because he was all she had. Because she'd been allowed to love Bannon, she was able to love Gyhard. It had never occurred to her that she could love more than one person at a time.

Suddenly released, Gyhard cautiously extended his control. *Vree?*

Her answer wasn't so much in words as a tentative opening of final barriers neither of them had realized still existed.

Becoming concerned by the lengthening silence, Bannon pulled back until he could look down into Vree's eyes. He'd looked into them too many times in the darkness to need light now. "Sod off, Gyhard. This is my time, not yours."

Gyhard stopped her as she started to stiffen. *Bannon's right,* he murmured, and withdrew as far as possible.

Releasing a breath she couldn't remember holding, the air leaving her lungs in a long shuddering sigh, Vree touched the comfort of Gyhard's presence and rubbed her cheek against Bannon's shoulder. The last time she'd held her brother, only her brother, their relationship unwarped by the training that made them blades of Jiir, she'd been seven and he'd been six. "Be my brother again."

"Just a brother with a sister? I wouldn't know how." He pressed his lips against the soft cap of her hair. "And neither, sister-mine, would you."

Vree sniffed and glanced over his shoulder at the shadowy figures of Gerek and Magda, peering at them in concern from the circle of light around a second lantern. "It doesn't look that hard."

"Magda!"

Karlene's urgent summons spun her around. "Oh no!" Diving forward, she helped the bard lower Enrik to the ground. "What's wrong? What is it?"

The body is dying.

"We know that, but ..." Suddenly grabbing his shoulders, she shook him, hard. "Stop it!"

"Magda!" Karlene grabbed her hands and broke her grip. "What are you doing?"

"He's trying to die!"

"What?!"

"When the body dies, he's free! Enrik, you've got to hang on! Just for another minute or two!"

No.

"Yes!"

NO!

"I said, Yes!"

Ears ringing, Karlene caught Magda's chin, forcing her head up. "Magda, calm down! You're Vree's only chance. You can't fall apart on her now."

Vaguely aware that her mother was Singing a circle of fire kigh to light the yard, Magda stared across Enrik at Karlene. "Vree's and *Gyhard's* only chance," she snapped.

Karlene's mouth twisted into an approximation of a smile. "Yeah. Him, too."

Jerking her head away from the bard's touch, Magda pressed her fingers against the inside of Enrik's muscular wrist. His pulse felt thready, distant from her touch. "I can't let him die."

I am dead. Let me leave!

Leave? She could've smacked herself. Of course. There was no reason for the dead kigh to remain. "We have a bard here who can Sing you out of your body."

The body dies.

"No, it won't." It should have seemed stranger than it did, reassuring a dead man, but it had been a strange day all around. "We have a kigh without a body of his own to replace you."

His eyes met hers, and she looked away. Some things could be borne; some things could not. *If I am free, the body is dead.*

"But ..." Then she understood. It worked both ways. If Karlene Sang Enrik's kigh out of his body before Gyhard's kigh was in it, the body would die. Therefore, Gyhard had to share the body, however briefly, with the dead man.

"All right." Vree looked from Enrik to Magda. "Explain why that's dangerous."

"We don't have time ..."

Vree's jaw set. "Then explain quickly."

"But ..." Realizing she had no choice, Magda threw up her hands. "Okay. Quickly. You know that living kigh don't like to be around dead kigh, especially not dead kigh acting like living kigh. *We're* all a little numb, so Enrik by himself isn't enough to cause us a lot of trouble but *we're* not stuffed in the same body with him and Gyhard *will* be. He might fling himself out again."

"Then I'll grab him again."

Magda sighed, spitting out a wet curl. "He might be caught in Karlene's Song and end up Sung away."

"I'm not going anywhere," Gyhard declared.

"What I'm trying to say is, he might *die*."

As Bannon's arm tightened around her shoulders, Vree closed her eyes for a moment. "And the alternative?"

"Things stay as they are."

"No." That decision had already been made. "Do what you have to do."

"I don't have to do anything right away," Magda reminded her gently, "you do. You have to push Gyhard out of your body and into Enrik's."

"Like giving birth," Bannon offered when Vree hesitated.

She elbowed him hard, just below the ribs. "That's sick."

Doubled over, gasping for breath, he managed a shrug.

"Vree, hurry! I'm losing the pulse!"

Do I have to make eye contact?

Gyhard nodded. *I'm afraid so.*

Ignoring the lines of sweat dribbling down her sides, Vree dropped to her knees and shot a warning glance at Karlene. "Are you ready?" When the bard nodded, she looked into Enrik's eyes. Over the years as a blade of Jiir, she'd looked into the eyes of the dead countless times—this time, the dead looked back. All the dead. "I can't . . ."

Death as practice. Death as profession. Death as escape.

There were too many. She could feel them gathering her into their company.

Vree!

Gyhard's terror jerked her back. Still teetering on the edge, she gathered up all her remaining strength and shoved everything she thought to be him through the dead and into Enrik's body.

Bits of her went with him.

Bits of him were left behind.

He didn't throw himself from her as Bannon had, but he went nevertheless.

Surprisingly, the actual doing of it hurt less than the fear of it had.

When at Magda's nod, Karlene began to Sing, Vree watched the dead man's kigh flicker and disappear. One by one, the dead of memory followed. When they were gone, Enrik's eyes held only the lifeless reflection of the surrounding flames.

The body breathed once. Twice. No more.

"NO!" Screaming in rage, Vree flung herself forward. "Get back here, you slaughtering carrion eater!" With every word she slammed both fists down on the broad chest.

"DON'T! YOU! DARE! LEAVE! ME!"

Warm fingers closed around her wrists and pulled her hands to either side. She pitched forward, barely stopping herself from smashing face first into Enrik's body.

"Vree ... please stop." She knew the voice although it had never sounded so weak. "That ... hurts."

"Gyhard?"

A swollen tongue dragged across cracked lips. "Wish you'd stop ... calling me ... carrion eater."

Pulling easily free of his hold, she sat back on her heels, her hands laced together in her lap as though she were afraid to touch him. "Gyhard?"

"Yes." He tried to cough and didn't quite manage it.

"What's wrong with him." Vree grabbed Magda's arm. "He sounds so ..."

"Dehydrated. His body needs water."

"That's all?"

She wrinkled her nose. "Well, he could also use a bath."

Staring up at Vree's face, trying to memorize every curve, every line, Gyhard attempted a wink. "Remember the bath ... at Elbion's?"

Magda was almost positive Vree blushed although the firelight made it difficult to tell for certain.

"What about Enrik?" Gerek asked, leaning forward for a closer look.

One palm resting lightly on Gyhard's forehead, Karlene shook her head. "He's gone."

"Witnessed," Annice said softly. "But what about Gyhard? Did sharing the body with a dead kigh hurt him?"

Before Magda could answer, Vree stared fixedly at Gyhard's face, searching for pain that went beyond the physical. "*Did* it hurt you?"

"No." Gyhard closed his eyes and felt the lingering awareness of being dead and trapped in life. It felt surprisingly like the guilt he'd shared a hundred midnights with. "But I ... remember."

Karlene rocked back on her heels and stood. "All things being enclosed, I'm glad that's over."

Bannon caught her as she stumbled. "Is it?"

"It is for Enrik." She yawned and nodded down to where Vree and Magda were ministering to the abused body Gyhard now wore. "And it looks like Gyhard survived." The events of the day would be recalled and discussed in the Bardic Halls for years, but at that moment, Karlene was too tired to care. "Now, we've just got you two to worry about."

"What two?"

"You and Gerek. You, Your Grace," she said pointing a finger at Gerek, "were supposed to bring Magda back to Elbasan from Bartek Springs. I don't imagine Her Royal Highness is going to be too happy about your disregarding her wishes. And you," the finger moved to point at Bannon, "were given a direct order to bring Vree and Gyhard back to the Emperor. He's not going to be happy with you."

"All things being enclosed," Gerek muttered, scratching at the new skin on his shoulder, "I think I can deal with whatever Her Highness throws at me."

Unexpectedly pale, Bannon shook his head. "To disobey an Imperial order is treason."

Annice, still anxiously watching her daughter, snorted. "You leave the Emperor to King Theron, and you leave His Majesty to me."

"We thought it best to bury Kars' body with the others at the timber-holding."

"You're sure he's dead, Annice?" Theron locked eyes with her across the table. "You're sure this is over?"

"I'm sure."

"Good." He scowled at the bowl of clear broth and pushed it to one side.

Annice pushed it back. "Although there are a few loose ends."

"Of course there are." Throwing a crested linen napkin over the bowl, he glared at her. "Annice, I am not eating this slop, so you can just have a server take it away. I want a good thick chowder and an ale."

"Neither of which, I've been told, you can have." Putting her elbows on the table, Annice levelly regarded her brother and her king. She suspected he'd agreed to a private lunch immediately upon their arrival in order to circumvent the dietary order of his healer. As Lilyana had taken her aside and given her quick but explicit instructions, it wasn't doing him any good.

"You've been told," he repeated, crumbling a dry biscuit in disgust. "That's never stopped you before. You were *told* to remain at Ohrid."

"Stasya was there to give early warning if necessary and the Ducs of Ohrid were holding the pass long before you put a Bardic Hall in the keep—Pjerin was quite definite about that. *My* abilities were needed elsewhere."

"Which does not change the fact that you disobeyed a direct order."

"I couldn't stay there, Theron. Not when I *knew* what Maggi was going to do."

"You could have sent word, told me. You're quick enough sending the kigh about for other reasons."

She spread her hands. "I didn't want to chance having to disobey yet another direct order."

"I don't see what difference that makes," he muttered grumpily. "You're a bard. Bards are supposed to keep me informed." After a moment he sighed and sat back in his chair. "Oh, all right. The lot of you destroyed a very real threat to my people; I suppose that's as much defense as you need." Unexpectedly, he smiled. "Considering the lives this Kars had already taken and the ones he could have taken, I am very grateful he was stopped. I'd order a public celebration," he added brushing crumbs off his lap, "but I don't want the public to know about the whole horrific incident until the bards have had a chance to present this undead kigh thing in such a way as to cause the least amount of panic. I don't suppose you or Karlene had a chance to come up with anything on the way back to Elbasan?"

"On the way back to Elbasan," Annice repeated dryly, "Karlene and I spent our time answering questions from other bards—Kars' laying to rest having reverberated across the entire kingdom. The only time we got a moment's peace was when we were inside an inn, on the second floor, with the shutters closed, and blankets over our heads; at which point we were so exhausted all we did was sleep."

"And the others?"

She stared down into the red-brown surface of her soup, remembering short tempers and long silences brought about by exhaustion and emotional overload. The only high point had been watching Vree and Bannon attempting to reclaim their past, using Gerek and Magda as their template for a sibling relationship. "I can give you a full recall," she offered, "but you wouldn't enjoy it much."

"Then you can wait until after lunch." Theron sighed, removed the napkin, and picked up a spoon fancifully carved from a piece of narwhale horn. "Not that I'm enjoying lunch much. Magda has straightened things out with the Healers' Hall?"

"If she hasn't, she soon will."

Theron snorted, amused. "She's got that whole place wrapped around her little finger. What about the two doomed lovers? Who, not surprisingly, have been the inspiration for some truly bad ballads."

Delaying her response with a mouthful of broth, Annice thought back on Vree and Gyhard. From the little she'd seen, it hadn't looked good—Vree had ridden as far from the cart holding Gyhard and Magda as she could. Could love endure being ripped apart as theirs had? Had his moment of sharing a body with a dead kigh changed Gyhard in Vree's eyes? Annice shook her head, both in answer to her own thoughts and Theron's question. "I don't know. But, if they want to stay in Shkoder, you should give them some show of appreciation in return for taking care of Kars."

"Show of appreciation?"

"Land, money; you know, the usual."

"The usual? Annice, this is not something that happens quarterly." He raised a hand to cut her off. "I'll see that they're suitably rewarded—perhaps I'll speak to the Duc of Bicaz about that empty timber-holding. What about young Otavas' bodyguard?"

"I expect he's back guarding the prince's body." She leaned forward slightly, Theron having finally directed the conversation where she wanted it. "The Emperor arranged Otavas' visit, you know, in order that Bannon would have a reason to be in Shkoder."

"No, I didn't know," the king growled. "And how do you know?"

"Bards know everything." Then her teasing smile vanished. "His Imperial Majesty wanted the boy to kidnap his sister and take her back to the Empire."

"Why?"

"Because he only found out that Gyhard was alive after he—they—left the Empire and Gyhard was apparently involved in a number of treasonous acts against the Imperial Throne."

His eyes narrowed as the brother disappeared within the king. "I assume you're referring to the rebellion he instigated as Governor Aralt and his intention to murder an Imperial Prince in order to take over his body?"

"You know about that?"

"Kings may not know as much as bards," he told her grimly, "but we're kept fairly well informed. I had been assured, however, that His Imperial Majesty thought Gyhard had died."

"Bannon blamed Gyhard for the loss of Vree, and he . . ."

"Decided to get even?" When she nodded, Theron shook his head. "Wonderful. An immature assassin. That aside, I was also informed that if Gyhard paid for those crimes, it would destroy Vree."

Annice spread her hands. "Vree and Gyhard are now separate people. Bannon could now take Gyhard back to the Empire without *physically* destroying Vree."

"Physically," Theron grunted. The emphasis made the alternative obvious. "What do you want me to do, Annice?"

"Intervene with the Emperor on Bannon's behalf."

"Intervene with the Emperor on behalf of an Imperial assassin refusing a direct order to deal with an Imperial treason?" Grasping the edge of the table, he leaned toward her, just barely maintaining a grip on his temper. "I don't think so."

She reached across the luncheon dishes and laid a hand over one of his. "Then intervene on behalf of a brother who doesn't want to hurt a sister he dearly loves."

Theron looked down at their hands then up at her face. He struggled silently for a moment then sighed, knowing when he'd been flanked. "I'll speak with Karlene. She knows the particulars better than anyone; perhaps we can work something out."

"What I find most curious, Majesty, is that the Emperor went to so much trouble." Karlene frowned down at the plush carpet covering the floor of the king's office, seeking answers in the pattern that turned and looped around upon itself. "Why send Bannon secretly when he could have just sent a message to you to have the traitor returned?"

"Perhaps he assumed I would agree with the bards that the innocent body worn by the traitor would not be destroyed. Understandable, since it was a pair of Shkoden bards who assured him Gyhard had been destroyed."

Karlene looked up to find the king regarding her with something less than approval. "But, Majesty, you did agree with the bards or you'd have sent them back the moment you were given my recall."

"The moment I was *eventually* given your recall," Theron amended.

Standing quietly to one side, Kovar winced.

"But since I have been assured from the beginning that this is a bardic matter," the king continued, shooting an unreadable look at the new Bardic Captain, then turning his gaze back to Karlene, "I would like to hear a bardic solution. With your help, and the help of my niece, Vireyda and Albannon Magaly and Gyhard i'Stevana have done Shkoder a great service and I would prefer that none of them be sent back to the Empire to be executed for treason. I would also prefer not to have to explain to His Imperial Majesty that Bardic Oaths supercede oaths sworn to him when he demands that I have you and Gabris executed for harboring a known traitor."

Karlene slowly shook her head. "He won't demand it, Majesty."

"That fond of you, is he?"

"No, Majesty. But if he were going to do it, he would have already done it. The Emperor wanted Gyhard back in the Capital, but he wanted it done quietly. He wanted something and he wanted as few people as possible to know about it. He has to want Gyhard for something more than merely treason."

Theron's brows rose. "Merely treason?"

Kovar stepped forward before Karlene could answer. "What does Gyhard have that's worth such convoluted planning?"

The office fell silent as the two bards and the king spent a moment in thought. When Theron's stomach growled, he remembered his consort in tears, his heir pitched suddenly onto the throne, long lists of instructions from his healer, and innumerable bowls of broth. "I know," he said, remembering the pain, and terror, and the cold weight of death pressing against his chest.

"Eternal life?" Magda looked around the room at the king and the pair of bards and pulled a wet curl from the corner of her mouth. "Well, I *suppose* His Imperial Majesty might think that Gyhard had the secret of eternal life. I mean, he has lived a *very* long time moving his kigh from body to body, but it's no secret how he did it."

"How, Magda?" Theron demanded, eyes gleaming. "How?"

Recognizing where his interest originated, she smiled a little sadly. "All it takes is a fear of death so complete that you'd do *anything* to escape."

"There must be more," Kovar protested. "Or we'd have kigh jumping out of the dying all the time."

The young healer sighed. "You don't understand. You have to be willing, if only at that moment, to do *anything*." She stepped toward the desk. "Majesty, when you thought you were dying, did you fear death so much that you would have given an innocent life to survive?"

Theron slowly shook his head, left hand rising to twist his collar button. "No."

She nodded, satisfied. "And I don't think His Imperial Majesty would either."

"But there are those who would," Kovar pointed out.

"Those sorts of people," Magda replied, wondering why it was so obvious to her and so apparently difficult for anyone else, "are not the sort with the strength to throw themselves into the heart of their fear over and over again."

"But if Gyhard is such a person ..."

"He isn't." Frowning, she reconsidered. "Well, I guess he *was,* but he isn't anymore."

"Magda, true love conquering all is a bardic tale." When she started to bristle indignantly, Theron leaned forward and held out his hand. "Child, the known path to immortality would be too great for anyone to deny."

"He doesn't have to *deny* it. He can't *do* it. When he was willing to die rather than take over Prince

Otavas' body it was because he'd found something he couldn't do—which, I would like to point out," she added, chin lifting, "had *less* to do with the prince than it did with his *love* for Vree . . ."

In spite of the seriousness of the situation, both bards hid a smile at her tone. The young healer had matured a great deal since Vree and Gyhard had come to Elbasan, but she was still only seventeen.

". . . at which time he lost his all-encompassing fear of death."

"You don't know that, Magda . . ."

"I *do* know that. I just spent *days* helping him anchor his kigh in the body he now wears."

"So he'll grow old and die just like the rest of us." Theron sighed. "Does he know?"

"Does it matter?" Magda demanded. "Immortality now has a price he's unwilling to pay. Why diminish him by telling him he couldn't pay it if he wanted to?"

After a long moment, Theron nodded, and sat back in his chair, thumb tracing the design of the crowned ship carved into the broad arm. "Why indeed? Which brings us back to the problem of His Imperial Majesty."

"The Emperor is a realist, Sire. He realizes that, occasionally, the birds he flies will miss their strike."

The other three people in the room blinked at Karlene in confusion. She cleared her throat sheepishly. "Sorry. You get into the habit of hawking analogies around the Imperial Court. Why not tell him that Gyhard is now just a man, no longer immortal and, furthermore, a man wearing a Shkoden body which cannot be executed for a treason committed by the body of an Imperial citizen. If you will not allow Bannon to remove Gyhard—in his new body from

Shkoder—then whether or not Bannon is disobeying an Imperial order becomes irrelevant."

Theron snorted. "He won't like that much."

"For what it's worth," Magda offered earnestly, "I really, *really* don't think we could have stopped Kars without Gyhard and Bannon."

Within the masking of his beard, the king's lips twitched. "So I've been told." Twisting the ivory button between his fingertips—they'd stopped pulling off when his tailor began sewing them on with sailmaker's thread—Theron examined Karlene's suggestion from all sides. "It does have the advantage of being the truth," he said at last. "And it does solve young Bannon's problem, as even an Imperial assassin can hardly be expected to start a war by taking the man out of the country if *I* won't allow them to leave. However ..." He glanced over at the beautifully detailed map that covered one wall of his office. Shkoder was a small country, bordered on three sides by mountains and the fourth by the sea. It was smaller than three of the Havakeen Empire's seven provinces and the Empire was running out of room to expand. "... we'd best come up with a way to sweeten the pot."

In the long, paneled corridor outside the king's private office, Magda fell into step beside Karlene and sighed. "I'm worried."

Shortening her stride, Karlene glanced down at the top of the healer's head. "About what?"

"Vree and Gyhard. Vree never came near him all the way back to Elbasan."

"She also never took her eyes off of him."

"Are you sure?"

"I'm sure," Karlene told her with sardonic emphasis. "Trust me, I would've noticed if she'd looked away."

Magda glanced up at the taller woman. "You like her, don't you? I mean, not just like but ..." She could feel the blood rise to her cheeks.

"I could be a little in love with her, yes."

"Gerek, too," Magda said as they walked through a set of double doors and out into the public areas of the palace. "He's with Her Royal Highness, so I guess I'd better wait for him in his suite."

"Do you think he's going to need a healer?"

"Not unless he's forgotten everything Tadeus ever taught him about charm." She smiled up at the bard. "Thanks for reassuring me about Vree and Gyhard."

"No problem." Karlene stood and watched the young healer effortlessly move through the crowds and wished she felt as reassured. As much as she might have wanted to believe otherwise, His Majesty had been right—true love seldom conquered all outside of a bardic tale.

"I had thought you understood that I wanted your sister and the assassin returned directly from Bartek Springs?" The Heir of Shkoder leaned back and locked eyes with the Heir of Ohrid over steepled fingers. "I believe my exact words were, 'I neither want my cousin with her unique and irreplaceable talents endangering herself by confronting this bardic abomination nor do I want an assassin with two not entirely stable kigh wandering around Shkoder.'"

"Yes, Highness, but after speaking with my sister, I realized she was right."

"And I was wrong?"

Gerek dropped gracefully to one knee. "And that you had less than complete information, Highness."

Onele's smile held edges that flayed. "I assume it never even crossed your mind that as there was a bard readily available I would like to be informed of any new information you acquired?" Her fingertips beat out an irritated staccato beat on the arms of her chair.

"Yes, Highness, it did cross my mind, closely followed by the fear that, should you still want me to return Magda and Vree to Elbasan, I would have to disobey a direct order."

"You would *have* to disobey a direct order?"

He inclined his head. "Yes, Highness, and I in no way wanted to put either of us in that position as we both believed we were acting for the good of Shkoder."

Onele stared at him for a long moment. Someday, when she was Queen of Shkoder, he would be Duc of Ohrid and the relationship between them would determine the security of her borders. "Get up, Gerek," she said at last. "And the next time, if it is possible, I should like to be consulted before you decide my instructions are no longer relevant."

Gerek's teeth flashed within the dark frame of his beard. "I guarantee it won't happen again."

The Heir accepted his assurance with a laugh. "I'd rather hear a guarantee that the abomination is truly gone."

"The bards and my sister are quite certain that he is, Highness." Frowning, Gerek tried to recall his sister's somewhat confused explanation. "Magda says his kigh has gone back into the Circle."

Onele rolled her eyes, an expression that reminded Gerek very much of her aunt. Although Annice would have probably snorted as well. "The priests keep tell-ing us all things are enclosed, but I doubt sharing the Circle with such a man is going to make them very happy."

Having heard a small fraction of Kars' story, Gerek was surprised to find himself feeling sympathy for the ancient Cemandian. "He was what circumstances made him, Highness."

"Aren't we all. What about the others? The assassins?"

"Bannon has returned to his position with Your Highness' cousin, Prince Otavas. Vree . . ." He paused. "Gyhard was under Magda's care most of the way back to Elbasan. Vree seemed to be avoiding him."

"How unfortunate after all they've been through." The Heir of Shkoder cocked a speculative brow. "But I wouldn't have thought an Imperial assassin avoided anything."

"Highness, I am sorry but I didn't know what else to do but throw myself on your mercy." Down on one knee, Bannon stared fixedly at the carpet between Prince Otavas' feet. His Highness had been with a cousin when the seven of them had gone their sepa-rate ways upon arriving back at the Palace, giving him time to bathe and change. By the time the prince re-turned, he'd decided to tell him everything, from the moment he'd met with the Emperor until the moment the prince had welcomed him back. When he finished, he lowered his head until his forehead rested on his bent knee. "Highness, His Imperial Majesty gave me an order that I cannot obey."

"Are you saying that your inability to cause your

sister pain outweighs your oaths to the Empire?" Otavas asked softly.

Mouth dry, Bannon swallowed nothing and nodded.

"But this Gyhard i'Stevana is a traitor to the Imperial Throne."

"Highness, when Gyhard was Aralt, he was a traitor to the Imperial Throne, but *this* Gyhard's only a man that my sister loves."

"He is the same man."

"No, Highness. I'm not the same man I was before I went into Ghoti. You're not the same man you were before Kars. Gyhard's not the same man he was before ..." Bannon's hands closed into fists but he managed to finish the sentence. "... he fell in love with Vree."

"And she loves him?"

Bannon sighed. "Yes, Highness."

"Look at me."

Bannon looked up.

The prince met his gaze and held it. "You are disobeying an Imperial order and yet you returned here to me, risking arrest, risking being sent back to the Empire and a traitor's death. Why didn't you run?"

Surprised, Bannon opened and closed his mouth but no sound emerged. "It never occurred to me, Highness," he said at last. "Who would guard your dreams if I was gone?"

"Who indeed." The prince's brilliant eyes grew more brilliant still. "So for love of your sister, you refused an Imperial order and you returned to Elbasan for love of me?"

Had Vree felt this way, Bannon wondered. As if she'd been fighting her way *out* of a walled town? "Yes, Highness."

Otavas smiled. "Then, in order to keep you in my service, I have to keep you from being executed for treason."

"Yes, Highness. You'll speak to his Imperial Majesty?"

"I doubt that just my speaking to father would be enough." Love. Otavas repeated the word to himself; first in Shkoden and then in Imperial. Assassins could fall in love. And if assassins could fall in love, then anyone could. His voice rose and his eyes shone. "I have an idea."

Princess Jelena stared at Otavas in astonishment. "You want us to what?"

"Be joined. But not right now," he added hurriedly at her expression. "Look, Jelena, we both know we're due for political joinings. Shkoder is a small country, the Empire isn't. It can only benefit Shkoder to have closer ties. If when you're Queen, your consort is an Imperial Prince, well, that'll secure your borders for at least another generation. You're not quite fifteen, so nothing's going to happen for three years anyway, but wouldn't it be nice to have the threat of being joined to a perfect stranger taken away?"

Her eyes narrowed. "And what about us?"

Otavas backed up a step and wondered why he'd ever thought she was shy. "Us?"

"You and me. Especially you." She poked him in the chest. "Give me a reason that isn't politically based or you can just go home and have His Imperial Majesty join you with some fat old man in the Third Province whose ancestral lands happen to have access to a natural harbor."

"How did you hear about him?"

"The bards told me!"

His brilliant eyes sparkled. "You were asking the bards about me?"

"Tavas!" Smacking her palm down on the sketches of strange machines that lettered her desk, she glared at him. "I want a better reason than politics!"

"All right." He captured her hand. "I like you. A lot. Someday, if we give it enough time, I'll probably love you."

"Probably?"

"And even if I don't, I can't think of any way I'd rather spend my life than beside you, staring at the stars." When he bent his head to kiss her hand, she changed her grip and nearly pulled him off his feet.

"Come on."

"Where are we going?"

"To tell Grandfather. It is customary when you suggest a joining with the second in line to the throne, to inform the King."

"But you haven't given me an answer."

"Don't be ridiculous, Tavas." Her smile held a promise of shared exploration into the unknown. "I'd decided we were going to be joined during Third Quarter Festival."

Head reeling, the Imperial Ambassador left the king's office and hurried back to his own, his speed making the sweep of his robes against the polished floor sound like excited whispering. He had a great deal of work to do and was very grateful that his carefully worded communique would be sent through the almost instantaneous services of the Imperial fledgling still at the Bardic Hall.

His Imperial Majesty had to approve the joining, but that, he was sure, would be a mere technicality.

When Gabris bowed and left the room, the Emperor stared reflectively at the scars on his wrist. "So," he murmured without turning, "I have lost my first hawk."

"And the chance of immortality, Majesty?" Marshal Usef asked from his place to the right of the throne.

"Flown as well."

"You believe them, Majesty?" Greatly daring, Usef shook his head. "King Theron may be sheltering the traitor in order to gain the secret for himself."

"No. The Shkoden bards with their circles, and their connected quarters would never allow so dangerous a skill to continue to exist once they became aware of it." The Emperor frowned, reflecting on all he'd just been told. "It seems unlikely that the exact circumstances that created such a skill will probably ever occur again."

Marshal Usef shifted his weight but remained silent.

"So tell me, Marshal, would you be willing to die over and over, in order to live forever?"

The marshal thought about it for a moment. He had been in battles on his way to the command of the First Army and he'd seen a great many soldiers die in a great many unpleasant ways. "No, Majesty," he said at last, "I would not."

"Nor would I." The Emperor sat back and grinned. "I have lost the potential for an unpleasant immortality, Usef, but gained a hold on the Shkoden crown. Not an entirely bad trade."

"So you will give your permission to the joining, Majesty."

"Give it?" The Emperor laughed. "I've already sent them a pair of assassins, hooded and jessed, as a betrothal gift."

"Vree?" He would have thought she hadn't heard him approach except he knew better. "Every healer in the Hall took a poke at me and it seems they agree with Magda. This body took no permanent damage from holding Enrik's dead kigh."

"Good."

Reaching out to touch her shoulder, Gyhard let his hand fall back to his side. "Are you avoiding me?"

Vree stared out the window of the Bardic Hall at the wall around the Citadel and shook her head. "If I was, you wouldn't have found me."

"You barely spoke to me on the way back to the city."

"Magda said you needed to get settled in the body."

"And?"

"I was afr ... I thought if I came too close I might pull you back here, into me."

"And we don't want that."

"Yes." She swallowed and closed her eyes. "Yes, I do. I missed, miss you, so much."

"I'm still here." Greatly daring, he gripped her arms and turned her around. His heart pounded a little less violently when she didn't object. He had no desire to end up on the wrong end of her reflexes. When she looked away, he sighed. "Is it the body?"

"What?"

"The way it looks?"

Holding her elbows, she shook her head. "I like the way it looks."

"Is it because of Enrik? Have I changed since touching him? Since touching death?"

"No."

As she didn't appear to be wearing her daggers, he lifted her chin until her eyes met his. Her skin was as soft as he remembered and her eyes as dark. "Are you still afraid I'll leave you?"

"No."

Her breath lapped warm down over his hand and Gyhard didn't think he could bear it. He'd waited so long to hold her. "Then what? Are you afraid of me? Of what I was? Of what I've done? Of what I did to Kars?"

"Of you?" She broke from his touch and stomped across the room and back. "Of you!" she repeated. "Of all the arrogant . . ." Then she saw he was afraid of exactly that—of what he did to Kars and the possibility of him destroying her as well. The anger left her as quickly as it had arrived, leaving her shaking and confused. "I'm not afraid of *you!* Not you. You . . ."

Stepping forward, she grabbed his arm. "You, I'm sure of. How could I not be. We know more about each other than any two people ever have." Her fingers dimpled the smooth curve of muscle, warm and resilient under her hand, and she forced herself to meet his gaze. His eyes, his new eyes were an indeterminate shade under brows that slanted down at the corners and up over the center of a crooked nose. It was a stranger's face, familiar because she so intimately knew the life that animated it. "I'm afraid of me!"

"Vree, do you love me?"

"You know . . ."

"I need to hear you say it."

She closed her eyes and touched the bits of him that remained with her, then opened them and took a deep breath. "Yes. I love you. But . . ."

Gyhard rolled his eyes; he should've known that was coming.

". . . I'm not used to having feelings."

"That's a load of ratshit. You always had feelings. You were just trained not to notice them. Now they're all breaking training at once."

Her gaze tracked the edge of his jaw, slid down the corded muscles of his throat, and lingered where his pulse throbbed just under the skin. "I feel like the first time I ever walked a roof. Like the next move is going to topple me off and when I hit the ground I'll break into a million pieces. Or like the first time I ever held a throwing dagger and I almost cut my own fingers off because it was so incredibly sharp and I didn't know how to use it."

"Do you know what I'm afraid of?" Gyhard asked softly. "That now I'm out of your head, you won't want me."

She took a step closer and breathed in the scent of soap and sweat and clean clothes. Of him. "I want you. I just don't want to fall off the roof."

"If you fall, I'll catch you."

She snorted. "You're up here, too."

"Then I'll jump after you."

"And if I cut someone's fingers off?"

He closed his hand over hers. "Won't happen."

"What makes you so sure?"

"I won't let it."

"You can't stop it! I can't stop it! Don't you understand, it's completely out of our control!"

"Is that why you practically ignored me on the way back to the city?" he demanded incredulously. "You didn't want to lose control in front of an audience?"

Vree had a sudden image of what would have happened had she surrendered to need surrounded by two bards, Gerek, Magda, and her brother, and hurriedly shoved it aside. "You don't understand!" she protested, cheeks flushed. "I've spent most of my life learning control, it's not that easy to surrender it!"

"I do understand. Like you said, we know each other better than anyone ever has. But you're not an assassin anymore; if you lose control, what's the worst that can happen?"

She stared at the walls, at the ceiling, at the empty hearth, anywhere but at him.

"Uncertainty might kill assassins, Vree, but it's the state the rest of the world lives in." His free hand cupped the side of her head, the callused edge of his thumb tracing the full curve of her lower lip. "You'll get used to it. And you'll never need to be uncertain of me; we're a part of each other."

Leaning into his touch, her tongue followed the path he stroked. "It's not like it was."

Gyhard swallowed and looked at the moisture glistening just above his thumb. All at once, the room seemed a great deal hotter. "It's better," he assured her, adding hoarsely, "there's no audience now. Maybe we should lock the door and see how much better it's going to be."

"Maybe . . ." She could feel the tempo of his heart quicken, and her heart began to beat in time. "Maybe we should."

"Karlene told me once that there would be no happy ending," he murmured against her mouth.

Teeth closing around his lower lip, she pulled her fingers from his because she wanted to use both hands. "Karlene," she said, finding certainty in opposition, "was wrong."

Tanya Huff